PERSEPHONE RISING

KATE GLASS

Beartown
Press

Fast-paced and engaging! *Persephone Rising* by Kate Glass delivers a gripping tale of survival, secrets, and the bond between siblings in a crumbling future Chicago. Perfect for fans of dystopian adventure.

—Millie Copper

Author of the bestselling speculative series *Havoc in Wyoming*

For those who view books as their saviors—yet simultaneously commit to living bravely and purposefully in the real world.

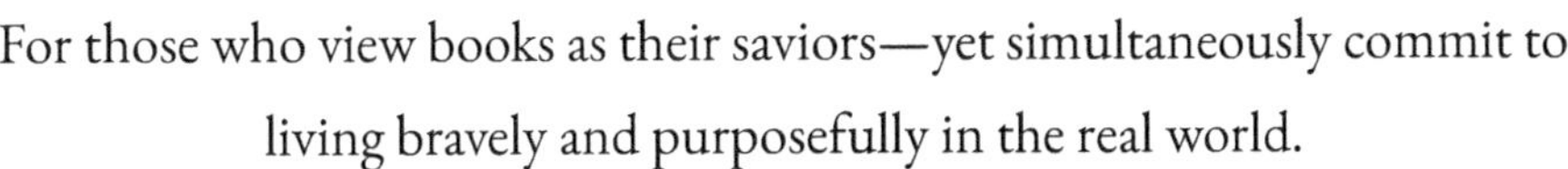

And for my family, who continue to support me.

New Chicago, U.S.A.

May 2073

We are starved of resources, of beauty, of hope. The fault is in ourselves. Our instincts say destroy, take, protect what is ours! We do so to nature's detriment. Only by surrendering to the Earth will we reclaim it.

-Mons Vega, Prophet for the earth

1

CLERA

Automatic doors whoosh. Clera Diaz and her fellow shift workers spew forth from Perkine Skinpad Industries. Soul-weary, Clera sighs and squints into the sun. It's been four years since she schooled out and began work there. Four years imprisoned behind concrete walls away from books, the sun, freedom.

She brushes strands of golden-brown hair from her eyes. Day blends into day blends into day—an endless cycle. *We Slummers scrabble for a few credits, for a safe place to sleep, an occasional good cut of meat for the table. And for what? So we can return to work each day, perform the same mindless tasks, our backs bent a little lower, slowly deteriorating like the buildings around us.*

Cracked pavement stretches past the front gates and ends at a busy thoroughfare. It bustles with smart cars, electric trams, and folks just getting off work, picking up laundry, heading to dinner. Overhead, delivery drones buzz like giant insects, and elevated trains zip past. New Chicago pulses with life even as it sags under layers of dirt and despair. It's the glowing heart of America, the new capitol city, the most populated, crime-ridden place in the U.S.

Her home.

Of course, not all New Chicago crumbles. She hears the old mansions up north have been replaced with smart homes. In vids she's seen, strips along Michigan Avenue gleam, their prefab buildings mirrored to reflect the sun, while rooftop gardens spill greenery over glass-railed balconies. But that's not her Chicago. Hers is grimy and smells like spoiled cabbage. Still, it's home. Familiar. Safe in its own way.

Clera dodges two young scrulls on the corner, heads bent close over the leth pipe they share. Its subtle, bittersweet fumes mingle with smells of refuse and rust. Her empty stomach churns. She jaywalks across a busy intersection, earning an empty smartcab's angry flash of lights. If she had money, she'd pay to reach the apartment faster. Mama will be there, sick again with that nagging cough. Clera always feels better when she's with Mama.

She picks up her pace. Secondhand clothing stores, web cafes, and virtual reality shops stretch in an endless line. Clera trips on an empty bottle and almost goes sprawling. There's a stitch in her side and a picture of Mama in her head, curled in bed, a mug of chamomile tea forgotten beside her. Or maybe she'll be well enough to watch for Clera's return from the fourth-story window? But probably not. Sickness has taken its toll.

BOOM!

The ground shakes. Tires squeal. Black smoke boils into the sky between the buildings ahead of Clera. Pedestrians turn to look, hands over mouths, frozen. Clera recoils, her end-of-shift trance shattered. Her heart stutters, then pounds double-time because the explosion came from where she's headed.

She takes off at a run.

"Watch it!" a man shouts, pushing Clera out of his way. Her little brother Elio would have stopped and yelled some obscenity, but not Clera.

Her building can't have been hit, can it?

Businesses give way to identical row houses. Smoke wafts toward her, and sirens wail. A tang of burning plastic clings to Clera's nostrils. Spray-painted gang slogans scrawled across brownstone walls signal that she's almost home.

She turns onto her block, slows to a jog, then a walk, lungs burning. She wishes she could go back to this morning, when she was just heading off to her shift, brain filled with nothing more than the last chapter of the novel she'd been reading the night before. One with a strong heroine, an adventurous girl who scoffs at danger.

Smoke *is* coming from her building. It pours from the left side about halfway up. Walls are missing from several apartments, their contents clearly visible. Tattered bed sheets blow in the wind, and burned clothes lie in the rubble that used to be a sidewalk leading up to arched front doors. Wait. Those aren't clothes. They're *bodies*.

A scream rises in Clera's throat. She bites her lip and joins the crowd of gawkers. She looks up, counting windows through a veil of tears. *One, two, three, four.* Where the smoke is thickest, that's her apartment. Right in the bullseye of death.

The police—or clinks, as Slummers call them—corral people, push them back, say it isn't safe. An elbow pokes Clera in the ribs, but she barely notices. She's trying so *intensely* hard to believe this isn't her building, or that Mama went to work after all, covering a later shift, because she *can't* be here.

2

ELIO

Elio feels pressure on the back of his head, and fingers bite into the muscles of his arms. Through blurry vision, he sees a plastic bottle float past his sneakers. He's underwater in the shallows of Lake Michigan. The beach has been closed all summer due to algae blooms, so no one is coming to save him. No one ever comes anyway. His heart pumps so loud it might burst from his chest. A buzzing fills his ears. His body tells him to suck in air, but he can't. He'll drown.

Though he wants to keep fighting, Elio goes limp. The hands holding him loosen. The pressure on the back of his head eases. That's when he rears, comes up gasping, cracks his skull against what feels like cartilage.

The boy behind him cries out and releases him. The other one yells something, but Elio's ears are clogged, and the words elude him. He twists and swings. He's not as big as the Steelheads, but he's wiry and strong from working the streets, performing dangerous maintenance jobs the execs leave for the desperate so they don't risk expensive bots.

He's saved up almost enough credits to buy into the Arcade. He won't let a couple of wanna-be gangsters ruin it for him.

Elio's fist connects with a jaw. The tall, blond kid falls on his rear in the foam. The hulking, black-haired one Elio head-butted hunches in the sand, blood pouring from his nose. Elio blinks to clear his vision and make sure Hulk is out of commission. He is, for now. Elio turns back to Blondie and gives his ribcage a kick. Normally, he'd run, not risk a fight, but he saw Blondie put Elio's digi-ring in a jacket pocket, and he needs it back. All his personal information is stored there—and all his credits.

Blondie isn't hurt bad, and he's already trying to rise. If he rights himself, the Steelhead will have a five-inch height advantage and thirty-plus pounds on Elio. Even Elio's rage may not overcome those odds, so he hooks a foot around the bully's ankle. Blondie falls on his butt again. Elio kicks him in the head a few times. The kid grunts and seems to pass out, but he could be faking—holding his breath and waiting for his chance. That's what Elio would do.

He tries to push coherent thought through his oxygen-deprived brain. If the tall kid is playing him, he'll go for Elio when he reaches for the jacket pocket. It's the expected move.

The sun winks off something on the bully's neck. It's a chain the Steelheads wear, heavy links of copper. Elio crouches over Blondie and scoops three fingers between skin and metal. He twists.

Blondie's eyes fly open. He raises his head above the ebbing tide, gulps a breath, and claws at Elio, but he's too late. Elio's other hand has already found the switchblade at the tall boy's waist, slid it out, and pressed it above the necklace, where an artery pumps beneath skin.

Hulk makes a move toward them. Crimson snot pours from his nose, the back of his hand bloody where he wiped it away. His eyes are already bruising. Tears stream down his cheeks. "Another move and I'll slice him." Elio controls the tremor in his voice. He pretends he's ten feet tall, not five-nine.

Hulk hesitates. There's no fight in him. He's felt pain, and he doesn't want to feel it again. Elio can see this in the bully's eyes, has felt that same pain plenty of times himself—in the locker room, the back alley, the school bathroom. Before he learned to fight, that is. Now it's not about winning or avoiding pain. It's about controlling the rage that rolls over him like a fireball and threatens to make him into a mindless beast who only wants to punch and kick. He can't let that beast out; can't let it change him. He feels it lurking beneath his skin, but he makes himself release the necklace. Elio scrounges inside Blondie's wet pocket for the ring. It's there, his whole life in one metal, auto-fitting band with a tiny black screen.

Elio's fingers curl around his treasure. He pulls his hand from the pocket and jumps away from the Steelhead. Blondie sits up but doesn't make a move. Elio could hurt him worse than he already did, but he's not going to be that person. He breathes deep from his belly, lets air out to the count of ten. The rage recedes a few ticks. Soon, the shakes will replace adrenaline, and he needs to be long gone before then. He turns and sprints away.

They won't catch him even if they try. He's always been fast. He's built rangy, lithe like a cat. No, they'll bide their time, hoping to run into him again, but they won't because he's done working for the execs in Steelhead territory. He'll take his digi-ring to the Arcade, buy a full-year membership so he can play any time he likes and as much as he wants. They have contests, and he's good. Or he thinks he can be, anyway, because he has fast reflexes.

Elio stops to rest in the dark alcove of an industrial building where he can't see the water anymore. He slides the ring onto his left middle finger, where it flashes and tightens to fit. He shakes curly, dark-brown hair from his eyes, but it falls back, too long and needing a cut. *Mama will do it when I get home once she's done yelling at me for being late.* He's about to move on toward Armour Square when there's a loud boom, and the ground shifts under him. He scans the snaggletooth skyline where the sound came from. A dark rope twists into New Chicago's pale sky.

What in hot hells is going on? Elio sets off at a jog, though his legs feel like rubber. Some instinct drives him faster than he really needs to go, probably. The explosion has nothing to do with him. He hasn't eaten since this morning and really wants to stop at the first food truck he sees, an Asian man selling hotpot, but a sense of urgency drives him on. Usually, he's trying to escape from home to avoid Mama's nagging questions and Clera's resentful looks, but not now.

When Elio finally turns down his street and sees his building, he stops. It looks like a bomb went off inside, and maybe one did. Missing walls fade in and out of smoke haze, the innards of people's homes hanging over broken bricks and down the sides like guts. Flames lick from windows. The police are already putting up yellow caution tape and clearing out onlookers. A few people argue with them.

Elio stares in horror at the blackened exterior. He recognizes Mama's home-sewn, iris-print curtains fluttering through glass shards. They're stained with soot, and he knows suddenly that she is gone.

Horror clogs his throat. He wants to gag. Throw up. Scream. He drifts forward, pulled by some invisible line, and he can't resist the motion.

Does Clera know? Is her shift over? Could she have come home early to check on Mama? Is she dead?

Then he sees his big sister. He can't mistake her long hair, brown with golden highlights, or the way she holds herself, like she's trying to become smaller.

Elio rushes up to her. She's at the back of the crowd, still dressed in her gray work jumpsuit. He only has to push one old guy aside to tap her shoulder, but he hesitates. He wants to stay in this moment, to keep it from spilling into the next—the one where she turns and tells him their mother is gone, and they've only got each other now.

3

CLERA

The man in front of Clera shouts in a high, hysterical voice at odds with his whiskey barrel chest and pronounced jowls. She recognizes him. Mr. Mustafa. He lives down the hall from her. No. *Lived.*

"I have to get up there! My father is inside. That's my floor!" He jabs a finger upward. "I pay my rent! You clinks have no right to keep me out!"

The policeman, who looks barely older than Clera, has red cheeks and peach fuzz on his chin. He wears the olive-green uniform they all do. It looks like wool, too warm on this weirdly hot May day. There's not even a breeze off the lake. Smoke blankets them. Ash drifts and settles on her eyelashes. It lands on Mr. Mustafa's bald head, too, but he doesn't seem to notice.

The clink says, "Sir, have you looked at the building? Half of the left corner is just gone. It could fall at any time. We have instructions to keep onlookers away until the investigators and structural engineers can come in to assess stability." He holds both arms wide as though he can single-handedly keep back the dozens of people who freeze to listen. The crowd outnumbers the clinks, but policemen have buzz sticks, and worse, micro-cameras that record everything you do and relay it back to Central so they can come for you later.

Clera feels sorry for the clink. It isn't his fault someone blew a hole in her home. He's only following orders.

Mr. Mustafa shouts, "I can tell you who did this! Don't need any piss ball investigators. The Steelheads have been running a leth lab right below my place for over a year. I called about it. Told the super. No one listens." His face reddens during this speech, then crumples like a deflated balloon. A sob bursts from his throat.

Clera places a hand on his worn work uniform, squeezes, whispers, "It's all right, Mr. Mustafa. It's all right. You won't do your family any good if you get arrested."

She isn't sure he hears her over the crowd noise. Mr. Mustafa shifts, and she drops her hand. He steps back, forcing Clera back, too, though she wants to duck under the clink's arm and run through the arched doors, up three flights of stairs and down a hallway that might not exist anymore. *And Mama will come rushing out our front door, miraculously unhurt.*

"Clera!"

The voice wrenches her from the daydream. She turns and breathes out her little brother's name like a prayer. "Elio."

Until this moment, Clera realizes she wasn't sure he was still alive. He *should* have been at school, but sometimes he skips. Where does he go on those days, and why? He doesn't talk to her anymore, not like when he was little and hung on her words. She misses that little boy. This seventeen-year-old looks so unfamiliar that she catches her breath. He resembles Papa, with dark brown eyes and lashes too long for a boy. He has more beard growth than the young clink. It shadows a jaw that isn't round anymore.

"Elio?" Clera says his name again like a question—like she must reassure herself that her brother isn't some faceless stranger.

He studies her faded gray work jumper, grimy from the ash. "Mama? Is she . . ."

Clera can't answer. She just shakes her head and looks up. A few bricks roll off the yawning hole that used to be their outside wall and fall atop a growing heap of rubble.

An older clink hops on top of his patrol car and raises a bullhorn to his lips. His voice whines and crackles. He adjusts the volume and tries again. "This building is sealed until further notice. If you don't live here, return to your homes now or you will be arrested. If you DO live here, you will need to find other accommodations for the night. Anyone trying to enter this housing unit will be arrested. You can find lists of deceased posted at your local PD in the next forty-eight hours. Do not be a hero. Do not abuse my officers." The sergeant directs his gaze at a pretzel-thin lady wearing pink slippers who grips a clink with white-knuckled claws.

Someone yells, "What about our things? Clothes, money, food? And where exactly are we supposed to sleep tonight?" Others murmur agreement. The air shimmers with potential violence. Someone tugs Clera's elbow, and she looks back to see Elio jerking his head.

She doesn't want to leave. At the same time, she wants desperately to be anywhere else. Clera lets Elio pull her from the ragged fringes of the mob, across the street, into a shadowed alley. "We have to go now," he tells her, voice urgent.

Clera starts to argue, a reflex action she barely controls. He's right. They'd only get arrested if they stayed. Desperate people who've just lost their homes might turn violent at any minute. Or they'll head to the first public shelter they can find. The nearest stands only a block from her workplace. It will fill up quickly, and she doesn't know where there's another one. Clera gives Elio a quick nod. "Follow me."

———◦———

Clera and Elio stand in line at the homeless shelter. A supervisor scans their digi-rings to check for criminal records, then makes them breathe into the drug analyzer for signs of leth. She isn't sure Elio can pass these tests, but he does, and in less than an hour, they find themselves inside a cinderblock building she hoped never to enter.

The manager, an older man with a chest-length beard and bones poking out in every direction, waves them toward two cots pushed against the gray cement wall. Frazzled mothers, crying babies, and sad-eyed children occupy most of the other cots. Clera doesn't see anyone she knows from her building and wonders where ancient Ms. Lewenski from next door ended up. She plops down on a cot which sags beneath her weight.

Elio drops to the other cot, then jumps up. "I can't just sit here."

She's used to this itchy mood. "Go take a walk. Bring back dinner if you can."

After he leaves, Clera stretches out. She stares at a fly-spotted light on the ceiling. Her thoughts return to her neighbor.

Clera remembers Ms. Lewenski sneaking her mints at the store and lamenting, "With Social Security bankrupt and no family, what can I do but work?" Extra skin crinkled the corners of her eyes. She'd smile even though she had nothing to smile about and stroke Clera's cheek. "Ah, my girl. You're a good one. If I'd been lucky enough to have a daughter like you, I'd be able to retire. You'd have taken care of me, wouldn't you?" Clera always agreed, though she'd heard this question a million times.

The memory extends, sharpening like an icicle.

Business was slow. It was winter, and a storm rattled the glass door, snowflakes trying to get in. Six-year-old Clera wished she weren't wearing mittens so she could feel the old lady's dry, bird-bone hands, so different from Mama's plump, callused ones.

"Clera, I see in you myself sometimes," Ms. Lewenski had told her.

"You like the books, eh? I notice you walking past with your arms full of old stories on your way to the library. Reading is a grand thing, but only if it doesn't take the place of living. When you're old like me, and all your chances have gone, it's fine and right to curl up with a good book, but at your age, with your whole life before you—" She paused and squeezed Clera's mittened hands. "It would be a shame if you spent your life in novels when you could be experiencing a real-life story, one that has only begun. Living life is a risk, but hiding away is a bigger one. You only get one book of your own to star in! Don't be afraid! Make your life count for something."

Clera had pulled back, uncomfortable. What did Ms. Lewenski mean, "Don't be afraid?" Mama and Papa and her Grandma Buela would always take care of her. The cozy fourth-floor apartment in Armour Square was all she had ever known and all she needed.

Another, darker memory pushes into her mind, contradicting the first.

Clera sees herself at six again, taking trash to the incinerator in the alley one night. A male voice called to her. She turned. The sinking sun silhouetted the stranger, whose shadow stretched toward her. She stepped back and almost tripped over a rusty piece of metal that hadn't made it down the chute. He slunk closer. Closer. "Hey, little girl," he crooned.

No! Clera thrusts the vision away and sits up. She wraps her arms around herself but feels panic creeping in anyway. Her throat closes. The blood in her veins cools and thickens, circulation slowing, like she's dying. A veil falls across her vision. Her heart pounds, and her limbs feel as heavy and useless as steel girders. She's dying. Oh God. Exactly like before. But she *didn't* die the last time she felt like this. *I talked myself down. That's right. Take a breath. Relax. Imagine water shushing toward the shore. And the seagulls. How they soar and dip on air currents.*

Reality rushes back. She's safe in the homeless shelter, even if she has nothing but the clothes on her back. She pulls in a long breath, and the darkness recedes.

Counting her blessings affords little comfort, though. Her family has disappeared one by one. Buela and Papa succumbed to the latest pandemic three years ago. And Mama . . .

She can't think about that right now. Clera still has Elio, and she clings to that thought.

4

CLERA

"Clera, where are you?" Elio jolts her from reverie by snapping his fingers in her face. He sets two bowls of stew in foam cups at their feet. How long was he gone? An hour? Two? While he was out, a woman tried to steal his cot, but Clera scowled at her and pretended to reach for a knife.

Elio nods at the food. "I went to the soup kitchen next door. Better wait a bit to eat. It's hot. Oh, and they were out of plastic spoons, so we'll have to slurp it from the bowls."

"What are we going to do, Elio? They only let people sleep here one night. Then they kick you out. And what if Mama's out there on the streets? What if she escaped the destruction somehow, and she's looking for us?"

"Clera." Elio stills, the soup forgotten in his hand. "You know . . . we both know that Mama isn't . . ." He can't go on. Silence stretches between them. She watches while he swallows his emotions and holds on to a fragile control. She wants to rub his back but doesn't dare. Any show of empathy might shatter them both right now.

Elio clears his throat. "We'll go if they kick us out, then come back early enough to get a spot again. Or we'll find another shelter." He leans back on his elbows and stares at the ceiling. A whiff of something foul wafts off him.

Clera focuses single-mindedly on her brother to avoid more thoughts of Mama creeping in. "Why weren't you still at school when the explosion went off? It was only three o'clock. And why do you stink like day-old fish?" Her mind races ahead. She answers the second question herself. "You've been down at the docks."

Elio sits up again, sighing. He sniffs his collar and winces. "Do you want the truth, which will upset you, or the same lies I've been telling Mama for the past months?"

Clera winces at the mention of their mother, then pushes Mama behind a walled-off part of her brain. "Tell me what's real."

"I haven't been in school for most of this year." He shrugs. "I know I was supposed to be the one to make it to graduation, but I couldn't take it anymore. You should've been the one to finish."

"I wish I could have! You know dropping out wasn't my choice, right? After Papa died, we needed the money, so Mama got me on at the factory. But you? We had such high hopes! You could have made something of yourself, Elio, with your smarts."

"This is why I didn't tell you." He can't look at her. The tightness around his mouth signals an impending explosion. "Maybe school was different for you, Clera. But for me, it was hell."

"Surely, that's an exaggeration. You—"

But he's shaking his head, interrupting her. "No." He grinds his teeth, pauses for control, softens his voice. "Did you ever learn anything from those sad excuses for teachers?"

"It isn't their fault. I make more credits at Perkine. And with all the drugs and fights going on, well, *I* wouldn't want those jobs."

"I'm not blaming the teachers, just telling you why I had to get out. Part of the reason, anyway." Elio's eyes dart to her face but don't stay there.

Clera's thoughts spin. She's trying to remember a day Elio didn't come home sullen, unhappy, sometimes black and blue. "You were bullied. I should have realized. I think I did. Mama would ask you sometimes where you got this bruise or that one. Why didn't you tell her something was wrong?"

He glares at her. "What could Mama have done? Or Papa, back when he was alive? Nothing, that's what. It's what all boys go through when they're small and weak. Survival of the fittest, right? Maybe it's different for girls. You kept your head down, didn't even try to make friends."

Clera wants to deny this but can't. She's never been able to lie, and he's right. She thought he hadn't noticed her staying up late, reading under the covers. By the time she entered secondary school, Mama had given up urging her to meet up with one of her classmates. Clera spoke more to Ms. Lewenski and the school librarian than she did to kids her own age. She hadn't been exactly happy in school, but she hadn't been picked on, either. You can't bully someone you don't know exists. If she could have stayed long enough to graduate, she'd have tried for a scholarship at the local trade school.

The angry light leaves Elio's eyes. "Look, I have credits. I've been working for the city execs, doing the nasty jobs no one wants. I've been saving up for an Arcade membership, but I can spare a little to keep us going until they let us back into the apartment. And you can keep your factory job. It'll be okay."

"The Arcade, Elio?" Clera frowns. Now isn't the time to nag him about wasting money on video games. She sucks in a breath. "You're right. I'll go to the Skinpad factory tomorrow. Are you still working for the execs?"

"No. Today was my last day. Pretty sure I can't beg for my job back, either, so don't ask me to."

"Fine. Then you can stop by the PD and check the casualty lists, just in case." Her voice wobbles. She clears her throat before adding, "And go by the apartment building. Maybe some official will be there with a timeline for moving back in."

"Clera, you saw the building. Do you really believe that's going to happen?"

The housing authority will probably condemn the place, but she can't let herself think like that. There are waiting lists a mile long to get housing in New Chicago and plenty of people sleeping on the streets. That *can't* become Elio's and her fate. She won't let it.

Mama's face flashes across Clera's vision. She imagines what it must have been like inside their apartment when the explosion ripped through boards and brick. She sees the surprise on Mama's face, the *horror*, like it's her own. Clera balls her fists until nails bite into flesh. "We'll cross that bridge when we come to it."

Buela used to say that. Oh, how Clera wishes she were here. She'd been so feisty but bighearted as well. She'd always found the positive side to every problem, so that's what Clera will do. Elio needs her. She can't fall apart thinking about "what ifs."

She clasps her brother's hand. His fingers are larger than hers now, but she's still the oldest by two-and-a-half years, so she tries to reassure him. "We'll work it out, little brother. At least we have each other."

Elio's hand slides from her grip. He nods. "Wish I had a toothbrush." He glances around. "Doubt this place gives them out for free."

Clera picks up the foam cup, sips, and grimaces. Toothbrushes aren't all they need. How will she look, going to the factory tomorrow in her rumpled uniform and finger-combed hair? Oh, well. One bridge at a time.

Elio drains his bowl in a long gulp and sets it beside his cot. He pushes off his shoes, grabs a thin mylar blanket, and lies back. Clera finishes her soup and does the same. It's still early, but there's nothing to do but sleep.

She tries, but images of explosions, brick and mortar collapsing, and bodies scattered in the street like trash keep her awake for a long, long time.

Maybe Clera sleeps poorly because of nightmares, or perhaps it's because the cot sags in the middle, and she can't get comfortable. But for whatever reason, she drifts in and out. Dreams meld into memories. She stirs at dawn with the most recent recollection still vivid in her mind.

Five-year-old Clera had been asleep when the front door squeaked, waking her. She tiptoed from the bedroom and padded into the living room to stand beside Papa, who stood with his back to her at the open doorway. He wore his robe and held a broom in one hand. A man faced him from the hallway.

Clera recalls details: a scraggly beard, a tangle of necklaces, a blue headscarf, a snake tattoo, a gun.

"Clera, go back to bed. Now."

Papa made the command. She ignored it. The rest of the conversation is fuzzy but went something like this:

The young man said, "Who's this, now?" He squatted so he could see Clera better.

Her father tried to push her behind him, but the stranger caught her shoulder and held her in place. "You can tell me, little girl. Don't be afraid."

"Clera," she finally said. "Why are you here past bedtime?"

He laughed and released her. "That's funny. Past bedtime. Ha!" He stood and tapped his gun thoughtfully against his jaw. He looked at Papa. "If you don't have the money, maybe we can take payment in some other form?"

"No!" Papa's angry retort made Clera jump. "You're taking credits from your own people. Can't you see that? I knew you when you were a little boy. You weren't like this."

"Like what?" The stranger smiled. "Pathetic? Weak? This is the world we live in, hom. You join the strong and let them protect you, or you die. It's simple, like adding two plus two." His gaze shifted back to Clera. "Can you do that, little girl?"

"Four?" Clera ventured.

"She's pretty and smart. You give her to me, and it'll buy your family's safety for a year at least. What do you say?"

Papa had raised the broom, but he didn't strike the man. Something important seemed to hang in the balance, like air crackling just before lightning hit. Clera stepped in front of her father. "Leave him alone."

"She's sassy, too. I like that."

"I'll pay," her papa rasped. He pushed Clera aside. "If you stay away from my daughter."

The stranger shrugged. "Sure. Whichever way you want to play it." But his black eyes lingered on Clera.

Papa propped the broom against the wall and tugged off the ring he always wore. The young man took it and rummaged in his cargo pockets. He pulled out a pad, tapped on it, and swiped the ring across. He tucked the pad back into his pants and held up the ring. Papa reached for it, but the bad guy only held it away from him. "If you change your mind, you know where to find me."

His hand opened, and Papa snatched the band from a grubby palm. He thrust it on his finger. "That won't be happening. Now get out."

•◦•

Twenty-year-old Clera opens her eyes. The memory lingers like a bad aftertaste. She wonders how she could have been so brave back then, and when did she change? Would Buela be disappointed if she saw her granddaughter now? Would Papa? Clera squints at the window, where a rising sun pries at bent, plastic blinds. It wants to get in, and she doesn't blame it. Clera buries her head beneath the crinkly blanket.

Even the shelter seems better than what's out there.

5

SOLAST

Solast Bahri watches the fruit seller from under the hood of her jacket. It smells of smoke and body odor, too hot for this sunny day. Her newly shaved scalp prickles with sweat. Shoppers pack the cordoned-off street on this first market day, so her strange attire won't be noticed. The upper-class wives wear capris, sleeveless blouses, and straw hats. Teens dress in a retro-grunge style, and the oldsters sport long sleeves to cover sunspots and cancer scars.

Sol edges closer to the hydroponic tomatoes and strawberries. Her mouth waters. It's been two days since she ate. She eyes the seller, a paunchy, bald Hispanic who yells at his female helper in Spanish and agitatedly flaps his arms. He's perfect. If she must steal, better it's from someone like him. She's met the type plenty in the Barrens—men best left in the nineteenth century.

A young man bumps into her. He's so busy watching vids behind his mirrored smart glasses that he doesn't notice. Sol hunches, buries her hands in giant pockets, pretends to examine a shiny red tomato with a seam running like a scar near the stem. The seller turns to answer a young mother's question. Sol absently fingers her own scar, given courtesy of Anton the day her father was executed. It forms a pale line across her sharp cheekbone. *Eleven years ago. Has it really been that long? Was I ever that young?*

The mother clutches her child with one hand and picks up a pint of strawberries with the other, asking about freshness. Sol casts about. Midmorning shadows from New Chicago's skyscrapers darken the busy street. Identical kiosks run in straight lines down the thoroughfare. There's a constant hum of voices and movement.

Despite her almost six-foot height, she's beneath notice in her drab clothes. She scoops several tomatoes into a pocket, then leans forward and pretends to check imperfections on a melon while a carton of strawberries slides into the other pocket. Oblivious, the seller rubs his scalp and urges his helper to find more bags. Sol saunters off. She wants to hurry but makes herself loiter, pretending to examine a display of cheap tungsten jewelry and a rack of synth suits.

She strains for sounds of pursuit, a cry, a change in the crowd's lazy Saturday rhythm. Without thinking, she steals several beef sticks at the last stall before slipping into an alley. Her pockets are full. She walks down the stinking, trash-strewn concrete tunnel until she finds an alcove dark enough to hide her. There she pauses, withdraws a tomato, and bites into it. Her hands tremble. Juice runs down her chin.

The hydroponic fruit reminds her of summers from her childhood when she and Father tended rows of vegetables, hauled endless buckets of water to keep them alive in August heat, then reluctantly donated the harvest to the commune. *That's how it works*, Father had told her when she complained this wasn't fair. They *had* gotten to eat some of their harvest at the community table. *We aren't capitalists*, Father had tried to explain. *What we have belongs to all*. But Sol had seen Anton's container house, and it dwarfed everyone else's. Once she'd looked through his window and watched him feast on pork roast—meat the rest of them rarely saw.

Sol's shrunken stomach tightens as she finishes the tomatoes and starts on the strawberries. She'll eat everything standing in the alley doorway, not risk having her haul taken by some scrull in the park. She's too thin, but there's no one in her life to look beautiful for, so who cares? It isn't that she doesn't eat, simply that regular meals aren't something New Chicago offers to people like her. She saves the meat sticks for last. They were an afterthought. She was rash to take them on a moment's whim, but she's gotten away with it. Again.

How long? Will the clinks catch me next time? Or the time after? Throw me back out in the Barrens? Or into some dark cell to be forgotten?

She remembers the hope she felt when she'd first bribed her way past the gates of the city meant to keep out chaff like her. The only job had been sewer work for the execs. Three years of it. But she survived and finally snagged the nursing job at the clinic. Too bad it folded two years ago and dumped her back on the streets. She's twenty-eight now, and what does she have to show for her life? Regrets. Loads of them. And the burning revenge that keeps her going. If Anton is somewhere in this morass of humanity, she'll find him. Then she'll kill him.

Sol sucks the spicy salt from her fingers. She wanders the streets through the afternoon, slipping through alleys, dodging traffic, always alert for danger. She ties the jacket she nabbed off a dead leth addict around her waist and lets the sun bathe the dusky skin of her arms. After an especially cold winter, its touch feels like hope. But she knows better than to believe it is.

Only at dusk does Solast Bahri slink back to the cardboard and tin space she's carved for herself beneath the maple tree in Freedom Park. The place was reclaimed and renamed decades ago, only to slip back beneath the litter and ramshackle Slummer huts that cover every foot of trampled grass. As she passes between two sagging tents in the fading light, a hand grabs her wrist. Without thought, she catches the attached arm, bends, and flings the assailant over her head. He lands with an *oof* behind her on his back. She whirls, crouches, and balls her fists, but the man lies still. His chest rises spastically. Maniacal laughter drifts toward her over the caws of the crows.

"Fecking leth sucker." Sol turns away and crawls inside her meager shelter. Anger curls around the flame of revenge. In the background, despair wafts like a foul odor she can't shake.

6

ELIO

Clera shakes Elio gently.

His fists fly up.

She hisses and pulls away. "I'm headed to the factory. Meet me back here after my shift at three."

"Okay," Elio mumbles. He falls back into his dream, only it's not a dream but a memory.

His father was mad—no, disappointed. He'd caught seven-year-old Elio beating up the neighbor boy, who was a head taller than him and had been stealing his lunch money for the past week. Elio didn't plan to attack the kid. It just happened, like it always did. He never knew when the devil in his brain would turn his vision red. During those times, he might do anything. There was no thought involved, only action.

Papa yanked Elio off the older boy by the back of his shirt. Even then, Elio kept punching the air until the bully scuttled crying to his apartment. Papa set Elio down and whirled him around. "What are you doing, boy?"

His father's words sapped the heat from Elio's cheeks. His thinking brain returned, and he fumed, "That boy stole my money. He'd keep stealing it, too, if I didn't do something."

Papa let Elio go. "So, you planned this all out, did you? Decided fists were the best way to solve this problem? Or did you react without considering your actions at all?"

"Well, I . . ." Elio stuttered.

"That's what I thought." Papa squatted in the hallway so they could look at each other eye to eye. "Elio, we've talked about this. You can choose how you react to the bad stuff, eh? Like a thinking person or like a wild animal. Which are you?"

Elio was pretty sure he was a wild animal, but he answered, "A thinking person?"

"Right." Papa sighed, then touched Elio's chest. "I know there's a good boy in there. Use your passion to make the world better, son, not to destroy it. Okay?"

The memory wavers. Perhaps Elio falls asleep, for suddenly he's underwater, looking up through a watery veil. His chest burns, and he *has* to breathe. He opens his mouth and sits up, gasping. Tears, not water, stream down his cheeks.

He blinks at the cinderblock walls of the shelter. Sunlight filters through a grimy window. The dormitory is empty. At the far end, a man wanders in and stops when he sees Elio. "You still here? Rules are to be out by nine."

Elio rubs the wetness from his cheeks. He bites his cheek and keeps his temper in check so he can get back in here tonight. He pushes his shoes on, thrusts the blanket aside, and stands. His ribs hurt from the fight yesterday, and he's hungry, but what's new? He mumbles, "Sorry," and heads out of the shelter.

The soup kitchen has closed, so Elio stops at a cafe on route to the PD and taps his digi-ring on a paypad to buy a stuffed pepperoni roll and bottle of water. He hates spending money on mundane things. Maybe he'll pay for his Arcade membership while he still has some credits left. But what if things get worse, and he and Clera need that money? When does Clera get paid next? It's monthly, but he doesn't know the date, and he doubts she has many credits on her digi-ring. Seems like Mama and Clera use their paychecks as soon as they get them to pay rent and utilities.

Elio follows the road he's on. Traffic is light. A few leth-heads recline against buildings in a drug haze, but they thin out as he nears the station. Police hover cars pull out of the lot, sirens flashing. A vaguely familiar woman stares at the digital sign just outside the front door. She brushes his shoulder, crying as she hurries away.

Sunlight soaks into his skin, but he barely feels its warmth. Nearby, a crabapple tree stuffed with pink blooms sits on a small square of grass. There's no greenery where Elio lives, only concrete. He'd like to rest on the bench under the tree and pretend he's rich and carefree, but he can't. He has to do what Clera asked, though his feet feel leaden.

Dragging forward, Elio stands in front of the sign, where notices track across the screen. Fines for illegal parking were just raised. Deportations from New Chicago are ramping up. The station will close early tomorrow to celebrate President Bendurin's reelection.

Elio could care less about parking and less than less about Bendurin, who's managed to stay in office since Elio was born thanks to "term limit extensions." Elio doesn't follow politics, but he remembers Buela fuming about the country's downward spiral. *How dare we call ourselves a democracy still? How?* He's passionate like she was. Not *only* hot-headed. Not *always* bad.

The sign changes. There's a list, long but alphabetical, so Elio's able to skim through to the "D's" before it changes. He doesn't think Mama will be there yet, doesn't believe in the clinks' competence or efficiency. And she's not. Something lifts in his chest until another list composed of injured taken to hospitals flashes across the board. Again, no *Alita Diaz*, which can only mean one thing. There was nothing left for emergency workers to find.

Mama. Is. Gone.

Elio's chest pinches. Maybe some secret part of him dared hope she'd been out getting cold medicine when the explosion hit. But no. She'd been home. Elio tells himself she didn't suffer, but the words ring hollow.

He wishes he had a picture of Mama. All their photos were in the apartment. The images in his head will fade until he won't remember the shape of her face or her smile. That's what happened with Papa and Buela.

A sob pushes up Elio's throat. He turns from the sign and grinds his fists against his face. *No more.* But another sob erupts, so he hurries into the crabapple's deep shade and hides himself while he cries. Fragrant blossoms shiver above him. He'll hate that smell forever.

Once Elio regains control, he heads for home. There will be more pain waiting there, but best to get it over with.

7

CLERA

With no alarm to wake her, Clera's late for her early shift. She pulls her fingers through tangled hair, but the wind sends strands flying again. She has enough credits left on her digi-ring for breakfast and maybe lunch yet decides to skip eating.

Her brain feels fuzzy as she navigates the steps leading to the factory grounds. Pain stabs at her chest—not a heart attack, simply her old friend, panic. She pauses, breathes, counts down from one hundred. It works for now, and she proceeds. A sign attached to the fence proclaims: "Penzine Industries: Makers of Penzine Skinpads. More reliable than your own brain!" Below this, in tiny black print, is President Bendurin's stamp: an eagle clutching a snake, and beside his emblem a note: *This business is authorized for trade.*

Inside the fence, trash flutters against chain links. The cement yard with its stone benches is empty. Front doors slide open as she nears, familiar yet somehow creepy. Clera shivers. She's been on a horror kick at the library, gobbling up thick novels by some guy called King. She survives the factory by living inside books, but now is not the time for flights of fancy. She'll be lucky if her boss, Mrs. Apochek, doesn't notice she's tardy and dock her salary.

Clera swipes her digi-ring across the check-in kiosk screen and glances at the clock on the wall, which tells her she's not *too* late. She proceeds to the elevator that will take her to the fifth floor, where bots work mindlessly, spidery metal fingers aligning filaments along elastomer plates to create control boards for Skinpads. Her job is to check their work. Bots make more mistakes than you'd think. Buela's voice drifts through her head: *Technology! We were better off when we had less!*

Mrs. Apochek interrupts this thought by bellowing her name.

Clera jumps. She can't help it. The woman's voice grates. She bears down on Clera between two assembly lines of metal arms that twist and jerk, twist and jerk, as they pick up microscopic parts and place them. Workers in gray jumpsuits blend into shadows far across the huge, echoing room.

Mrs. Apochek's arms perch on wide hips. She halts in front of Clera and glances pointedly at the Skinpad attached to her inner arm. The epidermis there glows. As a supervisor of supervisors, she qualified for a company Skinpad and doesn't like anyone to forget it. It's almost funny how she waves her arm around, trying to get noticed.

But right now nothing about Mrs. Apochek seems humorous, and Clera braces herself.

"You're late, and we had an issue on your line. I had to take care of it," Mrs. Apochek snaps. Her two chins wobble indignantly.

"Th . . . thank you," Clera stutters, not knowing what else to say. When Mrs. Apochek stares at her with slits for eyes, Clera feels she must explain, though that's the last thing she wants to do. "You probably heard about the leth lab explosion yesterday afternoon? That was in my apartment building. It's sealed off, and I had to sleep in a shelter. I don't have an alarm, or clothes, or anything really." Her voice shakes.

"Hmph." Mrs. Apochek continues to eye her suspiciously. Her right hand drops to her Skinpad, and she starts tapping.

Checking out my story. Like I'd lie about a thing like that. Clera concentrates on the blood pumping through her veins and waits. Fear turns to annoyance. She wants to tell her boss, *if you're so concerned about my tardiness, why don't you let me get to work?* But she doesn't.

Mrs. Apochek looks up. "I'll expect you to come here clean and unwrinkled tomorrow. Penzine has standards to uphold. You are now half an hour late, which is a twenty-credit dock."

Clera opens her mouth to object, but her boss is already talking again. "No excuses, or I'll file a complaint upstairs. Now get on it." She turns and marches off like a drill sergeant, high stepping in her shiny boots.

For a moment, Clera watches. She pictures a ceiling fan flying off its bracket and falling on the woman's head with a satisfying clunk. There's no pity in Mrs. Apochek. She's the job, and the job is her. Clera hates Perkine's soullessness. She could stand the boredom, the isolation from other people, the mindless tasks, but the *feel* of the factory is like touching cold metal. She dies a little every time she walks through the front door. Yet Mama never complained.

Mama. She's worked downstairs in the packaging department for many years. Clera would often picture her there and feel better, but now there's a void beneath Clera's feet and in her heart. How will she stand it?

Find a spine, Clera tells herself. *You* have *to stand it. Elio needs you. If you can't get back into the apartment, there's nothing but this job. Better a crappy job than nothing.* Yet she isn't sure she believes that anymore.

Work flows normally until the afternoon. Clera meets her friend Luz in the lunch line. They sit together in the cafeteria, eating flatbread with soy paste and drinking cups of strong coffee.

Luz hugs her and says, "I'm sure your mama will be found alive, Clera. Medra's family made it out."

"And what floor were they on?" Clera asks around a bite of bread.

Luz purses thin lips and wrinkles her forehead. "First floor, I think."

"Not fourth floor."

An awkward pause follows. Luz clears her throat. "I'd offer to take you home with me, but we're ten people crammed into a three-bedroom apartment. Bedro would never let me." She shakes her head sadly.

Clera's friend married her high school sweetheart after schooling out. She already has a one-year-old, and they live with Bedro's extended family. Clera can't imagine how crowded Luz's place must be and cringes at the thought of sharing such close quarters. "No worries," she tells Luz, meaning it. "Elio and I will be fine. We're sleeping in the shelter again tonight, and then—" What? She can't finish. She doesn't know.

"You'll find something." Luz pats her arm. Her hand is dry, nails bitten down to red skin. Dark circles underscore her eyes.

After fifteen minutes, the bell sounds to clear out. Sighing, Luz gets to her feet. Clera follows her to the conveyor belt and deposits her tray on the rubber treads. Luz gives her a hug before they part ways.

On the elevator, a red-eyed, gray-haired woman sniffles and clutches a tissue. When she sees Clera, her eyes widen. She makes a choking sound and pulls Clera close. Caught off guard, Clera accepts the embrace for a few seconds, then eases back. She recognizes the woman. It's one of Mama's friends from packaging—Gina Torrez, she thinks. "What's happened?" Clera asks with a sinking feeling.

Gina swallows another sob and takes a trembling breath. "You don't know?" She blinks. "But you must. Your apartment building . . . it's *been leveled.*"

Cold starts at Clera's forehead and oozes down to cover her whole body. She's frozen, joints locked, her brain stuck between gears. She tries to make her mouth work and fails.

Gina reaches for her again, but Clera evades the woman's touch. The elevator door starts to open, but Clera jams the *CLOSE* button and holds it. "What are you talking about?"

Gina shrinks back at her tone.

Mama's friend rubs the tissue under her nose, straightens, sucks in air. "My husband left a message on my tablet. I was looking at it over lunch and saw the note. You remember that we live in the building next to yours? Heral was driving by on his route and saw the city execs with their dozers and wrecking balls. He was scared they'd accidentally take out our building, too. You know how close together they built those places."

Once she pauses for breath, Clera breaks in, no longer frozen but filled with shocked outrage. "Do you mean they just took down my home? Without checking for bodies, or investigating, or letting people in to collect possessions? With no warning?"

"The message wasn't long, Clera. I don't know details, but yes, I think."

"Why . . ." But Clera doesn't finish. The city wouldn't alert residents that their homes were about to be demolished. That might cause trouble. Another riot, maybe, like the almost-riot right after the explosion. "The clinks said they needed to investigate. They *were* going to investigate." She leans against the metal panel and closes her eyes.

"I assume your mother is on the death lists? And your brother?"

Talking feels like too much work, but Clera forces words out. "Elio's okay. I don't know about Mama. She was home. She was home." *She was home.* Clera sees the wrecking ball behind her eyelids. It bursts through the living room. Mama is in bed. The wall shatters, and the framed photo of Buela and Buelo crashes to the floor. The lead sphere blasting toward Mama cuts off her scream, knocks her out of bed and through plaster, wood, and brick. She's riding that ball clear up into the sky.

Clera shakes her head. *No.* That's not how it happened. Mama was already dead before the building was bulldozed. In her gut, Clera knew this, just hasn't acknowledged it until now. If souls can fly to the heavens, her mama's has done so. Is there life after death? Buela thought so. She burned candles for the ancestors and went to mass every Sunday. That belief must have been a comfort when she lay gasping for air two years ago, drowning in the fluids that filled her lungs.

"Clera? Dear?" Cool fingers wrap Clera's wrist in a gentle squeeze, then release her. Gina looks down at her with a nervous smile. "I have to get out. My shift's starting. I'm so sorry. I will truly miss Alita."

Clera jumps away from the button, and the door opens. Gina departs. A couple of workers get on, complaining about crappy lifts and how the maintenance crews must be slacking off.

Voices buzz like mosquitos in Clera's ears. The elevator climbs to her floor and deposits her. She feels like a ghost, like she's the one who died.

Mrs. Apochek is standing there. Clera runs right into her. It's like colliding with an elephant.

Her supervisor frowns. "You're late from lunch," she barks.

"The elevator wasn't working." Clera's excuse sounds lame in her ears.

Mrs. Apochek leans in. "Are you high, girl? This company doesn't allow leth smokers on its property. If that's what you've been up to over lunch, it's straight to the unemployment lines for you."

Clera has never once thought of trying leth. In Buela's day, they called it meth, and it was toxic stuff, just like the modern version. Buela said it turned people into walking skeletons. Leth is even more addictive, and Clera would never risk experimenting with the drug. "I'm not an addict." Her voice comes out angry again. She can't help it.

"Watch your tone," Mrs. Apochek snarls. "I'm taking twenty more credits off your account. No, thirty, for disrespect." She taps on her company pad, then holds it out so Clera can swipe with her digi-ring.

"No."

"Excuse me? Are you refusing a direct order?"

"Yes."

Those monosyllabic answers flummox the supervisor. She stutters, searching for a response while Clera watches stone-faced.

She could try to explain. *My home's been destroyed. My mama is almost certainly dead. I don't know where to go.* But she doesn't bother. The Penzine Skinpad Factory has never cared about her before. Why would they now? She's numb, and it's a good place to be.

"Well, then, we'll just see. I'm calling up the general manager, and you can talk to him." Mrs. Apochek nods to herself in satisfaction and taps again on her pad.

"I don't think so." Clera's voice sounds oddly calm and rational in her ears. Maybe she's going crazy. "I want my last paycheck before I go."

Mrs. Apochek laughs in her face. "You can talk to the big boss about that. He's waiting for you upstairs."

"I don't think so," Clera repeats. She's gone too far to turn back now. A flutter of panic rises in her belly past the apathy.

"Don't expect any money from the company. There's plenty willing to take your place, you know."

Clera's laugh is dry. "I expect so." They stare at each other. Mrs. Apochek blinks first.

"I never saw the like." She turns on her heel and stomps off.

Clera calls for the elevator.

8

ZAVI

There are plenty of untrained people in New Chicago who could have done this job, Zavi reflects as he repots cucumber seedlings. He's seated in his medical hover chair. The uniform of Fadel Arboretum and Greenhouses, a green shirt and slacks, fits loosely over Zavi's shrunken frame. He's started weight training alongside physical therapy sessions, but it's slow-going. A constant, dull pain wraps around his reconstructed spine. The doctors say he's doing great, that the ache will fade, but he isn't sure.

His healing injuries remind him every moment of the air rail accident that killed his parents and made him a cripple. The trip from Grandfather's compound outside the city should have been an easy, safe one, but the world is messed up. Earther saboteurs blew the rails, leaving their telltale mark behind, a circle within a circle, transected by a spear, on the toppled cars. Zavi's car didn't take a direct hit, but it fell off the track. After waking from a weeks-long coma, the doctors informed him that Mother and Father had been thrown from the transport and died instantly. Was that supposed to comfort him? It didn't. Their absence carved a hole in his chest that, unlike his spine, would never heal.

He remembers nothing of the attack. They said his amnesia might be permanent, and he hoped it would be. The fanatic terrorists, with their anti-space and anti-technology Earther agenda, were never caught. They'd faded back into the Barrens, those vast, unpatrolled and poorly governed rural areas outside New Chicago.

At least I still have Grandfather.

———◆———

Elijah Fadel had been at the hospital when Zavi woke. He'd left his billion-dollar pharmaceutical industry in the board's hands so he could sit at Zavi's bedside. Zavi remembers well their conversation the day before the hospitalist released him into Grandfather's care.

"We need to talk about your future," Grandfather had said. He sat upright in a chair drawn close to the bed, cane propped beside him. Thick white hair flowed almost to his shoulders. Blue eyes identical to Zavi's shone with familiar intensity.

Zavi pushed the button that raised the bed so he could meet that gaze squarely. "I've got my master's degree in botany. I was going on to study for a PhD like Niklas did." Niklas was Zavi's cousin—his mother's brother's son—and five years older. They lived far away in Sweden, yet Zavi, an only child, had always looked up to Nik like a big brother.

Grandfather's eyes never wavered. "You know that isn't possible now. At least not in the next year. You need time to heal. Physically, but also emotionally. You and I have a great grief to cope with."

Zavi swallowed away the tears always so close to the surface. "But what will I do? I can't just sit around. I'll go crazy. My mind needs something to focus on besides—you know."

"I do." Grandfather shifted his rangy frame. "I certainly do. That's why I've procured you a job. Nothing intense. Something you can manage while attending physical therapy sessions."

"A job." Zavi rolled the thought around in his brain. There were plenty of career opportunities in Grandfather's labs, but none for a botanist.

"Do you remember touring the Fadel Arboretum and Greenhouses when I first opened it in New Chicago? Well, Albero Harris, the director, has assured me he has a place for you there. You'll be a regular worker, overqualified for the position, but it's not a taxing one. You'll stay occupied in a field you love while you heal in mind and spirit."

"I don't know if my spirit *will* heal. I can't imagine not missing Mother and Father. Moving on."

"That's because you are young." Grandfather's gaze softened. "You've never known such a loss, but I have. And you're right. When people we love pass, the missing pieces change us forever. We never stop feeling the absence, but we do learn to move past it. We have to."

"*I* have to, you mean." Bitterness leaked from Zavi's voice.

"Both of us do." Grandfather paused. His eyes drifted away to focus on a painting of the ocean hanging from the wall. He cleared his throat before adding, "I can't lose you, too."

After Grandfather left, Zavi sent Niklas a message on his Skinpad. It was the first time they'd been in contact since the accident.

Hey, Nik. I heard you came out for Mother and Father's funeral. Sorry I missed seeing you.

Niklas responded almost immediately.

Well, it's not like you could help being in a coma. I'm so sorry for what happened. How are you?

Better. They're releasing me tomorrow, and I have a botanist job lined up through one of Grandfather's pet projects. The docs say I should be walking again in the next six months or so. Miracles of modern medicine, right?

Yeah.

The cursor flashes maybe thirty times before Niklas comes back. Words roll across the screen.

I don't know if anyone told you that I've been selected to join the biology team aboard the starship *Lycka*. I'm on route to Mars as we speak. We left soon after the funeral. I thought maybe I should stay with Father, but he wouldn't have it. We're going through the ARH, little cuz! You know, that Martian wormhole the Mars colonists discovered? In less than a year, I'll be living on a whole new planet!

Zavi's heart stopped, then resumed beating double-time. His fingers flew over the keyboard.

How can you leave knowing it's probably forever?

He hit send and immediately wanted to take back the accusation-filled message, but it was too late. The time lag between sending and receiving was almost nil, thanks to a new quantum messaging app.

Niklas responded immediately with words Zavi still remembers.

Don't be like that, little cuz. This is the opportunity of a lifetime! And we don't know I won't come back. We don't know anything, really. I'm sorry to hit you with this when you're down,

but try to be happy for me, okay? I think of you all the time. One day we'll be together again. I promise.

Zavi memorized those words even though he didn't believe them. They echo through his mind now until brash laughter interrupts the memory. He blinks, and he's back in the greenhouse. Two female workers several aisles over glance his way, then whisper and move off.

Zavi puts the cucumber seedling aside and stares without seeing through the glass wall of the greenhouse. Trees sway in an ever-present wind outside. Inside, fans hum.

The vacuum in his soul hasn't mended yet. It probably never will. He opens a screen on his Skinpad and finds Nik's address in his *favorites* list. He begins to type.

9

CLERA

Clera loiters at the razed area where her building stood only yesterday morning, sandwiched between two identical apartment units. Her heart is an empty drum. Yellow caution tape outlines piles of rubble. Here and there, a cloth fragment waves in the breeze, a teddy bear pokes his head above broken bricks, and someone's coffee cup sits, miraculously undamaged, atop a splintered board. A breeze whistles between buildings, the sound lonely as ghosts.

No one is about. It's a workday, and everybody works—except her, because she quit—when she and Elio most needed her credits, too. She tries to dredge up regret, but nothing comes. It's like her brain's been shot up with Novocain. Leaving the factory feels inevitable, something she knew was coming but didn't let herself think about. Yet if there had been no explosion, would Clera have stayed, unhappy? Maybe. She's always done what she was told. Always taken the safe path. Not like Elio. Even when he was little, he'd rush into trouble like a knight into battle.

Clera sees no bodies at the disaster site—no bones or blood or severed limbs. Her mother and many others must be decomposing beneath the remains of the building, though. She can't imagine a better scenario, and her stomach turns at the thought. They've been buried as neatly as corpses in a graveyard. The housing authority has already forgotten Clera's home existed, and the clinks are too busy to investigate. Those who caused the explosion must have died in it, too, which ties things up nicely. And the world moves on.

Yet Clera is stuck. For the first time in her life, she has no idea what to do. Only Elio keeps her planted in reality. They could leave New Chicago, strike out past the border wall and risk the Barrens. Or they could look for other work here in the city, maybe even start their own business. But what would they do? They aren't trained for anything. The crowded metropolis hems them in. Clera wants to flee, hide, lose herself in a book and pretend this isn't happening.

But she can't, and she needs to quit wallowing. A solution will appear. It always does, right? Hopefully, the answer to her problems won't mean sacrificing who she is and disappointing Mama, Buela, and Papa. She imagines them watching up in the clouds, waiting to see how tragedy will change her.

The library. She'll go there. Elio won't expect her back at the shelter until after three, so she's got time. South Side Public Library usually makes Clera feel better. It's a run-down, flat-roofed structure built when Frank Lloyd Wright designs were popular. The red brick building must be a hundred years old.

The library sits wedged between a laundromat and a smoke shop. A parking lot sprawls along the front, and cement steps lead up to a glass door. The handicapped-accessible ramp gives the place a kindly feel. Or maybe Clera gets that vibe because it's always been her escape.

A bell chimes when she walks inside and through a metal detector. The detector used to keep patrons from stealing books, but that was long ago. For Clera's whole life, this place has been so much more than a library. Homeless people linger on the sagging sofas in the reading area during cold winter days. Slummers too poor to own even cheap internet tablets surf the web at banks of old-fashioned computers clustered in the back. The librarians hold free classes here, host craft times for kids, and there's a multi-purpose room where old people exercise on Saturday mornings.

Clera draws in the smells of dust and paper. The library has just opened for the day, and it's deserted except for Mrs. Moriarty, the head librarian, and two young girls shelving books. Rich people don't read like this anymore, picking buckram-bound volumes off shelves and thumbing through rustling pages. They don't know what they're missing. Clera loves to curl up in a corner and feel the heavy weight of a book on her lap.

Mrs. Moriarty looks up from the circulation desk and smiles at Clera. She's a thin black woman with slanting eyes that suggest part-Asian heritage. Reading glasses hold straight black hair behind her ears. Her long fingers flutter over a keyboard. They pause as she says, "Good morning, Clera. I'm surprised to see you here. Aren't you working?"

"No." Clera hesitates. She could lie, but she's too tired. Her jumpsuit gives her away, anyway. "I just quit."

"Oh!" Mrs. Moriarty's voice reminds Clera of velvet, soft and deep. The librarian rises, edging around the barrier that separates them. "It was your building that was destroyed, wasn't it."

Clera nods, unable to speak. The older woman's arms encircle her. This hug feels different from Luz's brief squeeze or Gina's semi-hysterical embrace. Mrs. Moriarty's arms are muscled. They hold Clera firmly while something inside her breaks, and suddenly she's sobbing into Mrs. Moriarty's blouse. The librarian smells of incense. When Clera finally pulls away, for the moment, she's okay.

Mrs. Moriarty puts one of the girls in charge of circulation and pours Clera and herself cups of herbal tea in the back room. Bins of blunt-edged scissors and cups filled with markers rest beside squares of felt on a long table. Someone has been covering paperbacks at the laminator in the corner, and a burned plastic smell lingers. A small window looks out on an alley, where a scabby old apple tree attempts to grow.

Clera sips, swallows, asks softly, "Do you need any workers here, Mrs. Moriarty?"

The librarian looks sadly back at her. "I'd hire you in a minute if I could. But if anything, the city's cutting jobs like mine. Calling libraries 'unnecessary.'" She shrugs, sees Clera's worried look, and adds, "That sort of talk has been going on since the advent of the Internet. We simply ignore it and carry on."

"I need to work, Mrs. Moriarty." Clera folds her hands around the warm mug. "I shouldn't have been so hasty to leave the factory, but I just couldn't . . ." She swallows hard.

"Of course you couldn't," the librarian soothes. "The place you need to go is Job Recruitment. I'll look up the address. The Internet is good for something, eh? Do you have a place to sleep tonight?"

"Yes. We'll be fine." Clera makes her voice firm. Mrs. Moriarty has a family of her own. They share a tiny apartment not far from here. The librarian held a party for library club there—one of the happiest times of Clera's life. The apartment had smelled like incense, too, and a tiny, wrinkled Indian lady sat by the front door. Two small children chattered in a back bedroom, sometimes poking their heads out and giggling.

Clera smiles at the memory. A little later, she leaves with the essence of warm tea and soothing arms still lingering. She heads back toward Perkine Industries but turns off before she reaches it onto a road buzzing with traffic. It's near noon.

There's a plate of cookies and fruit in the waiting area of the small office labeled "Job Recruitment." Clera e-signs some documents, and when the receptionist's back is turned, she takes a banana and three cookies from the counter. She settles down to wait.

It's a long wait, but a vid-screen provides entertainment, spewing out the latest news: the fanatic Earthers are holding another rally, arsonists have burned a downtown strip mall, and NASA has almost finished constructing *Calliope*, the U.S.'s first, gargantuan starship. Clera munches stale cookies and listens.

"NASA has set a July deadline for completion of *Calliope*. While three-fourths of its shuttle berths are already spoken for through NASA's strenuous vetting program, a full fourth of berths are to be filled via lotteries. According to NASA's chief engineer, this will ensure a varied colonist gene pool to travel through the ancient, Martian-made wormhole that scientists have nicknamed the ARH.

"Last year, Norway's starship, *Loki*, launched through the ARH after data from the probes, *Pioneer I* and *Pioneer II*, revealed Goldilocks planets in the red dwarf solar system on the other side. Sweden's *Lycka* will soon reach Mars and follow her. While *Pioneer III* has not yet returned, nor has word from *Loki* reached top scientists yet, the U.S. government and NASA have deemed our own launch of *Calliope*, to be followed soon after by *Thalia* and *Urania*, a worthwhile endeavor and as safe as can be expected. Excitement has been building over the past year."

Clera wonders how the government can spend so lavishly on space travel while Americans starve in the streets. She almost sounds like an Earther, and the thought makes her wince.

The camera pans to an orbital shot of the U.S. Space Station, where drones are hard at work putting finishing touches on the behemoth called *Calliope*. Its whale-like structure is attached to girders. Along the curved side, indentations mark empty docks where space shuttles will attach. The back of the whale's belly slowly rotates. Glass that must be radiation and asteroid-proof allows the camera to cut to a close-up inside, revealing paths, tree-studded lanes, circles of bushes. She's read about this. It's a huge, rotating park. The spin will create artificial gravity essential for long space flights. Orchards and gardens will supply food for colonists. Even farm animal embryos are making the trip.

It's fascinating, but Clera has more pressing things to consider. She finishes eating the banana and has risen to throw the peel away when her number is called.

A woman who reminds Clera of Gina, only a decade younger and twenty pounds lighter, escorts her into a small office. She settles Clera on a metal chair and eyes her from behind a matching metal desk. Fake tulips decorate the top. An abstract painting on the wall depicts a vast, frothing ocean. Clera's sure she's seen that print before, maybe at the free clinic?

The woman scans Clera's information and looks up. She folds her hands on the desk. "You have no skill set," she informs Clera. "I have no jobs for unskilled workers."

"Oh." Clera tries to ignore the sting of those words. "I'm a hard worker and reliable. I can learn fast."

The woman's face remains unchanged. "You quit your last job, at the . . ." She looks down. ". . . Perkine Industries Skinpad Factory . . . today?"

"Um, yes. It's a long story." *Or a sad, short one.*

"Well, jobs don't grow on trees, you know." The woman sighs. "You see, we're in a recession. Do you know what that means?"

Clera grinds her teeth at the woman's patronizing tone. "Yes, I know. But I'll do anything."

"I don't have 'anything.' What I have is 'nothing' for unskilled workers. I'm sorry."

Clera won't beg. She rises and holds out a hand to shake. Her mind scrambles. She'll find another recruitment office. Something will turn up.

Yet trepidation tightens her belly. It threatens to overcome a grief that stretches as wide as the ocean in the picture. She hadn't thought fear could overtake sadness so quickly, but it did.

Clera didn't die in that explosion. She lived, and she wants to go on living.

For Elio. But also for herself.

10

ELIO

Elio leaves the place he called home for eighteen years, a flattened square of rubble now. Numbness creeps into his bones, and he's glad for it. Enough tears. He forces himself to take stock, makes a mental to-do list.

First, he checks with the local housing authority to see what accommodations are available near Clera's factory so she can walk to work. The waiting list for apartments is a mile long. He doesn't add his name.

Elio notices a park across the street. Buela told him once that there used to be many parks in New Chicago, but most have turned into drug deal hubs, gang territory, and refugee camps. This one is the last sort. Tents and shacks made from pallets, cardboard, and sheet metal cover most of what used to be open, green lawn. There's a public restroom, rusty swings, and a sandy square with netless poles on each side. The clinks probably gave up trying to root people out years ago. Elio doesn't know how the park residents survive New Chicago's cold, windy winters. He doesn't want to end up there.

He passes his old school. A chain-link fence topped with razor wire surrounds the ancient two-story building. Windows stare like blank eyes. Around the left side, a delivery truck loiters at a ramp, its back open as a worker hauls boxes of supplies into the kitchen.

Elio stops, hands gripping the metal fence. Those green dumpsters beside the truck jolt him into dark remembering.

He recalls standing behind the lunch counter wearing a disposable apron and vinyl gloves. In exchange for a free lunch, he served and cleaned up after rowdy hordes of secondary students each day. "Retard" Renato, so-called because of a stammer and perpetual goofy grin, worked alongside him. Elio was bullied because of his size, but huge, gentle Renato had it worse.

The bell rang, and students sauntered out of the cafeteria. Elio started wiping down tables. He looked around for Renato, shook his head, and continued cleaning up slopped milk and crushed chips. Where the hells had that big goof gone? Elio would be late for geometry, though did he care? The instructor had given up actual teaching after the first few weeks. He was an older guy with a comb-over and sour expression—ex-military.

Elio was sweeping up when Renato emerged from the kitchen followed by the cooks, Lena and Carmen. Renato carried a platter with a lit cake on it. He led the cooks in an off-tune "Happy birthday, to you . . ."

Renato set the platter on the nearest table, and they huddled around it. "Happy birthday, dear Elio, happy birthday to you!" Renato clapped. "I made it myself. Blow out th . . . the candles!"

The cake was square and lopsided. Goopy frosting dripped onto the platter along with candle wax. Elio made the same wish he always did, that he would reach number one on the Arcade's billboard someday. He bent and blew.

"Did you make a wish?" Renato asked, full of exuberance.

"Sure."

Lena cut the cake into wide squares and told Elio, "We'll get you excused from class, and don't worry about the cake." Her eyes slid to Renato. "He had supervision."

Elio sank onto a bench and dug in. Carmen sat beside him. She was only a few years older, but he would never make a play for someone employed at the school. Fantasies weren't off limits, though. She and Lena chattered while they ate. Renato's cake vanished in two bites.

Lena said, "Hey, big guy, will you take the garbage out?"

Renato nodded, crumbs dusting his mouth. He rose and disappeared into the kitchen, emerging a few moments later with two bursting bags. He went through the side door that led to the dumpsters. Two minutes passed. Then five.

Lena stacked their plates and rose. "Guess we'd better get back to work."

Carmen asked, "Shouldn't Renato have finished by now?"

"He probably got distracted by a butterfly or something. Elio, will you go get him?"

"Sure." Elio got up. "And thanks. I really appreciate the cake."

Carmen nodded and blushed. He wondered if he should take a chance with her, after all. Elio turned and pushed through the outside doors.

At first, he didn't see Renato. He walked over to the dumpsters and peered in. Renato's garbage bags rested on top of a smelly, fly-specked pile. Elio looked around. Nothing moved. He caught a whiff of leth smoke.

He edged around the dumpster and stopped. Renato's scuffed loafer poked out from the other side. Elio forced himself to keep circling until Renato's body came into view. He lay on his side, one arm stretched above his head. Blood flowed beneath him and soaked into the gravel.

Elio's breath caught. He ran to the prone form and knelt. "Renato!" He nudged the boy onto his back.

A dark stain spread across Renato's shirt. His face was flour-white, and his eyes stared without seeing. Renato's wide, always-grinning mouth sagged open.

Elio turned away and threw up all the cake he'd eaten.

He wiped his mouth, hesitated, then forced himself to look at Renato's still body. He bent and shook a large shoulder. "Renato! Renato! You big idiot! Wake up!" When the boy didn't move, Elio raced inside the school, yelling, "Help!"

Adults took over, and in the hubbub, Elio slipped away. He ran until he reached the shore of Lake Michigan. Up the beach, familiar sea walls rose above the water line, built thirty years ago to keep out high tides. Water pooled across his sneakers. He imagined wading in until scummy waves covered his head. He'd keep walking until he couldn't hold his breath anymore. Air would bubble out of his lungs, and he'd float softly until the water sang him to sleep.

Instead, he sat in the sand and watched boats slip past. He wrapped his arms around his knees while a band of sorrow squeezed his chest.

That was the day he quit.

⁕

Elio shakes off the past. Memories are why he avoids this area.

He heads north, visiting a secondhand store along the way. There he purchases a large duffle bag, spare clothes for himself and his sister, and sheets that smell like laundry detergent, so at least they're clean. He stops at a corner grocery and buys peanut butter, flatbread, bottled water, apples, protein bars, and plastic silverware. He adds a pack of gum, toothbrushes and toothpaste, hand towels, a brush, and two chocolate bars as an afterthought.

The duffle bulges. He loops it over his head so it'll be harder to steal and treks north again. Before he knows it, he's standing among skyscrapers he's only seen from a distance for most of his life. The sky between them is white with haze. The tallest building blocks the sun and wind.

Elio wanders. He's unfamiliar with this part of New Chicago and leery of the humped forms propped against cracked walls, or men huddled on corners, or even the street kids who rush into traffic, offering to clean windshields. Traffic lights blink a frenzied red, yellow, and green.

There's a constant hum, sometimes joined by sirens or warning honks. Overhead, the Loop, Chicago's aerial transport system, arcs past, carrying mass transit cars away from him at a hundred miles an hour. Elio generally knows what's in downtown New Chicago. He locates the Chicago River and the River Walk and a few streets whose names he recognizes: Michigan Avenue, State Street, and Congress Parkway—which, ironically, was named long before the United States Congress resided there. The new White House has taken over Millenium Park. The buildings here are old, gothic, and reek of history. Museums abound, and pedestrians wearing expensive smartsuits join the homeless on crowded sidewalks.

A gaunt, scar-faced woman in a hoodie bumps into Elio. She mumbles an apology and hurries on. Elio checks his pockets before remembering there's nothing in them to steal. He pauses out front of a small building. It's constructed totally of black slate, with a high, steep-sloped roof and tall, narrow windows. In swirling metal script, a sign reads, *New Age History Museum*. On a digi-sign next to a pathway, golden letters flash: *Grand Opening! Free for one day only! Featured: The Martian Collection and 3-D vid-showing: Revelations from the New James Webb.*

Intrigued, Elio follows stone steps to an open door and walks in. Electronic music wafts toward him from hidden speakers. A lady at a slate desk that matches the exterior calls out, "Would you like to buy a pass? Yearly passes are on sale today!"

"Uh, I'm just here for the free exhibits." Elio jerks a thumb backward to indicate the sign he saw.

"Well, if you change your mind, I'll be here." The perky lady has bright green glasses and hair piled into a messy bun. Elio nods to her, then follows signs that lead him down a shadowed corridor which opens into a gallery. Track lighting highlights each numbered section of the free exhibit. Elio has always been interested in astronomy and welcomes this brief distraction from his life. The first lighted display reads:

2047 – *Mars One begins permanent space colony on Mars.*

Black and white pictures reveal a crater-pocked land. White pods dot the landscape, and a tiny human in one of those old-fashioned puffy jumpsuits astronauts once wore plants an American flag on a rise behind the colony. There's a lot of writing on plaques. A space helmet and red rocks sit under display glass. Elio moves on to the next part of the exhibit.

2051 – *Mars colonists explore caves under Arsia Mons preparatory to building safer habitats below the surface. They discover ancient artifacts dating back 3.8 billion years, when Mars had atmosphere and seas, proving that intelligent life once existed on the red planet.*

Again, Martian artifacts are displayed under glass. They look like rusty metal sculptures with wheels. Wingless dragons decorate the sides. He skims the descriptions and strolls ahead.

2053 – *A massive earthquake rocks Mars. Its epicenter is Arsia Mons, and it buries many excavating colonists in half-finished tunnels. An unidentified object, previously obscured by advanced Martian technology destroyed in the quake, appears in Mars' sky near Deimos.*

The famous earthquake. Did the colonists trigger it with all their digging? No one knows for sure, but it set events in motion that have led to the building of starships and catapulted human exploration of the solar system ahead at light speed. Elio's finger traces a ring that shines among twinkling stars in a blown-up photograph. It looks like a huge wedding band with symbols carved into the shiny rim. *The ARH.*

2054 – *Scientists identify the UO as having some characteristics of a* *theoretical wormhole. It is judged benign and nicknamed Alice's Rabbit Hole, or the ARH, after Lewis Carroll's* Through the Looking Glass. *The first probe, Pioneer I, traverses the wormhole.*

Elio hurries on until he's devoured the whole exhibit. There are even blueprints of the first starship, Norway's *Loki*, which by this point has followed *Pioneers II* and *III* through the ARH and into a brand-new solar system, hoping to colonize. There's a model of Sweden's starship, *Lycka*, too. The United States is running behind, but the last part of the exhibit explains how they plan to catch up by building three starships at once. The first, *Calliope*, is set to launch soon, and a final photograph shows the U.S. Space Station surrounded by metal girders holding a partly finished ship.

Elio exits the room and blinks in the hallway's harsh light. He takes a few deep breaths before returning to the lobby, knowing he spent too much time in the museum, but he can't regret it. As he leaves, the desk lady sings out, "Come back any time!" and he thinks he might.

Outside, Elio's thoughts drop back to earth, and he heads west. The Mars exhibit recedes, replaced by a twenty-foot-high billboard advertisement at a busy intersection. Elio smiles. He follows the directions on the ad. Soon the vaulted roof of what used to be a music venue but is now New Chicago's famous Arcade rises before him.

The billionaire Dec Gaston owns Arcade Entertainment, Inc., so the building, which sprawls like a vast island oasis amidst a concrete sea, is well kept. Reflective glass covers most of the dome. Digital billboards flash contests, deals, and A-list gamer stats from atop steel posts. Clera's disapproving face pushes into Elio's mind, but he shrugs the image away. He approaches the front doors, hesitates only a second, and walks inside.

The world changes. Fans whir, and lights flash beyond security gates. Snatches of tinny music reach Elio's ears. A guy wearing smart lenses sits behind shatterproof glass to Elio's left. He looks up when Elio doesn't scan his ring and enter the arcade. "Can I help you?"

"I need a year's membership pass," Elio says, palms sweating.

"Sure thing," the clerk replies in an easy-going voice. He pushes a pad through a hole in the glass. "Scan your ring, right there."

Again, Elio sees Clera and hears Papa's voice urging him to control his impulses but ignores them both. He knows he can win these games with his fast reflexes and quick mind. He could make tons of credits—maybe end up on those digital boards out front.

Elio swipes his ring and watches his credits drop to almost zero.

But it will be okay. Clera has a job, and before long, he'll be making money again, too.

Elio glances at a clock behind the counter guy. It's only one p.m. He longs to start playing right now, but he resists. Maybe if he finds housing before he meets up with Clera at the shelter, she'll be less mad when she discovers his gaming membership.

The sun feels too bright after the dim lighting of the Arcade. Elio scans the area to get his bearings. He's west of Millennium Park. There's a spacecraft museum right across from the Arcade and a public library down the street. Clera would like that. If they lived nearby, she'd need transportation to the factory, but he'll worry about that later. He saw some old buildings that might be apartments not far off. He heads that way.

When Elio gets closer to the apartments, he realizes what used to be an area of chic cafes and shops with housing above has fallen into disrepair. The stores are empty husks. Broken glass and litter decorate sidewalks dotted with old gum. Last season's leaves clog the gutters. Though the blocks of red and tan brick buildings with scalloped corners might once have been beautiful, they look like haunted house material now. Graffiti mars alleyways, mostly scrawled messages signed by Second City. This is gang territory.

As if on cue, a voice speaks behind him. "Hey, there. You looking for someone?"

Elio whirls around. A boy about his age stares at him. He's a little taller, a little thinner, with sandy blond dreadlocks decomposing into fuzzy braids down his back. Amateur tattoos cover his arms. The boy wears baggy black pants and a short-sleeved button up, open to reveal a gray-white tee. He's got a digi-ring, but Elio would have known he was low-class without that. The only thing worth a second look at this kid is his necklace. The heavy silver links gleam.

"Hey, man. I'm cool!" the boy says.

Elio realizes he's raised his fists. He forces himself to relax.

The kid says, "If you're looking for leth, I can set you up. If you're with the Steelheads, better leave now so you can go in one piece."

"I'm not with a gang. Just checking out housing. My apartment building blew up."

"Wow, hom! That's bad luck!" The kid pauses, rubbing his chin where bristle sprouts. "My name's Bohdan. Boh for short."

"Elio." He nods and wishes he hadn't poured out his whole sad story.

"Where you from?" Boh asks.

"South of here," Elio offers, purposefully vague.

Boh doesn't press. "Well, if you have credits, Elio, you can walk a few blocks that way." He jams a thumb north. "But if you're strapped, you're standing on hallowed ground. The Second City call these old apartments 'Slavland' because a hundred years ago, Ukrainians lived here, see? Mexicans, too, I think. Anyway, this is free housing if you don't mind sleeping in condemned buildings with the rats."

"What's the catch?"

"No catch, hom. Occasionally, the clinks come through and chase out vagrants. And, like I said, there's rats. You could end up with not-so-friendly neighbors, too, if you know what I mean."

"Like murderers? Criminals?"

Bohdan shrugs. "Could be. People in free housing can't be picky. But looks like you know how to fight. If you don't own a knife, though, better invest. At least these old rattraps are out of the weather. And if you're lucky, your neighbors won't be right on top of you like in the parks."

"Do you live here?" Elio asks.

"Me? No. But I did before I joined Second City. My new family supplies quarters that are a little nicer than Slavland. 'Course, I have to earn my keep. If you're interested in joining, I could put in a word for you."

Elio hides what he's thinking behind a stony mask. "Thanks. I'll consider it."

Clera would kill him if he joined Second City. But maybe, just maybe, she'd accept these living quarters for now.

Bohdan smiles. He's missing a canine on top. "If you wanna talk more, I come by here on my rounds this time almost every day. You'll find me, easy."

Elio shakes Boh's hand. "Thanks again."

After Bohdan rounds the corner and disappears, Elio checks out the nearest building. Inside, rotting stairs lead up to a narrow hallway. The door at the end is half open. Dirt, broken chairs, and glass from shattered windows litter the wooden floor. Loose wiring hangs out of walls. Pale squares on peeling wallpaper show where pictures once hung. There's a small living room, a galley kitchen stripped of everything but a few busted cabinets, and a bedroom down a narrow hall. Something skitters into the gloom as Elio opens the door.

Miraculously, a metal-framed bed with a dusty gray mattress still crowds the small space. A breeze blows through an empty windowpane. Droppings dot the floor. It'll do. For now.

11

CLERA

Clera wanders through familiar streets. She pauses at Sacred Heart Cathedral, where Buela sometimes took her. The church stands out from the newer, boxier buildings that surround it. Flowering trees lead to elaborately carved front doors. Just inside is a foyer and a font of holy water, and past that, the sanctuary with its flying-buttressed ceiling and stained-glass windows depicting scenes from the Bible. A life-sized cross dominates the pulpit area. Jesus hangs from it, trapped and bleeding—a bit like she feels right now.

She shakes herself. It's sacrilegious to compare herself to Jesus. She's not hurt or sick, and she hasn't been convicted of a crime. She's only jobless. *Snap out of it,* she tells herself and moves on. Churches are supposed to offer sanctuary, but there's no way a priest will give her and Elio shelter for more than a few hours.

I'll have to leave South Side. She tries not to panic. The row houses, brownstones, and high-rise apartments, the corner grocery and stamp-sized playground only two blocks from her building, are comfortingly familiar. And the library! How can she say goodbye to Mrs. Moriarty? She'll have to bury her memories under bricks and mortar with Mama, or the pain will surely suffocate her.

Clera stops at Ms. Lewenski's shop. The floor tiles are worn and faded, the metal shelving scraped and dented. The store smells like coffee beans, orange peels, and cigar smoke. She looks for Ms. Lewenski behind the counter, but a young girl handles the register. Clera approaches her. "Where is the old lady who owns the shop?"

The girl shrugs and pops her gum. "Lewenski? We think she died in the explosion on Oak Street. By the way, she didn't own this place."

Clera's throat squeezes. "Who are you?"

The girl has long, stringy hair and a pasty expression. She tilts her head and drawls, "Shanda. I'm the owner's daughter. Ms. Lewenski was only the manager, you know."

"Oh." Clera feels rebuffed, unbalanced. Her friend was an underling, which makes her death even harder to bear, somehow, though Clera can't say why.

"Are you going to buy anything, 'cause I got work to do," the girl says.

"Yes, I am." Clera stifles a stab of anger. She turns and stomps down an aisle. Right away, she sees a sample box of truffles on sale. Mrs. Moriarty loves sweets. Clera uses her last credits to buy them, plus a card and a pen. Her credit account drops to zero on the girl's pad.

Clera heads to the library. She sits on the bench out front and writes a few words to the librarian, then tucks the card into its envelope and walks to the front door with a heavy heart. She should go in and say goodbye in person, but she can't, so she slips the gift and card into the book return slot. It's not like she's leaving New Chicago's South Side forever. Someday, when she's flush with credits and settled somewhere else, she'll come back.

But Clera doesn't know that's true. Elio and she might end up anywhere, following jobs, trying to stay off the streets. They might be forced into the Barrens.

As she walks toward the homeless shelter, the newscast from the job recruitment office flits through her head. She imagines flying away from

Earth on a shuttle to meet up with *Calliope* for its maiden journey to another solar system—a one-way trip reserved mostly for the rich.

Clera shivers. No way. Even leaving her neighborhood seems scary. Nothing changes for the better. Every cataclysm she's been through—leaving school, starting work at Perkine, losing Papa and Buela, then Mama and the apartment—have all been bad changes.

She approaches the homeless shelter, really hoping Elio's had better luck than her.

It's only 2:30 p.m., but there's already a line to get inside. Clera's pinched between a mother holding a crying, snot-nosed baby and a humpbacked woman who smells of dirty socks. She shifts on sore feet and wishes she could get out of her own rank clothes. Her last credits should have purchased something more practical than a goodbye gift, yet she's glad she spent them on the librarian. There are worse things than wearing a dirty jumpsuit two days' running.

Elio shows up just as the line finally starts moving. He cuts in to join her. A guy calls, "No holding places!" but Elio ignores him. Clera sighs in relief. She never knows when her brother will go off on someone. If they get kicked out of line, they'll be on the street tonight like those homeless people propped against walls, begging for handouts.

Clera greets Elio and looks him over. A full duffle is looped over his head. His dark, bright eyes return her stare, then shift away. "What?" he asks.

"You look almost happy. What's up?"

"I'm not *happy*." He's clearly *un*happy with her assessment. "But I did good today. I might have a place for us. I'll tell you about it when we get inside." He pauses, grinds out, "Mama's name isn't on any lists. She wasn't taken to a hospital, and she hasn't been found."

Clera nods, tight-lipped. "I think I already knew–" Clera gulps back the words and shakes her head, then changes the subject. "You bought something."

He looks down. "Yeah. You'll like this. Clothes for us both, toiletries, some food."

"Do we really have the money . . ."

He interrupts, annoyance knitting his brows. "Seriously, sister, give me a little credit. The clothes are from a secondhand store. The food is only basic stuff to keep us going until I find a job. Besides, we still have your credits, your job. We aren't exactly destitute."

"Yes, we are." Clera exhales. She stares at Elio's scuffed runners and feels heat climb her cheeks.

"What?"

"I quit." She makes herself look at him. "Don't ask questions, Elio. I already know it's bad, but I don't regret it. I couldn't work at Perkine another minute. I couldn't." She bites her lip to stop a sob from bubbling up.

Elio doesn't seem mad, only thoughtful. "It's for the best, maybe. I wasn't sure how you'd get to work, anyway, once we leave South Side."

She considers this, feels the truth of it. Resignation settles in her belly like a stone.

The line inches toward the door. The same tall man from yesterday scans people in. A father holding a toddler swipes his digi-ring. The pad beeps, and the supervisor shakes his head. "This is your third night. You only get two. Sorry."

"But it used to be five," the man stutters. He hoists the little boy higher in his arms. "There's nowhere else to sleep."

"Sorry," the supervisor repeats, shrugging. "We've had a big up-tick in people needing shelter. Two nights is all I can allow. But there's the parks. You should try them."

The father looks like he'll argue, but a bulky man with a holstered gun steps out of the entryway. The father's shoulders slump, and he moves out of line.

Clera whispers to Elio, "Did you hear that? We only get one more night!" She can't hide the panic in her voice.

Elio squeezes her arm. "It's okay, Clera. Just wait until we get inside, and I'll tell you."

She eyes him suspiciously. "Did you do something illegal, Elio?"

He rolls his eyes. "Just wait."

Clera does, but only until they're settled on the same cots from yesterday next to the cinderblock wall. Elio pulls a pair of frayed jeans and a pink tee shirt from the duffle and tosses them to her. These are followed by underwear and short boots that look like they should fit. She's impressed but ignores his offerings for now. "Spill it, Elio."

He settles back. "I guess you saw our apartment."

Her gaze doesn't waver. "I guess you know Mama isn't coming back."

"Yes." He doesn't look so cocky now. Her words seem to pull him back into that sea of misery where she's been swimming. Elio's jaw firms, and Clera knows he's working to hold it together. She waits patiently.

"We have to leave South Side, Clera. There's nothing here for us now."

"I know."

His eyes widen.

"What? Did you expect me to haunt the site of our flattened apartment building like a ghost until I keeled over and died?"

Elio shrugs. "I don't know," he admits. "You aren't too adventurous."

"This isn't some adventure, Elio. It's our lives. It's survival."

"Right." His mouth quirks up on one side. "So let me tell you my plan."

He describes how he went north into the heart of the city and how he found Slavland. He talks up the apartment, making it sound luxurious.

"Is there work there?" Clera asks. "Did you find a recruitment office and check it out?"

"I didn't see any," Elio admits. "One thing at a time, Clera. We'll have a roof over our heads and enough food for a few days. Something will turn up."

"Is this place safe?"

He hesitates. "Safer than the streets. It'll need some cleaning, but there's a bed. We can prop boards over the windows to keep out wind and bugs."

"What about rats? Cockroaches? How do we keep them out?"

His smile widens. "Are you kidding, Clera. We invite them in! Rat stew and roasted cockroaches for dessert! Yum." He pats his stomach.

The joke surprises a laugh out of her, but guilt quickly takes its place. *Survivor's guilt.* Clera swallows. She squeezes Elio's knee. "You did good. Better than me."

"Nah," he objects, but he looks pleased. "That factory was crap. You're well done with it."

Clera purses her lips. He's probably wrong, but what does it matter? They have shelter, fresh clothes, and food. She tells him, "I'll get us something from the soup kitchen tonight. My treat. Save the food you bought, okay?"

The world has a will. Can you not feel it like a pulsing in your brain? Can you not taste it like a saltiness on your tongue? Can you not sense it? An invisible being at your back, whispering. When we learn to hear the words, we begin to understand.

    -Mons Vega, Prophet for the earth

12

SOLAST

Sol is done with the parks. One day she'll let down her guard, and some scrull will have her. She'll become one of the faceless dead left to rot along some random embankment. But where to go? None of the employment agencies will take her, especially dressed like a Steelhead, with a shaved skull and scarred face. According to Father, once she was pretty. Tall and lithe, with shiny brunette hair falling to her waist, almond-shaped hazel eyes, wide lips. But her looks only attracted the kind of attention she loathed. Men wanting to own her. Men wanting to touch her. They didn't care about her mind.

Sol wanders toward the heart of downtown. Trains sail overhead on the Loop. Vehicles from smart cars to hovercraft dot the multi-lane arteries which run through the city. She's in the boutique section near Millenium Park, but the shops don't interest her. Nothing she can afford there, anyway. People get her attention. She's always on the lookout for Anton. He might not be in New Chicago, though. After he killed her father and marked her face, she'd run from the commune. Had he stayed on there after all these years? His ambitions seemed too large for a ragtag group of followers to satisfy.

She's lost in the past, not paying attention. Before she knows it, the crowds around her surge into a wave that picks her up and carries her with it into Millenium Park, where a mob chants and cheers. They wear face paint and tattoos in the shape of Earther logos. Sol puts her hood up and pretends to be enthusiastic, but inwardly, her skin crawls. She was careless, and now she's trapped in the horde.

A man jumps onto a multi-level marble fountain in the shape of jumbled cubes. Water spills beneath his feet. The surface must be slippery, but he hoists himself higher and higher until he stands at the top. Water bubbles up next to him in a small geyser before cascading down twenty feet to land in a wide, shallow pool half-hidden by the Earther cult.

Sol watches the speaker. There's something familiar about him. She edges closer, using her height to see over the crowd. Ecstatic chanting clogs the air. Heat, sweat, and a buzz of barely contained violence make her want to burst through the morass and run for her life, but she forces herself to stay. To look and listen.

The Earther leader raises his hands for silence. He wears all green, has short-cut hair, and could almost be mistaken for a clink. A single ring adorns his right hand. The Earther emblem, a circle within a circle, transected by a spear, is tattooed on his neck.

The crowd noise dies as he speaks: "Fellow Earthers, welcome! Here we were born, and here we will stay!" Loud cheers erupt, but the mob obediently quiets when he motions again. "I am Mons Vega! Proudly born in the Barrens, raised on real vegetables and river water, not bio-engineered poisons and plastic-fouled drink! The tainted air of forest fires and city smog chokes my lungs, but it has also lit a fire in my belly that cannot be quelled until every factory is dismantled, every tech giant destroyed, every satellite shot down from our skies. The Earth belongs to the Earth!"

The crowd chants this back at him. Sol follows along.

"And we will take her back!" Mons Vega continues. Again, the mob echoes his words. "We will save her from the venom that pollutes her! We will not abandon her in time of need! Down with *Calliope*! Down with NASA! Say 'yes' to restoring Earth to her pristine greatness!"

More cheers, but Sol has fallen quiet, though not because the speech strikes a chord. She, too, believes humans are custodians of the land and have a duty to fix the harm they've done to it. But at the same time, technology has accomplished great things. Can't these fanatics see that?

Sol shakes her head. It's not such thoughts that distract her. It's him. The man standing like a god atop his marble throne of flowing water. His hair tamed, his clothes fashioned in a new, military style so unlike the flowing tunics he used to wear. But she knows this Mons Vega. Knows him by the name his drug lord father christened him with before he left the southern cartels and made his way north, building a following as he traveled.

Anton.

Her father once looked up to him as blindly as those at this gathering, then betrayed him and suffered death for that.

As you sow, you shall also reap.

Mons Vega drones on. Sol edges away from the demonstration. She doesn't think Anton will recognize her after all these years, but she keeps her hood up just in case. Sirens wail in the distance. The clinks will be here soon to break up the crowd, and she wants to be long gone by that time. Her heart hammers with fear, elation, hatred. Finding Anton has been her driving goal for so long. She can hardly believe she's discovered him. But getting close enough to kill him will be hard.

First things first. Sol needs new lodgings. Safer ones. She adjusts her messenger bag on her shoulder and drifts through the streets. Before long, she crosses a parking lot as big as a city block before the sprawling Arcade. She was raised apart from video games. The place feels foreign, exotic even. Technology was forbidden in the commune. Sol only has a Skinpad because her job at the clinic required it.

Across the street from the Arcade sits an aeronautical museum. The shiny, blue-paneled demo shuttle in front draws her attention. She navigates the road, pauses before the life-size model, then moves around the building to the chain-link fence that encloses an array of decommissioned ships. Tourists emerge from the hatch of a rusty shuttle and shuffle down metal stairs. Sol blinks. An idea forms in her head.

13

CLERA

The next morning, Clera and Elio say goodbye to the homeless shelter and South Side. To the north lie skyscrapers, the river, ritzy restaurants and theaters. Papa took them downtown once when Clera was little. Elio probably doesn't remember. It was Christmas, and Papa's company gave him a small bonus. They'd visited a park—Millenium Park, maybe? And watched the execs light up a fir tree with so many bulbs it looked like one big sun. Christmas carols blasted from speakers, and Clera sat on Papa's shoulders and sang "Silent Night" while a cold wind whipped snowflakes into her face.

Clera and Elio are leaving everything behind. Each footstep feels like moving through quicksand. She knows they must do this, but which path is the right one? What would Mama think? Clera can never ask her mother for advice again. She's cut off from everything she knows, popped out of her shell like a chestnut.

Elio walks with a bounce to his step, but now and then he glances sideways at Clera with a creased brow. She wonders what's in that head of his. What isn't he telling her? She hopes he hasn't done anything illegal and that this place he's found is safe. Maybe she should be excited. After all, she quit her horrible job. She's moving on. But fear and sadness crowd out all other emotions. She'd welcome that numbness that sometimes blunts the knife's edge pressed against her heart.

Clera hasn't seen Elio cry. Maybe he mourns in private. She understands that, but if he's not letting his feelings out, he'll eventually explode or go off half-cocked and make some huge mistake. She's seen this before. *Be careful, Elio. Be so careful.*

They walk in the shadows of skyscrapers. Clera hates the traffic and bustling pedestrians, and she avoids eye contact with them. Before she realizes what's happening, some demonstration in front of a government building has folded them into its tight-packed, chanting crowd. The demonstrators wear shirts with photos of Earth on them and hold signs that say things like, "Save Earth. Don't abandon it!" and "You created this mess. Stay and fix it!" and "Instead of starships, build homes!"

Earthers. Elio grabs Clera's hand and pulls her away from the crush into a dark alley.

Panic flutters in her chest, but she breathes through it.

"You okay?" he asks.

Clera nods, and they move on.

Elio leads her west into what he calls "Slavland." How does he know the name? Has he met someone who told him? If so, why keep it a secret? The knot in her stomach grows.

He finally stops on a derelict block lined with deserted shops and cafes. Panes of plate glass lie shattered outside small businesses. A wrought iron cafe chair rests on its side beneath a ripped awning. The wind has risen and whistles down alleyways strewn with cans and wrappers. Elio turns toward a shop with faded words painted on the one intact front window: *Vlad's Ice Cream*, she believes it once read, though the *V* and *C* have mostly flaked away, so it looks like *lad's Ice ream* now.

Clera follows Elio inside. The place has been looted. Only an empty counter fronting a cracked mirror remains. Footprints disturb a thick layer of dust on the floor. Elio climbs narrow stairs at the back. She eyes the creaky staircase, shrugs, and follows him to the second floor and down a short hallway.

Elio swings open a door. He ushers Clera through ahead of him with a nervous, "Ta-da!"

She looks around. The apartment's living area melds into a small kitchen. Past it, a narrow hallway leads to a bedroom mostly occupied by a sagging bed. Clera edges around a pile of animal droppings and peers out a broken window.

Elio's words buzz like static in her ears. Clera closes her eyes, opens them again. The apartment is still there, lightless, mostly empty, dirty and destitute. Worst of all, Mama is gone, and without her, this place will never feel like the home her brother intends it to be.

Elio finishes his spiel. "I'm making a list of things we'll need. A hammer and nails, cleaning supplies, a couple of chairs and a table, sheets, rat traps. I know it looks terrible now, but we can make it better. Clera? Earth to Clera?"

She edges past him and walks back to the living room window. Below, a stray cat creeps from one shadow to the next. Clera steels herself and turns. *Keep it together. Be the big sister, the strong one.* "You did well. Once we clean it up, this'll be better than sleeping on the street." The words sound hollow. She rushes on, "Are you sure it's safe, though? There's no lock on the door."

"I'll add that to my list." Elio smiles. He doesn't seem to have noticed her tension.

Clera makes herself focus. "What list? You don't even have paper."

He taps his head. "It's all in here."

"I'm out of credits. Do you have any?"

"A few." He turns and sweeps turds into the hallway with his shoe.

She imagines ghosts lurking in dark corners and shivers. "I'll go out and look around the neighborhood, try to find somewhere within walking distance that isn't deserted and has jobs." She ponders a bit, then adds, "Those secondhand sheets won't keep us warm enough tonight. I'm finding us a blanket or quilt, even if I have to steal one. Also, I'd rather not sleep here without sweeping out the rat poop." She doesn't want to stay at all, but she can't tell Elio that.

He says eagerly, "I'll start looking for the things on my list. We'll meet back here at dusk or before. You won't get lost, will you?"

He's probably remembering that time when she was eight, and she turned the wrong way coming back from her first solo trip to the library. She'd gotten confused but stumbled across a fire station, and a kindly fireman had taken her home. "I'll be fine," she says. "I'm not a little kid anymore. Why's it called Slavland, anyhow? I didn't see a sign, and that's a weird name."

Elio shrugs. His eyes slide past her, and now she's sure he's hiding something. "I think I saw the name spray painted on a wall. This part of New Chicago was settled by Ukrainians, so that kind of makes sense."

And how does he know *that*? Clera frowns and bites her lip. No use asking. He won't give her a straight answer, anyway.

14

CLERA

Clera and Elio part ways. She turns onto the next street. *Right.* This block is also deserted and graffiti marked. Clera takes a left. *Left.* She notes the peeling "Lost" poster on a light pole to help her remember where she came from because, though she told Elio she'd be fine, she's horrible with directions. It's almost a disability. So, she keeps a running list of turns in her head and repeats them over and over: *Right. Left. Left. Right.* After a few more blocks, traffic picks up. A smartcab streaks by, its electric engine eerily quiet.

She's in a similar neighborhood to the one she left, but these shops are well kept. Some even have rooftop gardens. A few old people sit on cracked sidewalks under awnings playing chess or mah jongg. Blue solar panels shade a parking lot between cream-colored brick buildings. Laundry dangles on lines strung across alleyways. The sight feels old-fashioned and homey, and Buela's seamed face flashes before Clera's eyes. Feisty Buela, who taught her reading, safety, and how to be brave. Or she tried.

Clera pauses at a pink and blue-striped awning. A plastic cup with a domed top and straw sticking out decorates the glass window beneath. Loopy letters spell out *Boba Tea Cafe.* A grassy median divides the street in two. Opposite the shop, an oak tree towers higher than the buildings. It hasn't leafed out yet. Clera's neighborhood was void of trees and greenery, though she recalls old Mr. Rodriguez on the first floor setting out window boxes full of petunias in the summer. He probably survived the explosion, but where will he plant his flowers now?

Clera shakes her head. She must look lost, because a girl cleaning the interior of the cafe's glass door pauses, cleaner in one hand, rag in the other. She's Asian and close to Clera's age. Her hair swings in a short, shiny black bob. The eyes beneath slant merrily upward. She cracks the door and calls out, "Can I help you? Are you lost?"

"I'm . . ." Clera swallows. She lingered too long staring at the oak tree, called too much attention to herself. Still, this girl looks harmless. The words, "just thirsty," pop out of her mouth. She *is* thirsty. It's a warm day, and she's been walking all morning. Elio gave her bottled water and a protein bar before they parted, but she didn't want to drink or eat too much since she doesn't know when they'll have credits again.

"You've come to the right place." The Asian girl smiles.

"I don't have any credits. My . . . my home was blown up."

The words simply fall out of her mouth. They sound like something a little kid would make up and no one would ever believe.

But the girl's eyes widen. "Were you in that apartment building over on the South Side? Oh my God! I heard about that on the news! They already demolished it. The execs said it was unsafe, but some of the residents were protesting at the local PD. I watched the broadcast. It was awful. People were shouting and crying, and the clinks were standing there in a line with those bulletproof shields they use at demonstrations, not letting anyone inside."

Clera digests all this. "I didn't mean to tell you. It just kind of came out. I'm sorry." She gestures toward the tree. "I was admiring your oak. We didn't have trees in my neighborhood."

The girl sets down her spray and rag. She approaches Clera and shakes her hand. "My name's Soo Yun. My appa runs this cafe. What's your name?"

"Clera Diaz."

"Do you have family in West Town? Did they take you in?"

"No." Clera hesitates. Should she have lied? "Not exactly," she amends. "The homeless shelter would only let us stay two nights. We walked here this morning looking for work."

Soo Yun ponders this for so long that Clera opens her mouth to say goodbye. But the girl gestures. "Come inside. I'll make you a boba tea on the house. Appa won't care. Tea is cheap, and business is slow. If you don't mind, I'll sit with you unless a customer shows up, and you can tell me who 'we' is."

Clera's mouth falls open. Soo Yun's kindness ties her tongue.

The Asian girl adds, "Am I being too pushy? Appa says I'm pushy, especially with the customers. But you have to be a salesperson, right? To make money?" She sighs. "Not that we're making much, as you can see." Her eyes drift across the empty seats. Soo Yun's face falls, then brightens. "But early morning was good today. Saturdays, a few oldsters come in for coffee. Oh, yes, we don't only serve tea. I convinced Appa that we needed to diversify if we wanted to stay in business. So now we offer coffee and a few Korean treats like honey cookies and rice cakes. Are you hungry?"

As they talk, Clera finds herself ushered inside and pushed into a booth next to the window. Sunlight pools across the scrubbed laminate top. It feels good to rest her sore feet. "Yes, I am hungry," Clera admits. "But I didn't stop in front of your shop to ask for handouts. I really was just admiring the tree."

"Oh, I know." Soo Yun collects her cleaning supplies, then returns. "But let me treat you. Your payment will be telling me all about what happened. It's so boring here most of the time."

"Oh . . . okay."

Clera inspects the tiny cafe while Soo Yun disappears into a back room. Glass carafes, a stainless-steel flavoring machine, rows of glasses, and several electric teapots and jars of tea packets fill every inch of space behind the counter. A hand-printed menu hung on the wall lists teas, sodas, and coffee along with a soup of the day and the "kimchi special," whatever that is. Behind a display case set into the counter are rows of cookies, cakes, and packaged treats with calligraphic titles in Korean. They have English names, too, like "Pocky" and "Choco Pie." She stares in fascination.

Clera is studying a pair of carved wooden faces hung on the wall when Soo Yun returns with two boba teas and a plate of cookies on a tray. She plunks the tray on the table and sits down across from Clera.

"Those are Hahoe Masks," she tells Clera. "Have you never seen one?"

Clera shakes her head. The faces are shiny ovals with high cheekbones, squinty eyes, and painted black hair. They look kind of goofy, like cartoon characters.

Soo Yun shrugs. "Appa likes to keep things traditional. He says we have a niche, and if we modernize too much, we'll lose our customer base, but I don't know. I think mostly people come here because it's within walking distance and it's cheap. Well, the tea is good, too." Soo Yun takes a sip from her straw. The drink looks exactly like the graphic on the front window.

Clera eyes her boba tea with mistrust. What are those round beads clustered at the bottom?"

Soo Yun laughs. "You really don't know anything about Korean food, do you? Go on. It's safe to drink. See?" She takes another sip. "Those are tapioca pearls on the bottom."

Clera sips the iced liquid. It's sweet and cold and creamy. Delicious.

Soo Yun picks up a cookie. "Well? You like?"

"Yes, thank you!" Clera's so unused to charity that any other words dry in her throat. Why is this girl being so kind? Does Clera look as pitiful as she feels? Finally, she finds her tongue. "Who is Appa?"

"My father. He's gone right now, dealing with suppliers."

"Won't he mind me being in here without paying?"

"Oh, I doubt it. I'll just tell him you're my friend." Soo Yun shrugs. "And maybe that's true, right? Or am I being too pushy again?"

"No!" Clera says and means it.

"Now eat some cookies and tell me about what happened to you." Soo Yun pushes the plate toward Clera.

Though she doesn't want to, Clera feels obliged to explain her story. She starts haltingly, but speaking about the last two days gets easier the more she talks. She remains deliberately vague about her housing situation. Squatting must be illegal, but would Soo Yun call the clinks? As Clera concludes, a thought occurs to her. "Do you have any work available? I'm not skilled, but I'm a quick learner."

Soo Yun shakes her head and purses her lips. "Sometimes even Appa and I don't have enough to do here, and he can't afford to hire anyone besides the boy who takes over one day a week so we can have time off."

"Do you know anyone else who needs workers?"

"No." Soo Yun perks up. "But you can stop by the recruitment office. Or I know! Perkine Industries just opened a new Skinpad factory not far from here! I bet they need bot supervisors!"

Clera struggles to keep her face blank. She remained vague on *several* points of her story. The name "Perkine" sends her heart plummeting. She doesn't like remembering the confrontation with Mrs. Apochek. Though she can't afford to be picky, how can she go back to Perkine? Besides, when they scan her digi-ring, won't they see her work history? Perhaps her old boss has even filed a complaint against her.

"Thank you." Clera keeps her tone neutral. "Maybe I'll check that out.

And thanks so much for giving me food.”

"No problem.” Soo Yun pauses. “You have a safe place to stay, right?”

"Oh, yes,” Clera lies. “And I have my brother. We'll be fine.” She thinks of the filthy apartment and can't help adding, “The new place we're renting really needs a cleaning, but I'm broke. I don't suppose . . .”

Soo Yun jumps up. “Hang on.” She disappears into the back room and comes out a few minutes later with a paper bag.

Clera takes a last sip of tea and slides from the booth. She peers inside the bag to find cleaner, a few rags, a wrapped napkin, and an Italian soda. Swallowing her pride, she accepts the gift. “I'll pay you back,” she blurts, “When I have a job again. I promise.”

Soo Yun waves this away with a slim hand. She's shorter than Clera and stick thin, but there's an energy about her that fills up space. “Pay me back by returning, won't you? There's hardly anyone my age in the neighborhood. Seems like no one's having kids anymore, and only old people come in here. It made my day to sit and talk to you.”

"Well, okay then.” Clera hesitates. “I won't always have interesting conversation, though.”

Soo Yun laughs. “That's fine! I'm pretty sure I can talk enough for both of us.” She gives directions to the job recruitment office in West Town and sees Clera off with a wave.

15

ZAVI

Zavi sits at a table in the Boba Tea Cafe, a plastic chair moved aside to make room for his hover chair. He's stronger now, his muscles more defined, the ache in his back mostly gone. He sips his tea and accepts a plate of butter cookies from the smiling young waitress. *Soo Yun.* He enjoys seeing her sunny face. She's always in a good mood, always happy to see him. Or maybe that's the mask she wears for customers.

Zavi drinks and stares out the window. He's only now realizing how sheltered his life has been. This part of the city is dying. Not far away, a neighborhood the locals call Slavland has become gang territory. The Second City marred the old walls with graffiti, and no city officials come by to police the area or restore abandoned buildings. Zavi watches people stroll past, mostly oldsters hanging onto homes by their fingernails, afraid if they lose them, they'll end up in homeless shelters.

Soo Yun told him some of this. The rest he has witnessed with his own eyes. He sees the worry behind the young waitress' smiles and guesses the Boba Tea Cafe won't survive much longer. Too bad. The kimchi special is perfection—just the right blend of garlic, ginger, and heat. Soo Yun approaches and refills his mug. "You seem stronger every day," she comments. Her slanted eyes settle on his biceps. "Before long, you'll be entering body building contests."

He forces a laugh, but when she retreats, the now-familiar loneliness settles across his shoulders. Work is good, at least. The director of Fadel Arboretum and Greenhouses, Albero Harris, reminds him of his own father, though perhaps a sadder version since gangs murdered his little sister last year. The other workers keep their distance thanks to the Fadel name he carries, yet they aren't unfriendly. Zavi hasn't made real friends at the arboretum. He was raised in a luxurious compound as a spoiled only child. He's traveled the world, had a five-star chef prepare his meals, never lacked for anything. That richness left him unprepared for his life now: dreams of a PhD put on hold, a body broken, and worst of all, parents lost forever. And Grandfather is too far away to see every day except through video chats, which isn't the same.

To distract himself from his thoughts, Zavi scrolls through the news. The stories don't raise his spirits. There have been riots in the Canadian refugee camps. No one wants to take in former Maldives nationals whose islands are five feet underwater. The photo of a deep-blue mountain lake at Glacier National Park in Montana dominates one page, but the headline reads, "Last Glacier Disappears Despite Scientists' Best Efforts After Hottest Summer on Record." The most optimistic story Zavi can find is an article stating a band of men trafficking young girls in South Side have been apprehended.

The chat feature on Zavi's Skinpad buzzes. He picks up, and a grainy picture of Niklas materializes. Zavi's cousin has shorn his tangled golden locks—the envy of all the girls when they were teenagers. He's lost his tan after months of space travel, but that lopsided grin on a wide, mobile mouth remains the same. His blue eyes still sparkle with mischief, and that charisma Zavi always envied is still there, an indefinable aura of energy and goodwill.

"Niki!" Zavi tries his best to sound upbeat. "Still at Arsia Mons?"

"Only for a week or so more. This might be our last video chat, little cuz. It'll be radio silence once I'm through the ARH. You're looking good."

"Am I?" Zavi raises his eyebrows. "How much of me can you see on screen?"

"Enough to know you're bulking up." Niklas squints. "You might actually have more muscles than you did before."

Zavi notices Niklas doesn't add *the accident*. They never talk about the wreck that killed Zavi's parents and Nik's aunt. Niklas must be hurting, too, but it's different for him. He's on the adventure of a lifetime and so certain he'll be able to return to Earth through the wormhole. *Too* certain. Lackadaisical confidence has always been his cousin's *modus operandi*. Zavi says, "I'm doing okay. Docs say I'll be on my feet soon. Get rid of the chair."

"That's great! And how's everything else?"

Zavi sums up his work, but there isn't much else to say. The lack only emphasizes the smallness of his life now. "What about you?" Zavi finally asks. He relaxes a little when Nik seizes the opening to rattle on about preparations to leave the underground city of Arsia Mons and make for the ancient Martian ring near Deimos.

"You should see this place!" Niklas shifts the screen to offer a view of the cavern where he sits at some sort of "outdoor" cafe. The place is huge, with red rock walls and pods pushed against the edges like seeds nestled into trenches for planting. "Mars One still has a colony up top, but the dust storms are wicked. It's much safer down here, though I must admit to missing the sun." The screen flips, and Niklas's face reappears. "Hey, we took a tour of the Martian ruins that were discovered when that big quake ruined those cloaking devices and revealed the ARH. Fascinating stuff! There are these Chinese dragon symbols on everything. No one knows what they mean. Do you think there could have been actual dragons on

Mars millennia ago?"

Zavi bites into a cookie and considers this. Restlessness stirs inside him. If the chance came, would he travel through the wormhole to discover brand new flora on some exotic planet?

No use dreaming about it. He won't leave Grandfather. The old man has already lost too much.

Niklas gives Zavi a long-distance tour of the underground, multi-national city. Zavi is glad to let his cousin talk, to focus on something besides himself. When they finally say goodbye, Nik's face grows serious. "Hey, Zavi. You know I'll be thinking of you even when I'm far away, right?"

"You're already far away."

"You know what I mean." Niklas hesitates. "I need to know you'll be alright."

"I'm fine." Zavi is pretty sure the words emerge with confidence. He forces his mouth into a smile and repeats, "I'm fine now, Niki. You go off and explore your new planet, and when you come back through the ARH, I'll be waiting."

They end the chat. Zavi sits back. His hands wrap around the cup of now-cold tea. The loneliness Niklas' presence held at bay rushes back, stronger than before. He leaves the last cookie on the plate, pays at the counter, and whirs out in his hover chair.

16

CLERA

Clera notices blankets hung out to dry on a line stretching across an alley. It's early afternoon, no one about. She steps into the shadows between buildings. Though she's never stolen anything in her life, the blankets hang within easy reach if she jumps. They're dry, clean, and probably smell like sunshine. She leaps and grabs.

A blanket falls, taking the rope and other blankets with it. They land in a jumble on the gravel. Clera stuffs a blanket into her bag, but it spills out the top. There isn't time to worry about discovery, however. She races down the alley, heart pounding, and ducks into a doorway just as someone hurls indignant curses out an open window. Clera huddles, panting, until the voice fades. Then she races out the passage's far end and melds into a crowd of pedestrians waiting at a tram stop.

Clera draws in on herself, but no furious footfalls sound behind her. The tram pulls up, and the crowd recedes like water sucked back into an ocean. Suddenly she's alone, exposed, not sure if she can find her way to their new apartment without retracing her steps, which she will not do.

She sighs and turns down the street. As she walks, Clera looks for "help wanted" signs in windows but sees none. Nor can she locate the job recruitment office for West Town. Her adrenaline rush fades, and with it, her optimism.

A kid on a hoverboard zips past, brushing the bag she holds. For a moment, she thinks he's trying to steal it. Clera clutches the bag to her chest and realizes she's standing in front of a public library.

It's bigger than her branch but has the same look: a red brick facade and a wide, gently sloping roof. A bank of windows looks out onto lilac bushes. Bees buzz around lavender clusters. Clera walks up to the door, hesitates, then pushes her way in. The air smells papery. A fan hums. She approaches the desk and asks if her library card will transfer to this branch. The librarian is a tiny, middle-aged woman wrapped in a sari. Gold hoops dangle from her ears. She thrusts a pad toward Clera, who swipes her digi-ring.

The woman turns the pad around and studies it. "We need an address, and this indicates that your old one has been deleted. Tell me the new one, and you should be good to go."

"Oh." Clera should have foreseen this. She could make something up, but what if the computer flags a fake address? She'll be too humiliated to return. In the end, she says, "Thanks. I'm new here and afraid I can't remember. Guess I should memorize that!" She smiles with fake cheer. "I'll just browse today."

Clera scurries off. She passes through an arch into the children's section. Worn couches in primary colors surround a rug printed with the ABC's. A few adults rest on the couches. Clera deduces from their threadbare, dirty clothes and hodgepodge bags and bundles that they must be homeless. She's surprised the children's librarian lets them stay. Probably, once kids pour in after school, she won't.

The librarian is busy shelving books and doesn't see her. Does Clera look homeless, too? She wonders when she'll have a shower again. She doubts Elio thought about water when he chose their new living quarters.

She wanders into a third room. Rows of computers stand

wall-to-wall—the ancient tower kind—not laptops. They're probably super slow, but she sits down anyway and clicks the "Welcome to West Town Public Library" button. Several other people work nearby, but none glance at her. She e-signs a pledge not to surf porn sites or use the computers for more than an hour. A timer has already started in the screen's corner, so she guesses she'll be kicked off if she tries to linger.

Clera brings up a map and locates the local job office, then finds the old Ukrainian sector, the Boba Tea Cafe, and a few other interesting spots like a green blob marked *Fadel Arboretum and Greenhouses* bordering Slavland. She commits this portion of New Chicago to memory and returns to the job recruitment office link. When Clera navigates to the website, though, a message flashes on the home page: "This office is temporarily closed to job seekers. We are sorry for the inconvenience."

How can a job office be closed to job hunters? When she skim-reads the local news, she begins to understand. New Chicago and other large northern cities have become migrant hubs. In the old days, the poor and desperate only overwhelmed cities on the U.S.-Mexico border. Now those people have stopped coming, but with Arizona and Texas topping one hundred and twenty degrees for much of the summer, people are migrating north. Add those pushed out of what used to be Florida and Louisiana as the ocean crawls inland, and maybe New Chicago starts to look like the promised land.

At least that's what the article suggests. This city is no utopia to *her*. She skims more and catches the phrase, "Promised Land," used again, only this time in an article about Mars and the ARH's potential to open new frontiers. Clera reads:

In coming months, Norwegian officials expect word back from their starship, Loki, the first ever to travel to a new solar system. Loki's mission is to make orbit at Vishnu, one of two "Goldilocks" planets in the red dwarf system. Vishnu is second-distant from the system's sun. Pioneer I *reports that water covers 70% of its surface, making this planet the most desirable new "promised land" of a new frontier. According to Dr. Ghatak, chief engineer on the* Pioneer *missions, while Vishnu is NASA's number one choice for future colonization, the other planet in Genesis's habitable zone, Ganesha, shows promise, also.*

Swedish Lycka *follows* Loki *through the ARH next week. The United States' own starships*: Calliope, Thalia, *and* Urania, *have forthcoming maiden voyages in the coming two years.*

Billionaire Dec Gaston, the exec behind the hugely successful Arcade Industries, plans to launch his Arcade lottery for berths on Calliope *any day. Top gamers will compete to fill the remaining slots not already reserved for scientists, specialists, and the rich. Gaston remarks, "It's the least I can do to help the lower-class youth of our cities. Without the lotteries, they'd have no hope of raising themselves out of poverty through immigration to a new planet. Winning a sim game might even gain some lucky kid a pilot's seat in* Calliope's *defense and exploration division, since our sims are built to mimic real shuttlecraft controls."*

Clera loses interest when the article goes on to discuss space-oriented philanthropies Gaston promotes. She skims to the bottom, where hyperlinks direct her to other news: *Canada Closes its Southern Border; The New Cold War for Control of the Arctic Enters its Fifth Year; Marsica, the Newest Martian City, Nears Completion*; and *Northern Africa Declared Uninhabitable.*

I guess New Chicago isn't so bad, Clera thinks glumly. She moves on to the newspaper's classifieds, but there's no "help wanted" section. Maybe employers don't use newspapers to advertise? But what about the millions of Slummers without Skinpads or other ways to access job apps? Weights press on her shoulders like she's trapped underwater with no way to rise, no way to breathe. It would be easier to let the water in, to drift down and let currents rock her to sleep.

Clera shakes off her bad mood. It's nearly four, and the computer screen fades to black. She heads outside and squints into the sun, picturing her route to Slavland. Southwest is Soo Yun's cafe, farther south and a bit east, Slavland. Clera believes she can find a larger street than those she traversed earlier and save time getting back.

She sets off and soon recognizes the artery she's looking for. Traffic lurches along in stops and starts. Overhead, mass transit trains whoosh past. The train tracks swing south and disappear around a distant skyscraper. Clera turns right and walks along a littered culvert. She thinks back to the Boba Tea Cafe and meeting Soo Yun—the highlight of her day. She wants nothing more than to return to the little tea shop and sit in a sunny window while honey cookies melt in her mouth and Soo Yun chatters.

But though she's been invited back, Clera won't go until she has credits in her account. Otherwise, Soo Yun will offer more charity, and she's already done enough. But how to get credits? Maybe Elio and she will have to leave New Chicago, after all. The Barrens loom only miles from the walls that enclose city limits. She knows little of them except that they cover millions of acres between America's largest cities, a no-man's-land of lawless renegades and drug runners.

That's according to her high school geography teacher, anyway. She doesn't want to test the truth of his words firsthand.

17

ELIO

Elio heads north. He stops a stranger for directions to the nearest job office, but when he gets there, a sign glows red in the window: "No Admittance. Closed Until Further Notice." Across the street, a homeless shelter that's a copy of the one they stayed at last night sits dark and quiet. A few ragged drug users shoot up out front, and Elio hurries by before they notice him.

He veers east, unsure of what to do now. None of the shops are hiring. A small refugee park sits between a bargain retail center and a silicon manufacturer. Tents and makeshift shelters obscure the grass. Elio has to pee, but he doesn't want to wander between cardboard and tin shacks looking for a public bathroom. He's too clean to fit in. If someone thinks he has credits, they might cut his digi-ring from his finger to get them.

Someone emerges from a tent to hand-pump water into a jug. *Water.* That'll be a problem in the Slavland apartment. This thought coincides with a partial solution. Old gas stations litter the city. Elio remembers Papa reading him a book about truckers and how they'd shower at such places. You paid some credits—or dollars back then—and a shower door swung open. You had ten minutes to luxuriate under a pounding stream of hot water before you hopped back in your eighteen-wheeler and drove down the road.

Elio wanted to be a trucker so badly until Papa told him those jobs didn't exist anymore. Planes, drones, and high-speed cross-country trains deliver goods nowadays. Transportation trucking used gas or diesel, and those fuels are illegal.

Elio had asked, "But why couldn't someone figure out how to convert all those trucks to hydrogen, Papa?"

He shrugged. "I was pretty young when the last truckers hung up their hats. Part of it was politics, I suppose? Part of it poor business choices. Not getting on the bandwagon soon enough."

The words only confused Elio. Soon after, he changed his dream to becoming a fighter pilot.

He walks on. Where two multi-lane boulevards intersect, one of those sprawling, ancient truck stops sits. Semi-trucks exist only in scrapyards, yet the place still operates. Elio goes in. Sure enough, a hallway in the back leads to bathroom stalls *and* shower stalls. It takes five credits for a ten-minute shower. Elio wants to feel that water massaging his flesh, but he isn't dirty enough yet, and he's got more important things to do. He leaves, buying nothing. The clerk's suspicious gaze follows him, but he doesn't care. He's found out what he needs to know.

Next, Elio stops at a construction site and offers to do grunt work, but the foreman shakes his head. Northeast, the city's heart throbs. Before he knows it, he's standing in front of the Arcade. It's an unusually warm day for mid-May, and sweat sheens his skin. The interior will be air-conditioned. He's got his yearly pass. Maybe he'll go in for a bit and check the place out.

Elio nods to the guy behind the shatterproof glass like he knows him, scans his ring, and saunters through security, heart pounding with excitement. He's wanted to join the Arcade since he was ten and Daz Brighton, a finalist in the International e-Games, spoke at school. There were no funds to bring people in, but Daz had gotten into legal trouble and had to make public reparations. Elio had dreamed of stardom in the games ever since.

But a poor kid from the South Side couldn't afford to join the Arcade. Some played on occasional day passes, yet what good was that? You had to practice constantly to get anywhere. And you had to do it before you hit your mid-twenties and reaction speeds dropped. At almost eighteen, Elio was in his prime. Draining his account to buy that yearly pass had been a necessity.

The vast hall past the gates is dim. Colored lights in the high ceiling provide a festive atmosphere, though. Jumbled sounds—whistles, bells, and dings—rebound off walls lined with consoles. Near the hall's front, there's an RPG area of players hunched on couches next to shelves of laptops. Other gamers stand in shooter play kiosks off to the sides. They whoop, curse, and sway as though dodging bullets or lasers. Elio meanders through the games, checking them out, noticing the glass counter with prizes displayed beneath, the flashing lights when someone gets a top score, the side room with booths and concessions almost empty. According to a sign at the cordoned-off entrance, you can't take refreshments into the playing area, so why bother eating?

A few little kids pass him, but most people in the Arcade are teenage boys. A few dazed-looking parents trail children clutching wads of tickets. Is this a weekend? Elio doesn't know or care.

A twinge of guilt hits him. Clera's face forms behind his eyes, but he brushes the vision away. He won't stay long. He's just feeling things out, finding his place here. After all, if he can become a top gamer, it'll be worth missing a little time looking for work. Of course, winning means playing the Arcade more than a little. His mind skitters past that point. He's got an adrenaline buzz going, and this is a needed break, a temporary lift from the heavy weight of living. If he thinks about Mama, he'll start imagining it's him buried beneath mounds of rubble. Though he knows she was dead before the wrecking ball came, his mind twists reality into nightmares. He barely slept last night because of them.

The Arcade distracts Elio from the horror of the last few days. He's ready to win.

To his left, digital tickertape scrolls across the wide arch of a side room. Names and scores zip past. On a monitor set into the wall, the billionaire, Dec Gaston, founder of Arcade Industries, speaks. He wears a fancy suit and waves his hands a lot. His brown hair molds to his skull, and his teeth flash blindingly white.

". . . . can win a chance at the lottery! It doesn't matter your social status or how many credits you've got! Become a high scorer on the sims, and join the elite group destined for a chance at a berth, kiddos! A berth on *Calliope*, that is!" An AI-rendered picture of a starship replaces Dec. The image drifts closer, and the perspective changes. A camera circles the exterior of a finished ship. *Calliope*, green letters on the hull proclaim. The vid turns the hull transparent. Elio sees right into the starship's guts, where simulated humans walk down curved hallways in grav boots, sit at shiny booths in dining areas, clink cocktail glasses at the bar, or enter a bulbous part of the ship which spins slowly. This section is so large that the people inside probably don't even realize there *is* a spin. Elio read somewhere that centrifugal force creates artificial gravity. It's a park, he realizes in amazement. There are paths, orchards, open spaces where people throw frisbees, a simulated blue sky and golden sun on the slope of the ceiling.

Next on the vid, a shuttle slides gracefully into one of many slots on the exterior. Other slots are already filled. *Shuttle berths*, Elio thinks.

When Dec's face replaces the starship, Elio frowns. He wants to see more of *Calliope*. "Can you imagine? The chance to win a SHUTTLE, which you will fly YOURSELF up to the U.S. Space Station, where you will rendezvous with *Calliope* in your assigned docking berth! And how is this possible, you may ask? Look around. What do you see?" His hand sweeps across the screen, redirecting Elio's gaze into the sim room.

"Simulators, Gamers. Simulators. Designed to imitate shuttle controls exactly. So, by playing the sims in this special room, you'll be training for free! Well, not exactly free, since you paid good credits to get into the Arcade, right?" Dec winks at the camera. "And what's the catch, you ask? There is none. Five hundred and fifty berths aboard *Calliope* are unspoken for. They go to common folk through a lottery system. And, thanks to the maneuvering of Yours Truly, a full two hundred of those berths will go to winners of the Arcade lottery! So, get to playing, Gamers! And may the best man or woman win!"

The screen goes dark. A voice speaks at Elio's shoulder. He jumps, his thoughts in outer space. Dreams of flying among the stars have taken him far away.

"What a bunch of baloney," a female voice scoffs. "It's probably rigged. There are no free rides. That's what my uncle says, anyway."

Elio turns, blinking, to stare down at a petite girl with brunette hair and pale eyes. Her eyebrows arch like birds' wings. A thick, fraying braid hangs over one shoulder. She's wearing an oil-smudged jumpsuit and work boots. The girl only comes to Elio's shoulder. She'd be kind of pretty, with her pert, upturned nose and glinting eyes, but in that dirty suit, she stands out like an alley cat among pampered Siamese.

"What are you talking about?" Elio asks, frowning. He's annoyed that she interrupted his daydream, her voice a needle that popped the pleasant fantasies in his head.

The girl shrugs. "Uncle Bas says I should stay far from the Arcade. It's a credit suck. Kids gamble all their money away in here when they could be earning a real living."

"Not all of them. Some kids win. Didn't you notice the top gamer scores when you came in? Don't you watch the e-game Olympics on the vids?"

The girl eyes him with a condescending tilt of her head. Though she's short, it feels like she's staring down at him when she replies, "Are those real people, though? Anything can be AI'd. And even if they are—" She holds up a hand when he tries to interrupt. "How many of these poor fools will win anything?"

"So, what are you doing here, then, if the Arcade is so bad?"

She shrugs again and gives him a full-on smile complete with dimples. This goes a long way toward melting his aggravation. "I like watching," she says simply. "It's like going to a circus. All the lights and sounds, the feeling of excitement. It's a nice break from the aeronautical museum across the way where I work." The girl holds out a grimy hand. "I'm Mila Aguilar, by the way. And you are . . ."

"Elio Diaz," he replies automatically, taking her hand. It's lost in his, but her grip makes him wince.

Mila laughs like she knows this and releases him. "I haven't seen you here before, Elio Diaz. This your first time?"

He doesn't like to admit it, but he nods. To change the subject, he asks, "How is it that a girl your age gets a job at an aeronautical museum? That doesn't seem likely."

"I'm not lying, Elio. Uncle Bas got me the job after I graduated last year. He's head curator at the museum, and he was my guardian until I turned eighteen. My parents died in the last flu epidemic." She says this matter-of-factly.

"So did my . . ." but Elio stops himself, instead asking, "What do you do over there?"

She looks down at her oily jumpsuit. A Skinpad glows faintly under the left sleeve. "Isn't it obvious? I work on shuttles. Decommissioned ships come in from all over the United States, and I help take out the good parts—engines, compressors, air-flow systems—so the museum can resell them. The shells are placed in the Graveyard—really the back lot—so tourists can pay money to tour them. But a girl can't work all the time, so on breaks I cross the road and come here. I'm probably wasting my pass by not playing, but there's not enough time during my breaks to get much gaming in. Probably just as well."

"You don't look old enough to have graduated," Elio says.

"How old are you?" Mila shoots back.

"Eighteen." *Or close enough.*

"So, are *you* graduated, Elio Diaz?" She says his name in a sing-song voice, like it's a joke.

"Schooled out," he mutters. The lie comes easily because it's almost true. He should have schooled out like Clera and gone to work in a factory. A lot of kids didn't stay in public school past sixteen. "Now, if you don't mind, I'm heading in to play the sims so I can 'waste some time' and 'never win a single credit back.'"

Mila only laughs again and raises one of her perfect eyebrows. "Suit yourself, Elio Diaz. Maybe I'll come watch you sometime."

She turns away. He lets out the breath he's been holding. He doesn't know whether he hates Mila Aguilar or feels attracted to her. Either way, she's quite annoying, and he doesn't want anyone observing when he plays for the first time. He won't be any good. Still, he knows he *can* be good if given a chance. Elio watches Mila's backside as she retreats, curvy even under her gray jumpsuit. She disappears behind a circle of dance game machines, and he enters the sim room.

There's an open console in the corner. Elio slides into a plush, faux leather pilot's seat. He adjusts the chair with a button on the side and begins reading directions on the screen. There are a *lot* of them, though, and his ADHD brain grows impatient, so he scans his ring above a flashing arrow and presses START. The chair vibrates. It's connected to the main screen, a huge, hooded, curving pane that wraps halfway around him. This makes Elio feel like he's really in a shuttle. So does the robotic computer voice which announces, "Are you prepped and ready for takeoff, Captain Elio?" Cool. It even knows his name.

He answers, "Yes."

The voice goes on, "Your mission is to break up a cluster of troublesome asteroids headed for Earth. Are you up to the task?"

"Yes."

"Good. Strap in and start your engine, pilot."

Elio does as instructed. Though there are a lot of buttons on the dash, the start-up one is large and green. Easy enough. When he pushes it, the chair rumbles beneath him. A dark screen lights up, showing him the runway. A robot holding a flag in one hand and chocks in the other runs off. Elio takes the wheel in both palms and feels for pedals with his feet. He's never even driven a car, but it's obvious what to do. He pushes down, and the runway rushes toward him.

Or rather, his shuttle rushes down the runway. Blinking lights on the tarmac light up as he approaches, then sails by. Suddenly, a red warning siren swirls on the underside of the hood. The robotic voice says in its weirdly calm monotone, "Warning, Captain Elio. Pull up immediately to avoid launch failure."

Elio is already tugging the wheel toward his chest as the message repeats, but he's too late. The chair jolts and vibrates like it's trying to throw him off. The screen erupts in flame, and the siren above his head dims. After the screen fades to black and the chair stills, a simple message slides into view. "You are dead. Want to play again, Captain Elio?"

Elio sighs. He knew this wouldn't be easy. He's reaching for the start button when someone gives a hoot of laughter next to him.

A guy bends down and says, "Bad luck, hom. Didn't you read the instructions first?"

"Do you mind?" Elio retorts, heat rising to his face. He takes a deep breath to calm himself and adds, "I don't need onlookers, *hom*. Go find your own game."

"Hey, you mad or something?" The guy bends even lower. Back to its home position, the screen casts blue light across a smooth jaw, straight nose, flashing eyes. The interloper's a teenager close to Elio's age. His black hair gleams like it's been oiled, not a strand out of place. He wears jump pants and a mostly unbuttoned silk shirt over a white tee shirt. His hands are bare. A Skinpad glows faintly beneath the skin of his inner wrist. He's not a Slummer.

"I'm Juke. Well, that's what everyone calls me, anyway. And these sims aren't for beginners, if you know what I mean. You've got to study the directions if you want to get good."

Elio's anger trickles away. He shouldn't snap at this kid. Juke's probably right. Maybe he can help. Elio swallows his pride and admits, "I'm new to the Arcade, and I'm not much good at reading instructions. I mean, I can read fine, but after about five minutes, the words swim, and I get a headache."

Juke says, "Hang on a minute." He disappears but returns in less, dragging a chair he found from who knows where. He sets it next to Elio's control chair and leans his elbows on his knees. "Look, if you want to learn, I can teach you."

"What's the catch?"

The boy shrugs. "I'm out of credits, but I don't feel like leaving yet. It's fun helping newbies."

"You look like you can afford a year pass. Why don't you have one?"

Juke winces. "My dad. He says the Arcade is addictive, so I only get day passes, and only on weekends."

So, it is *a weekend*, Elio thinks. "I don't have extra credits to pay you."

Juke looks over Elio's ratty jeans and faded shirt. He arches an *oh, really?* eyebrow but doesn't comment.

Elio likes him better for that. "Okay," he says. "Show me how."

Juke is a good teacher. He's patient and answers all Elio's questions, though Elio knows some of them are dumb. He doesn't admit that he's never played vid-games at all, simply listens carefully and does what Juke tells him. He's a great listener, and he won't forget, just like he remembers the maze of streets that make up New Chicago.

Several hours later, Elio has managed multiple successful take-offs, shot down some asteroids, and even made one landing without crashing. He's still on apprentice level, but he's improved a lot.

A claxon goes off somewhere in the main hall, and a piped voice calls out, "We have a new high game score!" This jolts Elio back to reality. He asks Juke what time it is.

"Four-thirty, hom," the kid says. "You gotta be somewhere?"

"Yeah," Elio says. "And I'm gonna be late. How long is this place open, anyway?"

Juke's lips widen into a grin. "The Arcade never closes, hom, as long as you have credits."

Elio slides out of the sim. He shakes Juke's hand. "Thanks for the help. Maybe I'll see you around."

"I'm here every weekend until the credits run out. I'll buy you a drink next time if you come back."

"Oh, I'll be back." Elio offers up his biggest smile, and it's actually genuine.

18

ELIO

Elio can't go back to their new shelter empty-handed. He edges south, avoiding the noise and traffic of major roads. Will Clera worry when he's late? Will she return with supplies or even a job offer? What will he say when she asks what *he* accomplished?

He didn't waste his time. Juke taught him a lot at the sims, and with practice, Elio will start winning tourneys.

He wanders into an industrial sector. Rectangular concrete buildings with flat tops dot the streets. Fenced storage yards filled with a hodgepodge of materials and equipment crowd the space between buildings. Elio spots a smaller business through an alley. A delivery truck has pulled up inside an open gate. The building's back door yawns open. No one is in sight, so he moves closer.

Elio hesitates at the open gate. If he's caught trespassing, he'll claim to be lost. He passes through, swerves around blocks of landscaping granite and unopened, bubble-wrapped pallets, and sidles up to the back door. Voices drift toward him from some inner office. He peers into the room.

It's a staff room. There are a few scuffed metal tables, a coffee pot on a cluttered counter, a pad on the wall for clocking in, and a janitorial closet, its door propped open by a bot that died before reaching the dock. Elio skulks across the room and peers inside the closet. A motion-sensor light flicks on, making him jump.

Cleaning supplies line steel shelves: towels and plastic bottles filled with solutions, scrubbers, and trash bags. Elio pulls a bag from its box. He reads a few labels and fills the bag with cloths and cleaners. A toolbox sitting on a shelf catches his eye. He pulls out a hammer and nails, then a wrench and screwdriver set. He adds these to his haul. A dustbin and brush hang behind the door. He takes those, too, and tops the pile off with boxes of masks and rubber gloves.

Back in the staff room, Elio spots a half-eaten carton of donuts on the table and grabs a couple of them. He hurries outside with the trash bag slung over his back and looks around, a half-baked story ready on his tongue. But the yard is still deserted, and he makes his escape without getting caught.

With the bag slung over his shoulder, Elio continues south. He munches on chocolate-frosted donuts and pushes aside twinges of guilt. The black plastic bumps against his shoulder blades and makes him look like a truly homeless person. Elio gives up job hunting for the day. It's past five, the end of the workday for those unfortunates who pull weekend shifts or seven-dayers.

He's got to get work, but how? He only sees two choices: get in touch with Bohdan or reapply with the city execs. After seven months on their payroll, that's the last thing he wants to do. He might not survive it. Crawling through toxic sewers and swinging off the sides of high-rises on a windy day aren't conducive to living a long, healthy life. Hells. The execs won't even let their bots do those jobs. Elio recalls the day when he finally quit. He'd been sent down a service shaft below the streets fronting the river. A clog was causing the street above to flood. His job was to find and remove the blockage by whatever means possible.

He was wary. Only last week, two workers didn't return from the sewers. They were found several days later floating face down off the shore of Lake Michigan. Bite marks covered their bloated bodies. The news anchor never identified what made those puncture wounds. Alligators? No way. Some new breed of monster? There were always rumors of unsanctioned genetics labs flushing rejected experiments into the sewers.

Fitting his gas mask more firmly against his cheeks, Elio crept forward. His headlamp cast eerie shadows over algae-encrusted walls. He bent low and followed a current until the water sloshed against a mud-mix of trash, leaves, and sticks. Raising his shovel to dig, he paused. A sound like metal grating echoed through the tunnels behind him. He remembered how the air coming from the tunnel he'd just passed chilled him with something more than cold. How imagined eyes stared out from the dark.

Elio'd brushed off the feeling, but now he swung around and listened. Was something there? He retreated a step. Then another. Soon, he passed the hole that branched from the main tunnel. *Glurp, Glurp.* Water gurgled. *Snuff, snuff.* Something was hunting.

Elio's retreat turned into a run. He looked back once and saw a pair of glowing eyes almost upon him. The eyes lurched forward. He swung his shovel. *Thunk.* The orbs blinked out. He doubted he'd killed the monster, simply stunned it. He panted, splashing on, relieved to see the iron ladder up ahead. Gripping slick rungs, he'd climbed. With every step, Elio expected to feel a claw on his ankle, a tug pulling him backward.

Now, days later, he shakes his head to clear the memory. It's the reason he never went back, and he can't regret that decision. Execs couldn't care less about human workers. Workplace safety rules lapsed when the EPA and other watchdog agencies were cut. He's not big on rules and regs, but after the sewer incident, Elio wishes the government *did* care. In that tunnel was the closest he's come to dying.

Elio knows he's reached Slavland by the spray-paint scrawls on the sides of brick buildings, the deserted streets, smashed windows, and trash-clogged gutters. He picks up the broken chair beneath the ripped awning and hauls it with him. Another block and he's reached *lad's Ice ream.* Do others like him hide inside adjacent buildings? If so, they don't show themselves.

Clera sits on the curb, a black cat cuddled in her lap. Is she worried about him? He hates to think of her scared, alone, and believing he's left for good—or been killed. These last couple of years, they haven't been close. He was miserable at school. Keeping that secret, then more secrets when he dropped out, created distance between them. Besides, Clera was with Mama at Perkine, exhausted every night and probably hiding secrets of her own.

Elio hasn't really looked at his sister for a long time, but he does now, before she notices him. She's hunched over, focused on the stray. She reminds him of Mama—long, wavy hair that catches the sun with strands of gold. Her cheek tilts toward the cat. She looks up when she hears his footsteps. The black feline stretches and slits its eyes. A large paper bag with a plaid blanket poking out the top rests beside her.

"Elio." She jumps up. The cat leaps from her arms and bounds behind a dumpster.

"Sorry I'm late," he mutters, wary of her mood.

But she smiles, eyeing the trash bag and chair. "You had some luck."

He doesn't contradict her. "Have you been waiting long?"

"Only half an hour or so. I was a little late, too."

"Let's go upstairs." He glances at the second-story windows across the street. Anyone could be lurking there, watching and waiting like that monster in the sewer.

She wrinkles her nose but nods. "I hope you have a broom in your trash bag." She glances at it doubtfully.

"No," he admits as they duck into the shop, with its cobwebby corners and cracked mirror. "But I did find a dustbin and brush. Better than nothing."

He climbs the stairs. They creak ominously, and one gives a little under his sneaker. He'll have to look at that.

"Stole, you mean," Clera murmurs behind him. Before he can get defensive, she adds with a sigh, "I stole, too. The blanket, anyway. I didn't know if you'd find one, and I can't bear the idea of sleeping on that gross mattress with nothing on top but thin sheets."

Elio reaches the door to the apartment. He listens, then enters, eyes sweeping the room for any signs of disturbance. He needs to install a lock.

Clera asks for the brush and dustbin. Elio gives her a mask, too, and puts one on himself. He's pleased he thought of that. To plan ahead isn't like him. She spot-sweeps the main room floor. A cloud of dust hangs in the air, especially visible where sunlight pools from the window. They keep their masks on and sit cross-legged in the cleared space.

Clera reaches under the plaid blanket and pulls an Italian soda and cookies wrapped in an oil-soaked napkin from the bag. She offers Elio half the cookies and the soda. He hasn't eaten enough, and the snack barely satisfies his empty stomach. The carbonation in the soda gives an illusion of fullness, at least. He listens while she describes her day, disappointed she didn't find work though not surprised.

Elio improvises an account of his own day but leaves out the Arcade. When he's done, they fall silent. Clouds move across the sun, and a veil of gloom falls over them. Elio's been on a seesaw of hope and despair, but despair is winning out.

Clera plucks fuzz from the blanket. "What'll we do, Elio? We can't keep stealing everything we need. Eventually, we'll get caught. Besides, what would Mama think?"

Elio shrugs. Mama would be disappointed, but she's gone, and they've been left to fend for themselves. "We've only been on our own a few days. I'll go out again tomorrow. You can stay here and make this place livable."

A dry laugh escapes her. "If that's even possible! But okay. One more day." She hesitates. "I think we might have to leave the city. I wish I knew what was out there."

"Leave New Chicago?" Elio starts in surprise. He's never considered that notion, and he doesn't like it. The Arcade is here, not out in the Barrens. "That's a bad idea, Clera. We don't know anything about life in the rurals. How bad are things? How do people make it? Farming? I know nothing about plants or harvesting."

Clera admits softly, "I might enjoy growing things if that's what we ended up doing. Remember that aloe plant of Buela's? She let me water it and pluck dead leaves off. It was supposed to be a chore, but I liked it. I liked seeing something survive because I cared for it."

"That's different from living off the land, and you know it. I thought I was the reckless one." Elio tamps down annoyance. He can't afford a fight right now, especially the kind where he ends up storming out. Where would he go, anyway? They need each other, so he's got to keep a lid on his temper. Elio takes Clera's hand and squeezes it. "No matter what, we have to stick together. You won't leave me, right?"

"Of course not!" She squeezes back. "But we should be realists. There's no work."

"Give me more time. Just a day or two. We have enough food for that, and we have shelter."

Clera sighs and nods. She drops his hand. "I'm too tired for another trek right now, anyway. We could use a few days to think and to rest. It's so unfamiliar here, Elio. I feel like we *did* leave New Chicago, though we've only moved across town. This place even smells different."

He laughs. "Yeah, like rotted garbage."

She smiles. It's a milk-toast smile, as Buela would say, but a smile nonetheless.

"Have a little faith," Elio whispers. He's pretty sure he's talking to himself as much as to his sister.

19

CLERA

Clera stares at the ceiling. She and Elio lie as far apart as possible on the lumpy mattress. They haven't shared a bed since he was very small. She has vague memories of cuddling with him under a quilt until he turned five and announced he was moving to the sofa bed in the living room. Part of Clera cheered this news, but another part missed his warm little body.

Nights are still cool. She layered her clothing before lying down, meaning she's back in her work jumpsuit. Still, Clera shivers. She should be *under* the blanket. How can Elio sleep so soundly? A million thoughts run through her mind, foremost the one thing she didn't tell him.

She hadn't come straight home after the library. Instead, she loitered on a crowded street. Cars stalled in the end-of-day crush. She watched a little boy run between them and peer in windows, rag and washing spray in hand. A driver transferred credits to him after he cleaned a windshield. Up ahead, a little girl sprayed another set of car windows.

Clera thought of her zeroed-out checking account. Other than sex work, she couldn't think how to fill it, couldn't imagine trading her body for credits. Despite all her reading, she was still innocent. Too busy for a relationship, she told herself, but the real truth? She didn't want to be with another Slummer. Clera wanted an educated man in a smartsuit, loafers, and with a glowing Skinpad beneath his perma-tan. He didn't have to be good-looking, just cultured.

It would never happen.

Clera had pulled herself from daydreams, taken a cloth and cleaner from her bag, and strode into traffic. Her heart thumped, and she almost ran back to the curb. But instead, she knocked on a window and held up her spray. The woman inside frowned and shook her head. She tried the next car. Then the next. Some people yelled, "Fec off!" through bug-splattered windshields. Some made angry swiping gestures, and one even gave her the finger.

But once she'd started, she couldn't stop. If she did, all this would have been for nothing. An old man leaned out his window and told her to get off the streets and find a real job. *You're too old to panhandle!* Elio would have dented the man's fender with his fist. Clera only blinked furiously and turned away. Traffic inched forward at that moment, and the man's car almost ran over her foot.

At last, a young mother in the back of a smartcar took pity on her. She motioned Clera over, let her wash windows, then tapped her Skinpad. Clera swiped it, and once the woman's ride moved on, she scanned her account summary. Twenty credits.

She'd hurried back to Slavland, insults still ringing in her head, and swore she'd never try earning credits that way again.

In the dark, Clera stares up at bare wires hanging out of the ceiling. Why hadn't she told Elio? He wouldn't have laughed or scoffed. He might have been angry, though. Some scrull could have pulled her inside a vehicle and made her vanish. How many kids were snatched off the streets every day and sold to human traffickers? Maybe her height and age would have saved her, maybe not.

She wraps her arms tightly around herself and shivers. Perhaps she dozes. A creak of rusty hinges brings her upright. Elio goes rigid beside her. He puts a warning finger to his lips. Moonlight streams through the window, bathing his face.

He rolls off the bed and gestures for her to stay put. Clera shakes her head and follows him down the hallway. Elio grabs a hammer from his garbage bag on the way. She has no weapon, but she's confident in Elio's fighting skills. He's been in plenty of fights, anyway. She doesn't know if he won.

They peer into the living room. Nothing moves, but the front door gaps wide. Beyond, the corridor's ominous quiet turns her throat dry with fear.

There's a scrabbling sound. Clera clutches Elio's arm and points. The black cat she petted earlier hunches next to the wall and shakes something caught in its jaws. She moves past Elio and calls, "Kitty . . . here, kitty."

The cat trots over and drops a dead mouse at her feet. Clera releases a breath and grimaces. She scratches the cat's ears, and it arches its back. "Good kitty. Good kitty."

Elio closes the door. He props the broken chair in front of it. "I need to get a lock," he mutters, then turns around and adds, "We should keep that cat. It'll help with rats."

Clera examines the sleek feline. She runs hands over silky fur. "I think it's a boy," she says. "We should call him something strong. Maybe Duro?"

"If we keep him, he'll have to feed himself."

Clera smiles. "It's not a question of 'keeping.' He can go in and out as he pleases, probably. He's a cat, after all."

"We'll see once I board the windows and put a bolt on the door." Elio heads back to the bedroom, mumbling, "Hope I can get to sleep again."

Clera leaves Duro to his meal and follows. She sleeps easier after that, though her brother moves restlessly beside her.

The next morning, sunlight streams through cracks in a freshly boarded-up window. Clera can't believe she slept through Elio fixing the chair and blocking the empty window frame. He must have gone scrounging around the neighborhood for boards. He tells her he's jerry-rigged a latch for the front door, too. It won't keep human intruders out but will do for stray animals.

Elio hands Clera a protein bar and a bottle of water. He says, "I'm going out to look for work. You okay here?"

"Yes." The protein bar tastes salty-sweet, but she's not hungry. Just tired and muddle-headed and depressed. She forces out, "I'll go, too, in a little while. I need to clean some more."

"Be careful, okay? And don't let that cat add more poop to the floor."

Clera feels Duro's warm weight on her legs where he must have slept. She smiles, her sadness lifting a little.

Elio walks into the hallway and pauses. "It'll be okay, Clera."

"Isn't that my line, little brother?"

He doesn't look at her.

She frowns. "Hey, don't do anything stupid, all right? If anything happens to you—" She can't finish.

He forces a grin but still doesn't meet her eyes. "Same to you, sister." And he's gone.

20

SOLAST

Sol sits on a bench in a shaded picnic area adjacent to the aerospace museum. She waits for closing time and thinks about Mons Vega. No, *Anton*. The Earthers in the communes were all expected to take "spirit names" once they passed their twelfth year. Sol had been five when her mother died in childbirth, ten when her father first heard Anton speak at an Earther rally and joined the commune, twelve when she discarded her old name. *Anna*. That's right. She had been *Anna*. The name no longer conjures powerful memories, only a twinge of longing for parents many years gone. Her father had become Ridge. A good name. Rugged and earthy, like him.

But Anton kept his name. Sol thought she understood why. He wanted to remain apart, to solidify his mystique. But why switch that name now? Had he needed anonymity?

A group of tourists walk past her on a winding sidewalk. The sun dips behind tall, mirrored buildings to the west. Sol rises and slips through the front door of the museum. Inside the dim foyer, the desk lady talks to someone on her Skinpad. It's easy to sneak past her into the vast room beyond, duck into a shadowed place between kiosk and wall, and wait for closing time. Once the manager quells the lights and she hears footsteps retreat and locks clunk, she emerges. Sol finds the side door that leads outside to where old ships sleep. It doesn't budge when she pushes it.

She looks around, finds a narrow hallway. Amber emergency lights flood its walls with soft color. The hallway leads to several closed doors. The first proves to be a staff room. Inside, key cards are tucked into carefully labeled cubbyholes on the counter next to a coffee machine. Handy for the workers, but not too secure.

Sol runs a finger along the labels, reading. She finds several cards in the slot labeled "Graveyard" and deduces this is the outside area of dead boats. She pockets a plastic square. The next slot reads, "Prototype." Inside lie two gray remotes instead of key cards. She ponders a moment, then slips a remote into her pocket. Voices filter through the door.

Her heart leaps. She jumps away, crouches behind a couch, and waits with held breath. The sounds fade. She cracks the door, looks both ways down the empty hallway, and steps out. *Clunk.* Somewhere in the empty museum, an outer door has unlocked. Sol hurries toward the displays. She reaches the metal door leading into the Graveyard and peers through the glassed-in part just in time to see two ragged Slummers, a man and woman, ascend a ramp to one of the shuttles. They disappear through the hatch.

She considers her options. How many homeless have found this place and camped here? If she follows the couple into the Graveyard, will they spot her leaving in the morning? Who else might be out there? She wants a safe, deserted place to sleep. This isn't it. Fingering the remote in her pocket, she turns away from the metal and glass door.

A little more searching reveals a service entrance that leads to the picnic area Sol used earlier. She sits down on the same bench as before and watches the sky turn pale blue, then pink, then black. A sprinkle of faded stars appears. You can't see constellations much in the city. Not like in the Barrens, where her father taught her Orion, Casseopeia, the Pleiades, Betelgeuse, and the Dog Star.

She misses those days, or some of them at least. Not everything about the commune was bad. The midwife, Cress, trained her to help deliver babies and showed her herbs that would cure common ailments like fever and colds. She'd eaten well and blossomed in the warm sun and fresh air of the countryside. Winters had been brutal, though. She and Father were never warm. And the longer they stayed, the more disillusioned he became with the Earthers. Long before that fateful seventeenth birthday when Father challenged Anton and died for it, she'd seen the Earthers for what they were, too. A cult following a man who'd built himself a little kingdom. Equality for all meant no one starved, but only Anton got the best meat, the best shelter, the finest clothes.

Seeing him again after eleven years brings a rush of memories. Sol doesn't want to remember anything but her hate for Anton. She shakes her head to dislodge the painful past from her brain. Once the traffic dies and lights in the apartment building across the way blink out one by one, she edges around the museum until she stands before the prototype shuttle. She walks underneath, and it curves over her like the belly of a giant bird. She runs a hand over the smooth surface and steps out. The solar panels covering the sleek craft look dull beneath a single security light.

Sol searches for cameras but can't find any on the front of the building. It's a small museum. Not much inside to steal, and not in a rough part of the city. She fishes the remote from her pocket and pushes the button. A hatch opens, and stairs roll down.

<h1 style="text-align:center">21</h1>

<h2 style="text-align:center">CLERA</h2>

Duro follows Elio out. Once they're gone, the walls close in. Clera's heart rate increases and sweat beads her forehead though she's still cold. Her chest feels tight, and she recognizes the signs of an oncoming panic attack.

Fear slams into her, irrational yet unstoppable. She tells herself she's safe—not on the street or buried under rubble. But her body doesn't believe her. She gasps for breath yet can't get enough. Her hands clutch the blanket. She might really be dying this time.

Clera digs her fingernails into her skin. *Get a grip on yourself. You've got to pull your weight. Mama needs you to watch out for Elio. It's your job to protect him. That's what big sisters do.*

She claws with her nails. Blood wells on her arm. The pain brings reality closer, and the panic recedes. *You aren't dying. You're having a panic attack. It will pass.* She keeps repeating this, and eventually, it does. Her heart slows. She strips her work uniform off and stands at the bedroom window. The sun finds her through cracks between boards, and its soothing heat banishes the last of her terror.

Clera spends the rest of the morning cleaning. She piles tools and other supplies against one wall, then fills the garbage bag with debris. In the living area, she sinks gingerly down on the chair Elio mended. It feels firm. He did a good job.

She looks around. With rugs and furniture, this place might become livable if only they had water! A weird sense of calm settles over Clera. Duro scratches at the door, and she lets him in. He saunters past, rubbing against her shins, and wanders down the hallway. He hops on the bed and stretches out. She can't help but smile. "I'm leaving you inside no matter what Elio says." She scratches his ears. "I'm taking the trash out. Be back in a minute."

Clera unlatches the front door and hauls the bag into the hallway. It bumps down the stairs behind her. She feels a momentary pang as she stands before the glass door leading outside. Can she leave without her legs freezing up again? *Move it,* she tells herself in Buela's no-nonsense voice. Once she's on the sidewalk, a breeze wafting across her face, she feels better.

No one is about. Clera rounds the corner into an alleyway and heaves her bag onto the dumpster's rim. She shakes it until all the dust, rodent turds, dead cockroaches, and bits of glass and plaster have fallen into the bin. Dots swim across her eyes, and suddenly she's in another alley. Acid rises in her throat. She closes her eyes, waits to the count of ten, opens them. Her breath whooshes out. The nightmare sinks back into the dark place where she stores it.

Forcing her jaw to unclench, Clera saves the bag and goes back upstairs.

It's a little past noon. A plan swirls in her head. She considers, then brushes her hair, splashes water on a rag, and wipes down her face, arms, and legs. If only she had some mascara. Oh, well. Clera pulls the door firmly shut behind her as she leaves.

Nothing moves, but she imagines eyes watching behind empty windows. Surely, she and Elio aren't the only squatters around—unless something keeps the others away. Clera shivers despite the cloudless spring day. She wants to return to the apartment and hide there until Elio comes home. But if she does that, she'll spend the afternoon with nothing to occupy her mind except dark imaginings. She'll picture Elio lying face down in a ditch, his blood running into the gutter, or something even worse.

Clera keeps walking until she sees cars parked along curbs, a few people strolling down sidewalks, and the huge oak tree that marks the spot where the Boba Tea Cafe resides. A bell tinkles as she enters. Today, a wisp of a man stands behind the counter. It must be Soo Yun's appa. He resembles her in build and in the slant of his nose. "Hello. Welcome, welcome. Can I help you?" His voice carries a slight accent, and Clera wonders where he grew up.

"I was hoping to see Soo Yun." Clera walks up to the counter. "But I'll take a cup of black tea." It's only two credits, the cheapest thing on the menu. She hates to spend anything, but she promised herself no more handouts.

The man calls into the back room and turns his attention to the teapot behind him. He fills a porcelain cup with dark liquid and pushes it across the counter. Clera scans her ring and adds an extra credit. Just then, Soo Yun materializes behind her appa, tying an apron about her waist. When she sees Clera, pleasure widens her almond-shaped eyes. Soo Yun turns to her father and rattles off a high-pitched speech in Korean.

"Ah," Appa nods, shooting Clera a glance. "Your new friend."

Tension melts from Clera's body. *Friend.* She's had so few friends. Now she knows Soo Yun wasn't simply being polite yesterday.

"Go, go," Appa shoos his daughter away with the rag he holds. "You take lunch break now, Soo Yun."

Soo Yun lifts a hinged section of the counter and steps out. Her father hands her something wrapped in thin white paper. "Come, let's sit outside," Soo Yun tells Clera. "It's so nice."

Clera looks around the empty cafe and hopes the midday rush has already come and gone. Customers are few, and she wouldn't wish her own jobless situation on anyone else. She follows Soo Yun to three metal tables set beneath the pink and blue awning. Clera places her tea on a table and slides a chair out. Once they settle, Soo Yun immediately launches into a tirade about a rude woman who refused to accept that an order of chai spices had been delayed and that she'd have to settle for a different drink.

So, there *were* customers today. It's nice to worry about someone besides herself for a change. Clera makes appropriate sympathetic sounds while Soo Yun rambles on and gobbles down her sandwich. Finally, she draws breath and looks at the cooling tea that Clera hasn't touched yet.

"Aren't you going to drink that?"

"Oh." Clera lifts the cup and takes a sip. The black tea is bitter. She never drinks any kind of tea, and she makes a face.

"Don't you like it?" Soo Yun asks. "I can get you something else."

"No! It's fine." Clera doesn't want to admit that's all she could afford, so she adds, "It's a little hot, still, and I'm not used to tea."

"What are you used to, then?"

Clera remembers Buela and her cinnamon-spiced chocolate. She describes the drink to Soo Yun, who purses her lips. "Ooh, that does sound delicious. A little more fattening than Appa's black tea, though."

"Like you need to worry."

Soo Yun laughs, and Clera thinks, *This is how friends talk to each other. They chatter about inconsequential things, tease, and giggle.* She wants to pretend she's a rich girl out for a lazy weekend meet up, but Soo Yun's next words bring her back to earth.

"Have you found a job yet?"

Clera stares into her tea. A watery reflection looks back. She shakes her head.

Soo Yun sighs. "Have you tried the Skinpad factory?"

Clera considers lying, but she wants to be honest with Soo Yun, so she admits, "I just left Perkine in South Side, and it wasn't a friendly goodbye. They weren't sympathetic to my new circumstances."

"Oh, yes, your apartment. Did you know anyone who died in the blast?"

Clera is silent for a long time. Finally, she wills steel into her words and answers, "My mother."

"Oh, no!" Soo Yun's hand covers Clera's. "I'm so sorry. Can you talk about it?"

After a moment of hesitation, Clera does. To her surprise, she doesn't break down though her voice wobbles a bit.

When she's finished, Soo Yun says, "Horrible Perkine! Of course, you can't work there again!" She pauses. "My mother is also gone. I don't remember her, though. I was only a baby when she died. You were lucky to have had parents throughout your childhood. And a brother, too! What of him?"

It's easier to talk about Elio. Clera drinks her tea, which tastes better with each sip. She chatters as much as Soo Yun. Eventually, she draws breath. "But I'm keeping you from work. I'm sure you've overstayed your break."

"Do you see any customers? The cafe will be fine without me."

Just then a man appears. He's seated in a hover chair, the kind disabled people use, and it's so quiet he's reached them before Clera notices him. His sandy, short-cut hair falls over one eye. He wears loose khaki pants and a tee shirt. His eyes are so blue that Clera can't look away. Few people in New Chicago have eyes the exact tint of a summer sky.

Soo Yun scrapes back her chair and rises. "Hello, Zavi!" She offers her hand, and the man squeezes it. "I didn't think you were coming. It's well past lunchtime."

He shrugs. "I got busy transplanting some tomatoes at the greenhouse. Lost track of time."

Clera likes Zavi's voice. It's deep and musical. She can't take her eyes off him. He's not handsome, exactly, though his tanned skin and light hair make him memorable. Muscles cord his arms, which are covered with sparse golden hair.

Soo Yun introduces Clera. Zavi takes her hand, his skin warm against hers. She pulls back too quickly and hopes he doesn't notice her reaction, how his touch sends electric shivers down her spine. More than ever, she wishes she could have showered and put on makeup before going out today!

Zavi has already turned back to Soo Yun. "What's the special today, or have I missed lunch at the Boba Tea Cafe entirely?"

"Of course not!" Soo Yun turns and proceeds Zavi inside. Clera picks up her empty teacup and follows.

Zavi parks his chair at a table. She stands awkwardly waiting while her friend goes to fetch his food.

"So, are you only visiting? I haven't seen you here before, Clera."

"I'm new." She can't think of anything else to say and feels her cheeks heating. It's ridiculous, but she can't control it.

He ignores her discomfort and makes a few remarks about the weather. Clera hides a sigh of relief when Soo Yun shows up with a bowl of what might be the "kimchi special" and an Italian soda. They exchange a few more pleasantries. Then Soo Yun says, "I will let you eat in peace, Zavi." She jerks her head for Clera to follow and heads toward the back of the cafe.

"You're working, now. I'd better go," Clera calls after her.

Soo Yun glances over her shoulder. "Are you sure?"

Clera's gaze slides between Zavi and Soo Yun. She hurries closer to her new friend. "Soo Yun . . ."

"What? You wish to stay longer? Please sit here as long as you want."

"Our water isn't working," Clera mutters, low enough Zavi won't hear.

"Oh no! You should have said before. Do you need to fill a plastic gallon from our sink?"

"Well, yes, that would be wonderful. But actually, it's been a few days, and I . . ."

". . . you need a shower. Of course. Follow me right upstairs. That is no problem at all."

"Your father . . ."

"Appa won't care as long as you don't use up all the hot water. Come along."

It's that easy. Five minutes later, Clera has stripped naked in the upstairs apartment bathroom. Hot water massages her skin and washes dirt and sweat from her body. She only wishes she could wash away the memory of the last few days as easily. By the time she towels off and returns to the cafe, Zavi has gone.

22

CLERA

Clera thanks Soo Yun and her father. It's too early to go back to the apartment, so she heads southwest. She doubts she'll get lost if she pays attention to street names. Before she's walked a mile, the new division of Perkine Industries rears up, a copy of South Side's factory down to the razor wire fence and the sign: "Perkine Industries: Makers of Perkine Skinpads. More reliable than your own brain!" Below this, a smaller sign proclaims: "Help wanted! Livable starting pay! References required."

She doesn't know how "livable" that pay really is. Most of her salary went to rent. Clera's fingers twine in the metal fence links. *I should go in, at least see if they'll take me back.* She thinks of Luz, with her baby and predictable life mapped out. Clock in. Mind the bots. Clock out. Day after day, huddled in a cave of metal parts and air purifiers, starved of sunlight.

Not yet. Clera pushes away from the fence, the violent motion producing a rattle. She can't attempt a return to Perkine until she's down to her last option. A little voice in her head mocks, *Aren't you already there?* She ignores it and walks on. Soon she's back in the abandoned areas, with their red spray paint and broken glass. Is this still Slavland or some other neighborhood taken over by gangs? It doesn't feel safe, but at the same time, she likes walking down a deserted road with no one to bother her, no snarled insults or jeers, no too-curious looks or assessing eyes.

Something buzzes. She looks around but can't find the source. Buildings shadow the street—old, crumbling brick Victorians that might have been respectable middle-class homes two hundred years ago. Now their paint is scraped, their shingles curling. Cement stoops sag like tired shoulders. Messy red symbols mar the old facades. They aren't street art, more like secret signs that Clera doesn't understand.

She sees movement ahead. Two girls dart into the street. A manhole cover lifts, and a head pokes out. An arm waves the girls forward. Moments later, the girls vanish like rabbits down a hole.

Buzz. The noise comes at her from both sides, high up and too loud to be insects. It sounds more like drones. Clera picks up her pace and is within fifty yards of the maintenance hatch when a woman bursts from behind a bus stop shelter. Clera calls out, "What's going on?"

The woman's head snaps around. She's gaunt, hollow-eyed, and wears the soiled clothes of the homeless. "Get off the street!" she shouts, runs to the manhole cover, and stomps on it. "It's the war games! You can't be out right now. Didn't you see the signs?" Beneath her boot, the cover lifts.

Clera frowns. "Do you mean the spray paint marks?" But the woman has already slipped below. Clera runs to catch the heavy rim before it settles into place, but she's too late.

The first pigeon-sized drones appear. They swarm into the street, flying toward her fast. More buzzing sounds erupt behind. Clera whirls to find another pack. She's trapped between them!

Pellets spray overhead. Something pops and smokes in the cloud of metal bodies. A drone drops from the sky and crashes a few feet from Clera. Metal slivers somersault toward her. Pain shoots up her lower arm, and blood drips onto her fingers. She runs for the only cover she sees, a pair of mostly disintegrated root cellar doors.

The cellar is a black hole. Clera's foot splinters the first ladder rung leading down. More wood crumbles, and she's falling.

She lands on her back in a pile of sticks. Air rushes from her lungs. Eight feet above, a square of light reveals clusters of drones, fire, smoke, and more pellet sprays. Small explosions and the whines of propellers fill her ears. Her breath comes back in a whoosh. Gasping, she scoots into a corner away from the open trapdoor. Her ankle throbs, but her arm only stings a little. *I'm okay.* She repeats this mantra like doing so can make it true.

While the battle rages overhead, Clera looks around. Empty shelves line the cellar. There's one broken jar in the opposite corner and probably tons of spiders. She swats at her hair, but only wood splinters fall out. A drone shrieks and falls through the opening. It spins in the pile of ladder rungs and spits sparks, then dies.

Clera pulls her legs up and wraps her arms around them. Now she understands where the homeless in Slavland live, at least. Not in the abandoned, condemned apartments. They're in the sewers. But why? Is it safer down there? She doesn't know, and not knowing is going to get her killed.

Clera does understand one thing. She'd rather live in the place Elio found than like a rat under the streets.

The firefight ends about ten minutes later. A tang of smoke fills the air. Surviving drones zip away, and the streets are silent once more.

Clera tests her ankle. It hurts. She can walk on it, though. She tries jumping for the cellar opening. Her palms brush the edge, but she loses her grip and falls back, landing on her good leg. Pain shoots up the injured one. *Oh, hells. Am I going to die down here trapped like an animal?* She calls up, "Hello! Help!" not even caring if some Second City gangster hears her. Better to take her chances than starve to death surrounded by spiders.

"I'm here! Can anybody hear me?"

A minute passes. She calls out. Waits. Calls out.

Miraculously, a head appears, silhouetted in the opening. "Hang on," a familiar voice shouts.

"Zavi?"

"Yes, it's me."

There are scrabbling sounds. Arms stretch into the hole. "Can you reach? Take hold of my hands."

He must be on the ground, out of his hover chair. She stands on tiptoe to grip his palms. His muscles flex, and he pulls her up, grunting with effort.

Clera's head clears the opening where Zavi kneels. Muscles strain in his neck, and his mouth is a grimace, but he keeps lifting until her armpits emerge. He falls back, bringing her to land on top of him. He frees her wrists, and for a moment she doesn't move. Every nerve in her body tingles with relief. And possibly something more? His body is hard and warm, and she's pressed along its entire length. "Oh!" She rolls off him and sits up.

Zavi sits as well. His so-blue eyes regard her with surprise and consternation. She blinks at him, then stares at the empty sky. Belatedly, she dusts dirt and cobwebs from her hair and clothes.

"Are you hurt?" He holds up his hand, stained with her blood.

"What?" Clera glances at her arm. "It's nothing. No, I'm fine. I can't believe you're here."

Zavi picks a dried leaf from her hair and tosses it away. He's grinning. "I'm not used to finding damsels in distress hiding in dirty cellars, I'll admit."

Clera's brow wrinkles. "I guess I'm lucky." She wishes her voice didn't sound so breathless.

He rises stiffly to his feet and offers her a hand. She accepts it, and he hauls her up.

"I thought you were paralyzed," is all she can think to say.

"I was until six months ago when I had an operation that fixed me. Spinal and brain implants. I can walk, but I still use the chair when I go any distance."

"Oh. I'm sorry." Why can't she get her tongue to work around this guy? He's probably not that much older than she is and shouldn't be this intimidating. Her thoughts are like scrambled eggs, a jumble she can't sort out. "Thank you for rescuing me," she finally manages.

"You're welcome." Zavi studies her. His light-colored eyes lend to his face an intensity that makes her even more self-conscious.

Clera shakes her head and asks, "Why were you in this abandoned neighborhood? I mean, I'm grateful, but it's such a coincidence. I met you in the tea shop, and then you left. I followed maybe twenty minutes later, and here you are!"

Zavi turns and gestures towards the end of the block. Past the next intersection, the buildings fall away. There's a high, black metal fence interspersed with thick stone columns, and beyond that, a rolling green common dotted with mature trees. She recognizes oak, but there are other kinds, too, some peppered with white blossoms, others just leafing out in pale green. She sees a stripe of blue in the far distance, maybe a lake.

"I work there, at Fadel Arboretum and Greenhouses."

"Oh!"

Zavi grips the back of his chair with one hand. "I was at the perimeter fence to check on some bushes I planted, and I heard the drones." He frowns. "The Second City don't usually play their war games so close to the park. I don't like it."

His comments only raise more questions. Before Clera can figure out which to ask next, there's a whirring sound. Two lanky boys on hoverboards zip out of an alley and turn their way. They pull up when they see Zavi and Clera. Tattoos cover their arms, and thick chains swing from their necks. He hisses, "Get down!" and pushes Clera behind the floating chair, which doesn't come close to giving enough cover. Her bad ankle falters, and she yelps.

Zavi doesn't notice. His eyes have fastened on the hoverboarders. Suddenly, there's a stun gun in his hand. Clera clutches her ankle and peers around the chair. The boys remain where they are, boards bobbing. One shouts, "You're on our street, cabron!"

"These streets belong to New Chicago," Zavi shouts back. He points the gun their way. "You're way too close to the park. You get any closer with your kid games, and the police will start paying attention. I'll make sure they do."

"No games. Training. We got no time for games. The Steelheads are coming, and when they do, we got to be ready. You're lucky we aren't taking you down right now. Maybe you're a Steelhead sent here to spy. Maybe we *should* take you down, and your pretty girlfriend, too."

Zavi takes a few jerky steps toward the boys. "Like I said, I work in the park. If anything happens to me, Fadel Industries will come down hard on you. Your boss won't be happy if he finds out I had to teach you a lesson, boys. Best you leave now. I'm going back in there." He nods toward the fence.

The bigger boy nudges his board a few feet closer. "We can't go until we collect the drones, or what's left of them. We got orders."

"Which don't include hassling Fadel workers," Zavi snaps. "We'll leave first, and you won't touch us. Then you can get on with your 'work.'"

Neither of the Second City gangsters says a word. Clera gets to her feet, favoring her good leg. Zavi shoots her a quick glance, but his gun stays trained on the boys. "You hurt? Better take the chair. I'll be fine walking this far."

Clera thinks she should help, but how? She slips into the floating chair.

It sinks a little under her weight and bobs up again. There's a simple keypad on the right armrest. When Zavi steps forward, she pushes a green arrow, and the chair follows. The Second City hoodlums watch warily as they approach. Zavi's gaze flashes between the boys and the road beneath his feet, where remnants of drones lie like crumpled insects. Though the stun gun won't do much good at this distance, the punks seem to respect it. Or maybe they're afraid of Zavi. Does working at the arboretum somehow give him protection from the Second City?

Zavi edges past the hoverboards. He tells Clera, "Keep going until you reach the fence. Then turn right. The gate is a little way down."

"Will you be all . . ."

". . . I'm fine. Go."

She does, but with her head craned around so she can keep an eye on Zavi, who backs after her. The Second City boys make no move toward them, and once they reach the intersection, Zavi faces forward, looks both ways, and hobbles across. Clera waits for him near the park's perimeter.

"I told you to get to the gates," he says.

Her back stiffens. "I'm making sure you're okay. I'm not leaving you."

"What, because I'm a cripple?" He seems half-angry, half-frustrated. He holds her gaze for a few seconds before his eyes slide away. His jaw clenches. "Sorry."

Clera studies Zavi. Who *is* he? They watch the boys gather broken drones into messenger bags strung across their shoulders. Zavi sighs. He tucks the gun into a holster hidden beneath his shirt. Clera glimpses his ribcage and belly for a split second before the shirt falls back in place. She feels the pull of his magnetism again but shakes it off.

Zavi leads her toward a gate twenty feet away. He walks like he's in pain.

"You can have your chair back."

"You need it more than me."

Clera wants to argue, but he may be right. Her ankle still throbs.

She catches up to Zavi at the gate. A sign reads, "Fadel Arboretum and Greenhouses." The entrance is locked, but he looks up at a camera half-hidden atop a column. A red laser scans his retina, and the gate swings open. He slips in. Clera hesitates only a second before pushing the green *forward* button.

23

ELIO

Elio arrives at the Arcade before it opens. He's first inside and aims straight for the sims. He's got a plan—stick to one type of game to get better faster. All the games have contests and potential winnings in tournaments, but only the aircraft sims offer an added bonus: entry into the starship lottery. *The chance to win a shuttle and berth on* Calliope*!* Before he viewed Dec Gaston's vid, he thought he only wanted to become a top gamer, but now visions of *Calliope* dance across his vision. His dreams have expanded to include flying past the edge of the solar system and exploring a new planet.

What would Clera think if he told her? Can he convince his sister this is their real ticket to a better life? Not some nothing job in New Chicago? She's not very adventurous. He'll need to be persuasive. But first things first. Elio settles into a sim and adjusts the seat. The robotic voice welcomes him, and he receives his mission.

After a couple hours of playing, Elio leaves the sim to grab water from a fountain. He ate a protein bar on the way over, but it's not holding, and his stomach growls loudly.

"Wow!" comes a familiar voice at his elbow. He turns to see the girl he met his first time at the Arcade. She's still just as dirty but doesn't seem ashamed of it and holds out a hand. "Mila from yesterday."

He shakes. "I remember."

"You were pretty distracted, so I wasn't sure. How's it going?"

"I'm learning. A guy named Juke helped me figure out the controls."

"Oh, him." Mila rolls her eyes.

"What?"

"He's just such a player. Female, Male. Doesn't matter. A real charmer."

Elio's back stiffens. "Juke didn't come on to me. It's not like that."

"Hmmm. Do you want him to? Or are you into girls?"

Elio can't believe the nerve of this female. He wants to ignore her but feels like he has to answer. "I'm a straight shooter, not that it's any of your business." Does he sound experienced? Mature? He hopes so, but the truth is he's only been with one girl—one night for fifteen minutes. He can barely claim he lost his virginity.

At least Mila has the sense to look down and blush a little. "It's only that I might be interested . . . in you, I mean . . . not Juke, and I don't want to waste my time, you know?" When she looks up at him again, her eyes have softened into what *looks* like timidity.

"You're playing me," he accuses.

"What? I'm not. Really."

He stares at her until she sighs and turns away. She shoots over her shoulder, "I didn't mean to offend you. If you want to be friends, I'm good with that." She tips her chin. "See ya."

"Hey, wait—" But she slips into the crowd and disappears.

What the hells just happened? Did Elio miss a signal, or perhaps ten? Maybe he shouldn't have let Mila go. Does he want her back so he can say, *Heck yes, let's go out?* Or is Mila Aguilar best forgotten?

Elio goes back to the sims. He's gained two levels already, though he suspects as the game gets harder, his progress will slow. He wishes Juke were here. He could use some advice on how to shoot down this flying raptor that keeps dodging his guns. Oh, well. Elio can figure things out on his own.

At one o'clock, he walks away from the Arcade. He's promised himself that he'll only play half the day and look for work the other half. The job recruitment office is still closed. He wanders. Finally, he stumbles across a new Perkine Industries facility. He almost goes in, then changes his mind. The way Mama and Clera described their work, he doubts he can do it. His ADHD brain chafes at repetitive tasks. He'd screw up royally and get himself fired.

Elio begs the boss at a construction site to let him help unload pallets. It's a rinky-dink operation, so there aren't bots for heavy lifting. When he finishes, the man adds a few credits to his account. They aren't enough. It's time to explore his last option, the one Clera won't like. His feet lead him back to *lad's Ice ream*, and after a short wait out front, Bohdan comes walking along like he promised.

He wears the same baggy black pants and button-up. His hair is even frizzier, and he hums and bobs to music in his earbuds. When he sees Elio, he grins and taps his ear. "My man, Eli."

"It's Elio."

"Is this a chance meeting, or did you consider my offer?" Bohdan stops, hands tucked into his pockets.

Elio swallows. *Clera will HATE this*, one half of him thinks. The other half argues, *don't tell her*. And the loudest voice of all says, *you can't go home with only thirty credits and no hope for more. What else are you going to do to make money?* He doesn't trust himself to speak, so he just offers a clipped nod.

Bohdan's smile grows. "Right on, hom. You can take over my route today. Easiest money you ever made. Let me tell you where to go." He points down the street and gives directions. There are three stops. It'll be fast, so Elio should be home by five. Bohdan pulls a hand from his pocket, and he's holding a switchblade.

Elio stumbles back a few steps. His fists curl into weapons, but the other boy shakes his head.

"No, hom, I'm not attacking you! This is how the Second City do it. Blood brothers, you know? It's like a pact. Otherwise, how could I trust that you won't run out on me with the goods? You do that, and the Second City are coming for us both. But you deliver like I described, and you're one of us. You can come live like I do as part of the family."

Elio forces his bunched fists to uncurl. "No, thanks. My sister can't know about this. That's the deal. And nothing between you and me can involve her."

"That's sage." Bohdan nods. "She's a little uptight? No problem. Your blood is what I need. Not hers."

"Fine." Elio sticks out his hand, remembering an old-time book he read where the boys cut their palms and mixed blood to become brothers.

Bohdan grabs his wrist. Elio holds still, anticipating pain. He doesn't like Boh's fingers pressed against his skin, but the gangster only makes a quick, shallow cut under the elbow. He puts the knife away and pulls a swab and baggie from the same pocket, dabs the wound, then drops the swab into the baggie.

"What did you do that for?" Elio asks.

"I told you. I need your blood. My boss will take the DNA from your sample and run it through his system. Then, if you try to cheat us, we'll be able to find you. Not that you would do that, right, Elio?"

"Right," Elio echoes, but regret twists his gut. He pictured Second City and the Steelheads as gangs of ignorant, leth-brained thugs, not high-tech organizations. He covers his worry with a smile. "So, what am I supposed to deliver, Boh?"

From a larger cargo pocket, Bohdan withdraws three brown-wrapped packets. "They're all the same. Drop each one where I say, and the last guy will pay you."

"Sixty credits per bag, right?"

"Yep. Can you remember the directions?"

"Not a problem."

"Good. Good." Bohdan bounces on his feet. "You change your mind about living with the Second City, let me know. These buildings aren't safe, Elio. Sometimes they just fall. Boom! No warning. And sometimes someone shows up and decides they want your place instead of finding one of their own. If that happens, they're not leaving you around to come steal it back. The smart homeless live down there." Bohdan points at the street.

Elio frowns. "What, you mean in the sewers?"

"Yep. We call those people rats. Being part of Second City isn't the worst thing that can happen. Tell your sister that, eh? And see if she changes her mind about us."

"Sure, man." Elio tucks the packages into his pants pockets. "I better get going."

He thought he liked Bohdan when they first met, but now he has a bad feeling. He's half-tempted to tackle Boh and get that swab, but he doesn't.

Elio needs the money.

Bohdan salutes him, and Elio heads off, sensing the guy's eyes on his back. He's relieved to turn the corner and disappear.

24

CLERA

Clera follows Zavi up a path trimmed with red and yellow tulips. She feels bad making him walk but doesn't think her ankle can take the exercise. Before long, they reach a domed building with a wide front veranda. Polished stones create swirling patterns on the floor. Empty lounge chairs and wooden folding tables are scattered about. Zavi shuffles inside. Clera passes through carved wooden doors after him. Display cases and terrariums huddle under the glassed dome. Palm trees and bougainvillea shoot toward the roof. A bird flies off a palm frond into the humid air, chirping.

Zavi glances back at her. "There's a first aid room down this hallway. I'll fix you up."

Clera barely hears him. "What is this place?"

"It's for tourists. Just one arm of the complex. We charge admission for the History of Plants displays and the atrium. Not much, but it helps. There's a big cost to running the arboretum and the greenhouses. We sell crops periodically, and our flower business brings in decent credits, but we give a lot away, too."

He walks down the hallway and turns right. Clera follows him into a room with a blue cross on the door. It looks like a doctor's office with an adjustable, papered bed. Cabinets line the walls.

"Hop up." Zavi pats the bed.

"Are you a doctor?" Clera half jokes.

"Only of plants." He smiles and opens a cabinet. While she eases from the chair onto rustling paper, he retrieves a compression tube, bandages, and antiseptic.

Clera gingerly raises her leg and props it on the bed. Immediately, the throb in her ankle lessens. Zavi's hands are gentle yet firm as he removes her shoe. She bites her lip but doesn't cry out when he massages the joint. There's something intimate about his touch. He's not a doctor, only a man.

"You're swollen," he says, glancing up. "But nothing feels out of place. Hopefully, a compression tube will get the swelling down."

Zavi removes her sock. Clera stares horrified at the sweaty, dirt-stained thing lying in his palm. It must disgust him though he doesn't show it. *She* must disgust him, too. She's everything he isn't—poor, uneducated, and so clumsy to have fallen into that cellar, to not have realized what was happening when the drones appeared.

He slips the cloth tube over her lower leg and studies the buttons on the side. This is smartcloth, not ordinary wrap like Mama would have used at home. Clera has never been to a doctor, but she reads. She knows what Slummers are denied. Skinpads, doctors, good meds, and so much more. They might as well be living in another century.

One button tightens the cuff. It melds to her skin's contours. She feels a prick, then heat spreading into her toes. Zavi says, "There. I've administered a painkiller and anti-swelling meds. The tube will also alternatively heat and cool to get the swelling down faster. You should keep it elevated if you can. How does it feel now?"

She clears her throat. "Fine."

He dabs antiseptic on a ball of cotton, cleanses the cut on her arm, and tapes a bandage over it.

"Thank you. I think I'll be able to walk home now."

His brows come together. "I'll drive you."

She can't let him see where she lives, so she shakes her head. "No, it's fine. I'll be fine."

"Why won't you let me help you?"

"You have!" But she knows what he means and thinks fast. "It's not a safe neighborhood. I'm still looking for a job, so we don't have much money." She can't hold his gaze. "You'll think less of me if you see it."

He doesn't answer.

Sweat gathers under her arms. Finally, she looks up.

Curiosity, not pity or condemnation, fills his eyes. "Okay," he finally answers. "But I'm not the kind of guy to judge. Can you at least contact me so I know you made it home safely?"

"I don't have a Skinpad."

"Right." He considers. "Meet me at the Boba Tea Cafe tomorrow at noon, then, if walking isn't too painful. I want to know you're getting better."

She should protest, tell Zavi he already helped more than enough. He's probably thinking, *Poor slum girl, trying so hard to look and sound respectable. She's galaxies apart from my world.* Clera doesn't want to be attracted to him. No good will come of it, yet she replies, "Fine."

She leaves by the side gate. He sees her off in his floating chair. She feels his worried gaze on her back and tries not to limp. She hardly needs to. The tube's temperature system, support, and pain meds have made her feel almost normal. Still, once she rounds a corner, she slows. Clera studies the sky for drones, listens, watches for men wearing heavy chains around their necks. But she makes it back to *lad's Ice ream* without incident. Upstairs, she lies down on the blanket and rests. This apartment feels like a haven compared to what's out *there*. Streaks of afternoon sunlight break through the window boards and stripe the bed with light.

Duro curls up on her stomach and purrs. She pets him and waits for Elio.

A door creaking and footsteps jerk Clera awake. Alarm jumps in her chest until Elio calls out, "It's me, Clera. Sorry I'm late. I stopped at a discount store for more supplies."

Her brother appears in the doorway, arms laden with bulging green recycling bags. He sets them on the bed and plops down. The smartwrap hides beneath Clera's pant leg, and he doesn't notice anything amiss.

Elio takes a couple of blankets from the bags, followed by two inflatable pillows. He pulls the cord on one. It puffs up like a helium-filled balloon. He tosses it to her. "Here."

Clera tucks it behind her head. "What else did you find?"

He pulls out foldable solar panels. "I can set these up on the roof where no one will see. They connect like Bluetooth. No wires. See?" He shows her. "We can use them with this light or that camp stove." He pulls out more items. Elio has bought bananas, eggs, and cans of beans. There's a pair of plastic plates, a dishpan, utensils, and cups. He's thought of everything. Last, he displays a real e-bolt to put across their door. He shows Clera how the electronic lock works, and they set it to open when they press their thumbprints to a pad.

"That wasn't cheap," Clera remarks.

"If we're going to be here awhile, we'd better feel safe. And comfortable."

Clera doubts "safe" is something she'll ever feel again, but she doesn't argue. Instead, she squeezes his arm. "I'm not criticizing, Elio. Just wondering where you got the money for all this." She gestures to the items spread across the flannel blanket.

"I didn't steal." His voice is flat, his look sullen.

Clera sighs. Her brother can be so difficult. She's used to him misunderstanding her. "Of course you didn't," she soothes.

"I got a job, Clera."

She forgets everything else. A weight falls from her shoulders. "You did?" She grins. "Where? How?"

Elio concentrates on peeling a banana. "There was a construction site. I talked with the boss, and he hired me on. It's a big job. He should be able to keep me through the summer and fall."

"Where's this at? I walked all over and saw nothing big going up."

Elio breaks the fruit in two and hands her half. He tucks the peel into an empty bag. "I had to walk back toward the skyscrapers."

It's a vague answer, but Clera doesn't press. She takes a bite, chews, and swallows. "I'm glad you had some luck because I haven't had any at all. Sorry." She finishes the banana and sighs.

Elio rises and starts putting things away. "I didn't show you the folding table and chair I bought. They're out in the living room. Everything's cheap, but better than nothing."

Clera doesn't want to talk about furnishings. She wants to explain how she stumbled into the Second City's war games and how Zavi pulled her from the cellar, but she holds back. Elio will worry if he believes she's been in danger. Maybe he'll be afraid to leave her to work, and he *has* to work. At least one of them must succeed in this new world. It should have been her. She's older. But so far, she feels like the weak one, the helpless girl.

Tomorrow, she thinks, gritting her teeth against the twinge of pain in her ankle. Something will turn up.

25

ZAVI

He can't forget the way Clera looked in the cafe, with golden-brown hair spilling over her shoulders. And in the cellar, with dirt smearing her cheek and panic in her eyes. When he reached for her, he didn't feel like a cripple or a failed, broken man. He felt strong.

She is obviously from the lower classes. No Skinpad. They probably have nothing in common, yet something inside him sings when he sees her. Can she hear it, too? Or is this some stupid, one-way crush? It's been over a year since he's been in a relationship. Maybe that's made him a little crazy—or turned him into a romantic. How Nik would laugh if he could see Zavi daydreaming about Clera. Someone he barely knows. Cute, sure, but not girlfriend material.

Still, he's glad he'll see her again. He wants to know if she's okay.

Zavi finishes out the day at the greenhouse and starts up the road to his bungalow. Down the way, a man is just leaving another worker's house. Zavi believes it belongs to one of the supervisors. Gab, maybe? Zavi hasn't spoken to the man and only briefly been introduced. He takes a second look at the departing visitor, who's thin as a leth smoker, fingers weighted with rings, a messenger bag bouncing at his side. His black boots stir up dust. He tips his chin at Zavi when he sees him watching.

Embarrassed to be caught, Zavi returns the gesture and makes his way home. There was nothing blatantly wrong with the guy's appearance, yet a sense of unease lingers. He lets himself in, does his exercises, pulls a ready-made dinner from the freezer, and sinks onto the couch to eat. Alone, as always. It will be nice to meet Clera for lunch tomorrow.

26

CLERA

Clera plans to meet Zavi in the cafe at noon. Despite the new lock on the door, she slept poorly. Visions of floors sliding into ceilings and walls covering her like coffin lids haunted her dreams.

She wakes before dawn to scratches and meows. Duro wants out. Clera forces herself to get up and unlatch the door. She imagines gangsters wearing silver chains lurking outside, but the hallway yawns empty.

Elio sleeps on while she dresses. She wishes she had more clothes. How can she meet Zavi wearing secondhand jeans and a shirt with tomato stains on the hem? Elio finally rises, grumbles a greeting, and munches on crackers before he leaves for work.

Clera doesn't like being alone and wonders where Duro went. She scrubs floors all morning on hands and knees until it's time to meet Zavi. Panic flutters inside her but then subsides. No time for an episode. She sets off to the Boba Tea Cafe, and her ankle barely twinges in discomfort.

Soo Yun is serving coffee to an old couple in the corner booth when Clera arrives. She watches while she waits. The customers remind her of residents from her old apartment building who'd sit outside in lawn chairs on sunny days. Sometimes the men would pull out checkerboards, or the woman would knit. The same scene could have played out a hundred years ago. Coastlines might sink beneath the ocean, deserts might become uninhabitable, and starships might leave Earth for new solar systems, but nothing ever changed in the slums.

Or almost never.

Clera orders tea from Appa and takes a seat at the sunny window booth. She catches Soo Yun's gaze and waves. Soo Yun's quick smile warms Clera better than any sunlight.

Soo Yun tucks an order pad in her apron and approaches. "You look like you've been crawling around in an old attic. And is that blood on your jeans?"

Clera knew she looked bad, but not that bad. Her heart sinks. She gives a mental shrug, then fills Soo Yun in on yesterday's events.

Soo Yun's eyes widen. "You can't catch a break, can you? I have some old clothes upstairs." She glances at the elderly couple. "Hang on."

"Wait!" Clera calls her back. "You're way too short for your clothes to fit me."

"Oh, they aren't mine." Soo Yun winks. "They're my sister's. She left New Chicago to work in a commune several years ago. It's a little outside the walls but not quite in the Barrens. She's taller than me. I think her old clothes will fit you."

"But won't she want them when she comes back? I should pay you."

Soo Yun shakes her head. "My sister won't care. We don't hear from her much. She's got a new family, a new life. And truthfully, you'd be doing Appa and me a favor by taking the clothes. They only remind him of painful things. My sister deserted us. She and Appa fought, and no one will admit to being in the wrong. Even now." She sighs.

Soo Yun's life had looked so easy, so idyllic, even if she did have to work in the humble cafe. But everyone has problems, Clera supposes. She accepts Soo Yun's offer and changes into a sundress upstairs. With a box of old clothes at her feet, she slips back into her booth just as Zavi shows up.

The flowered, flowy dress makes Clera feel almost pretty. His eyes search her out, and he steers over to her. His mouth opens, then closes, one corner creeping up. "Don't you look nice."

Clera wonders if she overdid it. She used an old mascara sitting on the sink in Soo Yun's sister's bedroom. She also clipped her hair back with barrettes rummaged from a drawer. Hopefully, this won't attract the wrong kind of attention when she heads home.

Zavi stands and sets a brake on his chair. He slides into the booth opposite Clera.

Soo Yun scurries toward them, looking from one to the other. "So, you two might know each other better than I thought?"

"The cellar," Clera reminds her. "Zavi wanted to meet here and check on me."

Soo Yun nods and turns to him. "Having your usual?"

"Bring two. Clera needs to try a bowl of the special."

"Wait a second," Clera says. "Are you talking about that kimchi stuff? I don't think . . ."

Zavi breaks in, "Bring it, Soo Yun. If she doesn't like the special, I'll order something else for her."

Clera acquiesces, but in her head, she tallies what she owes Soo Yun and now Zavi.

He interrupts her calculations by asking, "How is your ankle? Did you walk here on your own?"

"Yes, and it's much better, thanks. I should be able to give you back the smartwrap in a few days."

"I hope you won't be cutting through Second City territory to get home today."

"Is there a way to tell I'm in gang territory other than by the abandoned buildings?"

Zavi leans back and folds his arms. "They spray paint symbols on the walls. It's an archaic means of communication. Untraceable. Anonymous."

"You've had dealings with them."

"If by 'dealings' you mean 'run-ins,' then yes. As you saw, their territory borders the park grounds."

"Does your boss worry the gangs might take it over one day? Lots of people seem to have been driven from their businesses."

His eyes flicker. "I'm not in the know. I only work there tending plants. By the way, if you're still looking for a job, I could get you an interview."

Clera perks up. "Really?" Then her hopes fall. "But I'm not trained to take care of plants. I don't have any experience with botany."

Zavi unfolds himself and leans toward her. "We need to work on your interviewing skills, that's for sure. What *are* you good at?"

Telltale heat warms her cheeks even though he's joking. She focuses on the question, not on the way he smells like sandalwood and soap. "I did well in school until I had to quit and start factory work. I can read and perform basic math." She wishes she could say something to really impress Zavi, who seems so far above her. Given a different roll of the dice, she might have been born into a middle-class home, gone to college, made something of herself. But that's not been her life. Mama and Papa did the best they could.

"A good start," he says. "I'm guessing you're also well-spoken, reliable, punctual, and good with people." He sips his water.

Clera is startled into a laugh. "You sound like a quote from a resume. Is that really what people say at interviews?"

He shrugs. "Of course. Didn't you have to speak to some boss before you got your factory job?"

Clera remembers back. "Mama just asked her supervisor, and I was hired the next day."

"Do you miss it? Factory work?"

She coughs on a sip of tea. "It was horrible. I couldn't imagine doing it the rest of my life. So boring and sunless."

"Plenty of sun in a greenhouse." Zavi does that one-sided quirk of his mouth. Clera's eyes fixate there.

She realizes she's staring and blinks. Her gaze drifts to the old couple. Their heads bend close as they share sips of their boba tea through straws. "I think I'd like working around plants. Buela had an aloe vera that I cared for when I was little. Seeing something grow from a seed is kind of a miracle. There weren't any lawns, let alone growing things, in my old neighborhood."

"Did you know there are around two hundred and fifty kinds of aloe, but humans only cultivate four of them? Amazing, really, considering all the uses."

"Buela had me rub a leaf on my tongue when I got canker sores." Clera studies Zavi over her teacup. "You sound like you know a lot about plants. Did you learn about the aloe vera by working at the greenhouse?"

He leans back in his seat, one hand wrapped loosely around his water glass. "I have a college degree in botany. A year ago, the plan was to start my PhD. But life interfered." His eyes grow distant, and the hand not holding the glass clenches. "I was riding a high-speed train to New Chicago with my parents. It derailed. I survived, barely. They didn't. My spine was crushed, but luckily, my grandfather paid for treatment. This body you see is the new and improved version of the limp and broken one of a year ago." Behind his smile, sadness lurks.

Clera wants to tell him she understands that pain, but her own is still too fresh. "I'm so sorry." She can't find words to comfort Zavi any more than she can find them for herself. Clera's thoughts veer toward all she's lost, but she grits her teeth and closes that door. "At least you still have your grandpa," she tells him.

And I still have Elio.

Soo Yun comes out of the kitchen with two bowls sitting on hot pads. A spicy aroma wafts up as she sets them down before Zavi and Clera. "The kimchi special!" She makes a flourish. "Enjoy!" She starts to say more, but Appa calls from the back. She shrugs and retreats.

Clera wonders how well Soo Yun knows Zavi. She might have dated him. She might have a crush on him. Clera hopes there's nothing between them. *Like you should care. It's not as though you're going to ask him out.*

He expertly pinches a piece of cabbage dripping red sauce with his chopsticks, pops it into his mouth, and waves a hand, mouthing, "HOT!"

Clera studies the mass of noodles, cabbage, and bits of pork in her bowl, then prods it with her chopstick. This uncovers some fried egg on the bottom. "I don't know how to use these." She holds up the wooden utensils.

Zavi swallows, takes a sip of water, and coughs behind his hand. "It's perfectly fine to use the fork."

"But won't I look uncultured?"

He leans so close that his cologne overtakes the spicy food smell. He whispers, "I'm pretty sure we're alone."

But it's you I want to impress. "Maybe I'll wait until it cools."

"Chicken." Despite the heat, Zavi digs into his food.

Clera blows on a bite and nibbles. The eggs and noodles cut the spicy sauce. "Yum," she mumbles.

They eat in silence. Zavi finishes and wipes his chin with a cloth napkin. "So why did you end up moving to West Town?"

Clera bites her lip. Losing her home and mama feels like raw, gaping wounds. She doesn't want to talk about them, but she doesn't want to make up lies, either. In the end, she relates the facts of the explosion in a toneless voice.

He's staring at her way too intently by the time she finishes. "You say that without a trace of tears. Maybe you're still in shock." After a lengthy pause, he adds, "I'd say I'm sorry, but that doesn't cut it. There are no words, really. Speaking about the train wreck still chokes me up sometimes."

She shrugs. "I don't mean to sound unfeeling. I just don't want to blubber into my food. Besides, you should only break down in tears with people you've known for at least a year."

"Is that a hard and fast rule, or is there room to negotiate?" To her relief, he laughs.

She smiles back. "We might negotiate . . . some day." Is she actually flirting?

"I'll hold you to that, Clera Diaz."

Suddenly, they're sitting way too close, and he's eyeing her way too perceptively. She feels like a bug beneath a microscope, every flaw laid bare for inspection. Clera swallows. "So, when can I come for an interview? And what do I wear?"

"I like that dress you have on today. And if you stop by around five, Albero should have time for you. Go to the front gate on the east perimeter, and the security staff will buzz you in."

Clera wrinkles her nose. "Why does Fadel Arboretum and Greenhouses need such tight security?"

"Have you been to almost any of New Chicago's parks? They've all been taken over by homeless camps. Don't get me wrong. We have plans to help the homeless, but controlling how it's done is important. We have to protect our staff as well as the tourists and vegetable buyers."

"I see."

Clera opens her mouth to ask more questions, but Zavi says, "Come by later, and I'll give you a better tour if you get hired. Then you'll understand." He glances at his Skinpad. "I have to get back, but see you at five?"

She nods and watches while he sinks into the floating chair, waves to Soo Yun, and heads out. Clera follows Zavi's progress through the window until he disappears from sight.

27

CLERA

At quarter to five, Clera skirts Second City territory and arrives at the main gates of Fadel Arboretum and Greenhouses. An elaborate sign invites her to "Come inside! Retreat within a lush rainforest, learn how to forage for food, or visit the History of Plants display. Donations welcome!"

A nervous flutter tickles her stomach. At least she looks presentable. How can she ever repay Soo Yun for the clothes? Smoothing her hair, Clera rings a buzzer next to the closed gates. A few moments later, an open-topped hover car pulls up. A bulky man in a green jumpsuit and utility belt jumps out. He taps a code into his Skinpad, and the gates slide open. He asks for Clera's name, taps something else, and gestures for her to hop in beside him. The gates shut, and a lock clicks.

Clera feels like she's entered a prison, though it makes sense that the arboretum has to vet its guests and keep out the bad guys. That's the reasonable answer for all the security, right? She looks around at rolling green fields, just-leafing trees, the far-off domed building, and she's reassured. This place isn't Perkine, and it's certainly not a jail. She can leave any time, but why would she want to?

The security guy doesn't speak, yet he's not unfriendly, either. He hums under his breath as he directs the hover car along a dirt road. A blue strip off to the left becomes a lake with an island in the middle and a stone bridge connecting it to the rest of the grounds. Sparrows cluster on the grass and rise in a tornado of feathers when the hover car drives too close. Across from the lake, torn-up ground forms a stadium-sized rectangle. Cranes work there, placing white cubes the size of train cars in neat, measured rows.

They pass the worksite, wend under a shady canopy of trees, and stop at the building Clera visited yesterday. Her escort says to proceed inside and gives her directions to the boss's office. What was his name? Albero? Should she call him that? Or stay quiet until he introduces himself? Yes. Definitely. Quiet. That would be best.

She enters the building and wonders if she'll see Zavi. The last visitors filter out, leaving the place empty except for a security guard. Her boots click on terracotta tiles. She reaches a door marked: "Albero Harris, Fadel Arboretum and Greenhouses Director."

Albero Harris. Mr. Harris. Dr. Harris?

The door swings open before she can knock, and the director waves her in.

He looks half African, half something else—maybe Italian? He's got a narrow, hooked nose, huge, dark eyes, and full lips that curve into a smile as he gestures Clera toward a chair and slides behind a mammoth desk which matches his girth. Clera imagined him wearing a smartsuit, but he's dressed casually in cargo pants and a knit shirt. A pen sticks out of his breast pocket. Candy wrappers lie crumpled on the synthetic wood top of the desk.

"Welcome, Clera . . ." He glances at something on his Skinpad. ". . . Diaz." And the interview begins.

Clera never gets the chance to tell Mr. Harris that she's punctual, reliable, or any other adjective her addled brain can retrieve. He wants to know about her past, about the apartment explosion, about Buela's aloe vera plant and the flower box her first-floor neighbor so carefully tended. He wants her to ask *him* questions, but all she can think to say is, "Are you familiar with the Boba Tea Cafe not far from here? There's a huge tree in the median right across from it, and I've been wondering what kind of oak it is."

Mr. Harris tells her it's probably a pin oak, then rambles on about oak trees and their mythical beginnings.

Clera loves Albero Harris. Does he have this effect on everyone?

Finally, Mr. Harris says, "Well, shall I see you tomorrow bright and early at eight a.m.?" He pushes back his chair and rises, so she does the same.

"Am I hired?"

"You were hired the moment Zavi Fadel spoke up for you. Didn't he say?"

"Zavi . . . Fadel." Clera's world tilts. She clenches her palms into balls and takes a breath. "Isn't that the name of this place? Fadel Arboretum and Greenhouses?"

"Right you are." Mr. Harris cocks his head at Clera's confusion.

"So, Zavi is not just a worker here?"

"He *is* just a worker, miss, but he *also* happens to be the grandson of this place's founder, Elijah Fadel. Botany runs in Zavi's blood. His mother, rest her soul, was a leading Swedish chemist on the tumor eradication team that took Elijah's collection of rare Amazonian canopy plants and transformed them into a marketable cure for cancer. His father was part of that team, too. I believe that's how they met."

Now Clera understands where Zavi's dark-blond hair came from, but the rest! Why hadn't he told her?

She manufactures a smile, shakes the director's hand, and makes her way out, only to find Zavi sitting on the veranda waiting for her. He rises and waves, but she doesn't wave back.

"Want to take a walk?" he asks. "I'll show you the grounds, and you can tell me about your interview."

She nods, still in a daze. Zavi navigates the steps to the lawn without his floating chair. "You're walking?"

"I need practice. Three miles a day is my goal—split up, of course. I hope to be rid of the chair by fall. I'll be a bit slow. Do you mind?"

Clera joins him on the lawn. "No. Of course not." Being near Zavi sends a confusing mix of heat and chills zinging through her body, but she hardly notices. Zavi is rich. Unreachable. A nice guy who's taken pity on her, but not a potential boyfriend. He hasn't led her on. She stupidly confused kindness with possible interest on his part. He's more educated than she, more worldly, more sophisticated. Way too—everything.

"I thought we could take this path through the grounds, if that's all right?" He points toward a winding, cobbled track that curves past the admin building/museum. "Are you feeling okay? Or did something go wrong with Albero?"

Albero. They're on a first-name basis. Mr. Harris probably *had* to hire her, which might explain why he didn't ask tough questions like *where did you work before*? And *why did you leave?* "I start tomorrow morning bright and early." She tries to look enthusiastic, to appear properly grateful.

Zavi frowns. Sunlight catches strands of his hair, making them shine like golden threads. "You don't seem unreservedly happy about working here. I thought you were desperate for a job?"

"I am! And so grateful for this chance, really!" She finally meets his eyes and feels tears spring into hers. She blinks them away. "It's just that I . . . I didn't realize that you aren't simply a worker here. You're the grandson of Elijah Fadel. The founder."

Zavi's face goes from concerned to carefully blank. "I know who my grandfather is. But you're wrong about my position. I *am* only a worker here. Did Albero make me seem like more? I don't get any special privileges, I assure you."

"No. He was fine. When he said your last name, it took me aback. You never told me. I had a picture of you that wasn't right. I'm still processing it."

His voice turns bitter. "So now my secret's out. I'm not simply Zavi the shrub planter. I'm a rich, spoiled kid from the suburbs. Your opinion of me is officially ruined."

Clera lays a hand on his arm. "That's not it at all."

How to tell him she *likes* him? They've only known each other for a few days. If she admits to a silly infatuation, what will he think? Will their budding friendship die? "Zavi, don't be mad. I'm so grateful that you got me this job. I'll do my best so you don't regret speaking up for an almost total stranger. If you want to be friends, that's what I want, too. If you believe I'm superficial, only seeing you as a name, not a person, then I'm truly sorry."

He looks down at her hand resting on his forearm. She draws back. The muscles in his jaw have relaxed, so maybe she's convinced him.

Zavi takes Clera by the elbow and steers her down the path. "Let's just be Zavi and Clera, shall we? It's so much less complicated."

She doesn't know if she can do that, but at least he isn't scowling at her now. To change the subject, she points toward a cluster of cottages behind the domed building. "What's that?"

"Worker housing. That one at the end is mine. I'll show it to you sometime."

But not now because that would be *too* friendly, Clera imagines him thinking. Zavi *is* still annoyed, yet he's decided to give her a chance.

They walk around the lake, through a wood and stretch of new saplings, tagged and protected by mesh fences and tubes around their trunks. Zavi leads her to three large greenhouses. As they walk down aisles of sprouting tomatoes and cucumbers, tiny petunias and marigolds, and a host of other plants she doesn't recognize, he introduces her to a couple of employees busy watering, planting, and fertilizing. He nods toward a ruddy-faced, middle-aged man. "You'll be working in here under Gab." To the red-faced man, he says, "Gab, this is Clera Diaz. She doesn't know much about botany, but she's a fast learner."

Gab doesn't shake her hand. Maybe it's just as well, as soil blackens his nails and palms.

Am I a fast learner?

They emerge from the last greenhouse and wander near the worksite, where a crane operator places a white cube measuring about twenty feet across onto a concrete pad. It has no roof, but piles of metal sheets and trusses rest near the worksite. Some of the cubes already *do* have roofs. They start low and angle up, overhanging the opposite wall to form covered porches. "Are those to be more worker housing?" Clera asks Zavi.

He watches the crane hook swing free. A man in a hard hat yells something to the driver and gestures.

"Those are grandfather's latest project and one of his most important." Pride radiates through his voice. *Now* he doesn't care his last name is Fadel. "Grandfather got permission from the very top to transform part of the arboretum and greenhouses grounds into housing for the homeless. The 3-D printer technology has been around for decades, but no one in New Chicago ever thought of using it to solve the city's homeless problem until now."

Clera looks more closely at the structures. "I've seen other parks filled with tents and makeshift shacks. I was terrified I'd end up in one after our apartment building was razed. They're full of leth users and disease."

"This one won't be," Zavi says firmly. "We're taking applications and screening people. All residents will be documented and tracked. That's the price of getting in. The side gate we used will be their ticket inside. Retinal scanners will allow only residents to enter, and there will be strict penalties for letting in unauthorized guests."

"Like the Second City?"

"The Second City, the Steelheads, or anyone else who might make trouble."

"What a great idea!" Clera recalls the sewer people and her own condemned apartment. She remembers the drones and their pellet sprays.

Zavi gives Clera a real smile, and it's like sunlight coming out from behind clouds. "I know! And we'll have a community garden that residents can harvest food from." He pauses. "I'd like to see where you live sometime. I could drive you home."

For the second time, she refuses the offer. "It's not far, and the people we're staying with have night shifts, so they're probably asleep right now. I don't want to wake them by bringing a visitor by."

If he notices how she can't meet his eyes, he doesn't comment. She's not usually quick with a story like Elio. Clera used to see that as a positive, but now she isn't sure. Her life is upside down. Maybe right is wrong and wrong is right. Maybe stealing is okay and lies are necessary.

Her moral compass vanished days ago in a leth lab explosion.

28

ELIO

Elio leaves the Arcade early to meet Bohdan again, but the Second City thug doesn't show. He hangs out by the curb, watching the empty street. Do vagrants live in the sewers like Bohdan said? Finally, Elio gives up on Bohdan and decides to set up the solar panels he bought.

He climbs the fire escape to the roof. The remains of a garden—empty pots, dried up plants, and a coiled watering hose—decorate the graveled and tarred surface. There's a broken umbrella stand and a bench, too. Elio grins, looking forward to sharing this discovery with Clera. He wishes he could share other discoveries, too, but she'd kill him if she knew about the Arcade. He reminds himself why he plays. *To get into the lottery. To win money in the contests.* He's not good enough yet, but he will be.

Clera might like to do something with this garden space. Elio puts together the solar panels, then turns on Bluetooth so he can pair them when he goes back inside. He returns to the apartment, and soon the lantern and cooktop show blinking green lights. Perfect. But he doesn't have meat or vegetables to cook, so he sets out peanut butter sandwiches, crackers, and sliced fruit. Where is Clera, anyway? She's book smart, but she's got no sense of direction and is such an innocent that some creep could easily take advantage of her.

His heart leaps when the front door rattles. Clera trips the locking mechanism and comes in. When she pushes the door closed, the lock reactivates with a reassuring beep.

"Is everything okay? You're late."

She scans the table with its spread of food laid out. "You made dinner!" She sits down.

He shrugs. "Not a real one, but I did set up the solar panels, so once we get better food, maybe you'll make enchiladas?"

"Sure." She sighs and nudges her boots off with her toes. A long skirt brushes her feet.

He eyes the outfit. "Where did you get those clothes? You didn't steal them, did you?"

"Of course not!" She reminds him of her new friend, Soo Yun, talks about her other friend, Zavi, a disabled man who helped her get a job at the greenhouse where he works.

"That's great!" Relief and guilt war within him. *He* doesn't have a job, at least not a legal, regular one. Nor does he have friends he can tell Clera about unless Juke and Mila qualify. He's only met Juke once, and he doesn't know where he stands with Mila. "So, you haven't said much about this Zavi guy. Are you sure he's safe? Has he asked you for anything?"

Clera goes small and quiet, a sure signal she's irritated. "Not everyone is on the take. Besides, he can hardly walk."

He studies her. "What's he like apart from being a cripple?"

She picks at a loose thread on the flowered dress. "Just a regular guy, I guess. He's kind. A little older than us."

"Is he cute?" Elio can't help teasing a little. Clera's never had a boyfriend. Does she like guys? Maybe Zavi is acne-pocked, with greasy hair and a boil on his neck. That picture reassures Elio. He doesn't want his sister to get involved with a man. Not right now. A boyfriend would complicate things. He isn't sure *what* things exactly, but knows he's right.

Clera frowns. "I'm not going to answer that. It should be enough that I have a job. I might even like it. It's got to be better than working in that depressing Perkine factory."

"No doubt." Elio offers her a sandwich. He sits down and stretches his legs. They eat in companionable silence. Swallowing his last bite, he says, "We're going to be okay, Clera. For the first time since Mama died, I can feel it."

"I hope so." Clera looks around. The room is stark, featureless, and smells of mold. "I really hope so."

—◇—

Elio plays at the Arcade all week. Bohdan shows up Friday in front of the apartment with packages for him to deliver. Elio doesn't ask where Boh's been, and the gangster doesn't say. He's jumpy, but the deliveries go smoothly, just like last time, and credits roll in.

On Saturday, Juke appears at the Arcade. Elio sees him from across the main room, swinging through the security gates. Juke high-five's another guy, then weaves among the gamers. He smiles at a stocky girl aiming her gun at monsters on a screen, blows a kiss to a muscled man with a shaved head, and weaves his way toward Elio, who's standing by Dec Gaston's looping vid. He points a finger gun at Elio's chest.

"Yo, hom. How's your sim coming along?"

Elio plays it cool, though he's way better than when Juke first helped him. "I'm up to level four."

Juke whistles. Today he sports a pink silk shirt with a polka dot handkerchief sticking out of one pocket. His dark hair contrasts milk-white skin. Shiny shoes reflect Elio's face. "You been here every day? How are you pulling that? No school or job? Got yourself a sugar mama?"

"I work!" Elio tries not to take offense but feels his body tense. "I just don't waste time." He doesn't say how *little* he works. Juke's words hit too close to the truth.

"I promised to buy you a drink last time you were here, Elio. It is Elio, right? You ready for a break?"

"Sure. Thanks." They head to the concessions. Elio absently watches for Mila as they dodge gamers. He doesn't know if he wants to see her or not. Even when she was asking him out, it felt like she was mocking him.

Juke greets a few people along the way. One tall, skinny guy pauses long enough to kiss him on both cheeks like they're in Europe. Juke finds the last free table. It's noon on a Saturday, and the Arcade buzzes like a beehive. A mishmash of conversation, beeps, and whistles compete with the fans in the ceiling. Elio and Juke slide into the booth. There's an ordering column planted in the middle, and a cartoon face lights up on Elio's side. The AI brings out a menu on the bottom half of the screen. Elio studies it, then orders a burger, fries, and a soda. He can't remember the last time he ate such foods. He swipes his ring across the box beneath the price.

Juke says, "Let me buy you that drink. Ever tried a Lombago?" Without pausing, he rattles off his order and holds an arm up to the column to pay with his Skinpad.

"Is it alcoholic?"

Juke laughs like this is the funniest question he's ever heard. "I take it you haven't had one. Let me be the first to introduce you to something you will, I promise, love." He taps on the column. The cartoon waitress comes back, and Juke makes the drink order. This time, the waitress asks for ID, so this Lombago is definitely spiked.

Elio isn't sure how he feels about that. He wants to stay sharp. Nothing matters but being the best at the sims, and he's not letting anything get in the way. So, when two turquoise-colored drinks appear alongside the food order, he sips cautiously from the tall glass flute. It's half sweet, half bubbly, with a kick of something that makes his throat tingle.

Juke watches him and sips his own drink. "Good, yeah?"

"Yeah. A little too good. But thanks."

"Don't worry. Lombagos won't slow down your game, not unless you drink a lot of them. You might even find your reflexes improve, at least short term. That's why they're banned substances during the contests." Juke picks up a kabob stacked with chicken chunks and marinated peppers. He takes a delicate bite.

Elio digs into his food. He wants to close his eyes and savor every bite but feels he must pretend he eats burgers and fries all the time—though why Juke's opinion matters, he doesn't know.

Juke says, "Mind if I watch you play a mission when we're done?"

"Sure. Maybe you can give me more tips."

"I doubt it. Not if you've already mastered level three. I tend to play all the games, meaning I'm not an expert at any of them. But I don't have to be. I simply like the vibe of this place. I'm not here to win anything. Also, it's a good way to pick up dates."

"Looks like plenty of people know you," Elio remarks.

"I'm a friendly guy! But only some of them have dated me. Don't suppose you're interested?"

"What?" Elio almost chokes on his fry. "No. Not me. I'm more of a—" He shrugs.

"…traditionalist?" Juke supplies with a quirk of his mouth. "I thought so. I saw how you looked at Mila last time I was here."

"I didn't look at her any special way," Elio objects. Is Juke trying to get a rise out of him?

"Hom, you watched her ass with the attention of a dog slavering after a piece of steak the whole time she walked away from you last weekend."

Elio's cheeks heat. "I'm only human," he tries to joke. "Actually, she came on to me a few days ago, but I said no." He waits curiously for Juke's reaction.

It's immediate and explosive. "What? Hom! Why would you do that? Obviously, you liked the look of her."

"There's more to a girl than looks—although the grease monkey thing she's got going isn't super appealing. I don't know. Something about her set me off."

"Clean that girl up, put her in a slinky dress, and you'd have half the guys in here begging to touch her."

"Well, she doesn't wear a slinky dress." Elio feels dumb. Clueless. He's sure Juke thinks so, too.

"Have you no imagination, Elio?" Juke shakes his head and takes another bite of kabob. A sapphire ring glitters on his pinky finger.

Wanting to change the subject, Elio asks, "You dress like you have a lot of money, Juke. You from the exec class?"

If he wants to annoy Juke with such a personal question, he fails. Juke only grins. "Nah. My folks run a superchurch. The skimpy allowance they give me doesn't cover my rich tastes, though. My fashion sense requires that I hold down a job to maintain a certain standard." He rubs his collar between two fingers. "So, I dabble in the stock market and a few other things."

Elio leans in. "Like drugs?"

Juke's mouth purses. "What do you take me for, a leth-head? No, hom. I work for myself in a very *select* field of business. Most people don't know what I do. I probably shouldn't tell you." He studies Elio beneath a fringe of black lashes, suddenly serious.

"I'm good with a secret."

"Well, let's put it this way. If you ever have a technological problem and need a coding fix, I'm your guy."

Elio runs the words through his brain and does some *de*-coding. "You mean you're a hacker?"

"Shh. Not so loud." Juke casts around the congested, noisy concessions area.

He's so melodramatic. Still, Elio humors Juke and keeps his voice low. "So, what kinds of problems do you fix exactly?"

Juke's eyes fasten on him, bright and intelligent. "You need a grade changed at school? That's child's play. You need something bad taken off your record? Well, that's a bit harder. You want a pay upgrade or a clearance for something? That'll really cost you. I take a percentage for my work, and it pays for my swank style."

"Time in the clink if you get caught."

Juke hisses, "That's why I don't tell just anyone!" He can't hold his stern expression and grins sheepishly. "Don't know why I told *you*. You're easy to talk to, Elio. I guess that's it. Plus, quite obviously, you come from the slums, so why would you rat me out to the clinks? In fact, if you can ever afford me, you may well have need of my services one day."

"Do your parents know?"

Juke laughs so loudly that a couple of kids in the next booth turn to look. "Hells, no. What do you think I am, a scrull?" Again, he grows serious. "Do you believe me, Elio? Do you think I can perform magic with a keyboard and a screen?"

Elio isn't sure how to answer. Juke could be the biggest blowhard he's ever come across, or he could be telling the truth. Obviously, Elio's not that good at reading people. He sure read Mila wrong. So, he stays quiet.

Juke sits back and folds his hands across his belly. He tilts his head. "I like you, Elio. You didn't feed me an automatic line I can't trust. 'Sure, Juke, of course I believe you.' No, you're still assessing me, which is honest.

That honesty—well, it's refreshing."

"Thanks, I guess. I won't give away your secret. Hells, I don't know anyone to tell it to." Elio considers, then blurts, "Maybe I have a secret, too. One that could get me arrested. If someone is caught working for Second City, doing some small thing like playing delivery boy, what's the penalty? Do you know?"

Juke looks neither surprised nor repelled. His reply is prompt. "First, you're never just 'working for Second City.' If you work for them, you're one of them, and the penalty for being part of a gang is expulsion from the city. It used to be a short jail sentence, but the clinks are all full. And the Barrens? Well, that might be a worse punishment, anyway."

"Why?" Elio remembers how Clera thought of leaving New Chicago and making their way in the countryside.

Juke's voice falls to a whisper. "Hom, folks out there are starving. They've lost their hospitals, their local police, their delivery systems. Unless they live totally off the grid, they got no way to make life *work*."

29

ELIO

A summer of drought saps moisture from the air, then transitions into rainstorms that flood some areas and threaten to overtake Michigan Lake's seawall. The homeless die of heat or drown, but this has become the norm and doesn't make the news feeds. After months of practice, Elio wins his first contest. It's a small, local payout, but it tells him he's on the right track. He puts his name in for the Sims Tournament. It starts in ten days, the Big Deal that will get him into the lottery and give him a chance for a shuttle and berth on *Calliope*. She's headed through the ARH in the coming months and has become the center of all his plans and hopes. Bigger plans by far than he's told Clera about.

Now and then, Elio makes runs for Bohdan. Enough to keep him in credits and Clera from asking where he spends his nonexistent salary. She's doing well enough at the greenhouse for both of them. Plus, she seems happy. Their apartment has an actual picture on the wall, a tablecloth on the table, and a rug on the bedroom floor. It's starting to feel like a home. Not their old home. Not without Mama. But at least a haven from the world outside.

Elio meets up with Juke on weekends, but Mila avoids him at the Arcade. Did he hurt her feelings when he rejected her? *Why* did he reject her? Now he can't stop noticing the short, pixie-faced mechanic with the thick braid that swings as she walks. He likes to watch her. No other girl catches his eye. He refocuses on the sims and tries not to think about romance.

Mila's face intrudes, though, and he wonders if she'd show him around the aeronautical museum. The sims are cool but nothing like being inside a real shuttle, even if its working parts have been ripped out. One day, Elio sees an opportunity to talk to Mila, and he takes it. She's standing by the dance machines, watching a young girl stomp around on colored squares in a complex pattern. The song ends. Neon lights fade, and Mila pats the young girl on the back. "You've got the moves."

The girl smiles, waves goodbye, and skips off. Mila turns and runs into Elio's chest. She takes a step back.

"Hello," he says casually, like he hasn't been waiting for her to notice him for several minutes.

"Oh, hi, Elio." Her gray eyes flash some message he can't decipher.

"You've been ignoring me. Are you mad about something?"

"What? Why would I be mad? No." She shakes her head. "You weren't interested in me, so I moved on. That's all."

She's so up front. "I thought we might become friends, at least," he hates how plaintive he sounds.

But Mila's lips tilt up. "Most guys don't want to be friends. They want a date. Sex. And if you aren't into that, they find someone else."

The word *sex* throws him off. He takes a breath. "I'm not like that. I just don't have much time for girls. Getting ready for the games." He nods toward the digital ticker tape above the sims room. His name flashes across, the latest winner of 50 credits in the weekly sims contest.

Mila studies the scores. "Congrats. By games, do you mean the Sims Tournament? The one where, if you beat everyone, Dec Gaston puts you in the lottery to win a shuttle?"

Elio grins. "That's my hope."

"Your odds aren't good."

His smile falters. He remembers why Mila annoys him. Her words hit like darts. *Bullseye.* She's not trying to be mean, which makes the insult somehow worse. "Well, I'm going for it, anyway." In a millisecond, his body shifts from heat to ice. "Guess I'll see you around, Mila." He turns, but her hand catches his wrist, fingers so small they can't encircle it, yet she's not weak. He knows that.

"Hey." She steps toward him. "I keep making you angry, but I don't mean to. Uncle Bas says it's my nature to put my foot in it. I don't know how to lie, and I don't want to. I call things like I see them."

"It's okay." He disentangles himself and again starts to head off but suddenly pauses. "Do you ever give tours at that museum of yours? I'd love to see the inside of a real shuttle."

"Sure." Mila shrugs. "You could get in line with all the other tourists, or I could give you a private tour after hours. That would be much more intensive, and it wouldn't cost you anything." A smile teases her lips. Is she flirting with him?

He has no idea, but he's back on that tightrope again, unsure of himself or her. "You'd do that?" he finally asks.

"Why not? We're friends, right?"

"Right."

"How about tonight? I've got nothing better to do."

Elio considers what he'll tell Clera. If he says he caught an extra shift, she might buy that. Construction crews work on sultry fall nights. Maybe? "It's a date," he says, then regrets his choice of words. "I didn't mean—"

"Elio Diaz." Mila rolls her eyes. "Don't worry. I received your message loud and clear. You aren't into me *romantically*. Got it. No problem. Let's meet at six."

Clera accepts Elio's lie, and after dinner he heads to the New Chicago Aeronautical Museum. The sun pokes its head out of clouds, angling toward the horizon. The museum is a long, low building with a broad, sloping roof that resembles airplane wings. Chained to a cement pad by the front doors sits a life-size shuttle. Blue solar tiles cover much of the hull. It resembles an armored bird of prey: sleek and futuristic.

A display explains the ship in-depth, but the words swim after a minute. Elio reads far enough to learn the shuttle is a working prototype on loan from NASA that will become the new standard someday. He's studying the blueprint on the sign when Mila taps his shoulder, making him start.

Kind of jumpy, aren't you?" She grins, revealing those dimples.

Annoyance ebbs as quickly as it came. He considers what Juke said of Mila. A lot of guys would be flattered by her attention and take advantage of it. He imagines stripping that dirty jumpsuit from her curvy little body and wonders what she'd look like underneath.

"Earth to Elio. You have an odd expression on your face. Feeling okay?"

He's flustered. She does that to him. "I'm fine." But he doesn't sound fine, so he follows this with an apologetic smile. "I'm ready for my tour if you are."

"Sure." She regards him like she knows exactly what he was thinking. He follows Mila around the side of the building.

She scans her Skinpad, and a side door unlocks. They walk down a long hall into a breezy, high-ceilinged area, the lights dimmed now. There's an empty desk, security gates, and a stand where visitors can make donations. The hall is filled with kiosks showing photos of ships and tiny explanations he doesn't want to try reading. He's relieved when Mila passes them by and heads out a metal door into what she called the Graveyard.

Concrete walkways lead to various shuttles. You can climb portable metal stairs and step into machines that have sailed to the brink of Earth's atmosphere and farther. They date back clear to *Atlantis*. Mila leads him toward that ship first, saying, "The Kennedy Space Center sent this baby to us just before, you know, the island went underwater. It was one of our first. *Atlantis* flew thirty-three missions and orbited Earth around five thousand times before it was put out of service. Seems so old-fashioned now, but if you saw the preserved control room at Houston's Johnson Center, where the first Apollo missions happened, you'd be amazed at how ancient the computers look. They were big, boxy things. Must have taken a lot of trust to go on one of those missions."

She leads him inside *Atlantis*, and he can't believe he's standing right in the middle of history. It's cramped, and the bolts are rusting, but that only adds to the feel of antiquity. "You've been to Houston?" Elio asks Mila as he tries to take in everything at once.

"No. Afraid not." She runs a hand over the back of the pilot's chair. "But I've read everything there is on space travel. You can ask me any questions, and I'll have the answers."

So, he does. He might have trouble reading, but he's a great listener. Her answers only bring up more questions, and he's surprised to find himself enjoying Mila's company equally as much as touring retired shuttles. There are science research vessels, cargo ships, a sleek, executive tourist boat, even a fighter equipped with turrets and guns.

As they descend the stairs from the last shuttle, Mila says, "Soon we're expecting a new edition to the Graveyard, and I'm very excited. *Beatriz* is being retired here. She's actually pretty new, but now that solar is a practical alternative for short-range flights, the older fusion engines are being phased out. What a waste, I say. *Beatriz* is a science vessel, and she only made five trips. She's equipped with some solar panels, but nothing like that baby out front."

"The one that looks like a blue-scaled raptor? Is the new series already in production?"

"Not yet, but soon." Mila leads Elio toward a hanger backed against the twenty-foot fence that surrounds the Graveyard. "Geez, I haven't talked this much in a year. Hope I didn't bore you. Wanna see where I work?"

She glances over her shoulder at him. For being so short, Mila is a power-walker. Elio lengthens his strides to keep up. He isn't sure he wants to be finished looking at the shuttles, but he nods.

Once they pass through the hanger doors and automatic lights flicker on, Elio gets why Mila always looks so oily. He recalls she comes to the Arcade only on breaks, so she's never changed clothes first, and this place looks like a mechanic's shop. Tools line up neatly on workbenches and hang from pegs. There's a rolling diagnostic cart and lots of engine parts, fans, and other unidentifiable ship innards lying around seemingly at random. But there's no dust, and the floor is spotless.

Elio stops and stares. Mila spreads her hands. "Well, this is it. I guess not so interesting as the boats outside. Maybe you don't care to see the real work we do here."

"No, this is great!" And Elio means it. He regards Mila with new eyes. She looks different to him now, smart and skilled in ways he'll never be. To her, the Arcade is only a distraction from her real life. For him, it *is* his life. "You take ships apart, but can you fix them, too? Have you ever gotten the chance?"

"I could fix them, I'm sure, if I had the right replacement parts. That's my dream, to work in a shipyard, getting shuttles ready for liftoff instead of tearing them apart. I'd be building something, and wouldn't it be great to watch your creation take off and soar past the blue?"

"What would be great is *flying* out past the blue."

"You'd better win that Sims Tournament, then, Elio. You sure seem passionate about trying." She pauses in thought. "I saw how you studied that promotional vid Dec Gaston put out, and I've seen how you play. Not like it's recreation, but like it's a job. With determination, you know?"

"You've been watching me," he teases.

She tosses her braid. "Only when I was interested in you, Elio."

"So . . ." He takes a step closer. "You aren't interested anymore? Maybe you have a new boyfriend."

Can he score with Mila tonight? She invited him here, took all this time to show him around. They're entirely alone, and there must be a staff room somewhere equipped with at least a couch.

But her eyes narrow. She sounds peeved when she answers, "Why are you playing with me? Have you changed your mind about sex? Do you just want a one-nighter, like I could be any woman in a deserted hanger, and you'd go for it?"

That's so close to the truth he can't answer.

"I thought we were going to be friends, Elio, but you can't toy with me and expect that to happen. So straight up, what's your game?"

"Game? There's no game." He feels like a sims player on his virgin voyage. "I was joking." Was he? If not, he'd better say so. She's given him the opening, but he can't answer because he doesn't know. What does he want from her? A one-night stand? Surely not a commitment. "Mila," he sighs. "Don't be mad, okay? I'm sorry. I really appreciate you taking me here and spending time with me. I had no idea you were so amazing." He spreads his arms for emphasis.

Elio doesn't expect her to walk into them, reach up on tiptoes, and press her lips to his. They're warm and full, and his body reacts immediately. She steps back before he can deepen the kiss. He lets her go with a grunt of dismay and frowns. "Now, who's the tease?"

"I wasn't teasing, Elio. I like to move slow, that's all. I'm not some green girl, and I'm not a player." She shrugs. "I wanted to kiss you, so I did. You said a really nice thing, and it felt right. If I was too forward, well, I'm not sorry. Tell me 'no' if you don't want it."

"So, there's a chance you might kiss me again?"

Mila laughs. "You're so cute sometimes. I almost want to right now, but I think I'll wait. It'll give you something to look forward to." She throws that braid around, shows her dimples, and turns to lead him out of the hanger. Elio groans, but she only laughs. The sound echoes back and carries him out into the night.

30

CLERA

At first, Clera was nervous in her new job. She didn't know what to make of Gab or his terse directions, and he never complimented her when she followed them. But he didn't yell when she messed up, either—even when her over-watering killed some pepper sprouts they'd been about to transplant into the community garden.

She loves the greenhouses, how the sun pools at her feet as she walks down narrow aisles, removing weeds and dead leaves. She loves how the fans roar, how young branches caress her arms as she brushes past, how she gets to work by herself but doesn't feel alone like she did in the factory. Her skin darkens from the occasional outside labor, and her hair lightens to a uniform caramel color. Clera wishes she'd see Zavi more, but his work is in the arboretum. Still, sometimes he shows up unexpectedly and invites her to walk the grounds with him. She barely notices his disability now, and the floating chair has all but disappeared. Once or twice, they've met at the Boba Tea Cafe for lunch, but more often, Clera only visits with Soo Yun.

She hasn't run into any more Second City thugs or their drones, and little by little, she's starting to feel safe. The hole in her heart where Mama used to be will never heal, but new people help fill the cracks and shore up the broken pieces. Elio's job doesn't bring in steady money, but they're okay. She doesn't ask why construction isn't more lucrative. Maybe she doesn't want to know.

One day, Zavi takes her walking along a path lined with aspen and birch. Shadows dapple the trail. He stops at a statue she hasn't seen before. She believes it's the Greek goddess Persephone. Dressed in a flowing gown and wearing a crown of flowers, the goddess steps over licking flames, determination carved into her marble face. Her hands grasp at something just out of reach.

Zavi explains, "This statue was recently donated to us. Dec Gaston has been a big supporter."

Clera touches cool stone. She admires how the sculptor captured the fall of cloth and fire. "That's the mouth of Hell, I suppose? And Persephone is leaving Hades to come home to Olympus and see her mother."

"Right." Zavi sounds surprised. "That was the deal. She spent six months with Hades, then six months with her mother, Demeter. The Greeks used the story to explain the seasons. When Persephone left for Hades, Demeter would grow sad and let green things die. Thus, summer faded into autumn and winter. When Persephone reappears in the land of the living, Demeter celebrates with springtime and new growth. It's an appropriate theme for the arboretum."

"I only knew some of that," Clera admits. "My reading focused more on modern fiction and the occasional history book."

"What's your favorite novel?" Shadows play across Zavi's face.

Clera laughs. "How to choose? An epic love story like *Wuthering Heights*, maybe? I don't get to the library much now." She doesn't add that she can't get a library card without an address. She's only been back once. Curious about Zavi, she researched the Fadels on a public terminal. This confirmed her belief that he exists on another plane—as far from her as Vishnu, the planet where *Calliope* will travel next year. She sighs.

"What?" Zavi removes his hands from his pockets and takes a step toward her. "Is something wrong?"

"No, of course not! I can never repay you for getting me this job. I miss Mama, but things are better now."

"You looked sad. Or did I misread that? Maybe you have your own Persephone issues you want to talk about?"

"Persephone issues? As in some big, bad Hades wants to spirit me off to the underworld and force me to become his wife?"

"It's just a metaphor." Zavi grins helplessly. "Apparently a bad one. It's only that you looked so regretful there for a minute."

"You're wrong." Clera looks away and gathers her defenses. "Should we walk some more?" She steps off without waiting for an answer.

Zavi jogs to catch up, a sign he's almost healed. "Sometimes I think there's this whole other person in there." He taps her head lightly. "Someone I know nothing about. You won't let me see your life outside of work or the cafe. Why is that, Clera?"

"Why are you so interested?" she shoots back.

He grabs her arm and forces her to halt. "Because I like you." He looks more exasperated than moonstruck. They face each other on the deserted path like opponents squaring off for battle.

Clera's body goes still. "Wait a minute. You *like* like me?"

In answer, he moves close and bends toward her, head tilted.

Oh, hells, he's going to kiss me! She panics and almost steps back, but something holds her in place. Curiosity, maybe? Or the magnetism she felt from the moment they met? Zavi's hand comes to rest on her waist. He leans in until his lips touch hers, a brush soft as feathers. He pulls back just enough for her to feel his warm breath.

This thing between them will never work, but she wants him. So. Much. Clera reaches up, cups his neck in her palms, and answers the kiss.

When their lips meet again, he's less tentative. Both hands encircle her waist and move around her back to press her closer. Fireworks explode behind Clera's eyes. Her fingers twine in his dark blond hair. It curls about them, soft yet rough, like his lips, which grow ever more demanding. His tongue urges her mouth open. She stiffens, then relaxes into the unfamiliar sensation. Warmth curls in her belly, and she can't get close enough to him. Her thinking brain goes numb, and it's so good to let loose. To ignore the voice urging restraint and simply *feel.*

The groan in Zavi's throat brings Clera back to reality. He pulls away enough to mumble, "Should we go to my bungalow?"

"I . . . I . . ." Her hands move to his shoulders, then to his chest, where his heart beats a quick rhythm. She pushes her palms against him though her body screams to do the opposite. A one-and-done coupling isn't what she wants, is it? What if she falls in love with him, and afterward he finds out who she really is? *Just some Slummer who's been lying to him.*

"Clera?" Zavi holds her face in his hands and gazes down at her. She can barely breathe when he looks at her with that gentle concern.

"Please." She barely knows if she's asking him to continue kissing her or stop before he breaks her heart.

"Am I moving too fast?"

A breathy laugh escapes her. "No. It's not that. I only—" She pauses, then latches onto the first excuse that comes. "You're practically my boss. It doesn't seem right for us to . . . to have sex." Her words fall to a whisper. What they've started feels like so much more than simple physical gratification. A whirlwind of longing and regret swirls around her. She wants to be reckless, but that's never been her nature, and caution wins out.

Zavi's hands drop. He takes a step backward. "There aren't any rules about that sort of thing here." He bites his lip while he considers. "But if you aren't ready, or this isn't what you want, tell me now." When she doesn't reply, he goes on, "I'm not a cripple anymore. Maybe not an athlete, either, so if you're looking for someone with a perfect body—I have scars."

"I don't care about your scars. You *are* perfect." Tears shimmer in her eyes, and an ache clogs her throat. She swallows it. "There are things you don't know about me, Zavi, and I'm not sure I'm ready to tell you about them. I need time to think."

One side of Zavi's mouth tilts up. "What, are you a criminal?" At least his concerned look has retreated.

"No." Clera forces a smile and shakes her head. "But I'm not from your world."

"I don't care." His lips are suddenly on hers again. The kiss is fierce, brief, an explosion that dies as quickly as it ignited. She edges away.

"*I* care, Zavi. Like I said, I need to think."

He runs a hand through his hair. They stare at each other. Clera holds her breath, believing she might fall apart if he takes another step toward her.

But he doesn't, only nods, giving in. He holds out a hand. "Friends, then? Or still?"

She squeezes his palm. "Friends *for now*."

31

ZAVI

Zavi sits with his grandfather on the rooftop patio of the compound. Below are thirty-foot-high walls, mostly obscured by vegetation: pines, junipers, oak, and ash trees. Fall has created a motley display of oranges and golds in the courtyard. Red ivy clings to the stones, completing the illusion that Grandfather lives in an oasis, not a fortress.

A servant appears to offer them afternoon brandies from a silver tray. Grandfather takes his and sips. He watches Zavi from beneath bushy eyebrows. Zavi wonders if the old man lets them go wild on purpose to distract visitors from the eagle eyes beneath. Zavi sloshes brandy around in his mouth before swallowing, appreciating the notes of oak and caramel. His attention drifts past the compound walls to the rolling fields of the Barrens. Within sight is another walled fortress, the air rail station. A train, tiny from this distance, heads north on thin tracks that levitate above magnetic poles.

Grandfather has followed the direction of his gaze. "I think about your parents every day. Being so close to the station, I can't help it."

Zavi grunts. He doesn't want to talk about his parents. He's better now. Their memories feel more like splinters than shards of glass. Time is the best healer, and meeting Clera has helped, too. She makes him feel less alone. She doesn't seem aware that only a fragile shell protects the grief he carries. Or if she does notice, she has her own sorrow, and she avoids pressing him on his, unlike Grandfather.

"You look stronger," the old man remarks. Wind ruffles his white locks. It carries an autumn coolness and the hint of rain. Grandfather tucks a blanket around his legs.

Zavi inhales the ozone scent. "I am," he agrees. "I rarely use the chair now."

"I mean mentally. There's an energy in your step that was missing before. You appear almost happy."

Zavi stays quiet. Knowing the old man, his talk of Zavi's improved health might be a segue into some other topic.

"I have a promotion proposition for you."

"Oh?" Zavi's hand tightens around his glass. "I've been at the arboretum for less than a year."

Grandfather shrugs. "Surely, you want more."

"Are you talking about school? A graduate teaching job? If I apply now, it'll be another year before I can start my PhD, assuming I'm accepted."

"Of course, you'd be accepted. But I have something else in mind."

Zavi frowns. He hates it when Grandfather acts mysterious. He wishes he'd simply say what he means. But Zavi won't beg for clarification. Grandfather can't be rushed, and he loves to keep his schemes close to his chest, loves to keep people guessing. Even Zavi. Maybe especially Zavi.

Grandfather sighs, probably disappointed Zavi won't ask what this "promotion" entails.

Zavi doesn't care. He smiles a little, swirls the amber liquid in his glass, drinks. He considers and finally says, "Work at the arboretum is a little tedious, but relaxing, too. It's given me time to heal. I guess I never thanked you for that." He frowns, then makes a decision. "Also, I've met someone.

It may be nothing of consequence, but she's helping me get better. I'd hate to leave just when we're getting to know each other."

"Oh?"

Zavi feels color rise in his cheeks. He's relieved when the old man's eyes drift away to watch a hawk chase prey through the brambles outside the gate. "I'm not saying I'm in some serious relationship, but this *is* something I want to explore. If your promotion involves leaving the city, I might not want it."

"Tell me about this girl. Do I know the family? Where did you meet?"

"You definitely don't," Zavi admits. "And she works with me. Her name is Clera. I can't say much more. We're still in the getting-to-know-you phase."

"You can't or won't talk about her?"

A smile pulls at Zavi's lips. "Two can keep secrets, Grandfather."

"Ah, so that's your game. Maybe I shouldn't have brought up that promotion. I'm still working on it, which is the only reason I can't give specifics."

"Ditto." Zavi gulps a last swallow of brandy. It burns pleasantly in his stomach. He sets the glass on the balcony ledge.

Grandfather sighs. "You are entirely too much like me, Zavi. It's really quite annoying."

They grin at each other.

32

ELIO

Last weekend, Elio paid his entry fee for the Sims Tournament and won the right to enter the semi-finals by defeating an enemy squadron without dying once. His time, twenty-eight minutes and fifteen seconds, beat everyone else's by a good thirty seconds.

Today is the Day. The one that's driven him on, kept him from remembering all he's lost, held off despair. If he makes it through the semi's this morning, he'll go one-on-one in the last game for the chance to win that lottery. Dec Gaston will be here in person tonight to name the tournament champ, then pick the winning ticket. He's doing it the old-fashioned way—with names in a jar. Because, Dec says, he's a retro kind of guy. He follows this statement with the billion-dollar smile that appears in all his vids.

Elio understands that Gaston's charm is just for show and wonders if there's another reason the billionaire wants to choose a winner "the old-fashioned way." In the new commercial, Gaston raises a glass jar with *Mason* on the side. Buela had one like it in the refrigerator to keep their drinking water cold. No one on the South Side drank from the faucet. Buela boiled water and poured it into those jars.

Will Gaston play fair? Elio has to believe he will, though the drawing-from-a-jar idea seems a little off. Maybe the whole thing's a scam. It would be harder to cheat using computers to draw a winner, wouldn't it? But why would Dec cheat? Why would he care who gets a chance at flying out on *Calliope*? Most of the berths are filled. Gamers across the United States have names in that jar. This weekend's winning ticket—*his* ticket, Elio tells himself—is for the last berth. His final hope.

He's standing in line outside the sims room awaiting his turn to check in. Cameras and blinding lights fill the normally dark space and make Elio's temples throb. He rubs them, takes deep breaths, tries to calm his jangled nerves. An adrenaline rush is welcome, but if he lets anxiety wash over him, he'll drown in it. He'll lose.

Banishing this thought, Elio swipes his digi-ring across the check-in tablet. The guy in charge, backed by two buff security guards, points Elio toward his assigned sim console. It's not the one he usually plays. This bothers him, but he can't object. It shouldn't matter, anyway. The consoles are identical, right?

Elio slides into the seat and adjusts it. Camera lights can't penetrate beneath the hood that encloses the screen and seat. Tucked in the dim cocoon, his headache recedes to a dull throb. A kid he's met slips into a nearby console, and they nod to each other. Elio recognizes Arcade regulars but hasn't gotten too friendly. They're his competition.

Someone shouts, "Good luck, Elio!" from outside the room. He peers around the edge of his station and sees Juke and Mila standing together at the front of a crowd. They give him corny thumbs-ups. He smiles, feeling slightly less nervous. He's got friends here. He doesn't have to be alone.

The screen flashes to life. Instructions for the semi-finals scroll across. A familiar, droning voice reads them aloud, catering to the morons who never learned. *That's me.* He banishes this thought. *Nothing negative today. Winning is a state of mind.* He *knows* this. That stubborn confidence and dogged belief in himself despite all odds is what's gotten him this far.

Look what you've done in only a few months. These other kids have been playing for years, but you came in and blew most of them away. Only eight left in the semi-finals. Then two. Then a good chance at winning your own shuttle. He refuses to believe his name might not be drawn. That's how losers think.

The seat jolts and vibrates as he rolls down a runway. The screen becomes a tarmac. Grass and a few utility trucks drift past on both sides. This game's already different from the non-tournament one he trained on. The enemy isn't aliens but the other fighters in the room. He's not playing against a computer, but flesh and blood. Does that increase or decrease his chances? He doesn't know.

The seat tilts, and blue sky fills the screen as the ground drops away. It's Elio's favorite part, when he pretends he's flying a real shuttle, soaring into atmo and beyond. The screen sky pales, turns gray, then black. Stars switch on like lights, and he's in outer space. The players are supposed to fly in orbit, dodging space debris and small asteroids while they search out opponents. Last one flying wins.

Elio fingers the red button on his joystick. He steers right and follows the curve of Earth's blue-green sphere. Contestants have limited ammunition, so he can't waste any. He's got to make every shot count. The cameras, lights, and cheers from the crowd watching on big screens dissolve. It's just Elio, his craft, and the enemy. He can do this.

The first fighter shuttle comes at him from around an asteroid. Elio suspected someone might be hiding there, so he's ready. Laser fire streaks toward him, but he's already swerving. It flashes past his window, a little too close. The seat shivers, and the screen jumps. He loops to come up behind his opponent. *Wait for it. Wait for it.* Sighting crosshairs mark his target. They narrow, narrow more, lock on. Elio fires.

The fighter dodges at the last second. Elio thinks he's missed, but then a stream of smoke boils across his screen. It blinds him, and his heart lurches. Maybe *he's* on fire, somehow. He accelerates and flips on the rear camera. Flames erupt from the enemy fighter before they're extinguished in the vacuum of space. The enemy shuttle goes into a spin and plummets toward Earth. It hits atmo, flares, and vanishes. Elio switches his forward screen back on, now clear of smoke. A voice wafts through the speakers. "Congratulations, pilot. You've made your first kill, and you only expended 2.897 rounds of laser fire. You have 14.674 rounds remaining."

All eight players' stats light up on the screen. Two show red, their fuel and ammo gauges at zero. Five opponents to go. He focuses his attention back on the main screen just in time to see a fighter whizzing in out of nowhere, lasers blazing. Elio pulls up hard, veers left, then right, then left again. His ADHD brain takes over. His body reacts automatically before his thinking brain can process what's happening. Those lasers should have killed him, but by some miracle, he's evaded them. A glance at the rear view shows his enemy far behind. A glance at the stats shows the guy spent way too much ammo. *They aren't giving us enough. Much less than in the regular games.* It's possible that everyone left will run out of attack capability without blowing up any ships. What then?

Focus on the moment. Don't think about that. He fires thrusters and turns on his head. His sensors can't find a target, but the others must be out there somewhere. Elio flies on. A piece of an old satellite hurtles toward him. He's not watching for space junk. The metal clips his belly as he performs an evasive maneuver. The seat shudders, but a calm, robotic voice informs him that no real damage has been done. He sighs in relief and keeps searching.

Twenty minutes later, Elio stumbles upon a dogfight. He pulls up hard and slips behind a good-sized asteroid. His cameras adjust. If he stays partly exposed, he'll catch the end of the battle. It comes quickly. The fighters zip past each other and arc around to face off again. One fires. The other dodges without expending fuel. Elio calls up the stats. Looks like the second pilot already used his last laser rounds. He's dry. The first pilot fires again. The weaponless fighter erupts in flame.

Now, Elio thinks. The winner can't have much firepower left. Elio leaves cover. Sights come up on the screen, red circles that pulse as his gunner system homes in on the enemy. The opponent sees him. She arcs around and fires.

Too soon. You're fast but not patient enough. Your guns didn't have time to accurately pinpoint where to aim. The red pulsating circle becomes a steady curved line. *Now!* He presses the fire button. Lasers streak out ahead of him. A moment later, the opposing shuttle explodes. But the crafts are too close, and shrapnel streaks toward Elio. No time to gloat. He's too busy dodging flying metal. The screen bucks, but once again a mellow voice informs him no permanent damage has been done.

Four planes left.

No, two.

Somewhere out there, two shuttles have blinked each other out. He wishes he could have seen it.

Elio flies.

Space is so beautiful. Though it's not real, he pretends he's the last person in the galaxy. Stars shine like tiny campfires, and he imagines Mama, Papa, Buela, and Buelo sitting at one, watching him. Are they proud he's making something of himself?

The edge of the screen flashes. Confusion interrupts the daydream. Then he understands. It's his metal wing catching a glint of sunlight. The last two fighters come at him moments later from both directions. Have they teamed up? He doesn't believe that's possible. The consoles aren't linked.

Acting on instinct, Elio brakes hard. Laser fire streaks past the nose of the shuttle and leaves black burn marks along it. The seat shakes so violently he's sure they got him, but the screen doesn't fade into red fog like it does when a player dies.

The ships arc around and fill the whole screen. Their wings almost touch as they come at him, plenty close enough to lock on and fire. If he doesn't do something unexpected, he's toast. *Milk-toast.* Buela's voice floats into his ear. There's a smile in it, and Elio echoes that smile. He shuts down all systems. A warning light flashes in the screen's right top corner, but the game doesn't stop him. Free from thrust, his ship tilts, wobbles, and drifts randomly. Milk-toast.

Elio's opponents must think he's been disabled somehow. He imagines their thumbs hesitating on fire buttons. They don't want to waste ammunition if he's already dead. He wants so badly to power back up, to streak at them with guns blazing. The old Elio would have done it, but perhaps he's learning control. He counts to five and waits.

Now. Papa's voice, whispering in his ear. He flips the power back on, fires up his thrusters, spins and dodges at the same time. He ducks beneath the twin ships, pulls a tight turn behind them, and blasts all the rounds he's got left. Streams of light dance away. Exorbitant, reckless bursts.

Luckily, he doesn't have to keep this up very long. By the time he runs dry, both confused pilots have taken lethal hits. Their ships make soundless puffs as they hit atmo.

Disco lights and bells erupt in the sims room. Elio is back in the Arcade, back to reality. He blinks, dazed and triumphant. Someone helps him out of his seat. His legs shake. Outside the sims room, he hears Mila shouting a war whoop.

On to the finals.

Elio talks to a reporter, has his picture taken, and finally sneaks away to meet Mila in the hallway leading to the bathrooms. She wraps her arms around him and gives up her second kiss. It's longer and better than the first. When they come up for air, Elio murmurs, "What would you have given me if I'd lost?"

"I knew you wouldn't lose," she answers with a brilliant smile as she pulls away.

He lets her go reluctantly. "Where's Juke?"

"He said he had something he needed to do. You hungry?" She gestures toward a cooler she's set down against the wall.

"I thought I'd get a bite at the concessions."

"Are you crazy? You'll be mobbed. You're a celebrity now, at least a local one. I packed sandwiches. We can eat right here."

"In the hallway?"

"You too good to eat on the floor? At least we'll have some privacy." She sinks down and opens the cooler.

He notices she isn't dressed in her usual dirty jumpsuit. She's wearing tight black slacks and a silky black top, sleeveless and glittering with silver threads that bring out the silver of her eyes. She sits cross-legged and hands him a sandwich.

Elio drops down. "You look nice." He takes the food and unwraps it.

Mila slides a soft drink his way. "I'm off work today. Planned it that way so I wouldn't miss the tournament."

"Are you wearing that just for me?" He eyes her low neckline with appreciation.

"No. For that poor guy you shot down in the first five minutes." She rolls her eyes.

"Did you know any of the other semi-finalists?" He cracks the tab on his pop and takes a sip.

"Sort of," Mila says. She raises an eyebrow. "If you're wondering if I was close to any of them, I *could* tease you and say *yes*, but I'd be lying. I'm in your corner, Elio. Only yours."

Heat curls in his belly but doesn't stop there. Her words feel like sipping Mexican chocolate before a fire, safe in the old apartment. "Thanks, Mila. I appreciate that." He levels a look at her. There's no sexual edge, only him trying to show his gratitude. Mila's cheeks flush. This surprises and pleases Elio. He can't help adding, "There are several creative ways I could show my appreciation if . . ."

She slaps his arm but doesn't add a smart remark to dash his hopes.

33

ELIO

Compared to the semi-finals, the final competition is brief. Elio's matched against a girl, six feet tall and muscled like a bodybuilder. He catches a glimpse of her during their interviews but doesn't want to put a face to his opponent, so he looks away. It's Mila's image he focuses on as he climbs back into his game console.

Elio wishes Clera were here. He wants her to witness his victory, to share it with her. And where has Juke disappeared to? He didn't show up to congratulate Elio after the semis. It's not like the guy is his best friend, but still.

I'm thinking too much. Elio closes his eyes, breathes from the diaphragm, counts in his head.

Clears his mind.

This fight is in atmo above the city streets of New Chicago. The computer voice warns Elio that if he flies too high, he'll hit a force field that can destroy him as easily as laser fire. How high is that? Hopefully, his systems will warn him before he reaches max elevation.

Stats for him and his opponent appear in the screen's left-hand corner. There's his gamer tag, Zues604, and hers, Lilsbreath9. *Weird name.* The console revs up. *Focus, Elio. You're not done yet.*

It's different flying around without the endless breadth of space to cradle him. He spots Lil in the far distance, but she's not gunning for him, so he decides to test the limits of his cage. He's two thousand feet up when a warning voice says, "Careful, pilot. You aren't in outer space this time." He edges downward. Now he knows. Two thousand feet. Maybe Lil is out there doing the same thing as him, calculating limits. Elio drifts low. It would be easy to get distracted by the city spread before him, with its clusters of skyscrapers, winding river, motley neighborhoods with patchwork squares of green parks, and eastward, Lake Michigan. Golden flecks speckle the water. A few ferries cruise across blue depths, white wakes following like tails.

A streak of laser fire shoots along his wing. *Hells.* Lil has attacked while he gawped at the scenery. Elio drops, and a flare erupts across his screen. He's hit, but not fatally. The blast skimmed along the outer covering of the shuttle like a flesh wound. Elio kicks in reverse thrusters and swings around. His thumb hovers on the fire button, but he changes his mind and drops into the maze of buildings. He slips sideways between two skyscrapers. Let her chase him there.

Lil does. He's hoping she'll miscalculate and crash into the mirrored windows of a high-rise, but she didn't get to the finals through carelessness. She tails him so smoothly that he gives up on his original idea. Shooting skyward, he flies into cloud cover, levels, and turns toward the lake. His hands grip the steering column with white knuckles. At the water, he arrows down until he's almost skimming white-flecked waves. He decelerates to half power and allows Lil to fly closer—but not so close she can lock onto him.

Elio closes his eyes, imagines his next move. *Now.* He pulls back on the throttle and shoots straight up. The seat shakes like it's coming apart. He grinds his teeth and pushes his craft to her limits. If this were a real shuttle, the sudden g-forces would have made him black out, but it's only a sim.

In another violent maneuver, Elio spins and dives downward. The other ship swings into his periphery. Too close! He's surprised but reacts quickly. Instinctually. Not bothering to lock onto his target, he fires. A line of smoking holes appears in Lil's craft. He's so close he can make out her avatar through the cockpit window, a dark-haired girl with wide, staring eyes. They look at each other for a second before a panel flies off her shuttle. Elio swears and pulls up to avoid hitting it. He catches a round of returning fire.

A warning voice announces, "Your wing is on fire, pilot. Alert. Your wing is on fire."

The steering column bucks in his hands. He forgets about Lil and dives for the water. He rolls so the left wing slices through waves, and the warning stops. Thick smoke fills the screen. Elio increases elevation, wobbling. He turns and heads back to the landing strip where they started. The shuttle wants to spin, but he holds firm. The pilot's chair shimmies. Elio's teeth grind together, and he bites his tongue. Tastes blood. If he doesn't set his boat down quick, he's toast. And not milk-toast this time, but a raging pyre of *burned* toast.

The landing strip swoops into view. Elio flips the landing gear switch and eases toward the tarmac. The ground angles toward him but levels at the last moment. He bounces, pulls back on the throttle, and slows to a stop. Elio knows this near crash wasn't real, but his heart pounds like it was. He gives himself a moment to breathe. Only then does he glance at the stats on the screen. Lilsbreath9 has been destroyed.

———◦———

Elio barely remembers the next few moments. It's all noise, cameras flashing in his face, and reaching hands as security guards escort him down a back hallway to a theater he's never seen. It might be where the Arcade shows immersive movies, but today it's filled with spectators who want to see the live lottery drawing.

He can't believe he won—though he's told himself he would ever since he watched that first Dec Gaston vid. Winning has become a desperate obsession. Now that it's happened, he isn't sure what to think. The prize isn't credits, just this single chance for a new life.

The guards seat him up front in a roped-off area reserved for lottery ticket holders. People from all over the United States surround him, most of them teens. Two-thirds are boys. All are exactly like him, crossing their fingers and trying not to throw up. All are winners, but of something intangible. A chance. That's all anyone wants. Just a chance.

An announcer in a purple smartsuit and heavy makeup quiets the crowd with raised hands. He makes inane remarks and prepared jokes. Elio barely notices. *Come on. Get on with it.* His hands are balled fists. One of his eyes twitches. He still tastes the iron of his blood.

Finally, the announcer waves Dec Gaston out on stage, and the crowd goes wild. Some of them probably came only to see a celebrity, but Elio doesn't care about Dec. He cares about the marble stand sitting stage center. The Mason jar filled with slips of paper has been placed on top.

Dec looks older in person, a bit gray around the ears, a bit paunchy around the middle. As he approaches the stand, he holds up the last lottery ticket. Dec peers closely at the scrap. A dramatic silence louder than Elio's thundering heart ensues. Gaston waves the slip, then drops it into the glass jar.

He goes off on a rant about the value of the Arcade and competition, followed by another about his many philanthropies and how they've helped underprivileged youth. The crowd shifts restlessly. Dec finally pauses to wipe his forehead with a silk cloth pulled from a vest pocket and asks, "Are you ready to see who will be the owner of a brand new Class X Tourist Shuttle bound for *Calliope* and a new home on Vishnu?"

People cheer and whistle and hoot. It takes a moment for the announcer, who's been standing near Dec's side during this spiel, to silence them. Dec digs a hand into the jar and swirls the papers around for a while. Elio is annoyed. Can't the guy just get it over with?

Finally, Gaston pulls one slip out between two fingers and studies it. He smiles broadly and reads, "And the winner is Yara Okiro from New York City West!"

More wild cheering, but not from anyone near Elio. The faces closest to him dissolve into static. A scream builds in his chest. He feels an explosion coming. It takes all his willpower to push it back. He clenches his fists and closes his eyes. When he opens them again, Yara, a slim girl around Elio's age who looks part Asian, part Indian, is hurrying up on stage. Dec grabs her around the waist and embraces her. He plants a too-long kiss on her cheek and holds up her arm like she's the winner of a prize fight.

Elio barely notices. The world fades into static again. The crowd noise muffles. His best day ever has become the worst.

He doesn't remember leaving the theater, swept along by a raucous crowd. A few people pat his shoulder in commiseration. He ignores them. He wants to get home and pretend he never entered this stupid tournament. There isn't even prize money to console him. Fulfilling his dream was the prize, and that has gone up in smoke.

34

ＥＬＩＯ

Juke appears out of nowhere and plants himself in front of Elio. "We need to talk." He's not his usually flashy self, which gets Elio's attention and distracts him from his dark mood. He follows Juke outside. Juke hurries across the parking lot, taps his Skinpad, and a cherry-red sports car's lights flash. The locks click. Juke swings the driver's door wide. "Get in."

"I'm not going anywhere with you, Juke. I'm not in the mood for company."

Juke frowns at him over the hood of the low-slung roof. "There's nowhere else as private as my car, hom. What I have to share can't be known. I'm not asking you to go party with me, simply have a conversation."

Elio considers this. He feels like hitting something—or maybe jumping off a cliff. He doesn't feel like listening to Juke. And yet—what can Juke have to say that's so sage? Elio slides into the seat. He'll give the guy five minutes, and if this "conversation" doesn't go anywhere he wants to follow, he'll leave.

Juke slips in and pushes the door lock. A shiny black interactive screen covers the dashboard. The seat cushions conform around Elio's body and send a jet of cooling gel beneath his legs. Flower-scented air flows from the vents, and Juke hasn't even given a *start* command. He taps his Skinpad again, and the windows darken.

Elio asks, "What's so important that we had to discuss it out here?"

Juke lets out a breath. He checks the rearview mirror, settles back, purses his lips. His fingers thrum against his pant legs. Finally, he says, "I told you about my skills, right? How I make money? Most of it doesn't come from Mommy and Daddy, I can assure you." His voice sours.

Normally, such words would make Elio curious. He knows so little about Juke's personal life. But defeat fills all the space in his brain. There's no room for anything else. "So?"

"I've been interested in Dec Gaston for a long time. How he got his money. How he keeps it. The guy wasn't born rich. He's a self-made man, something almost unknown in this country. Do you follow pop culture?"

Elio scowls. "Not really."

"Well, Dec is known for being a ladies' man. His latest conquest isn't some glamor girl—more of a call girl, actually—a low-class sex worker out of New York City. Imagine my surprise when I learned that this girl was attending the New Chicago Sims Tournament, but not as some arm decoration. She was brought here as a games champ! A newbie phenomenon! Kind of like you, actually." Juke cuts a glance at Elio. Then he returns to studying the other cars in the lot. His fingers ball in a fist, flex, and continue drumming his thigh.

Cold coalesces in Elio's chest, spreading to his arms and legs.

"I've been suspicious about Dec and this whole 'I'm an old-fashioned guy, and we're doing this lottery the old-fashioned way' thing. It doesn't jive with his online persona. So, while you were playing in the finals, I decided to do some sleuthing. It was easy. I didn't need any hacking skills other than a lock override. Piece of cake. I saw Dec and his goons go into a green room off the stage and leave the Mason jar of slips locked in there. Once they departed, I jimmied the lock and read the slips."

"Hells," Elio mouths. He thinks he knows what's coming. Something he already suspected but wouldn't let himself believe.

"Oh, yeah." Juke's smile is hard. "I didn't take time to read them all, but every single slip I did study had the same name on it."

"Yara Okiro."

"The one and only. Call girl turned video game champ turned lottery winner. Trained through the sims to operate a shuttle, which she will now fly up to *Calliope*, where she'll claim a berth and leave her poor old planet behind." He sighs and shakes his head.

"But what about her boyfriend? What about Gaston? Why would he be so set on helping this girl get away from him? So far away he'll never see her again?"

"Oh, but he will see her, because he's going, too. I've actually known that for a solid month, though it's not public knowledge. I told you I'd been researching Dec. You didn't think that meant reading the tabloids, did you? My form of research involves hacking into personal communications, and Dec's had a berth booked on *Calliope* since last year."

Elio mutters, "Why did I bother competing? The deck is always stacked against a Slummer."

Juke shakes his head. "Hom! But you're great at the sims! One of the best I've seen, and there's still plenty of money to be had in other contests and tourneys."

Elio's mouth tightens. The urge to hit something unfreezes him. He sits on his hands to keep himself from breaking the windshield. "No. I'm done. Everything I try goes to crap." Familiar, negative feelings rush over him in a tidal wave—the precursor to self-destruction. He feels himself becoming the thing he hates, but he can't seem to stop.

Elio detests the pathetic whine in his voice but continues, anyway. "I tried to get a job. There aren't any. I tried the sims, and that hasn't worked out. The only luck I've had is—" He cuts himself off before he blurts out that he's running packages for Second City. He's not *in* a gang, only obligated to one, which might amount to the same thing.

He waits for Juke's rebuke. No one wants to hang around a loser. But instead, the other boy only asks after a quiet moment, "What about Mila? You two have a thing going now?"

Do they? And how does Juke know to ask? Has Mila told him something? Elio doesn't want to think about her. Doesn't want to remember how her mouth felt on his, how his hands conformed to the curve of her hips. And how he'd been hoping, once he won the tournament, that they'd celebrate with champagne in some swanky hotel. That black, glittery outfit floats before his vision, her thick plait undone and cascading down perfect, peach-sized breasts.

He closes his eyes. "She won't want a scrull like me. Why did I believe I could win that shuttle? Anyone else would have suspected the tourney would be rigged. Isn't that how life works for people like me?" He glances over at Juke, slick and polished as a vase on a shelf. "But you wouldn't know about that. You've never lived in the slums."

"I've got my own problems, believe me. Don't think you're the only one. Did you at least have good parents, though you lost them early?"

"They rode me pretty hard, but yeah," Elio admits. He doesn't want to remember Mama and Papa. He wants to wallow.

"Well, mine aren't what you'd call stellar." Juke's eyes turn hard as obsidian.

Elio acknowledges this with a tight nod. It's all he can manage. He swallows and returns to the topic of Dec. "Won't the public know Gaston rigged the contest now that his girlfriend has won? I mean, isn't that the logical conclusion people will reach? And won't the execs look into such an outcome? Or the feds? The tournament streamed all over the country."

Juke cocks his head. "You really are an innocent, Elio. Dec Gaston is a billionaire. He owns the feds. He owns this city's execs. He's one of the president's biggest donors. No one is going to accuse him of rigging anything."

Elio hardly listens. "There's no way out of the slums. I'm not on the South Side anymore, but I'm deeper in rat shit than if I still lived there. The more I try, the lower I sink. It's like struggling in quicksand."

Juke lays a hand on his shoulder and squeezes. "Let me think on this, hom. There's always an answer, but you have to be smart. Smarter than the execs and smarter than the rich guys." His voice falls to a whisper. "That's the secret to winning."

Elio reaches for the door handle. He's in no mood for advice. He starts to get out but turns back. "Hey, tell Mila I won't be around for a while, will you. And let her know this isn't about her. I'm just no good to be with right now."

"You should tell her yourself, Elio." Juke looks like he wants to add more. He opens his mouth, then clamps his lips together.

"I can't. It won't come out right. I'll mess things up like I always do. My temper takes over my mouth. I'll sound like some pouty child who lost his lollipop. *That'll* make her glad to see the last of me."

"Whether she wants you in her life or not should be her call, not yours. But I can see I'm not moving you." Juke exhales. "Don't do anything stupid, okay?"

Elio wants to laugh. Stupid is his middle name. He grinds out, "I'll do what I have to." He gets out and slams the door.

After he leaves, he doesn't go straight home. He wanders the streets hoping to pacify the monster inside. A light rain falls, turning the downtown streets into a shiny, blurred collage. The air smells of metal. A middle-aged woman in a synth fur stumbles out of a theater, her laughter shrill.

Heels clack on the pavement. The sounds strain his last nerve.

Elio hurries away from the bustling heart of the city. He'll never belong there, though it's his birthplace. He walks south along the river. Rain makes divots in the water. For once, the wind has died, and no ferries clutter the waterway. He leaves the skyscrapers behind and makes his way, eventually, back to the muddy lot that used to be home.

He feels nothing. Did he expect the ghosts of his parents and grand-parents to welcome him? To offer sympathy and advice? There is no peace here, only loneliness. Memories won't soothe his beast, nor can Clera. She believes he's been working, not gaming. And *definitely* not delivering packages for Bodhan. What was in them, leth? He's never tried it but might be tempted right now if it could close that black hole in his chest. Elio hasn't seen Bohdan in a few days or made any runs. The guy's gotten more and more erratic. Something's up, but Elio can't ask what. They aren't friends.

An old piece of yellow caution tape still dangles from a stake where the sidewalk leading to his building used to be. Mama's bones still rest beneath this soil, but they aren't *her*. He'll never hear her voice again. What he'd give for a scold or a hug or a cup of her famous Mexican chocolate. Nothing can ever replace what he's lost.

Elio sinks to his knees, covers his face with his hands, and cries.

Once our world was pristine. Simple. There were beasts of prey, and there were predators. Might made right. Then humans muddied the waters with their philosophies, their watercolor grays, their mathematics. They glorified nature while destroying it. Hypocrites. Leave the Earth to the Earth. Let well alone.

-Mons Vega, Prophet for the earth

35

CLERA

Clera waters the aloe plant she bought after work yesterday. It's small, but the pointed leaves are sturdy. She placed it in front of the boarded living room window and hopes the streaks of sunlight reaching between cracks will keep it alive. She shouldn't be using their precious jugs of water on plants, but this aloe reminds her of Buela, and she knows Elio won't mind. Clera has done what she can to make the condemned apartment into a mirror image of the one she shared with her parents and grandmother. She can't replace Mama or Buela, but she can mimic surroundings she remembers with the aloe plant, a cheap landscape print on the wall, the frayed throw draped over a chair.

Duro rubs against her ankles and demands to go out. She opens the door for him. Panic no longer snatches her breath as she imagines what might be lurking on the other side. Her heart doesn't race. As always, the hallway leading downstairs remains empty. Safe. Elio will be gone all day working overtime at the construction site, and Zavi said he needed to make a trip out of town. He didn't say when he'd be back.

Clera feels at loose ends. She decides to visit the Boba Tea Cafe and bring home two kimchi specials for dinner. Hopefully, Elio will like them as much as she does. The dish reminds her of Zavi, and she smiles. Her thoughts drift to their last encounter in the woods, and her whole body warms.

It isn't like she slept with him, but she would have. Right there, in the middle of a public place, outdoors on a bed of ferns, while Persephone looked down at them as she stepped from darkness into light.

Clera remembers clinging to Zavi, his touch dissolving rational thought, dissolving *her* and replacing the quiet, dutiful girl with a passionate woman. Had this other Clera always been inside, waiting for her moment? Her arms had *clutched* at Zavi, her breath unraveled in gasps. His had, too, hadn't it? And didn't he draw her closer, deepen the kiss, moan with helpless need?

They'd seen each other once more before he left. He was restrained as they walked along the forested paths, but when they found themselves back under the arms of Persephone, he'd given her such a look, eyes like blue flames. She traced his lips with her finger. When he hadn't moved, she'd followed the touch with her mouth.

They kissed only a few seconds before he drew back. Voice husky, he told her, "Clera, slow down. I still want this, but the timing isn't great."

"What? Are you hurting? I thought your spine was healed."

"It's not that." He half-laughed. "I just . . . there are things happening that . . . I'll know more after I see Grandfather this weekend."

"What?"

"I can't explain right now." His hands squeezed her waist, then set her aside. The embers still flamed in his gaze, but the rest of his body spoke a different language.

Clera felt foolish. Wanton. Disappointed. Embarrassed. She stared at him, saying nothing.

"I really like you, Clera, and if we're going to have a relationship, I want to do it right. There are things you don't know about me, and my future isn't clear right now."

He was correct. Of *course* he was. Hadn't she been telling herself this relationship could never work? Hadn't she basically said that last time they kissed? Yet she couldn't help the contradictory words that spilled out. "Am I too poor for you? When I kissed you, I wasn't thinking of money, Zavi."

"What? No." He'd shaken his head. "It's nothing like that."

"Then you'll have to be more specific." The last bud of passion died. Her voice came out sharper than she wanted.

"Let me go, for now, and I'll talk to you when I get back."

"Fine."

"Don't be mad."

She managed a smile. "Of course, I'm not. You go and do what you need to, and I'll be waiting."

This made him grin back with a hint of relief.

Clera hopes she didn't scare Zavi away. She considers this possibility as she makes her way to the Boba Tea Cafe. When she enters the shop, the scent of Korean spices envelopes her. Soo Yun stands at the counter. An old couple have taken the window booth where Clera first spoke with Zavi.

Soo Yun's face lights up. Clera smiles back.

"How is life at the greenhouse?" Soo Yun calls out.

Clera walks to the counter and fills her in except for the part about Zavi. She's relieved when Soo Yun doesn't mention him. "I need two kimchi specials to go."

"Sure thing." Soo Yun winks. "Zavi's made you into a believer, hasn't he. Boiled cabbage isn't too appetizing on its surface, but when you put our special Korean sauce on it, presto! Amazing." Her face falls. "Too bad more people don't see it that way. The business is struggling, as you can tell." Her voice sinks to a whisper.

Clera looks around, nodding. "I would talk the cafe up at my workplace, but I hardly see anyone, so I don't think it would help much. Do you have time to sit?"

Soo Yun shakes her head. "Afraid not. Appa has gone beyond the gates to meet my sister. Can you believe it? We haven't spoken to her in ages. Anyway, I'm the only one here."

"Oh, that's fine," Clera assures her, though she's disappointed. She wants to ask more about Soo Yun's sister but decides not to. If Soo Yun wanted her to know, she would have already explained. They chat about inconsequential things while her friend prepares the kimchi, puts it in boxes, and slips them into a bag.

Clera scans her digi-ring. It's a satisfying feeling to do so without wondering if the pad will reject her with an *overdrawn* notice.

"I hope things work out with your sister," Clera says, and then she's out in the sunshine again. Clouds rim the western sky, but the storm will probably hold off until tonight. Not wanting to go back to the apartment yet, she walks the streets—only the bustling places, where Arabic men sell kabobs from wheeled carts, electric trams whiz past on sparking tracks, and small children tug at adult hands and gaze longingly toward the taffy pullers and donut fryers. These people are the middle class, that sliver of New Chicago's population balanced between poverty and luxury.

Maybe I can be one of them. If I save enough, we could move to a real apartment. I'll take Duro and my plant, buy a security system, set down real roots, even marry someday. Her thoughts return unbidden to Zavi, but she banishes him from her mind. It's too soon. Way too soon.

Clera doesn't return to the apartment until her legs ache and she feels a blister coming on her right heel. She's tired and inattentive when she walks into *lad's Ice ream* and trips over a body.

She falls to her hands and knees and twists her head around. Empty eyes stare at her without seeing. Blood cakes a half-severed neck. The unfamiliar face is the color of chalk dust.

Clera rears back. She jumps to her feet, eyes darting every place at once: the dark stairway, the cracked mirror, the shadowy corners. Everywhere but at the body. She wants to run outside to escape, but is that any safer? Night's coming on. She wishes she had a weapon.

Edging away from the corpse, she forces herself to take a second look. The young man sprawls on his back. He's lanky. Poorly rendered tattoos cover his arms, and he's dressed in a blood-spattered tee and baggy black pants. His ratty dreads need redone. Blood pools beneath them. A broken metal chain lies next to the body. Is he Second City? Is his presence here a coincidence? Or a warning?

Clera dashes to the stairs. She takes them two at a time, unlocks the apartment, and yells for Elio, but she feels the emptiness even as she calls out. Her voice sounds thin in that hollow, lifeless space. She grabs a blanket from the bed and heads back downstairs.

The body still seeps blood, but there's no smell. Had she come home earlier, she might have witnessed a murder or been another victim of one. She starts to drape the corpse, to hide those lifeless eyes, but pauses when something white catches her eye. The stranger's hand resting on his stomach clutches a note. Clera snags it with two fingers, then lets the sheet flutter over him. She runs back upstairs, goes into the apartment, and slams and locks the door.

She can't draw in oxygen. Leaning against the door frame, Clera forces slow breaths through her nose. That helps. Maybe she's made the wrong move, hiding up here. She could go to Soo Yun at the cafe, but the idea of leaving the apartment makes her chest tighten with old panic. Besides, she has to wait for Elio. If only she had a Skinpad, she could contact him, warn him. But there's no way to let him know what he'll be facing when he walks in. She has no idea where the construction site is. All she can do is sit here and pray that the Second City aren't hiding outside, ready to jump her unsuspecting brother.

Clera sinks into a chair. She left the bag of food on the table. She opens it, then closes it again. The spices make her want to vomit. Swallowing, she pushes the bag away and tries to think.

Possibility one: the body has nothing to do with Elio. He'll come home, see the stranger, and help her drag the corpse outside to the dumpster. She feels guilty at that thought. The young man is someone's son, someone's husband maybe. They'll be waiting for him right now like she's waiting for Elio. Perhaps the murder victim was totally innocent, or he could be part of the Second City, but he doesn't deserve to be left in a pile of ancient food scraps and rat droppings.

Possibility two: Elio *does* know the dead man. He wasn't left on their doorstep accidentally but as a message. She remembers the slip in her hand. Suddenly, she doesn't want to know what it says, but she unfolds the note and holds it close to the dying light from the window.

Elio Diaz,

Congratulations on your promotion. Report to the L Train station located next to the old Ristorante Bona Fido tomorrow at ten. Hint: You might want to clear out of your unsanctioned housing SOON!

The note crumples in her hand and falls to the floor.

Duro meows. He slipped in behind her unnoticed. The cat bats at the note, then sets up a plaintive demand for the treat he's come to expect. Like a robot, Clera rises, scrapes leftover chicken onto a plate, fills his water bowl, feeds him. Afterward, she stands at the window, arms folded. She stares out between the boards. The only movement is the wind tossing old garbage down the deserted street. A few raindrops splat against shards of glass that still cling to the window frame. *Elio is part of Second City. My brother.* This thought ping-pongs around her brain, gaining speed and strength. Shock turns into anger.

And fear.

Where is Elio, *really*, right now? If he didn't tell her he joined a gang, what else has he left out? Or lied about? The construction job? At least it appears Second City haven't already killed him. She knows where the abandoned Italian restaurant sits, tucked behind an empty patio with bent iron railings near an abandoned subway hub.

Clera looks out the window for a long time. Duro curls on the bed and falls asleep. The pungent kimchi smell fades. Rain patters for a bit longer, then dribbles to an end, but her worry and rage grow and grow until she must stop herself from carving nail marks into her palms.

The lock clicks a little after Clera finally lies down, still dressed, tired but unable to doze. She jolts upright as her brother comes in. His footsteps tap down the hallway, but he doesn't call out. The solar lamp silhouettes him in the bedroom doorway. He's an outline, a paper cut-out, an almost-man she doesn't recognize anymore.

"Sorry I'm late," he mutters, moving inside. There's a crumpling sound when he steps on the note. "What's this?" He picks it up, flattens it, holds it close to read. "Clera—"

"Was any of it real? The construction job? Working overtime today?"

There's hardly a pause. "No." The bed squeaks as he sinks down on it, the note balled in his hand. He sounds exhausted. Defeated.

She holds on to her anger. It's the only thing keeping her from falling apart. "Aren't you going to say anything about the body?"

His head jerks around. "What are you talking about?"

"You couldn't have missed it. It's blocking the way up the stairs. *The body.* I covered it with a blanket."

"There's no body." He pauses, then adds slowly, "I might have felt something wet beneath my boots, though. I thought it was water from a leak."

She slides to the foot of the bed to study his face. For the moment, fear wins out over anger. "The Second City must have come back and moved it."

His voice finds her in the semi-darkness, charged with urgency. "Clera. Tell me everything. You aren't making sense."

So, she does. He makes her describe the dead man in detail.

Elio rubs his eyes. His shoulders slump.

"Did you know him?" Ice trickles into her voice.

"Yes. I was working for him off and on." He runs a hand through his hair. "I tried to get a real job, Clera. I swear. But no one was hiring. Bohdan showed up and offered to let me make occasional package runs for him. I was working for *him*, not Second City. I've never joined a gang."

"They seem to think you have." She glances at the note, then stares back at him, her words unflinching. "Drugs, Elio. How could you, when you see what they do to people? Have you forgotten those leth-heads huddled in doorways, frozen solid sometimes after a bad winter night?"

"It might not have been leth," he argues, but they both know better. He sighs. "I was desperate. Thank God they didn't hurt you."

"I was up here while they were a *floor below*, removing the body." Tears threaten to choke her, but she holds them back. "Why would they do that, Elio?"

He shrugs. "How would I know? Maybe he has a family down in the sewers. Boh wanted me to become part of Second City and go live with them. He said it would be better housing than this condemned building, but I refused."

"So noble of you," she scoffs and picks up the note he dropped on the covers. "And what about this end part? It sounds like a threat. We're being told to leave. Where will we go?"

"Forget about that for a minute, will you?" Elio swallows. "I haven't told you everything, and you might as well know all my secrets." He explains about the Arcade, his win that wasn't, the rigged tournament, where he's been for the past few hours.

It's too much to take in all at once. Clera's mind spins. Finally, she settles on the most surprising thing. "You want to leave Earth? To fly to some other solar system? And you never mentioned this before? Were you going to invite me along?"

"Of course! I didn't tell you because I knew you'd react this way. Come on, Clera. We both know how you are. You like life neat and tidy. You've got your routines, your safe places. And maybe that's enough for you, but it isn't for me. I want more out of this life. We get so little time, and I'm willing to risk what I have to make life worth living. Are you?"

Her rage dissolves like old snow under a spring shower. "I like my job at the greenhouse." The words sound pathetic, defensive, a poor answer to her brother's call to be brave.

"You aren't making enough to get us out of a condemned apartment. Even if you manage it, we'll be back living in some slum. And what will I do? Is there another job at the greenhouse waiting for me? Look around, Clera." His voice softens. "Can't you see what you've done? Even that old print you hung on the living room wall looks just like one Mama had at our old place. You're trying to recreate the past, but it's gone. Our parents and grandparents are gone, and so is our old life. We have to do what we can to create something new."

"But how, Elio? Not by joining Second City, surely."

"No." His brow knits. He sits, considering. "I messed up there. I'm going to have to meet with them."

"No, Elio!"

He takes her hands. "Clera, they won't leave me alone otherwise."

"But what if they don't let you leave? What if they own you now?"

"Then I'll have to do what they want until we can think up a new plan to get away. And by 'away,' I mean out of New Chicago. Either onto *Calliope*, or if nothing else, out of the city and beyond reach of the gangs."

"We don't know how far their influence extends."

"We've been ignorant about everything, Clera. That's our biggest weakness. But I'll start being smarter, I promise. Please, don't hate me." His voice sinks. "I need you."

She withdraws her hands. They sit cold on her lap, but the trembling has stopped. "I don't hate you, but I need to trust you, Elio. No more secrets. We're in this together. I'm going with you tomorrow."

"No!"

"Yes."

He falls quiet, then says, "Maybe we shouldn't be staying here tonight. That last part of the message sounded like a threat. What does 'SOON' mean, anyway?"

Clera ponders. "How about we pack go-bags so we're ready for anything and try to get a few hours of sleep. We can head out at dawn. If we have to find new housing, better to do it in daylight." She listens to her calm voice and wonders, *who are you?* Can she abandon this safe cave they've built? Maybe Elio's right. She holds onto the past when she should be looking to the future. When she should be thinking big, not small. As big as the galaxy, perhaps.

36

SOLAST

The prototype shuttle is the best thing that's happened to Sol since her return to New Chicago. It's the perfect home: pristine, comfortable, and she has the pick of six cabins to sleep in. Best of all, no one else has discovered it, and her theft of the remote that opens the hatch and rolls the metal stairway down has apparently gone unnoticed. The only bad thing is that she's been forced to become nocturnal. She waits until midnight to leave the blue-scaled boat while the neighborhood sleeps, then returns before dawn. She drowses the day away, which was hard at first but has gotten easier since she stole a sleep mask at one of the downtown boutiques. Later, she reads from the free app on her Skinpad, cleans up, plays games, and searches for signs of Anton on the internet.

Except he isn't Anton anymore. He's Mons Vega. A pretentious name. She looked it up. *Mons* is Latin for "mountain" or "celestial body." In astronomy, *Vega* is the northern pole star, or the ruling star, and in many cultures, a source of worship. *So you want to be a god, Anton? I can help you get back to the heavens, fallen angel, but you won't like my methods.*

She's all talk, and she knows it. Despite her research, she's not pieced together where Anton lives, his habits, or if he has a family. He's all over the chatrooms and media, but mostly as a news story, a mysterious vlogger, a nebulous ghost lurking among fanatic followers that seem to know as little about him as she does. He's clever, her nemesis. But so is she. One day he'll make a mistake, and she'll be waiting.

Meanwhile, Sol has gradually transformed the shuttle into a sort of home, if a spartan one. She has blankets, pillows, and one solitary succulent in a palm-sized clay pot that doesn't need much water. She leaves a shade cracked in her cabin to give it sun. Her food and water stay in the cargo space located beneath the floor of the hold. She keeps a few other valuables there, too: the silver crucifix her father gave her when she was ten, a bent and faded picture of the mother she never knew, a few spare articles of used clothing, the razor she uses to keep her head shaved and free of lice, the bucket where she defecates and urinates and which she carefully dumps down a storm drain each night.

Sol has explored every inch of the craft. It's a science vessel, she judges from the lab. Everything inside sparkles with never-used perfection. Up a flight of stairs, the bridge is one giant, sleeping computer, with leather smartseats and lots of handholds along the curved walls for nil-gravity. Sol longs to take a closer look at the controls, but thick windows bank the whole pilot's area. Even at midnight, they make her feel too exposed, so she remains on the main level.

Thank the sweet gods the clinic gave her a Skinpad, or she'd go crazy with boredom. Besides reading fiction from the free library app, she's discovered loads of articles relating to this boat. It's not just a showpiece to pull paying customers into the aeronautical museum. The ship can really fly. Those solar panels on the hull that make it shine like a sapphire (not that she ever gets to see that) constantly soak up radiant energy. If she knew what she was doing, she could fire up the engine and break free of the chains that tie the prototype to concrete. But she won't, of course. She hasn't the first idea how to pilot a shuttle.

Sol feels an affinity for the prototype, which she nicknames the *Blue*

Goose. Not a majestic name, but a fond one. She used to feed the geese by the pond at the commune. They could be mean, but she tamed them with scraps and loved the way they waddled along the shore, honking.

She's sorry this shuttle may never get to fly into the heavens and fulfill its destiny. Like her, it's chained to the ground, bound by fate to sit in front of the museum and watch the world pass by.

37

CLERA

Something buzzes like hornets swarming. The hum of tiny motors carries clearly through the broken window, and Clera's senses zing. *Drones!* It's still dark. She's been lying awake, thoughts spinning, but now she sits up.

Elio mumbles, "What's that noise?"

"We have to get out. Now!" She bounds to her feet, slipping on shoes and fumbling for her go-bag.

Then Elio's beside her, pushing his feet into boots. She thrusts a go-bag at him and in clipped tones explains the Second City war games while they hustle down the stairway. They push through the ruined shop's door into an early morning chill. Duro slides out on their heels and vanishes down the alley. A pink horizon signals dawn. The sky has paled, the stars winked out, but the pack of drones blinks like its own little galaxy. It flows down the street, approaching fast. The buzzing echoes in every direction.

She remembers the sewer grate and grabs Elio's arm. "Can you help me lift a heavy lid?" Clera runs into the street. They've only got seconds. She pries at the iron cover, and Elio squats and adds his muscles. The lid groans and shifts. They slide it aside just as the first drone lets loose a spray of pellets. The strike hits their apartment. Glass tinkles. Bricks fall. Smoke billows. The drones light up the side of the building. Something black and cigar-shaped flies through the front window. A moment later, an explosion shakes the ground.

Wood, bricks, and glass pinwheel outward. Elio grabs Clera and drags her into the hole. Somehow her feet find iron rungs, and she half climbs, half falls into the sewer. "Elio!" She stares up, terror raising her voice by an octave. His body blocks the light as he slips down after her. She's barely out of the way before he lands with an *oof*. His boots splash dirty water over her.

The smell of rot steals her breath. It must be ingrained in the pocked concrete. Light from above reveals that the tunnel runs both ways, so low they'll have to bend over to navigate it. But they don't run. They watch the pyrotechnics play out through the open manhole cover.

It's over quickly. The drones' humming fades until only the sound of crackling flames and the smell of burning wood remains. Smoke drifts into the sewer. Clera fans it away and coughs. Her eyes go wide. "Duro! He was out hunting. Come on. We're going back!"

Elio's eyebrows come together. He glances down the tunnel. Water drips somewhere, and dank air curls toward them. "I'll go first."

Debris litters the asphalt. Clera swivels to face their building, and it's like *déjà vu*—the gaping walls, peeled plaster, boards protruding like broken ribs. Thick smoke obstructs the view, but Clera knows the home she tried so hard to recreate is gone. Maybe it was never really theirs, but the sick feeling in her gut says it was. They've been left naked in the streets, exposed and vulnerable. Again.

"Duro!" she calls, but the black cat doesn't appear. Over and over she says his name. She only stops when Elio puts a hand on her shoulder.

"He's not coming."

Losing another apartment doesn't break her, but hearing those words almost does. *Duro's only a stray,* she tells herself. But hysteria bubbles up her throat, anyway. Before it can emerge, Elio turns her into his arms. His shirt smells like smoke. Everything does. But it smells like him, too—that familiar little-brother scent she's known all her life.

Clera doesn't cry. She pulls back and slips her hand into Elio's. He's staring at the flames, face raw with emotion. "My fault," he murmurs.

"No, Elio. It's not." She grips his hand hard. "Second City might have come for us whether or not you ran errands for them. We've been squatting in the middle of their territory like sitting ducks."

"No, Clera. Let me own this." He shakes off her touch. "We both know how I am. You always make the right choice. Everything so clear-cut. I'm the opposite. I can't see ahead, can't judge right and wrong like you. It's all muddy." He laughs, but there's no humor in it. "Maybe I'd have better luck if I did the opposite of what my instincts tell me."

"Elio, feeling sorry for ourselves won't solve our problems. We only have each other. Together, we'll figure out a new plan." She pauses, voice falling to a whisper. "But no more secrets, okay?"

He finally looks at her, eyes filled with self-loathing. "But what will we do now, Clera? Sleep on the streets? Go find a homeless shelter and hope there's room?"

She weighs her options. *You're not friendless. Not like before.* "I have an idea."

When she sets off toward the Fadel Arboretum and Greenhouses, Elio follows without asking questions. That's how she knows the depth of his despair. It douses the last of her anger toward him for lying, turns it into something tender and sad. Poor Elio. He's got so much talent and so little wisdom. But he was right about one thing. She *has* been trying to rebuild a past that died when Mama did. The one good thing she's done is find that job at the greenhouse.

Dawn brushes the lawns and trees with pearly light. They enter the grounds through the side gate, Elio slipping in on Clera's heels once the retinal scanner clicks the lock. A few early birds chirp, and an owl hoots a final call before heading to bed.

Elio blinks and emerges from his dark thoughts long enough to murmur, "This place is beautiful." He looks around. "It's like we left the city behind. I wonder why Second City doesn't claim it."

"Well, that's what all the fences and security guards are here to prevent."

"But they have drones, Clera." Elio frowns. Then he catches sight of the lake and points. "Wow! There's even an island in here! I can't believe you lucked into this job."

She supposes she *did* luck into it. "I'm learning a lot, you know. I think I'd make a great botanist. Mr. Harris, the manager, brought me into his office the other day to congratulate me on how fast I'm progressing." She doesn't mention Gab. He's never complimentary, yet he must have given a good report to Albero Harris, right?

Clera skirts the main building with its dome and wide veranda. She heads automatically to the bungalow where Zavi lives. She still hasn't been inside, but she's seen him going in and out. Marching up to the door, she raps, waits, raps again before realizing Zavi hasn't returned yet. She knew he'd probably be gone all weekend, after all. Elio looks at her with questions in his eyes.

"Zavi's house," she mutters. "But he isn't here."

"What now?"

Clera glances down the row of bungalows. She grimaces, then decides. "Let's try that one." She points. "It belongs to my boss. He's not super friendly, but I don't really know anyone else other than the director. Mr. Harris lives off site, I'm pretty sure." Before she can change her mind, she heads to Gab's place and knocks. After a few seconds, the door swings wide.

Gab stands there, still slipping a shirt over his hairy torso. He tucks a silver chain under the stretchy fabric. Stubble shadows his ruddy cheeks. Gab's dark eyes take in Clera before sliding toward Elio. They narrow, but then he blinks, and she isn't sure his expression changed, after all.

"I'm sorry to bother you so early, Gab. Our home was just bombed by Second City, and I don't know where else to go. I tried Zavi's bungalow, but he isn't back from his grandfather's place yet."

If her words surprise Gab, he doesn't let on. He turns to Elio and introduces himself. Clera feels young and clumsy as they shake hands. Again, there's a shift, something *knowing* in the way Gab studies her brother.

He turns back to Clera. "What do you want from me?"

"We need shelter until I can find another place to live. We lost everything except what we have in our go-bags." She holds hers up so he can see. When he says nothing, she adds, "We aren't lying. Second City came through the place we were staying with their drones."

"Then you must be squatters. Second City territory only extends through Slavland."

"Well, yes," she admits, feeling like a criminal.

Elio breaks in, "Look, man, are you going to help us or not?"

Gab looks him up and down. He steps aside and gestures them in.

Clera gives Elio a watery smile. The door closes behind them, and a dimly lit living room, sparsely decorated with a couch, rocker, and vid screen on the wall, comes into view. Past that, a counter separates the living room from a tiny kitchen with blue laminate cabinets and checked curtains on a bay window.

Gab points down a hallway. "You two can share the bedroom on the left and start looking for other housing when it's light. The bathroom is at the end." He sniffs. "Smells like you could use showers. Extra towels are in the hall closet. I'll be gone most of the day. Don't pry through my things."

How can Clera feel grateful, embarrassed, and affronted all at once? She almost wishes they *had* gone to a shelter. Or to Soo Yun's. She thought of Zavi first, because he's always on her mind. On impulse, she tells Gab, "I'm going to see if we can get into the housing on the Fadel grounds. If that works out, we'll be out of your hair in no time." The tremble in her voice ruins the air of confidence she tries to project.

He shrugs. "You'll have to talk to Albero about that."

Of course. "Right." She tips her chin up. "I'll do that first thing tomorrow."

Gab's smile is almost a smirk. He glances at Elio again, then turns his back on them and disappears into his bedroom. The door slams behind him.

Elio frowns. "That guy is your boss? He's a real scrull, isn't he?"

"Shhh. Keep your voice down. He's letting us stay here, isn't he?"

"I'd almost rather sleep under the stars or in that gazebo I saw by the lake."

That actually sounds nice, but Clera wants a shower. Running water for once. She'd put up with almost any humiliation from Gab to use his bathroom.

They both wash. By the time Clera emerges, it's dawn. Gab's bedroom door is locked, the electric scooter he rides missing from its parking spot by the lilacs out front. Elio rubs a towel through his hair and tosses it into a tiny laundry room across the hall from the bedroom they'll share. "I can sleep on the couch tonight if we're still here, Clera." He runs fingers through his shaggy locks.

"Your hair needs cut. And thanks. I'm tired of sharing a bed with you. No offense."

"Yeah? Well, you snore." He throws a couch pillow at her, suddenly grinning.

"Do not!" She throws it back, but he ducks, and the pillow hits a wall.

Elio picks it up and places it on the couch arm. He studies that pillow like it's a fascinating piece of art. "I have to go meet them, Clera."

"I'm going with you," she answers quickly.

"Absolutely not." He looks up, glaring. "There's nothing you can do to help. You'd only be a liability."

"But what if they're luring you out so they can slit your throat like they did your friend's?"

"Bohdan was only an acquaintance, and if they'd wanted me dead, they'd have already done it."

"So, what do they want?"

"Sounds like I'm part of the gang, Clera. I don't want to be, but I've been working for them. They have all my information, even my DNA." He describes how Boh took his blood. "We have to go along with this for now. But it's one more reason why we need to get out of New Chicago."

"Agreed," she says, surprising herself. Zavi's here. Her job is here. But Elio means more. Family means more.

"Good." Her quick acquiescence makes him pause. "Well, I'd better go."

She rushes to him and hugs him tight. Tears blind her. She whispers fiercely into his ear, "Be careful, little brother. Be so careful."

He pulls back, raising an eyebrow. "Not so little anymore."

"No." She chucks him under the chin. "I'll be waiting here for you."

38

ELIO

The subway steps lead down to a broken turnstile and empty booths where L line workers used to issue tokens. Elio slips through the turnstile. A few solar lights still flicker along the empty platform. A subway car squats on the tracks, the old ads on its side painted over with graffiti and Earther emblems. The other track stretches into darkness.

"You Elio Diaz?"

He turns. A woman stands where empty space existed a moment ago. She must have crept out of the tunnel. Her arms are folded, her face stony. She's taller than Elio and half again as wide. Her middle-parted, straight black hair and lined face give off a fierce expression, like an indigenous statue come to life.

"Cat got your tongue?"

"I'm Elio." He swallows.

"Come with me." She turns and retreats down the tunnel.

Seeing no choice, he follows.

The enclosed space pushes sounds back at him. His footfalls boom like drums. An oily smell mixed with refuse tickles his nose. The woman doesn't seem to care if she loses him, and she almost does. He follows by sound rather than sight. A door creaks open to his right. He stops, unsure. Past a triangle of light, a gruff voice asks, "You coming?" The woman's flat tones identify her as Native American. He thought all the reservation folks had retreated behind their razor wire and quit interacting with the whites once reparations were cut. Did desperation drive her to the city?

Elio hurries to catch up, trips on the iron rail, catches himself. A lit hallway leads away from the tracks. His escort passes several metal doors before stopping at one. She folds her arms and leans against the wall. "Go in. He's waiting for you."

Elio wants to ask questions, but his escort has turned into a statue again. He slips inside, heart pounding.

It's like he's entered an exec high-rise in downtown New Chicago—posh and spotless. A vid screen covering one wall projects photos of Earth that was: deep-flowing rivers which topple off cliffs, fields of rippling grain, seas filled with bobbing icebergs, polar bears lounging on top. There's a big maple desk, an overstuffed leather chair, a sideboard with glass decanters and cut-glass tumblers, and heavy armchairs. Behind the desk sits someone familiar.

Elio freezes. "You," he breathes.

A slow smile spreads across Gab's face. "Me."

Elio remembers Clera's boss pulling his shirt on when he answered the door and how he'd tucked a necklace underneath. *Stupid. I should have known then! Boh had a chain just like that. A Second City calling card.* But would knowing have mattered?

"So, you work for Fadel *and* Second City." Gab doesn't respond. "What do you want?" A muscle tics in Elio's jaw. He wishes he could knock that twisted grin off the man's face and take his sister far away from her precious job. She's been working for a gangster. Hells! For a killer, probably! Does her friend Zavi know? Is he Second City, too?

Gab points to one of the leather armchairs. "Sit."

Elio hates following that command, but Clera's voice floats through his head. *Be careful. Be so careful.* So, he drops into a chair across the desk from his enemy.

Gab folds his hands and places them atop a monitor embedded in the desk. His smile thins into a straight line. "Welcome to the family. We would have greeted you sooner, but Bohdan neglected to inform us that he had invited you in."

"He took my blood. Wasn't that enough of a heads up?"

"We didn't receive it until recently. Not until after we realized Boh had veered off the rails, subcontracted his job, and started keeping secrets. Maybe Bohdan meant to give us your DNA eventually. Maybe he forgot he had taken a sample. The boy was a drug addict himself, you know." Gab's shoulders lift. "It's all water under the bridge now."

Poor Boh. Elio had kind of liked the dread-head. "What do you want with me?"

"It's simple. You know Boh's route, and we need a delivery boy. Keep doing what you have been, only you won't be getting packages from Boh, obviously. It's quite convenient that your sister brought you to me. Saved me some trouble. Did Bohdan never tell you that Second City live with Second City? We're more than a gang. We're a community."

"He told me."

"Did he also warn you not to take lodgings in our territory without permission?" Gab studies Elio's face and answers his own question. "No, I can see he didn't." He sniffs and rubs his jaw. He's shaved, but his beard is already returning. "Well, no matter now. We'll get you and your sister a place to live right on the grounds of Fadel's park, close to my house. A few of the family are already there in the newly printed cottages. You may have noticed them when you strolled in without an invitation."

"Fadel owns the park, not you. Doesn't he have a say in who lives there?"

"But we own Fadel, so that's splitting hairs, isn't it?"

"What do you mean, you own Fadel?" A chill creeps down Elio's spine.

"It's more of a partnership, really. You don't believe the arboretum and greenhouses could exist right across the street from Second City territory without some cooperation, do you? Certain agreements have been made. We don't allow violence or drugs to pass through the fences, and Fadel provides housing and makes certain allowances for my people. Everyone benefits."

Something nudges Elio's mind. He's heard the Fadel name before. Clera's voice wafts through his thoughts. Zavi *Fadel* got her the job at the greenhouse, right? "Is Zavi part of this deal? Does my sister know about this?"

"I don't really care about Zavi Fadel. He's only a grandson. And your sister? Why would she know any more than you?"

Of course not. Stupid question. "She won't stay when she finds out you're using her workplace as cover for your gang. And I go where she goes."

"You go where we tell you." Gab flicks a finger at him. "When you went to work for us, you became part of the family. Here." He reaches into a desk drawer and draws out a heavy chain. It dangles from one finger. "This is for you." He holds it out.

Elio doesn't want to take it. Everything within him screams to loop those links over Gab's head and twist until the man's face turns purple. Elio breathes like Papa taught him. The red before his eyes fades. He takes the necklace, hesitates, then clasps it around his neck. It feels like a manacle against his skin.

Elio forces his face into a marble mask and stares at Gab. He won't explode. He won't run. There could be security cameras, alarms, guards—not to mention the tough-looking woman outside and Gab himself—to contend with.

Elio has been naïve and blind, but now he's got to be smart. Patient. A rabbit frozen in tall grass waiting for the chance to escape.

Gab lays out Second City's rules. Elio lets his mind drift. He pictures Mila. Annoying, intoxicating Mila. What would she think if she could see him now, slave to a gang? How far he's fallen from that single moment of triumph in the tournament! There must be a way out, but he can't see it. He also can't imagine being with her now. A strong girl like Mila won't tolerate weakness and defeat. Her attraction for him will die like an extinguished candle flame when she finds out about this.

Ironic, isn't it, that you want her so much more than you did a few months ago? No matter what, he can't have her now. Any association with him will put her in danger. Second City might use her as leverage against him. He needs to forget about Mila for her sake.

"Elio. Have you understood all I've told you?"

His head jerks up. Gab's hooded eyes regard him knowingly, like he realizes Elio didn't hear a word he said but doesn't care. *If I screw up badly enough to be killed like Bohdan, there will be another poor scrull waiting to take my place. There's no shortage of desperate men in this city.* Elio nods, afraid to speak, afraid of saying or doing something stupid.

"My lieutenant will see you out. Someone will come by the bungalow later today to move you into more suitable housing."

Elio can't breathe until he's back under the open sky. The raptor-eyed guard lady leaves him at the bottom of the subway entrance, and he makes his way alone from there. The sun blinds him, or maybe it's tears. He pulls in a lungful of fresh fall air and tries to forget how badly he's messed up.

Oblivious to what's around him, Elio walks. He doesn't want to see Clera yet. Miraculously, she forgave him for lying to her and supports him. But when she finds out how trapped they are, she might change her mind. At least he knows who her boss really is now and what Fadel's "philanthropy" entails. Until they decide how to handle that knowledge, they'll be housed, fed, and safe. Or as safe as anywhere in the city.

Elio meanders into the touristy downtown area. The streets open onto a square lined with art museums and theaters. Retrofitted lights chase each other around signs announcing, "For one night only!" and "Playing today, award-winning production!" On a plinth in the center of a broad cement plaza set with benches and e-bike charging stations, a giant vid-screen broadcasts local news. An announcer's head appears, tickertape words scrolling below, while an inset screen shows footage of a shuttle launching, *Beatriz* painted on her side.

Remembering what Mila told him about that shuttle, Elio stops to watch. Yearning twists his gut and makes his chest ache. He was supposed to be on a craft like that one, flying up to the U.S. Space Station, where *Calliope* is docked. Soon she'll be heading out, leaving him behind forever, and he sees no way to be on her now. Elio catches some of the words scrolling past. *Beatriz* has begun her last orbit. At its end, she'll set down at New Chicago's Aeronautical Museum to become another empty shell for tourists to gawk at.

What a shame! The boat doesn't look ready to retire. Will Mila be the mechanic who disembowels her? Probably. He wishes he could prevent that from happening. Thanks to the sims, he can fly any small spacecraft. But even if he could somehow steal *Beatriz* before the fuel was drained from her tanks like blood from a body, how would he get permission to dock on one of *Calliope*'s few still-empty berths?

Elio takes a last, wistful look at the soaring spacecraft and turns away.

39

CLERA

Clera sits outside Gab's bungalow in a plastic lounge chair, a glass of real tap water in her hand. She's taken a walk, washed her clothes, pulled weeds from the flowerbeds in front of the greenhouse, all to keep her mind from straying to Elio. Her brother scared, in the dark beneath the streets, confronting his friend's killer. Wait. He hadn't claimed Boh as a friend. Had he been? He didn't seem devastated by Bohdan's death, so maybe not.

Her thoughts leap back to the abandoned subway. She imagines the worst: Elio losing his temper, striking out, beaten and left for dead in some train tunnel. If he doesn't return, she'll likely never know what happened, and she can't think of anything worse. He's all the family she has, more important than Soo Yun or Zavi. Her parents and grandparents would expect her to save Elio from the Second City and from himself.

But she has no answers. Her stomach hurts with worry. Her brain feels like mice are running around in there, getting nowhere, like her plans end up nowhere. She can't see a way out. Not yet, anyway. But there's always a path. You just have to be patient, keep looking for it, and don't give up. She's good at waiting.

Elio finally appears around the curve of a footpath. Clera sighs and stands. She sets her glass on the ground and goes out to meet him, checking for cuts and bruises. When she finds none, she focuses on the heavy chain around his neck. Bohdan had a necklace like that.

She remembers Gab pulling his shirt on. So did he.

The truth hits her as Elio says, "Your boss is one of the Second City, Clera. I'm not the only Slummer working for them. You are, too." His tone isn't triumphant or condemning, simply a flat statement. She covers her mouth. Revulsion crawls over her skin. They stayed in his house, touched his things, and used his shower.

Elio takes her arm. Does he believe she might fall over? Clera doesn't feel like fainting. She feels like hitting something. A million questions form in her head. She homes in on the most important one. "Does Zavi know?"

Her brother leads her back to the bungalow and prods her through the door. "I don't know. Gab only said that Zavi's grandfather made arrangements with Second City—security for his pet project in exchange for housing and, in Gab's case anyway, a job. The Second City can't sell leth on the premises. The gang and their drones will stay away."

"He told you all this? What else did he say?"

They face each other in Gab's living room, arms crossed. Clera listens intently while Elio recounts all he can remember.

"You aren't leaving anything out?" She eyes him suspiciously.

"I promised no more lies, and I meant it."

"They didn't hurt you?"

"No."

"Well, there's that at least."

"I'm so sorry, Clera. About my bad choices, but about your job, too. It seemed like such a great opportunity, but now I don't know. How many workers at Fadel's park are gangsters? They hide these *things . . .*" He tugs on the silver chain, ". . . beneath their clothing, so who knows?" He frowns down at himself. "I feel like a dog with a collar. Maybe this necklace even has a tracker. I wouldn't be surprised."

"But you can remove it, right?"

"Sure, I can, but what good will that do? They've got my DNA, all my personal information. I can't go anywhere that they won't know. Gab says they have connections clear up to the execs, and that could be true if they've made a deal with Fadel." He slumps into an armchair. "I don't know how to get out of this."

Clera sits down beside him. Her stomach unclenches. Elio is back, alive and unharmed. That's what's most important. "We'll think of something. For now, lie low, and don't do anything rash. I know it's hard for you not to act on the first idea you come up with, but I'm asking you to give me time to plan."

"*Calliope* will leave soon, and I really wanted to be aboard her. All that training on the sims, and for what? The chance to lose a rigged lottery."

"Don't talk like that." She can't believe she's trying to comfort him about playing the Arcade. The old her would have scolded, judged, held it against him. But to make a better life, they *must* take chances. She knows this now, just as she knows her brother's strength *lies* in risk-taking. *Calculated* risk is *her* forte. So, she pats his arm and says, "You aren't alone anymore, Elio. We'll get away, but not today. Maybe not tomorrow. I need you to be patient while I think."

"Your idea of escape won't be moving to some new part of the city, right? Because I'm done with New Chicago."

She looks deep into his eyes. "So am I, Elio. So am I."

A man she doesn't recognize shows up a few hours later. He tells them Gab sent him to move them into one of the new 3D-printed cottages. They grab their bundles, lock the front door, and follow him to the other side of the grounds.

It doesn't look like many people have moved into the white, cubical homes yet, but Clera does notice a few signs of occupation—clothes strung from a line, a barbeque settled under a roof overhang that forms a tiny patio, a child's dirty rag doll splayed near a front door.

The man who came for them, an elderly guy with a curved spine and thinning hair, leads them to the third cottage from the end of the first row. He pulls a key card from his pocket and hands it to them. "Yours," he grunts.

Clera starts to thank him, but he's already turned his back.

She looks at Elio, who shrugs. "We might as well go in."

A flutter of excitement rises past the worry for Elio, the sadness at losing Duro, the trauma of displacement. A real house. Even if the Second City exact a price for it. Even if their neighbors might be criminals. *Like us*, she reminds herself and walks under the eave. Two plastic chairs and a little table sit before a black front door. She swipes the key. A green light flashes, and the door swings wide.

Inside the tiny house is a living area with attached kitchenette, and at the back, two bedrooms split by a bathroom. The place smells like vinyl and deodorizer. The floors are rubber planking, the furniture spare, modern, and new. Ugly brown woolen blankets cover the beds, a step up from the mylar blankets they used in the homeless shelter. There's running water, solar panels, a small refrigerator, and a tiny washer and dryer folded into a closet of the bathroom. It's smaller than Gab's bungalow but perfect.

Clera reminds herself that this place is no home, only a waystation. She can't let herself pretend otherwise. There is no going back to what was.

40

CLERA

That evening, Clera makes her way through the fading green shadows to Zavi's bungalow. Gab is nowhere in sight, thank goodness. She wonders how she'll take orders from him tomorrow like their relationship hasn't changed. Can she wear a mask of indifference she doesn't feel? That mask slips across her features now as she knocks on Zavi's door. She has things to say and hard questions to ask. They might not be what he wants to hear.

She knows he's home by the work jeep parked in front of his house. He opens the door at her first rap and smiles, eyebrows raised. Dark circles underscore his eyes, and his hair is tousled. He invites her in.

"You look tired." She glances around.

Zavi's bungalow is Gab's opposite. Though the floor plan matches, he's filled the space with native pottery, warm wood paneling, and plants everywhere, from cacti in painted urns and wandering ivy that creeps across door frames to common orchids with lavender pods just opening.

He waves Clera toward an overstuffed couch the color of rust. "It was a hard trip." Zavi sinks down beside her, not too close but not too far away, either. He turns at an angle to face her, motions smooth, expression pain-free as though his injury never happened. A thought comes unbidden: *For grandsons of billionaires, anything is possible. Maybe even death wouldn't stop you.* Another thought leapfrogs over this one: *Your world isn't mine.*

But seeing him makes her blood heat. Her body wants his despite all logic. Clera clears her throat. "So, what was hard about visiting your grandfather?"

Zavi runs a hand through his hair. "I'm his only grandson, his last living relative minus a few distant cousins. Grandfather likes to control things. Me, specifically. I know he only wants the best for my life, but especially since the accident, he seems to have forgotten that I'm a grown man with wants and needs of my own."

Do his eyes flash on the word, *needs*? Does he lean closer? She recalls how they parted and thinks this must be imagination. He was distant then, opaque. *Let me go, for now, and I'll talk to you when I get back.* She's ashamed of her innocence, her willingness to believe the best of Zavi, to throw herself at him, trusting she knew who he was when she doesn't know him at all.

"You said you'd have answers for me when you returned." She hears the tension in her voice and dials it down. "Did you get the information you needed this weekend?"

"I did, but maybe *directives* is a better word." He pauses, gaze turned inward, like he's picking apart words and parsing them together again, trying to find the best way to, what, let her down easy?

"You can tell me anything. I can take it." There's *definite* tension in her tone now, but she doesn't care.

"Grandfather booked me a berth on *Calliope*. I've got a job as director of the ship's biosphere. I leave in a few weeks."

Clera rears back at the flood of words. She doesn't know what she expected. An arranged marriage, maybe? A hidden girlfriend? That *he's* part of Second City? Or simply that he told his grandfather about their relationship and was shut down? Not this. Never this. "But you'd be leaving forever, wouldn't you? Is your grandfather going with you?"

"No." Zavi's voice darkens. "He sees no future here on Earth, yet he's staying to keep up the fight, do what he can. Like his housing project for the homeless. He says he's old, and this trip belongs to the young. You need to be energetic to colonize a new planet. Technically, he's right. The government has strict rules about allowing berths to people over age 45." Zavi shakes his head. "But grandfather has pull. He could have gotten around that."

How casually Zavi admits that his world is different, that money and power make their own rules. His words reinforce Clera's opinion of him and widen the gulf between them. She forces out, "Your grandfather is right. You're lucky to have this chance, way luckier than me and my brother. Do you know he's been playing the Arcade instead of working? He even won the recent sims tournament, that one where you get a chance for a shuttle and berth on *Calliope*."

Zavi frowns. "You mean Dec Gaston's rigged show? Where, coincidentally, his current girlfriend received a place by his side for the adventure of a lifetime?"

"So, word is out that the tournament was a farce, and Gaston will be on the ship, too?"

"It's all over the tabloids."

"Maybe you and he will become friends." Bitterness drips off the words. But it's not Zavi's fault he was born rich and privileged, or that his grandfather is using his money and influence to get his grandson off-planet before things become any worse. Clera can't even claim Zavi led her on. He was kind. He got her a job. And she paid him back by kissing him. For wanting *more*.

Zavi reaches for her hand. His touch sends tingles up her arm. She wants to hurl herself against his chest. Lurch away. Both at once. He says,

"Please don't be angry. I don't want to go without you. I don't want to leave if it means never seeing you again, Clera. I think I might be, I *am* . . ."

"Don't say it," she warns, pulling her hand away. "I can't bear this if you say you love me. Don't you see? It'll be even harder, though knowing what I do, it was already impossible."

"What do you mean?" Zavi leans back, frowning.

"I found out that Fadel has an agreement with the Second City, Zavi! They are protecting this place in exchange for free housing. My brother and I just moved into one of those new cottages, in fact. Because guess what? Turns out *we're* working with the Second City, too! At least my brother is. We want out, but we're trapped like you, only your cage is a starship. Ours is New Chicago."

"What? I don't—" Zavi falters. He rumples his hair, setting it more on end. He doesn't speak for a long moment but finally asks, "Who told you that my grandfather is working with the Second City, Clera?"

"Gab."

"Gab. Your boss."

"Yes. He's a Second City lieutenant or something. I don't really know how high up. All I do know is that he had our apartment bombed, then gathered us in like so much debris and installed us in one of those printed houses. But at a price, of course. Elio has to make drug runs for the Second City, or he'll end up as dead as the boy he's replaced."

Zavi's mouth falls open, and Clera's anger wavers. Maybe he didn't know about his grandfather.

A trickle of regret sneaks in. "I'm not mad at you," she finishes lamely. "Only at what your family stands for."

His disbelief turns to tight-lipped withdrawal. "And what do we stand for, Clera? Corruption? Unchecked opulence? Using any means to attain our ends? Funny, but I always thought Fadel Industries tried to help the poor, the dispossessed. That's the value Grandfather was continually drilling into me."

"Maybe he had to make a deal with the devil for the greater good." Clera looks down. She picks at a snag in her pants. Zavi didn't know about the Second City. She's deep-down sure of it, and she feels so bad for him. If she'd discovered Buela was secretly making pacts with gangs, how betrayed would she be? "You do believe me, right?"

"I don't know. Gab told you all this? What about Albero? There's absolutely no way he would be involved. A gang murdered his sister."

"I don't know about Mr. Harris. Gab said other Second City members are living in the new housing. He said your grandfather made a deal with them."

"But why would the Second City blow up your apartment? Was anyone hurt?"

Clera fills him in on the things she's hidden: her homelessness, Elio's failure at getting a job, how he started helping Bohdan and hoped the Second City wouldn't notice. But they had. And they'd arranged things so he had nowhere to go but into their fold. "I didn't tell you about our situation before," she finishes, "because I liked you, and I wanted you to like me. I didn't want you looking at me the way people stare at the homeless, like they're ignorant leth-heads, *lesser than.*"

"I wouldn't have, Clera. I swear." He whispers, "You don't think I'm working with the Second City, do you?"

"No," she says firmly. "I didn't know for sure until now, but no. You obviously didn't have a clue about Gab."

"I need to talk to him. And to Grandfather. There must be limits to the deals we'll make to keep this place safe. Why didn't Grandfather believe the gates and security squads would be enough?"

"When you have drones, gates and security people don't mean much.

And I think your grandpa wanted to keep drugs out of his pet project. The other parks in New Chicago are riddled with them. It's where a lot of the deals are made." She hurries on, "Elio and I don't do leth. We've never slept in the parks, either. We thought being alone would be safer, but in the end, nowhere is safe."

"I wish I could take you with me to the stars." His hands ball in his lap. He stares at them, only looking up when she speaks.

"You can't, though, can you? We wouldn't be registered for the flight. And you can't say no to your grandfather. You shouldn't because he's right. Earth is finished, or it will be soon, and he's giving you a chance to help create a new world. It's not something you can reject."

"Clera, you're too good." He slides over and draws her against him. Their knees bump. He rests his chin on her head. "Before I met you, I would have loved the chance to travel through the ARH and explore a new planet. Imagine the strange plants and trees that must exist there! The chance to perform groundbreaking research! But I don't want to leave you behind."

She breathes in his cologne and soaks in the heat of his body. "It's funny," she mumbles against his shirt. "Elio was so sure he could learn to fly on the sims and win the lottery. And he did win! But it doesn't matter. He's always wanted to soar above Earth and explore new places. It was me who was the coward. Me who wanted to play it safe. But that hasn't worked out so well for us." She pushes sorrow back down her throat.

Zavi's arms tighten around her. "I'm so sorry, Clera."

"Don't talk to Gab, okay? It won't come to any good. Neither will confronting your grandfather. He's doing what he believes he must, like Elio when he played errand boy for that murdered gang member."

"But what will become of you both? I can't leave knowing you're stuck here, a slave to some drug lord."

Clera makes herself pull away. "Yes, you can. I'm just some girl from the slums, remember? I schooled out at sixteen. I've been homeless. I've stolen. You'll meet other girls, college-educated, brought up in fancy houses like you probably were. Girls who can relate to you. Ones your family would approve of." She swallows.

He pushes back a lock of her hair. His eyes are sad. "But none of those girls will be you, Clera."

————— ·◦· —————

They don't sleep together. Their kiss goodbye is chaste. Final. She wants more, but it'll be harder then. She'll have a stronger sense of what she's missing. Better to hold on to her anger and bitterness. Better to be stone and protect the tattered remains of her heart.

Zavi's shuttle awaits him on his grandfather's estate south of New Chicago. It's fully automated, programmed to catapult him out of Earth's atmosphere and into space. Clera imagines the tiny craft arcing toward the U.S. space station and the goliath ship, *Calliope*, with its thousands of shuttle docks pockmarked along curved sides. She visualizes the starship, held in place by steel girders while drones with mechanical arms add the final touches.

She envisions *Calliope*, the first American ship of its kind, following her European sister ships toward that spinning ring of eerie lights scientists have nicknamed Alice's Rabbit Hole. When you go down a rabbit hole, you're diving into the unknown, taking a leap of faith. Clera is tired of watching others jump. When will it be her turn? And Elio's?

41

ZAVI

It's amazing how life can kick you in the face just when things are looking up. Zavi remembers being a kid, swimming with Niklas off the Greek coast of the Mediterranean Sea, their summer house a faint, chalky outline atop the cliffs. How simple life had been. How full of possibility. And now? The trip to another solar system he'd have given anything for once no longer appeals to him. He's lost people he cares about. The thought of losing more has changed his perspective.

Zavi recalls Niklas, his boisterous giant of a cousin, so cocksure they would meet again after he flew through the wormhole. *Lycka* is gone, sucked into the ARH, with no word since. What does it mean? Are communications impossible from the other side? *Loki*, the first starship to pass through, never came back, though *Pioneer I* and *II* returned. That's how NASA knew about the red giant system beyond the ring with its string of seven planets: Devi, Vishnu, Shiva, Sati, Parvati, and Ganesha. Two were judged habitable, and Vishnu, second from its sun, has huge green oceans. Is Niklas swimming there right now without him?

He should be excited about the chance to find out, but leaving Clera has ruined any possibility of that. She's come to mean something to him. What exactly, he isn't sure. He only knows that her presence warms him like she's the red dwarf star, and he's Vishnu. All he wants is to orbit around her and soak up her light. Is this a crush? He's had those before, and he doesn't think so. Guess he'll never know. Unlike Niki, he's not confident he'll be back on Earth anytime soon, if ever. He's said goodbye to Clera with no illusions that their parting isn't final. And when he tells Grandfather so long, he won't expect to see him again, either.

Zavi leaves his bungalow and walks through the woods to stand before the statue of Persephone. Looking up, he remembers that day with Clera when she kissed him—the surprise of it, the rush of it, an onslaught of desire pouring over him in a tidal wave. Now, he wishes he could be a marble statue, stone so hard and cold that no loneliness could touch him.

42

ELIO

Gab gives Elio access to a post office box in Slavland. Like everything in the area, the post office has been abandoned. Torch marks score its sides, and wadded paper and torn envelopes litter the tiles. Storage compartments hang open as though people panicked during some surprise catastrophe, dropped everything, and ran. At least some of them did. Rusty blood stains cover the floor.

Elio opens his assigned box and retrieves a brown-wrapped package. He's not supposed to look inside, but screw that. There's not knowing things, and there's *willfully* not knowing. Baggies of brownish powder lie atop their paper wrapping. Drugs. He's helping kill people by distributing this stuff, but what can he do? He has to protect Clera. If not for her, he might flee the city. But they're family, so he won't risk the Barrens. He won't abandon his sister.

Though he promised her he'll control himself and think before acting, it's difficult. Clera isn't the one breaking the law by making illegal drug runs.

Today's job is across the city on the South Side. Maybe Gab sent him there because he's familiar with every dirty street, sag-roofed business, and cracked sidewalk. Elio passes the homeless shelter where he and Clera spent two nights, Ms. Lewenski's darkened, boarded shop where they bought groceries, the library Clera loved to escape to. His goal is the pier, near the spot those Steelheads tried to drown him. It seems like ages ago, but it's only been months. He's turned eighteen. He and Clera have gained and lost several homes. He's won the sims and almost lost his life. Seen death up close and learned what it feels like to meet a goal only to have the prize ripped out from under him.

Why am I in Steelhead territory? Elio wonders for the tenth time. If Steelheads discover that the Second City are dealing on their streets, it might provoke a war. Maybe the Second City want one? They've sure been training, and not only with drones, but with practice clashes. So far, Elio's just the delivery boy, but how long until they give him a gun, and a commander sends him out to kill?

It's noon on a hazy fall day. Waves lap lazily at his sneakers. Seagulls tilt on wind currents, waver, dive for food hidden in the water. A motorboat whips by and swings around. The engine winds down to a gentle growl as the boat floats in, a white wake spreading behind. It grinds into sand. A man jumps out and wades to shore holding a mooring rope. The second man kills the engine, looks around, and slides into the water. He slogs past the first man. Elio steps from the shadowed pilings beneath the pier. The boat has no name, which fits what he was told to expect. It's sleek, made for speed, and he wishes he could try it out.

"The red kite flies high today," he calls to the men. An easy code phrase to remember, though he feels silly saying it.

"Wind's whipping from the west," the man not holding the rope replies. He's dark-skinned with high-boned cheeks and red-rimmed eyes.

Elio knows better than to make further conversation. He whips the package from his pocket and hands it over. A couple seconds later, the deal is done. The drugs disappear into the gangster's baggy pants. The man pulls a pad from his jacket and lets Elio scan his ring. Credits fill the *total* column.

No more is said. The dark man turns away and splashes back toward the boat. Both men clamber aboard. Elio retreats to the pilings. He'll stand there to watch the craft speed off.

He ducks beneath weathered gray boards. Seconds later, a shot rings out. He flinches, feet mired in wet sand.

Another crack. Elio slides behind a slimy piling. Water sloshes over his shoes. He peers out and scans the shoreline. There. Atop a swim shop, flat on his stomach, the sniper sights his target. The boat hasn't been fatally damaged. No one shot, either, judging by the jeers that echo back to Elio. Did the shooter see him, too? *Of course he did.*

The boat zips away and is soon out of range. The sniper turns to scan the pier and the beach. Elio cringes back, thankful he has cover, but he's trapped here. If he tries to leave the way he came, he'll be out in the open and easy to pick off. He hurries through pilings until the trash-strewn water reaches his waist. He's on the opposite side of the pier now and can't see the swim shop anymore.

Elio reaches dry land, steps away from the dock, takes a breath, and dashes up the beach toward a row of buildings that line a seawall. A shot whines again. Something whisks past his ear. He puts his head down and pumps hard. Another shot pings off a metal garbage can next to the empty lifeguard stand. The sand pulls at Elio's feet, slowing him down, but he makes it to pavement before the sniper fires a third time. Dodging a car, Elio darts between two buildings.

He keeps running. His lungs are on fire. Wet pants cling to his legs. A piece of seaweed stuck on his shoe tries to trip him. He weaves blindly through alleyways until finally emerging onto a busy street he recognizes. Elio slows, flags down a smartcab, slides in, and scans his ring. The dash lights up. A toneless voice synced to flashing pulses confirms his directions.

He sags back. His heart slows, breaths calm. He won't bother telling Gab about this. What does the lieutenant care if the Steelheads tried to kill him? It's only Elio's life on the line, and he's expendable.

He should get out. Leave.

No. Not yet.

Elio decides he won't tell Clera about the sniper. He goes to their cottage, washes the rotten fish stink from his jeans, and puts them in the dryer. He tries not to remember how he blew most of his credits on that cab ride. Maybe he'll clue in Gab about the shooter, after all. He needs protection. Do the Second City wear bullet-proof vests? Helmets? Will they give him gear that will make him stick out like a guerilla fighter at a little girl's birthday party?

He's moping over his bad choices when a knock sounds at the door. He peers through the peephole, and his eyes widen. Elio opens the door and ushers Juke into the living room.

Their last conversation didn't go so well. Juke patronized Elio with unwanted advice. He's frankly surprised to see the kid. Has something happened? His heart lurches. "Is everything okay with Mila?"

Juke smooths his perfectly slicked-back hair and ignores the question. A diamond gleams in his right ear. Is that new? What else has changed? Elio feels a pang of regret. He misses the Arcade. There was nothing like sliding into that sims seat and feeling it vibrate as he roared down a runway. And he misses Mila. Cares for her more than he thought he would. He was just realizing how much when he quit the Arcade. Elio'd like to go back, but he's tainted now. He can't risk involving others in this Second City mess.

Elio asks Juke, "How did you find me, not to mention get through

Fadel's security?"

"I came in through the front gates like any tourist interested in plants." He shrugs and grins. "To answer the first question, you were listed as recently having received one of the new Fadel homes for the unhoused. Nice work! Before that was a bit of a hole. Have you been living on the streets until recently? You should have told me, hom! And how did you afford an Arcade pass, anyway?" He wanders around the room, checking out the still-blank walls, the clean counters, Elio's unmade bed beyond an open door.

Elio gives up. He pulls two mineral waters from the refrigerator and hands one to Juke. He sits down on a stool at the counter and cracks the cap.

Juke stares at the bottle in his hand. "No beers? Not even a seltzer?" But he twists his cap and takes a long swig. He settles on the other stool. "So, tell me why I shouldn't be here."

"I thought you weren't listening."

"I always listen even when I don't like what I hear. You're lucky I don't take offense easily." He points the pinky finger of his drink hand at Elio.

"I'm trying to keep you far from this shithole I've made. I'm trying not to drag you down into it."

"Don't worry. The Second City won't want me. I'm not their type. They like the down-and-outs like you. People they can control. Of course, if they found out about my mad computer skills, I'd have to go into hiding. Speaking of which, I've been thinking . . ."

"I'm not interested in another gaming contest, Juke. Unless you can tell me how to get out of New Chicago and leave all this behind, you're wasting your time here."

Juke leans on his elbows. "I may not know how to leave, but I thought you might be interested to learn that, after some effort, I managed to hack a big game—the U.S. government's Aeronautical Science branch. It's a hobby of mine, poking around in the innards of important players." He traces a moisture ring on the counter with his finger.

Elio cups his hands around his bottle but doesn't drink. Why has Juke come here to tell him this? He ponders this and decides he knows. "You're offering your services. You think you can hack into *Calliope*'s manifest and change things. But I don't have a shuttle, Juke. And I can't pay you, either. So why bother with me?"

He shrugs, but a muscle works in his jaw. Juke isn't as relaxed as he'd have Elio believe. "Let's just say I have dreams, too. Maybe even the same ones as you."

"Like shipping out with *Calliope*? What about your parents?"

"My parents? That's rich. Perhaps they're the reason I want to leave, Elio. And maybe I simply want to get off this fell planet. Set out for new worlds. Go where no man has gone before and all that."

"Do you?"

There's a pause. Juke quits studying that wet spot on the laminate and looks up. His brown eyes flash with intensity. He doesn't answer.

"I don't have a shuttle. And I heard on the news feeds that the berths on *Calliope* are practically filled. There's almost no time left before the departure date."

Juke waves these facts away. "I know all that. I also know that you're a stellar pilot. And you're smart. If anyone could figure out how to get himself a shuttle, even if your methods are a bit shady, it would be you, Elio."

"Gee, thanks, but I'm actually not a skilled thief. Truth be told, I've never stolen anything of much value."

Juke grins. "There's always a first time if you want something badly enough." His look turns pensive. "What about your sister? Could you abandon her if a chance came up? Or would she go with you?"

"We stick together, Clera and me. I can't speak for her, but it doesn't matter because *I don't have a shuttle*." He glares at Juke in annoyance. "But thanks for thinking of me, really."

Juke misses or ignores the sarcasm in his voice. "I didn't believe you'd give up so easily, hom." He shrugs. "Well, I've done what I can. And I'm trusting you not to spread any unsavory rumors about my skills. Got it?" He swallows the rest of the water.

Elio takes a drink and eyes Juke. "Sure."

Juke pulls a white card from the breast pocket of his pristine shirt. "I'd give you my data via Skinpad, but you're stuck with that pathetic ring, so here. Don't lose it." He slides the card toward Elio, who picks it up. It's an old-fashioned business card. On it are Juke's name, title—*technical consultant*—and his address. Juke has written a sequence of numbers at the bottom of the card. "What's this?" Elio points.

"The front gate code. If you come, wait until after ten at night. The same code works on the front door. My bedroom is up the stairs, first on the left. Can you remember?"

Elio doubts he'll need to, but he nods.

Juke shakes his head. "I really wish you had a Skinpad. Keep that info on you, but don't leave it where someone else can pick it up. I'm trusting you with personal information here."

Elio lifts the card, waves it, and tucks it into his pants pocket.

Juke sighs and repeats, "It sure would be nice if you had a Skinpad like any civilized person."

"We can't all be rich."

Juke poses with an exaggerated hip tilt and blinks his eyes dramatically. "You know it, girlfriend."

Elio shakes his head but smiles.

Juke presses his arm. "Promise me you'll think about what I said. Don't give up, Elio." He rises, tossing his bottle in the recycle slot, then adds, "And little Mila is fine. Mad as hell at you, but, eh, could be worse."

"I can't lay my baggage on Mila. Tell her I'm trying to protect her if you see her, okay?" Elio rises, too, and follows Juke to the door.

Juke turns back before he leaves. "Mila is the last person on this earth who needs protection. Have you not figured that out? Oh, but you don't know her well, do you? Because you left before you *could* know her."

That stings, but Elio doesn't let it show. "Out," he says.

Juke flashes a grin and backs away. Elio follows him and watches Juke clamber onto a hoverbike. He waves goodbye and pushes the acceleration pedal. Silent as a soft wind, the bike takes off.

43

CLERA

Clera sees Gab transplanting seedlings when she walks into the greenhouse on Monday morning. She's nervous around him, but wasn't she always? Though he doesn't yell or criticize, he's never been friendly. Luckily, she knows what to do today and goes about her tasks without questions or conversation. She's watering a patch of zinnias outside when Zavi walks by with another worker. He glances toward her, then turns away like he missed her amid the red and pink blooms.

It's just as well. He'll be gone soon, and she'll be where? Here, still? She's had no luck conjuring up a plan to escape from the Second City. It's funny. Six months ago, Clera would have been happy for a 3D-printed house in a row of identical houses, exactly like she'd been ecstatic about the greenhouse work. But now, worry overshadows everything. Elio's unhappiness seeps into her. What does he do for the Second City? He doesn't talk about it, and she's afraid to ask.

After work, Clera sets off to see Soo Yun. The lunch crowd will have left, hopefully giving her friend time to chat. Clera hopes for a distraction from anxiety and fear, but she doesn't get it. Appa, not Soo Yun, appears at the counter when Clera steps into the cafe. He sees her and speaks Korean into the back room. Someone answers, and he waves at her to come.

In the kitchen area, Soo Yun and another girl wade knee-deep in boxes.

The second girl is taller and heavier. Her hair falls in black tendrils from a messy bun.

Soo Yun's usual bright smile is missing as she tells Clera, "This is my older sister, Ha Rin. The one who lives outside the gates."

Will Ha Rin recognize the outfit Clera wears as hers? Soo Yun's sister dusts palms on her jeans and pumps Clera's hand. Her black brows almost meet, giving her a fierce look that matches decisive movements.

"Soo Yun has told me about you. I'm glad you've been around to keep her company. There are so few children in this neighborhood."

"I'm not exactly a child!" Soo Yun objects. To Clera she says, "Ha Rin forgets that she's been gone for three years, and people change."

"What's going on here?" Clera asks. "Did a big delivery just arrive?" She eyes a cardboard box overflowing with Styrofoam.

"Ha! That's a good one," Ha Rin laughs like she made a joke.

Clera looks to her friend, forehead wrinkled.

Soo Yun frowns at her sister and tells Clera, "I'm ready for a break. Why don't we sit outside for a bit." Taking Clera's arm, she leads her away.

Ha Rin calls after them, "Don't take too long, Soo Soo," and Soo Yun winces.

Once they're seated at one of the metal tables under the pink and blue awning, Clera teases, "Soo Soo?"

Soo Yun rolls her eyes. "It's a baby name. I hate it." She wipes sweat from her brow. "I've been meaning to come find you, but then I realized I didn't know where you lived. I should have gone to the greenhouse. We're moving."

Clera goes still. "Moving. As in starting a new cafe in another part of town?" *Somewhere I won't be able to walk so easily.*

"I'm afraid not. Appa went to see my sister. But perhaps you knew that? And they finally cleared the air. You see, Ha Rin left three years ago because she wanted to be with a boy Appa did not approve of. They joined a communal farm bordering New Chicago, and we didn't hear from her until last month."

"That long? Why not?"

"Partly because they are both stubborn. Also because getting mail outside the city isn't reliable." Soo Yun sighs. "Apparently, my sister broke up with this boy over a year ago, and massive rainstorms flooded the farm fields last spring. It was the last straw. Most of the commune left. Ha Rin stayed, though. Like I said. Stubborn. But she did contact Appa at least, and when he went to see her, they worked things out." Soo Yun throws up her hands. "So now Ha Rin has returned, and I get to be the little sister again! Yay!"

Clera forces a smile, but inside, her heart freezes. Soo Yun was her first friend outside the factory, and now what will happen? "If you're moving, what will you do?"

"Ha Rin has contacts outside the city. She says there is another commune—all Korean—and they need a cook. It's state-sanctioned like her old commune, not as dangerous as those in the Barrens. These places supply fresh food to the city in return for licenses that give them perks such as free meds from New Chicago's labs. Appa misses the old country and hearing his native language spoken. And he's missed Ha Rin. The cafe here is floundering, so what choice do we have but to take a chance somewhere else?"

"At least you'll be together." Clera tries to smile but can't make her mouth cooperate.

"Hey, I wish I didn't have to leave, believe me!" Soo Yun covers Clera's hands. "But family is everything, you know? Even if they drive you crazy sometimes."

"I do know." Clera thinks of Elio. "I don't suppose there'd be any room for non-Koreans on your Korean farm?"

"Afraid not." Soo Yun cocks her head. "You've got a good job and a boyfriend. Why would you want to leave, anyway?"

Clera explains about Zavi as briefly as she can but says nothing about the Second City. No sense worrying Soo Yun. She withdraws from the other girl's touch and tucks her hands under her legs, steeling herself for the inevitable—that they'll lose touch and move on. Isn't that what happened with her factory friend, Luz?

Soo Yun looks sad. Maybe she knows this, too. Her eyes grow distant. "That Zavi. He is such a nice man. So kind, and so loyal a customer. But we should be happy for him, too, right?" Her eyes light up. "What a chance, to be traveling to a new solar system, to be the first to colonize a new planet! He'll be famous."

Clera wishes she could look at things this way. It's selfish, but she doesn't want what's best for Zavi or Soo Yun, not if it means they're leaving her. Though neither appears to have a choice, it still feels like desertion, like she's done something wrong to drive them away.

Soo Yun and Clera talk more but keep the conversation light. Soo Yun gives her a new address outside the city in case Clera ever needs help. She sends her off with a bag of honey cookies and a hug.

Clera looks back once, but the cafe door is shut. Soo Yun has already gone.

She wanders back to Fadel Arboretum and Greenhouses, but she doesn't go to the little cottage. The Second City owns it, owns *her*, and the house will never be home. Instead, Clera wanders into the woods and follows the footpath to the statue of Persephone. A few early leaves are starting to fall. They litter the goddess' shoulders and outstretched arms like showers of coins. The stone eyes emote yearning for the eternal summer a footfall away from her outstretched hand.

Persephone will never touch her desires. Clera feels like that. She's come so close to building a better life only to have it ripped away. Her boss is a gang lieutenant. Zavi's leaving, and he'll be so far away he might as well be dead. And now Soo Yun will desert her, too.

For the first time in her life, Clera wants to embrace change and take a chance. But how? She sits on the bench next to the marble statue for a long time. No answer comes.

44

SOLAST

Sol haunts Millenium Park. Even at one in the morning, old-fashioned lamps spill light onto concrete paths. A few smartcabs idle at curbs. Laughter drifts out of a dark alleyway, and Sol shivers and pulls up her hood. Anton was here once. Maybe he'll come again. It's a long shot, but she's got time.

A snuffing pit bull approaches from across the grassy plaza. Sol backs away, remembering half-wild canines from the Barrens. She turns onto a street filled with bars and restaurants, many closed at this hour. Jazz horns and the *tsks* of cymbals draw her toward a brick building with neon lights that flash, "Smoke and Blues." Through a grimy window, a few customers sit around tables, backs to her, while a trio of musicians croon and strum on the raised stage at the back.

Normally, Sol would move on, but she needs a bathroom, so she slips inside and heads down the hallway to her right. The restroom's trash bin overflows, and water drips from a broken faucet. Sol wipes the toilet before using it. Afterwards, she scrubs her hands and pushes against the exit door with her shoulder. A man's voice she'd know anywhere drifts toward her.

". . . be in your account on Monday."

Another male voice asks, "And that other thing you promised?"

Sol lets the door swing almost closed and peers out through a crack.

She can't see Anton at all, but the other man's profile is visible. She takes in his smartsuit, one manicured hand hanging loose at his side, a diamond winking on the pinkie finger, and graying hair smoothed flat against a pencil neck.

He's an exec.

What would an exec be doing in a low-class bar late at night–as out-of-place as a Slummer in some fancy boutique? She shakes her head, regains her focus, listens.

"... count on us to get it done. We aren't faithless." A note of derision colors Anton's words.

"Yes, yes," the other man replies impatiently. "The Earthers are noble humanitarians. Environmentalists." His voice grates on each syllable. He scoffs, "The good guys. Right."

"Do we have a deal or not?"

"I don't get why someone so into saving the planet would want to ..."

Sol strains against the door, but Anton cuts off the rest of the exec's sentence with, "The why is none of your business. This is a simple transaction. I don't need to know your reasons, and you don't need to know mine. In fact, better not to think too hard about that. You might suddenly grow a conscience."

The exec splutters, "What?" He clears his throat. "My reasons are clear. Life is all transactional, isn't it? Everything comes down to money in the end."

"Not everything," Anton replies with an edge to his voice. "But you didn't come here for a philosophy lesson. Are we good?"

"The paperwork has already been processed, and you should have a receipt and directions on your Skinpad by tomorrow morning."

There's a pause. Sol imagines Anton scanning his arm for—what? Should she jump out, attack before they know what's happening? If it was only Anton in the hallway, she might try it, though he's possibly better than her at martial arts. He taught her, didn't he? On the other hand, she has surprise and rage on her side.

The voices ceased during the debate in her head. She comes back to herself and bursts out the door, ready to drop kick the first person she sees.

But only shadows fill the corridor. Sol hurries down it, heart in her throat, and catches sight of the exec exiting out the front door. She scans the bar and sees Anton joining four other men at a table. Inked Earther emblems stand out against their pale skin even through the smoke haze. Five against one. Bad odds. She's lost her chance.

Sol slips out. The mocking notes of a mournful sax follow her. She glances up and down the street, but the exec has already vanished.

Questions follow her as she moves on to visit her nightly haunts. She needs to get Anton alone, not when he's surrounded by his fanatic friends. Still, she made progress tonight. Maybe the jazz bar is a favorite hangout of his. Perhaps he'll show up again, but alone.

And she'll be waiting.

45

ELIO

When the Aeronautical Museum's parking lot empties of the last bus, Elio trots to the front door and walks in. He's changed into his best black jeans and only button-down shirt. At the counter, a girl in a white uniform says, "Closing time is in five minutes. Please come back tomorrow."

But he shakes his head. "I'm here to speak to Mila Aguilar."

"Does she know you're coming?"

"Sure." Elio flashes his most charming smile.

"I'll just page her to inform her . . ."

"Unnecessary," Elio interrupts. He hurries toward the back of the kiosk-filled room, tossing over his shoulder, "I know where to find her."

If the girl objects or calls security, he's too far away to know. Pushing through the doors that lead into the Graveyard, he navigates the old ships in fading light. Construction bots are hard at work making space for the newest acquisition, *Beatriz*, due to land soon. They scrape the earth bare next to the far fence. He pauses to watch, but the bots' lights go out. It's quitting time for them, too.

Elio heads into the machinery shop where Mila works. Sweat dampens his palms. He has no idea what he'll say to her or even why he's here. Maybe it's because Juke told him to visit. She'll be mad, but he's used to that. He can take it.

At first, he doesn't see her. She crawls from beneath the wing of a shuttle. Oil smudges her cheek, and the dirty gray jumpsuit obscures her form, but he remembers it well enough. Even at her worst, Mila makes his blood boil. Elio calls, "Mila."

She stills. Her eyes rise to meet his from across the shop. She pulls a dirty rag from her pocket and wipes her face, but the smudge remains. Mila stalks toward him, pulls back an arm, and slaps him.

She could have hit harder. Elio steps out of range for another blow and rubs the stinging spot on his cheek. "I guess Juke didn't tell you why I've been staying away."

"What?"

"Um, did he?"

"Why are you here, Elio, when I haven't seen you in days? Talk fast. I'm headed home in a minute."

It dawns on him that he doesn't know where she lives. He pictures Mila at the museum or the Arcade, nowhere else. Maybe coming to see her was a bad idea. "Am I too late? Have you already found a new boyfriend?"

"That question implies *you* were my old boyfriend, a fact that isn't clear to me. Actually, there's lots of evidence to the contrary."

Oh, hells. "Look, I came by to apologize and to explain. Please. Can we go somewhere and talk?"

Her angry mask slips, and something else enters her eyes. Vulnerability, maybe?

"Mila." He puts his whole heart into her name.

"I was in your corner, Elio, and then you just dropped me. We can talk right here."

He takes another wary step back. "I didn't 'just drop you,' Mila. Something happened. What happened—it might not change your opinion of me, or it might make it worse. I don't know. But I need to say it. Because

I've been staying away to protect you."

A wrinkle appears on the bridge of her nose. She shakes her head like she's trying to clear it. "Do you know how little sense you're making right now, Elio?"

He half-smiles. "I might have some idea. You make me nervous."

"Start explaining so I can understand, or I *will* slap you again."

"I've joined the Second City." The confession spills out in a rush. Shame makes *both* Elio's cheeks burn. Part of him wants to turn away from this confrontation, but he's done with that. He'll face whatever comes.

Mila reads his thoughts. "You can't say something like that and not explain. Tell me the rest."

"So, you don't want me to leave?"

"I'm undecided."

He stares at her, wishing they weren't standing in the middle of a stinky shop with metal parts scattered everywhere and a noisy ceiling fan vibrating overhead. Sweat trickles down his back. "It's a long story, but if you really want to hear it . . ."

"I do."

Starting with the first apartment explosion, he tells her. Will she believe *two* of his homes have been destroyed? She listens, still as stone, giving nothing away. Her gray eyes rest on his face. He fumbles a little when he talks about accepting Boh's offer to deliver drugs. He admits he knew what he was doing, plays down his despair and emphasizes his rashness. "Mila, I felt like I couldn't come back to see you. If the Second City knew I liked you, they might use you against me for leverage. It's not safe."

"If that's so, why are you here now?"

He studies the oil-stained cement. "Juke said you were angry. I started thinking that sometimes when someone gets mad, it's really hurt in disguise. I couldn't stand you believing I didn't care about you, so I came. I hope I wasn't followed."

Mila steps closer. "Do you like me, then?"

"What?"

"You said, 'If the Second City know I like you.'"

"Oh, well, yeah. I might like you a little bit." A grin tugs at his lips. The pounding in his head is making him dizzy. He needs to sit down.

One more step brings Mila within slapping distance. Her boots crowd his field of vision. Her scent wafts toward him past the odors of oil and rusty metal—a sweetness like roses. He keeps his arms at his sides. It's hard to breathe. He feels tied to Mila with invisible wires. Elio can't look up. Mustn't look up. Has to see her—because she's not saying anything. At least she's not hitting him, either. When he does meet her gaze, he can't read her look.

"Follow me." Mila crooks a finger at him and turns her back. Her braid swishes as she makes her way across the hanger.

Elio follows.

There's a door he never noticed hidden behind a huge compressor. She opens it and waves him in.

Mila closes the door behind them and slides a bolt across it.

The room beyond is part living room, part bedroom, part kitchen. Prints of various spacecraft decorate the walls. A rumpled bed fills one corner of the space, an L-shaped couch and coffee table the other. A half-eaten sandwich rests on the table. Through another door past a row of cabinets and counters, Elio glimpses a shower and toilet. "You live here at the museum?"

She draws level with him, arms crossed, and surveys the apartment dispassionately. "You didn't think I lived with Uncle Bas, did you? He's got a new girlfriend every week. My uncle has two passions in life, this museum and long legs—the longer the better. He wasn't about to let a niece dropping into his lap interfere with his 'hobbies.' And I was happy to have this space. I like my privacy."

"Do you even see your uncle much?"

She shrugs. "He's at the museum during the day, usually in some back office. I know where to find him."

"Sounds lonely." He folds his arms, too, and tries to imagine Mila living here, parents gone, practically alone in the world. Elio has never felt that. He's always had Clera. He's been lucky.

Lucky. Wow.

Mila lives in a machinery shop and drops by the Arcade between long shifts for a little human company. Elio blew her off the first time they met. He's a wallowing, selfish little boy, unworthy of her notice.

Mila's next words bring his focus back to the present. "It is lonely sometimes, but you can be in a crowd of people and feel totally isolated, too. Like you were when you first came to the Arcade."

She doesn't look like she's about to hit him again anytime soon, so he grips her arms, unfolds them, and slides his hands down their length to squeeze her palms. "I don't know what's going to happen, Mila. My plans have all gone to shit, and I'm trapped in a gang." His grip tightens around her. "But I'm going to figure this out. I'm going to be free to make a life for myself. Do you believe me?"

In answer, she stands on tiptoe and brushes his lips with hers. That teasing touch hits him like a bolt of lightning. The pounding in his head evaporates. His nerves thrum, but she retreats before he can kiss her back. She sets him off-balance by winking at him. "I'm hopping in the shower."

"What?"

She disappears into the bathroom. Elio scratches his head. Does she really want to clean up, or was that an invitation? If he had more experience with girls, he'd know this answer. Or would he? There's no textbook for a woman like Mila.

Running water shushes beyond the door. Elio wavers, then mutters, "Hells. All she can do is hit me again." He kicks off his shoes, unbuttons his pants, and pulls his shirt over his head. He walks into the steamy bathroom, drops his drawers, and takes a fortifying breath.

He has imagined Mila naked, but the reality is so much better. Her slick skin reminds him of satin. She's all soft curves except for her shoulder blades, which protrude like the beginnings of wings. He's never seen her hair loose before. It clings in wet strands to her back. His eyes trace the line of her spine lower, lower, and he can't help himself. He reaches out and cups her round buttocks. When she stills but doesn't turn, he slides his hands around to her front, up over the ridges of her ribs to cover her breasts. As he imagined, they overflow his open palms.

He's quiet, breathing in the smells of shampoo and Mila. Elio presses against her back. She's so warm. Her hair tickles his chest. He waits for a signal, still unsure. Can she feel how much he wants her? But she makes no move. Is *he* supposed to? Elio tilts his head to whisper into her ear, "Mila?"

She turns in his arms. Water droplets spatter off their skin. He kisses her softly, and her lips mold to fit his. A moan slips between her teeth, and Elio forgets his doubts. Forgets to think at all. He deepens the kiss, kneads her bottom, cannot draw her close enough. He knows he's doing this right when she gasps and clings to his shoulders. When he lifts her, she wraps her legs around his hips. She's light as air, and they fit together like their bodies were created for this moment. Her back is to the tiles. He discovers her secret places, drawing more moans and gasps from her lips. By the time they join, he's already part of Mila, and she's part of him. The rhythm of their meeting sings in his blood. That wire of tension becomes a thread that ties them together.

Mila moves against him, rocks closer. Their lovemaking syncs with the beat of his pounding heart. Waves of pure feeling wash over him. Together, they drown in the depths of an ocean that should destroy them but doesn't. He realizes he's holding his breath and sucks in air. And yes, there's still oxygen in the world. Only it's not just his world anymore. It's Mila's too, and they're swimming through it together.

They crest the wave, her cry the pinnacle, his groan the ebb that follows.

Vaguely, he feels Mila bite his shoulder. Her thighs still clench him. He catches her lips with his own. They laugh.

It's over too quickly but still nothing like his first time—that memory a blurred image, this one a telephoto lens event.

Afterward, they dry each other off and sit on Mila's couch, eating leftover takeout from her refrigerator and drinking beers. Conversation comes easily. The space inside him which hopelessness filled now crowds with possibilities. He holds on to that feeling as long as possible but knows he can't fend off reality forever.

Elio finally kisses Mila and rises. She doesn't stop him. "I'll come back," he promises, though he doesn't know if he should.

Outside, cool night air fills his lungs and wakes him from this dream, but slowly, like a mother nudging her child into consciousness.

He whistles while he walks. Soon he's almost home, and thoughts of Mila mix with the beginnings of a plan for their future.

Footsteps warn him too late that he isn't alone.

46

ELIO

Elio whirls around, fists swinging. Gab darts out of the way and swears. "Where have you been? You're needed. Come with me, and no questions."

He begins to argue but notices the stun gun Gab holds. "My sister. I need to tell . . ."

"You'll do as I say. You're a soldier for the Second City now, and there'll be no backtalk."

Gab gestures with his gun. Elio considers running, but even if he escapes, they'll come for him later. He needs to consider Clera. Mila, too. Her face coalesces in his mind's eye. Those gray eyes. That curvy body. He shakes his head, knowing he shouldn't have slept with her, but he has no regrets. Everything will work out. He'll figure out some escape plan.

For now, he goes with Gab.

His old self wouldn't have accompanied Gab without a fight, but he's smarter now. More cautious. Why does the gang boss want him? If this were a drug run, he'd be sent off with a brown package. The Second City leader walks behind Elio and nudges him toward a familiar subway entrance. There are no packages.

When he sees the stairs leading down into darkness, he hesitates, reconsiders running, again decides not to. Gab's not going to kill him. He could have done that at any time, turned his stun gun on high power and sent volts through Elio until his eyeballs smoked. They descend the subway stairs and pass through the ruined turnstile. Gab commands, "Jump down onto the tracks. I'm right behind you."

They've only walked ten yards when forms materialize out of the gloom—the hatchet-faced indigenous woman and others he's never seen—mostly young men but a few girls, too. He can't make out their expressions. Gab's second holds an old-fashioned gas light which she swings up, blinding Elio.

"It's Gab, Catori. Put that light out of our eyes."

She lowers the torch. "It's about time." She eyes Elio like this is all his fault, like he missed a memo: *Meet in the underground tunnels promptly at nine o'clock.*

It's unfair, but Elio ignores her accusing look and slips into line. Catori leads about thirty of them through the blackness. No one talks. Feet shuffle, and sometimes a rat scrabbles away from their booted feet. Elio ignores the rodents better than he ignores the thoughts racing through his brain: *Do the Second City know I was with Mila? Have I put her in danger? What must Clera be thinking? Is she scared? Angry? Probably both.* He stayed with Mila way too long. That's on him.

Elio remembers his last delivery at the pier. Maybe what's happening now has something to do with the Steelheads. Gab called Elio a soldier. Hot hells! He's never even held a gun. All he knows is fist fighting. He has no desire to hurt anyone who isn't already pounding him into the ground. If someone hands him a weapon, can he look a stranger in the eye and pull the trigger?

They walk and walk. Under the streets, time loses all meaning. After a while, Elio hears the rush of a train on rails. They leave the tracks and enter a side tunnel similar to the one where Elio was taken before, maybe meant for maintenance workers. Catori ignores branching corridors and closed doors. She trudges on, her lantern still bobbing, though track lights along the walls illuminate the corridor. Finally, the line of silent figures turns right, into another hallway, and from there, passes through a doorway.

By the time Elio enters the small room, it's so crowded he almost misses the piles of weapons stacked against the far wall. Catori finally douses her light and begins passing out guns. Gab has disappeared somewhere, and Elio risks a whisper to the girl beside him. "What's going on?"

Her eyes meet his, then slide away. "We're attacking the Steelheads."

"Why?"

She chuckles grimly. "There has to be a reason?" Her gaze finds him again. She's got blue eyes and freckles. Her hair is done up in tiny black braids. "Are you new or something?"

"Yes," Elio grunts, accepting a weapon from Catori. She pays him the notice she'd pay a bug as she hands it to him and moves on to the next "soldier."

Elio stares at the gun. "I don't even know how this works."

The girl sighs. "It's easy, scrull. Just squeeze the trigger and fire. Oh, and try to aim at something first. Not me!"

He raises the muzzle. She pushes it roughly toward the ground and tells him, "This thing shoots laser bursts. They spread as they come out, so being precise won't matter much. Be sure you're shooting at the Steelheads, though."

"How will I know? It's dark out."

The girl laughs without humor. "Oh, you'll know." An explosion sounds directly overhead. "That'll be the drones," she adds.

Elio remembers how the Second City drones took out the squatter apartment. There's another boom, and dust falls from the lights like dry snow. His hand tightens around the gun, squeezing the rubber grip. He wishes he had a helmet and vest, feels naked in his jeans and button-down.

Wetness gathers under his armpits. Stale air chokes him in the tightly packed room. Elio's time with Mila feels like a dream, his budding plans a child's fantasy. Only this is real. There's no escape from the Second City or from New Chicago.

A few more explosions shake the ceiling before eerie quiet descends. Gab calls, "Move out. When we get up to street level, hit any target you see. We'll meet back here only when the Steelheads are gone."

Dead, he means, Elio thinks. The crowd around him shifts and thins. He stays at the back and leaves the armory behind the girl with the blue eyes and braids. Catori comes last, locking the door behind her and stomping after him. *She* has a helmet. They leave the tunnels, come up at the Green Line stop. It's still in operation. Ads stream from vid screens, and an empty train car lights up, waiting. But the subway patrons have cleared out. The credit kiosks are empty. Gab's Second City squad climbs the stairs leading outside and emerges into a war zone.

Flames erupt out of apartment windows. Security alarms scream from ground floor businesses, and broken glass litters the street. A few drones still buzz, emerging from thick smoke only to be swallowed again. Elio coughs and pulls his shirt up to cover his mouth. The Second City soldiers fan out, everyone scanning the scene. They move like ghosts among the remains of crumpled drone parts, fallen tiles and bricks, and scraps of fabric that might house bodies. It's too dark and smoky to tell.

Far off, sirens wail. The clinks are coming. Again, Elio resists deserting, sure Gab will know. Something moves within the haze, and Elio swings his weapon up, but it's only the blue-eyed girl. This is insane! How will he know who to fight?

Lasers burst toward him. He drops to the ground, but the girl isn't so fast. A stream of light catches her in the midsection and burns a hole straight through her stomach. She topples, shirt sizzling with sparks that quickly die. He scrambles up and runs to her, drops to his knees, and feels for a pulse though it's useless. Her glassy eyes stare at him yet see nothing. She's gone.

Another flit of motion, and he's swinging his weapon up and squeezing the trigger. A laser beam explodes from the muzzle. It cuts through the haze, then splits into ten smaller beams. They illuminate roiling smoke and dark shapes coming at him. The light dies. Darkness descends again. Someone cries out in pain. Did he cause it? He doesn't know. Elio surges ahead with his squad. His foot hits a solid object, and he trips headlong over it. The gun flies from his grip. He lands flat on his stomach, and his weapon skids out of sight.

Elio twists around and comes eye to eye with Catori. She lies on her side, helmet still on, a pool of inky blood spreading beneath her. She looks at him with the same fierce scorn she showed before. "Go, idiot," she mouths.

The sirens are closer. More screams, more laser flashes, and more bodies to maneuver around. Elio can't find his gun. He considers picking up a weapon left by some dead gang member but ducks behind a burning car instead. He unfastens the silver chain that marks him as Second City and tosses it through the broken car window.

"It's going to explode!" someone yells, and he realizes they might mean his cover, so he darts away and runs head-on into a Steelhead. It's Blondie, the kid who stole his digi-ring, the one he let live. The Steelhead recognizes him, too. His eyes widen just before he smacks Elio in the jaw.

Elio goes down, skull ringing, face throbbing. He rolls to get away, but Blondie's body lands on him. Fists pummel his ribs and stomach. Elio locks arms around the Steelhead and drags him into a bearhug, too close to throw a punch. They battle like wrestlers. Elio gets a leg around his enemy's calf and twists. Something pops, and the weight atop him shifts. He heaves up. Now he's on top. His fists thud against flesh, but only for a moment. Something drops next to Blondie's shoulder. *Click.* Poison plumes out of the tear gas grenade. Coughs wrack Elio, and tears stream from his eyes. His throat's on fire.

The Steelhead is coughing, too, their fight forgotten. Elio stumbles to his feet. He covers his mouth with one hand and wipes bleary eyes with the other. Fingers grab him before he can take two steps. A clink's olive uniform and steel helmet emerge from the smoke. A cuff clicks around Elio's wrist and flashes red.

47

ELIO

The clinks drive him and a bunch of others to the local headquarters in a transport meant to hold way fewer people. The van jolts and swerves—maybe purposefully—but the packed bodies cushion each other. Elio's arms ache from the cramped position the manacles force them into, and the rest of him feels like one big bruise. He's terrified and furious all at once.

After they reach the station, guards wielding stun sticks release the prisoners' handcuffs, take their clothes and toss them into boxes, scan IDs onto bar codes, then run everyone through chemical showers and body search them. Clinks leer at the girls but mostly ignore the men. Still, it's humiliating. At least by the time he's given a prison jumpsuit and thrown into a cell with a bunch of other reprobates, everyone has lost their stink.

Steelheads or Second City—gang chains mean nothing here. Everyone has been stripped of personal belongings. Only inked arms proclaim the allegiance of a few. Elio's skin is shiny clean, tan, unmarred by gang slogans. He's never regretted his bad choices more, but at least his flesh doesn't give him away. He pushes toward the wall, sinks down, and puts his head in his hands. A few others do the same, but some cling to the bars and shout insults at passing clinks. There are no vid screens here and only one communal toilet, right in the open, dark yellow stains in the bowl. The girls were herded into their own group cell.

This place looks like something left over from an old crime vid. Like much of New Chicago, it got stuck in the 2020s and stagnated while only select portions of the city evolved into sleek, smart neo-builds. There's a strip of posh shops along Michigan Avenue and another along the lake, a cluster in the heart of the financial district, and a few rich neighborhoods to the north. But most of the city is an open wound, exactly like this prison.

Though everyone went through the showers, rot permeates the concrete walls. It seeps out along with a chill that sinks through Elio's jumpsuit. The cold trickles through bone and sinew until it finds his despairing heart, where it settles.

He presses his head into his arms and tries to block out everything around him, but he can't evade his own voice. *Every decision I make turns out wrong. Why did I ever think I could win the lottery? Or that word wouldn't get back to the Second City that I was making runs for Bohdan? Clera would have known right from wrong. Not me.*

He replays every bad decision he's made, and there are many of them. Papa tried to help him curb his impetuousness and teach him right from wrong. He was so patient, and Elio repaid him by slinking around behind his back, or fighting, or stubbornly refusing to bow to authority. Elio imagines Papa's ghost hovering above, still waiting patiently for Elio to change.

Can he, though? What's the use? He's in jail, and he'll be here for a long time if the authorities don't ship him to one of the prison camps outside the city. Will he even get a trial? He wasn't wearing his chain when he was arrested. He could claim to have been in the wrong place at the wrong time, an innocent bystander caught up in a gang war.

The clinks won't believe him. No way. Even if he were innocent, which he's not, they'll see him as slave labor for their "rehabilitation" programs in the Barrens. In the old days, the term was "chain gangs." How appropriate. He smiles bitterly into his arms.

Elio's thoughts shift to Mila and Clera. What will they think when they discover he's disappeared? How will they know what's happened to him? Clera will believe him dead. That's where her worrying mind always goes. And Mila? Will she decide he's deserted her again? That he got what he wanted from her, and now he's moving on? And just when he may have thought up a plan to keep them together and get them all out of New Chicago. Far, far out, into a new world where they can start fresh.

But maybe his idea is a stupid, rash dream.

Elio tunes out the grumblings, groans, and grunts around him. He considers. *Really* thinks, though his rabbit brain isn't used to planning. Impatience rises, but he takes the deep breaths Papa taught. His mind settles. Details fall into place. He imagines every step of his plan, weighs consequences, and envisions what could go wrong. *Plenty*. But he's always been a risk taker, so that doesn't bother him. What does is that his idea depends on Mila and Juke. It won't work without them, and he hates relying on others.

Going it alone has been his error in the past. He rolls this revolutionary thought around in his head, and it feels true. If he had admitted to his parents that he'd been bullied at school, or if he'd told Clera when he couldn't find a job, his family would have tried to help. He might have been prevented from making the bad choices that landed him here. He pictures Mama, Papa, Buela, Clera. The despair coiling in his belly relaxes. It's still there, but not the cold, sharp thing it was.

A familiar voice pulls Elio from his ruminations. His head jerks up. He scans the crowded cell, finds Gab on a bench in the corner. The gang boss is busy promising to pull some poor scrull's legs off for tripping over his feet. Elio's vision goes red, but then Papa intrudes, telling him again to breathe.

He listens. He considers. When he's sure he has control, he rises awkwardly to his feet and pushes his way over to Gab.

"Move." Elio nudges the guy sitting next to the Second City lieutenant. The man scowls but shifts away. Elio sinks down beside Gab, closer than he'd like, but at least they can hear each other.

Gab didn't escape the battle unscathed. Fresh blood seeps from a head wound, and he clutches his right arm close to his side as though protecting it. He stares at Elio with unblinking eyes, their coldness as cutting as before the battle. But does fear flicker in those depths, too? Elio could kill Gab, and what clink would care? One less body to process through the system.

Elio considers wrapping his fingers around that ropy throat and squeezing. His hands clench into fists. The dragon inside him snorts and quiets. He isn't that person. He doesn't have to let circumstances control who he becomes. He's not alone, and he doesn't have to always use his fists. Elio pictures Clera's face, Mila's, even Juke's. The dragon sleeps.

He says to Gab, "I need your Skinpad."

And maybe he imagined that moment of fear in the commander's eyes, for Gab replies, "Fec off."

The words wash over Elio, meaningless. They are equals now, both trapped, both slated for a bad end. He smiles grimly. "I can take what I need, or you can give it. Only one way will hurt."

They stare at each other. Gab looks away first. He rasps out like he's in pain, "What, you want all my credits? You don't even have a ring to transfer them to. And if you think we're getting out of here, you're just a naive boy."

"I need your contact list from work. I need to send a message."

That gets Gab's attention. "Who?"

"Zavi Fadel. You have his number, right?"

Gab tries to laugh but ends up wheezing in pain. "Zavi won't help you. He might be a do-gooder, but he's a Fadel. His family's about as lily-white as they come, even if they did make a deal with the Second City."

"I don't need his help to get out. I need you to open a message to him on your Skinpad." Elio raises a fist. "One way or another."

Gab shrugs like he doesn't care, turns his forearm up so he can tap the glowing screen beneath his skin. Once he's opened a message box with Zavi's name at the top, he thrusts his arm at Elio.

Touching Gab's skin feels distasteful, but Elio makes himself do it. Letters glow beneath the epidermis. Elio writes,

Zavi, this is Elio, Clera's brother. I'm in jail. I need you to tell her to come with all the credits she has. I believe I'm in the South Side precinct. Ask her to hurry. I don't know how long I'll be here. And make her be careful. I'm sorry. Elio

He hits send and sinks back with a sigh. He's done all he can.

Gab retracts his arm. "You're a fool," he mutters. "Way beneath a Fadel's notice."

Elio only smiles. Gab is so far below *his* notice that the lieutenant can't say anything to wound him.

48

CLERA

It's like before, when they were in the condemned apartment, and Clera waited and waited for Elio to come home. He did—just before the drones attacked and forced them to run for their lives. This time, she's even more uneasy. She tells herself Elio is out walking or maybe at the Arcade, and if he's there, she can't be mad. Playing the sims taught him how to pilot a spacecraft. His plan was overly optimistic, but it had good points. At least he took a risk and reached for something better.

Not like her. She's got no imagination. Her mind gets one idea of what life will be, and she tells herself that's her only option. She makes the best of things. Security wins out every time. Settling wins out. But Elio has shown her that their lives can be so much more if only they reach for their dreams.

Yet in the end, Elio failed. Does that mean she was right? Can she be content working at the greenhouse, living alongside the Second City, trying to forget Zavi Fadel?

How ironic that he, not her brother, will travel through the wormhole! Elio would have given everything to win that shuttle and berth on *Calliope*. Maybe she would, too. Elio made the impossible seem possible. *Instead of weighing details and planning my every move, I should jump. My inaction isn't caution. It's cowardice. I've convinced myself I should accept my lot. Do I have to, though?*

If Buela's parents had thought like this, they never would have come to the United States back when it represented hope for the hopeless, a land of opportunity. It's harder to see that land now, yet maybe those chances still exist. Clera isn't happy living on this razor's edge, hiding behind closed doors that can easily splinter. She can't even use Zavi for cover since he's leaving. So, what now? *Jump, Clera. Jump.*

Abruptly, the childhood nightmare she banished years ago returns. She was in the alleyway. A man appeared. *Hey, little girl.* Clera starts to block out the rest, then steels herself and lets the memory unfold.

The man started forward. He was familiar, the same one who threatened Papa in their apartment. The one who wanted to *buy* her. He took another step. She backed away and almost tripped on the rusty piece of metal. She bent and picked it up just as the stranger lunged for her. His momentum carried him forward, the metal's pointy edge held between them. She thrust as he reached, felt the makeshift weapon sink through clothing into flesh.

The man gasped. His hands moved from her to his stomach. He stumbled back. His gaze fell to the dark stain spreading across his hands. She dodged around him and ran for the stairs.

She should have told someone, but she didn't. What if she'd killed the bad man? Would the clinks take her to jail? Would she ever see her family again?

The next morning, there was no news of a body or a murdered man, but she never encountered him again. She never went out alone at night again, either. It was the moment she began to hide.

Clera stares out the window, arms crossed. The memory doesn't terrify her like it once would have. Instead, she thinks, *you saved yourself, Clera. You were brave. Strong. Independent. And you can be that girl again.* Despite the sultry night, she shivers. Her reflection looks back through the glass like a translucent ghost. *What do you want?* Trying to recreate her old life has been a failure. She can't feel too sad about that. But what, then?

Freedom.

The answer rises like a spring of cool water. Freedom is all she wants. To decide what her life will be based on her own wishes. To reach for that dream without fear because failing is better than doing nothing. She won't let the past control her any longer.

She'll speak to her brother, tell him he wasn't wrong to hope for a better life. But where is he? Clera closes her eyes against the dark pictures her mind conjures: Elio hurt, bleeding out in some gutter, dead. He came home safe last time. It will be like that tonight.

Clera makes herself go to bed. Eventually, she sleeps, but not well. The next day is Saturday, her day off. Someone rapping at the front door pulls her from dreams. She scrambles up and reaches for clothing. Clera pulls a sweatshirt over her tank top, slips into joggers, and peers through the peephole. A familiar figure stands there.

She runs fingers through her tangled hair, takes a steadying breath, and swings the door wide. "What are you . . ."

Zavi pushes his way in. "We need to talk." Shadows underscore his eyes. He hasn't been sleeping well, either. He turns to face her.

She shuts the door and leans against it, suddenly afraid.

"I got a message from your brother this morning. He sent it sometime last night."

Zavi holds out his forearm. The words glow, letters with no audio. Clera reads with growing dread. "Oh, no."

"How soon can you be ready? I'll drive you. We'll try the South Side precinct first, like he said."

She touches his arm. "Zavi, you don't have to help. This is my problem, and I'll handle it."

He pulls away and shakes his head. "It's too big for you. How are you planning to get him out?"

"I've got credits. I'll use them all if I have to."

"But will they be enough? And if you empty your account, how will you manage until you get paid again?"

Clera tamps down panic, makes herself rationalize, not simply react. He's right, yet he's not. She shakes her head. "This is my brother's and my problem. We'll figure something out." She bites her lip. Elio's life hangs on the decisions she makes in the next few minutes. "I'll accept a ride, though. I need to get there as soon as possible."

Zavi frowns and doesn't answer right away. Finally, he says, "The prison system is broken. If you're with Second City or even suspected of being in a gang, you'll be lucky to get a trial. Slummers are being shipped to the Barrens every day."

"And what happens to them there?" she whispers, not sure she wants to know.

"On my last trip to Grandfather's estate, I saw a prison crew. They were working alongside the highway, setting up IEDs, I think."

"What? Why?"

"There's a rebellion going on out there. You wouldn't know if you only listen to news feeds meant for the public. The president doesn't like anything leaking out that makes his execs look vulnerable. But Grandfather knows people in power, so I get a different take on the state of the nation. Trust me, things are worse than you know."

"Then it's even more important to rescue Elio! We need to plan—" Her mouth snaps closed. *We? No, just me.*

"A plan?" Zavi repeats slowly. "Clera, tell me you aren't plotting something dangerous. Something that might hurt you or your brother."

"What do you care? You're going!" A sob rises in her throat. Every fiber of her being trembles. She's on the edge of falling apart. *But I won't. I can't.*

He steps toward her, pinning her against the door. His arms draw her close. She resists, resists, resists—gives in. She rests her head on his shoulder. Her cheek nestles into the hollow of his collarbone like it was meant to fit there. *For a minute, let Zavi help.* But she can't. He's leaving. She and Elio will *never* be his family or his responsibility.

Clera pulls away and swipes wetness from her face. "You can give me a ride, but that's all. I have to do this myself."

The note of finality in her voice must register because Zavi doesn't argue, only stares at her for a long moment, arms limp. His shoulders slump, and he nods. "Come on, then."

49

CLERA

Clera walks inside the precinct alone. This early, it's a quiet, cold place. Hardbacked chairs sit in a small waiting area opposite a line of dispatchers with tablets, earbuds, and bored expressions. Zavi waits outside. They argued about this in the car, but she won.

Clera approaches the oldest dispatcher in hopes she'll be kinder than the young man chewing gum or the sallow woman with the forbidding unibrow. She clears her throat. "Hello. I need to find out if Elio Diaz is here. He would have been brought in last night."

The gray-haired woman barely glances up. Her fingers fly over the touchscreen. "Cell 42."

The tightness in Clera's shoulders eases a little. He's here. "Can I see him?"

"Not without permission from someone higher up than me. Hang on." She taps some more and murmurs into her earpiece, then tells Clera, "Go down that hall to the counter at the end." She points.

Clera nods and follows directions. Harsh white bulbs light the corridor. A clink stands behind another counter. He sees her coming, pulls a metal box from its slot along a wall filled with identical boxes, scans a barcode along the rim, and sets it on the counter. As she approaches, he snaps out, "You're here for Elio Diaz's things?"

"I'm here for my brother, Elio Diaz, *and* his things."

"Right." The uniformed man has a round, bald head, jowls, and pink cheeks. He reminds Clera of the fairy tale about the three pigs. The clink pushes the box toward her and sets a plastic bag beside it.

"Can I open this?" She's confused, unsure.

"You need to transfer his things to the bag. We have to keep the box."

She lifts the lid and peers inside. There are Elio's jeans, shirt, underwear, digi-ring—everything. She looks up. "But he's going to need his clothes."

The man grunts. "Not where he's going. Everyone in his cell is being shipped out of the city at three o'clock today. Prison farm. It's standard anymore for gang members."

"Without a hearing?" She feels the blood drain from her face. "But my brother isn't even in a gang." She looks away.

The officer rolls his eyes. "Do you know how often I hear that from relatives? Sorry, lady, but there's nothing you can do."

Clera looks at Elio's dirty, blood-spattered clothing. The sight brings tears to her eyes. Knowing the next few minutes mean everything, she scrambles for words. "Wait. Just wait a minute. There's . . . there's something missing. I mean, if my brother was a gang member, wouldn't he have one of those chains they wear?"

"Maybe. But he could have gotten rid of it."

She shakes her head. *Lie better.* "No. My brother didn't wear a chain. He was in the wrong place at the wrong time."

The officer sighs. His jowls wobble. "Look, I'm not a judge. I get paid to run this counter, to manage prisoners' personal possessions. Take them or leave them."

"I don't believe you." She grips the counter. "You aren't working a beat, so you've moved up in the ranks. You have pull." She fumbles with her digi-ring, slips it off. The ring clatters onto smudged laminate. "Take everything I have, and give me my brother."

She doesn't believe he'll do it. Bribery only works in third world countries, not in the United States of America.

But the piggy clink eyes her offering, then her. "How much do you have?"

Clera shrugs. "Enough." She tilts her chin, defiant. She has no idea if the credits she's earned from the greenhouse job will tempt this man, but they *have* to be enough. There is no other plan.

He scoops the ring into his fist and turns his back. He disappears through a doorway.

Oh, God. What has she done? Her finger feels naked without her ring. What if he doesn't give it back? What if he drains her credits, then tells her the police don't take bribes? What if they arrest her for offering money in exchange for her brother? No matter how hard she presses her hands together, the trembling only gets worse. *Please, please,* Clera prays.

The clink is gone for ten minutes. Twenty. Clera paces in front of the counter. Down the hallway, someone emits an unearthly, animal sound. It's the same one she hears in her head, building and building, wanting out, but she clamps down.

The officer reappears. He tosses her ring to her, and she slips it back on her finger. It tightens to fit. She waits, breath held.

He gathers the plastic bag and the box holding Elio's things.

"Wait, what are you doing?" she asks.

"Go around the building to the side door. There's a little courtyard over there. It's where we release freed prisoners. Looks like he'll need his clothes, after all."

"You're letting him go." She hardly believes it.

The clink blinks at her, all innocence. "He wasn't wearing a chain, right? So, I guess we made a mistake. Elio Diaz was an innocent bystander in that gang fight that tore up two city blocks."

"Yes. Yes, he was. Thank you."

He grins, eyes flashing to her ring. "No, thank *you*. Better hurry. He won't be long."

She nods and flees from the clink's mocking face.

Outside, Zavi is still parked at the curb. Clera leans down and tells him through the open window, "I got Elio out. The prisoner exit is around the side."

Zavi looks relieved but not surprised, and she loves him for that. He believed in her though she didn't believe in herself. She almost reaches for him, then remembers they have no future. "Wait here." She hurries around the building.

A table and benches rest inside wrought-iron gates, where a thick metal door leads into the precinct. Clera paces. More time passes. Have they changed their minds? Was this all some cruel joke? But the door opens, and Elio steps out. His filthy clothes look out of place on his scrubbed-clean body. He sees her and blinks dazedly.

She runs to him and wraps her arms around him.

He hugs her back, then stiffens and draws away. "How much did it take?"

"I don't even know," she stammers. "It doesn't matter. You're here, and that's enough. Come on. Zavi's waiting in the car."

He grabs her hands and holds her still. "Clera. Gab's in there. He made me fight. Everyone left is being shipped out of New Chicago."

"I know." She nods. "I mean, I didn't know about Gab, but I knew about the prison farm. You don't want to get him out, do you? I don't think I could manage that. Maybe Zavi could."

"No!" Elio huffs out a dry laugh. "I'm just saying without Gab around,

I'm free. At least until some other Second City lieutenant comes for me. And I have a plan."

"Let's get out of here. Later we can talk." She pulls on his hand, and he follows her to Zavi's car and slides into the back with her.

Zavi stares at them through the rearview mirror. He and Elio have never met, Clera realizes.

"Zavi, this is Elio."

"Thanks for helping my sister get here in time." Elio leans forward and squeezes Zavi's shoulder.

"No problem," Zavi replies, voice neutral.

Clera wonders what he's thinking. Does he wish he didn't have to leave her? Or is he feeling relief that their almost-relationship is ending? She's grateful to Zavi, and sad, and rejected, all at once. Even if she wanted to talk to him, the words would tangle in her mouth. They drive in silence back to Fadel Arboretum and Greenhouses grounds.

50

ELIO

Elio spent a sleepless night in jail, and he's exhausted. Life feels like a dream as he shakes Zavi Fadel's hand and thanks him for his help. Fadel's grip is stronger than Elio would have thought, his palms more callused. Must be from working in the arboretum.

There's obviously something going on between him and Clera. Even in his trance-like state, Elio notices the looks that pass between them. He wants to ask his sister what she's been hiding. He wants to share his plans and see what she thinks. But first, a tiny nap. When they get home, he downs a double dose of pain meds and drops into bed.

Elio wakes to the smell of fried chicken. Stomach grumbling, he strips off his dirty clothes. Did he really sleep in those blood-stained, dirt-encrusted jeans? Pulling on fresh ones, he starts to leave his room, then pauses. His gaze lands on the black pants. Juke's card! He meant to take it from his pocket and store it in a safe place, then forgot. But it won't be in the clothes he wore to Mila's. He spots another pair of jeans on the floor. Elio falls to his knees and searches until he finds the white card with Juke's name, nebulous title, address, and gate code on it.

He exhales and touches his digi-ring screen. The hour glows and fades. Four o'clock! He didn't mean to sleep so long. There isn't much time to make his idea work. So much depends on other people. He doesn't like that part, but how did going it alone work out for him in the past, anyway?

Clera is just putting fried chicken, greens, and tomatoes from the community garden on their plates when he emerges. They slide into chairs at the tiny laminate table. So pristine, yet so *not home*. The stink of the Second City taints every molecule of air. He won't miss the cottage, except for having his own bed and running water.

"Hey, sleepyhead." Clera smiles. She picks up a fork and digs in.

She must be tired, too. He doubts she's slept much. "Clera, I'm sorry I made you worry. I swear I'm out of the Second City now. For real."

"Is that up to you?" She stares at him, not accusingly, simply asking. The skin below her eyes holds a bluish tinge. She's scraped her hair into a loose ponytail, but fronds escape to curl damply along her jawline.

"Yes, it is." He betrays no doubt. Raising his fork, he shovels chicken into his mouth. He bites into a tomato bursting with flavor. Clera added oil, vinegar, and parsley to the greens. It's the best meal he's had in a while.

She lets him chew and swallow a couple of times, then asks, "How?"

He takes a deep breath and pulls out Juke's card. He lays out the specifics of his idea, explains what could go wrong but also why they should try. Elio feels like a lawyer in one of those crime dramas. He keeps his voice level and makes himself consider his words before they spill out.

When he finally falls silent, she wipes her mouth and sets her silverware down. She takes a swig of water. "You've thought of everything, haven't you."

He isn't sure if she's being sarcastic or stating a fact. "Clera . . ."

"I mean it. I really do, Elio. I'm in."

His mouth falls open. "Just like that? But you're so cautious. I thought I'd have to argue with you, and even so, you'd probably say this is too risky. If you refused to go, I'd stay here, Clera. You know that, right? I'm not going off on my own anymore."

"I'm glad to hear that, but I did a lot of thinking, too, when you didn't come home earlier. We can't stay in New Chicago. Just because Gab is gone doesn't mean all the Second City are. They know where we live. They have your DNA, which means they have everything. And, well—" Her cheeks color. "Maybe I've been too stuck in the past. All that's left in New Chicago for me are old memories. I need to go out and make fresh ones."

"But what about Zavi?"

Her eyebrows shoot up. "What about him?" Her gaze falters, giving her away.

"It's obvious there's something more than simple friendship between you." He gentles his voice. "You can tell me anything. No more secrets, right?"

"He's leaving." She says it fast, almost angrily. "His grandfather got him a berth on *Calliope*. He'll be managing the biosphere. It's a promotion and a big responsibility. I'm happy for him."

"You don't sound happy. Maybe if my plan works, this isn't the end for you two."

But she's already shaking her head. "I can't think that way, Elio. Hoping for something like that will set me up for disappointment. If we do this, it's not for Zavi and me. It's for *you* and me. And that's why I'm saying yes. I need you to believe that."

"I do." He sets his fork down and squeezes her fingers.

She lets out a long breath. "We'd better pack our go-bags. I don't believe we're coming back. I hope you have a few credits because the clinks wiped mine out."

"Hopefully, we won't need credits. Pack as much food as you can."

The Arcade is their first stop. Elio times it so they arrive during the late afternoon when Mila often shows up. Clera can't get in without a pass, so she waits outside on a bench while he searches through the crowded, noisy gaming rooms. He doesn't find Mila at first and never sees Juke at all.

The big vid screen at the sim room's entrance isn't playing Dec Gaston anymore. The feed has switched to shots of the shuttle, *Beatriz,* cruising through outer space and angling ever closer to reentry. Clips of her end with a reminder that tomorrow is landing day, and she'll be coming down on the airstrip attached to the Aeronautical Museum. It also happens to be President Bendurin's birthday, so there's to be a big military parade after the landing. *Beatriz* will roll through the Graveyard gates and stop on the prepared pad. She'll be cannibalized for parts, and in a few months, for a small fee, tourists will stroll through her hollowed insides and imagine themselves on a space mission.

The parade is mandatory, which the emcee on the vid glosses over. He also avoids mention of the price tag, but with all the fireworks they're planning to set off, it's got to be exorbitant. What does Bendurin care since the cost comes out of public tax credits? Elio rewatches the looping vid, mesmerized by *Beatriz*'s slender white body traversing the black. She looks like a dove in flight. Mirrored windows shine from her bridge. Soon, if all goes well—

Someone taps him on the back. He turns, sees Mila, and hugs her with relief. She leans up to kiss him, but he forestalls her. "Is there somewhere we can talk?"

The smile flips into a frown. "Sure. In that hallway where I fed you during the tournament. Is that a bruise on your jaw?"

"Never mind that."

Mila weaves her way through distracted players. He follows in her wake. Once they're alone in the quiet corridor, he grabs her and presses his lips to hers.

"Are you too embarrassed to do that in public?" she challenges.

"What? No. Of course not. I'm just distracted." He fills her in on what happened after he left her. She brushes a finger over his tender jaw. "But you escaped. You're here."

He takes her hands. "I have more to tell—and to ask of you." He launches into the same speech he gave Clera this morning. If he can't convince Mila to join them, everything is lost.

After he finishes, he watches her, knowing he looks like a sad puppy pleading for scraps. A long tic of silence follows. Finally, she says, "Elio Diaz, there is more to you than meets the eye."

Mila's poker face makes him nervous. "Look, I know you have an uncle here, and you love your job, but . . ."

Her laughter cuts across his words, and his mouth snaps shut.

"Whatever gave you that idea?"

He's bewildered. "But you're so good at mechanics. I thought . . ."

She nudges him against the wall and stands on tiptoe, her face so close he wants to kiss her again. "I may have slept with you, but there is a lot you don't know about me. First off, I love aircraft. I love the way they look, their power, and how carefully they must be made so they won't come apart in space. I love engines, compressors, life support systems, and all the wires and tiny electronics that make up a boat. I love them like a doctor loves bodies."

"Okay . . ."

"But I'm no pathologist, Elio. I want to fix things, not take them apart, yet what do I do in this wonderful job of mine?"

"You disassemble aircraft?"

"Right! And you know what my dream is, Elio Diaz?"

He's slowly catching on. "To fly into outer space so you can work as a ship's mechanic."

"So I can *save* my patients, not disembowel them." She loops her arms around his neck and presses her length against him. She kisses him with such intensity that he knows she's in.

Elio mumbles against her lips, "But what about your uncle? The only family you have left?"

Mila settles against his chest and places her cheek over his rapidly beating heart. Her fingers play with his waistband, then move to rub his lower back. It feels so good that he's hardly paying attention when she answers, "Uncle Bas took me in. He taught me a trade, and I'm grateful. But he's got his own life. I'll write him a nice letter to be delivered well after our departure. That'll be enough."

Elio had worried about Uncle Bas. He wants as few people as possible knowing what they're up to.

Mila frowns. "What do you think Juke will say? I don't know if we have enough credits to pay him."

Elio recalls his and Juke's last conversation and smiles. "Let me worry about him."

"What do you have up your sleeve?" She punches his arm lightly.

"Has it occurred to you that Juke might want something other than credits?"

"You aren't going to give me a specific answer, are you."

"Nope." Elio grins. "Let's just say that Juke and I have already talked, and I only need to confirm if he was serious or playing with me."

51

ELIO

Elio and Clera have a few hours to kill before Juke's late-night visiting hours arrive. Elio looks up the card's address on a public map. They set off north, walking through neighborhoods they have never seen. The L line loops overhead, and increasingly fancy cars—many of them hover cars—traverse the streets. The homeless disappear. Streetlights shine like glowing fruit along tree-lined boulevards. Gated manors set well back from the roads replace apartment buildings and row houses. Some are retro designs from a hundred years ago. Others are geometric prefab wonders covered in solar panels or plastics so durable no hailstorm could dent them. Huge reflective windows and sweeping balconies decorate smooth, spotless facades. The landscaping glimpsed through iron bars is so well-tended gardeners must work overtime to keep up.

Elio and Clera have never witnessed such wealth firsthand. They walk without speaking for a long time. The buildings make Elio feel insignificant, then outraged. Do these people know about the parks full of tents and cardboard shacks? About corner drug deals and abandoned neighborhoods? About leth smokers who sleep in doorways and whole blocks where not a single green plant can be found?

Finally, Clera comments, "Your friend must be rich. Did you know?"

"No. Well, maybe. I never thought about it." Elio worries there's more he hasn't thought about, but this doesn't change anything. Juke, like Mila, is indispensable for his plan to work.

They hang out in a deserted park gazebo and stare across a perfectly round lake. Daylight fades into darkness, and faint stars appear. A fountain sprays into the air, and droplets hit the water and send ripples outward. A nightbird calls before falling silent. Time crawls by. Elio ponders the past months, of all he's lost and what he's found.

Finally, Clera says, "Is it time?"

He glances at his digi-ring and nods. They shoulder their go-bags and walk the last few blocks to Juke's house.

Elio reads the code Juke wrote on his business card and punches it into a pad at the gates of a sprawling mansion. A green light activates, and the gates open soundlessly. They slip through.

The house lights are off except for two on the second floor, so hopefully everyone has gone to bed. The estate looks like new construction designed to imitate a Tudor style, with faux bricks and a dark trim. Motion lights flicker on as they pass, and more lights bathe doorways and balconies in soft white. Lawns stretch away on both sides of the house, and a circular drive leads up to massive front doors overshadowed by a second-floor veranda. The place reminds Elio of a Shakespearean play he read in ninth year, where Romeo stood beneath a balcony and called up to Juliet.

The front door code gets them inside without triggering alarms. A wide staircase sweeps upward from the foyer. Elio swallows. Never has he felt more exposed. He smothers a moment's doubt. "Let's go."

As they climb, he studies photos on the wall. Each has its own tiny, hooded light, making details stand out even in the dark. Elio recognizes Juke as a baby, then as a young boy. He sees no siblings, just a clean-cut mother and father who look a lot like his friend. Elio pauses as the staircase turns. The photographs here are panoramic, their setting a mega-church.

In one, Juke's dad is on stage, backed by a white-robed choir, hands held aloft.

Elio looks at Clera, who says nothing, but her raised brows tell him she's thinking what he is—that Juke isn't just any rich kid. He's the son of Harmon and Judyth Burke, religious celebrities even *they* have heard of. Elio has seen plenty of ads for their church, Heavenly Assembly, on billboards and public transportation.

They reach the second floor, and Elio recalls Juke's directions. *First door on the left.* He raps softly. After a moment, the door opens a crack, and an eye appears. Elio is pulled inside, Clera on his heels. Juke closes the door like it's a fragile glass panel that might break.

"Hom!" he whispers, shaking Elio's hand. "Talk like my parents are listening on the other side of the wall, okay?" At Clera's worried look, he adds, "They aren't really, but it's best to be cautious." He pauses. "And who are you, lovely?"

Elio grins. He's used to his friend's flamboyance, but his sister looks like she doesn't know whether to slap Juke or smile at him.

Finally, she steps forward and holds out her hand. "I'm Elio's sister, Clera."

Juke ignores the hand and kisses both her cheeks. Elio rolls his eyes.

Juke wears a purple silk dressing gown and fuzzy slippers. He's removed his face makeup, and he looks more real somehow. His dark hair has a slight curl and falls softly over one eye. Shadows hide the planes of his jaws, and a tiny crescent moon scar mars one cheek.

Elio glances around, curious. Juke's bedroom is more of a suite, complete with a canopied bed, fireplace, couches, and huge floor pillows scattered across a plush rug. Parquet tiles in various wood stain colors provide contrast to the frills, ruffles, and gaudy beads that are obviously Juke's personal touches.

"What do you think?" Juke spreads his arms.

"Nice," Elio replies, mind on automatic pilot. He's focused on other things.

Clera says with a nervous tilt in her voice, "I hope we didn't come too late."

Juke scoffs, "No, ma'am. I rarely get to bed before midnight. Now is prime business time. Elio told you what I do?"

"Um, not really," she admits.

"Everything has happened quickly," Elio explains. "Do you have some time?"

Curiosity flashes in his friend's dark eyes. "Please. Have a seat." They sink into puffy couch cushions, and Elio recounts the last twenty-four hours. He leaves nothing out, and when he's done, Juke manages to whoop without raising his voice.

"Now that was a story worth listening to. I heard about the big gang takedown in South Side." He turns to Clera. "Good for you for going to the PD to bribe your brother out."

"The thing is, I had to use all my credits," she replies.

"And we need something from you." Elio leans forward. "Don't get me wrong. We have *some* credits. I just don't know what your prices are."

"So, you two are looking to conduct business."

"Yes." Elio clasps his hands. "Remember how you told me you'd successfully hacked NASA's aeronautical program?"

Juke nods.

Elio takes a breath. "Can you add Clera, Mila, and I to *Calliope*'s manifest?"

A low whistle escapes Juke's lips. "That is not a problem," he finally says.

Elio's shoulders relax. "*Beatriz* lands on the airstrip of the Aeronautical Museum tomorrow at ten. She'll be rolled into the Graveyard. That's the museum's outside area which houses all the retired spacecraft. Before she can be taken apart, she's got one final mission."

"You son of a spaceman! You're going to use your Arcade skills and fly her up to the space station! You've figured out a way to cheat the execs and hitch a ride to a new solar system!"

"Well, not without your help," Elio admits.

Juke's gaze turns inward. "It's not only names on a manifest they'll want. They need data on your shuttle. It's got to be connected to your personal data and entered into the logs. That way, once you get within hailing distance, *Calliope*'s AI can assign you a berth and draw you in with her tractor beam."

"I won't just—you know—pilot myself onto a landing pad?"

"No, see, the berths are tiny, and not too many pilots are that skilled. Rather than risk damaging the starship, the techs have rigged up this gravity pull that gathers you in like a mother embracing her baby. It lays you down neatly in your very own cubbyhole crib."

"How do you know all this?" Clera asks. She's frowning like she doesn't trust Juke's flashy persona and glib answers.

If he notices, it doesn't seem to bother him. Juke spreads his arms. "I'm on the net! All the time. And one of my particular interests is the space program. It's why I hacked the aeronautical division in the first place."

"So how do we get *Beatriz*'s information registered along with our names?" Elio wants to know.

"At takeoff. She's got communications controls on board. In the sims, you didn't need to know that because you weren't communicating so much as performing aerial maneuvers and shooting at enemies."

"It's impossible." Clera's shoulders slump. "None of us know how to do what you do unless you can give us a really quick lesson in computer hacking."

Juke laughs and looks at Elio. "She's funny." His expression grows serious. "You've got to understand it's taken me years to learn the mysterious ways of the cloud. They can't be taught overnight, and I wouldn't want to. But I do have an answer for you, never fear. And my answer is this. I want to go."

One side of Elio's mouth quirks. *Maybe I just want to get off this fell planet.* Juke hasn't changed his mind.

Clera blinks. "Excuse me?"

"Take me with you," Juke repeats more slowly, like he's talking to a small child, "and I will get you the clearance you need."

"But why would you want to leave Earth?" Clera's eyes take in the opulence around her. "You have everything here."

"No." Juke looks as serious as Elio's ever seen him. "I've got nothing. You notice those pictures on the walls coming up here? Not the portraits but the church photos?"

They both nod.

"Yeah. Well. I was born into a family of evangelicals with a capital E. Which wouldn't be so bad if they didn't believe that their names belong up there next to God, Jesus, and the Holy Ghost. Any wealth they acquire by tithing the crap out of other people is their Godly Due. Their ministry isn't about helping others. It's about helping themselves, and they've done a great job. Look around." He grinds his teeth and adds, "No one matters to my parents except my parents. I was supposed to be their perfect child, an example to all the children in their flock on how to raise a son. When they found me dressing up in girls' clothes in the bathroom one day when I was nine, I lost them forever. And they lost me. I broke the rules, betrayed the family. Now they let me live here and pretend to be what their tele-audiences want, but it's all a lie, and I've been wanting out for a long time."

Elio takes this new information in with growing empathy. He can't imagine having parents who don't accept you for who you are. Though he got in trouble a lot, he never felt unwanted. If he disappointed Mama and Papa, that was on him. He knew he'd done wrong. In many ways, he and Clera really have been fortunate. Juke might possess all the fancy cushions in the world, but he's short on family. "I'm sorry, man."

"Does that mean you won't take me?"

"No!" Elio and Clera burst out together.

Elio adds, "I mean that we feel for you, Juke. Of course you can come. Right, Clera?"

"Sure. We can't do this without you. Plus, it seems like we can help each other."

Juke's grin stretches to his ears. He ponders a minute. "If we're going to be bunkmates, you should know my real name. It's Felix. Felix Burke. But on pain of death, never call me that."

"Why 'Juke?'" Clera asks.

"You never heard of Chicago Juke?"

It sounds familiar to Elio. "Is that some old-fashioned music genre?"

"The best electronic music you ever danced to!" Juke agrees. "Here's the deal. We make this plan work, and I'll play you some Chicago Juke while we sail through the ARH. I might even dance."

Elio slaps him a high five. "It's a deal."

"All right." Juke rubs his hands, rising. "Down to business. There's no fee required in this transaction, so I believe a contract is unnecessary." He walks to the fireplace, pulls on the poker, and the entire insert slides sideways to reveal a desk laden with several keyboards and monitors. Juke rolls out a chair and sits. His hands fly over the keys. Elio and Clera draw close to watch code marching across the nearest computer's screen. After several minutes, Juke relaxes. The screen goes dark. Then a banner with *Calliope*'s photo and NASA's logo on it pops up. Juke enters their names into the manifest along with their personal data—texting Mila to get hers—and sits back. He swivels around to face them. "Done."

"That's all?" Clera asks skeptically.

"For now," Juke tells her. "Once you get us on board *Beatriz*, I'll have to enter the ship's data. After that, Elio can do what he's been training for all these months and fly us up to the stars!"

Gods, Elio wants that. He's imagined it a million times. The sims surely can't compare to the real thing. What will it feel like, bursting through Earth's atmosphere, defying gravity to float weightless in the vacuum of space?

Juke interrupts this daydream with a frown and a finger point. "But you two can't show up on *Calliope* wearing digi-rings. They'll know you're Slummers, and let me tell you, no Slummer is getting on board *Calliope* if her name isn't Dec Gaston's Current Girlfriend. No matter what he said in his fake vids, the execs who control the space program are a bunch of snobs."

"What do we do?" Clera asks.

"No problem." Juke's fingers fly over his Skinpad. He taps "send" and pauses, waiting for a reply. When it comes, he smiles. "Good old Henrik. I can always call on him in a pinch. My friend will be along shortly with his portable med kit to fix you up. You can sleep in my closet. We'll head over to Mila's between my parents clearing out for church service and the parade. Sound grand?"

"We're sleeping in your closet?" Elio asks.

Juke laughs and shuts down his monitors, then slides the fake fireplace back into place. He strides to a closed door and flings it open. Beyond is the largest dressing room Elio's ever seen. It's more like a second bedroom, complete with loungers and a dressing table. Juke's clothes stretch for twenty feet along one side, and rows of shoes adorn ceiling-to-floor shelves on the other.

"This will do." Clera grins and flops down on a lounger.

Juke tosses her a blanket and pillow he pulls from a dresser drawer. "Set your alarms, darlings!"

52

CLERA

Clera studies the Skinpad on the underside of her forearm. The analgesic hasn't worn off yet, and a half-numb, half-tingly feeling prickles her skin. The nanos Henrik injected have almost completed assembling themselves above a tiny silicone control board. They form glowing lines and control buttons she can use to text, watch feeds, set alarms—all the things she's not been able to access before. Lacking those technologies made her a Slummer. What is she now?

Clera doesn't know. The world feels full of possibilities. She has a chance to become someone new and leave her old life behind. Sadness and regret still color the world, though. She misses Mama terribly. Even Duro's absence pricks like a thorn. She wants to feel his purr against her chest and stroke his soft fur.

And what might Zavi and she have become? How ironic she'll beat him to the starship waiting in the black if only by a day or two. When he arrives, she's under no illusions that they'll find each other aboard a mothership filled with thousands of people.

Will she seek him out? Would he want her to? She doesn't know where they stand. Maybe Zavi has already moved on as he contemplates a future she's not a part of. He can easily find someone new, someone more attuned to his upbringing. He's whole again—a young, clever botanist with an impressive resume. And what is she? Maybe most people headed to *Calliope* already have job assignments. Clera doesn't even know how to get one. Also, how will she explain her presence on the starship?

She shakes her head. First things first. They have to *get* there.

Juke, Elio, and she eat bagels in Mila's studio room while Mila attends a meeting with the museum board. She told Elio that the execs are uptight about the morning's events. A small crowd of NASA enthusiasts have already gathered in the parking lot and along the runway. Nothing must go wrong.

Juke and Elio chat about the Arcade while they eat. Clera listens absentmindedly, her thoughts still on Mila. There's so much Elio hasn't told her! Most important of all, that Mila is obviously his girlfriend. Will he drop more bombshells?

There's a bumping on the door just before the mechanic girl backs in carrying a load of blankets, trash, and other assorted oddments. She drops her armful and groans. "It seems like every week lately I have to clear some homeless person's leavings from one of the ships in the Graveyard."

"What? Why?" Clera asks. She sits at one end of the L-shaped couch. Juke and Elio occupy the other.

Mila shrugs, her gaze wary. They're still in that awkward phase of getting-to-know-you. Being Elio's sister makes this worse. Mila probably wonders if Clera will be an ally or impediment to her relationship.

"Oh, some of the homeless have figured out that the shuttles make great places to sleep at night. I found cuts in the fence. They know better than to stay every night or for too long on one boat. Uncle Bas says we need more security cameras and an electrified fence. I feel sorry for the squatters, though. Must be desperate to come in here. Those ships have been stripped. They might keep the rain off your head, but they aren't comfortable."

Elio meets Clera's eyes. She knows what he's thinking. If it had occurred to them, they might have tried sleeping in the Graveyard. His gaze shifts to Mila and softens. Clera has never seen her brother wear such an expression. She shoves down a twinge of jealousy. It's been her and Elio against the world for so long, and she likes it that way, but Juke and Mila are necessary. If her brother likes them, she will, too, eventually. But right now, Clera feels like an outsider. The extra.

Mila plops down next to her and grabs a bagel from the coffee table. She takes a bite and eyes Clera. "Are you ready for this?"

Does she look nervous? Or is Mila simply making polite conversation? "I'll have to be. We all have to be."

"Right." Mila swallows and props her feet on the coffee table. "We should go out soon to watch *Beatriz* come down. She'll come to a stop in the Graveyard, where there's been a podium set up for a speech. The press will be there plus a big crowd. The crew will be introduced, and it'll take a while for the festivities to end. That parade for Bendurin should help clear everyone out, though, since we're all required to attend." She rolls her eyes.

"What's our schedule for getting out of here?" Elio asks.

"It's your plan," Mila shoots back. "But nothing will happen to *Beatriz* until tomorrow. After closing time today when it's dark will be the best time to steal her."

"What about fuel?" Juke asks.

"We only need enough to break atmo," Mila explains. "Elio should be able to steer us to the space station where *Calliope* is docked. He's trained on the sims to follow coordinates, and *Beatriz* will have those already locked in her system."

"Once we're close to *Calliope*, her tractor beams will pull us in," Juke reminds them.

"As long as you do your part, Juke," Mila says. "Sure you're up to it?"

Juke spreads his hands. "When have I not been, Mila darling?"

"Don't 'darling' me. This is serious. Not some fun high school prank. If we fail, we're all going to jail for a very long time. Your hack has to be perfect. *Calliope*'s AI can't suspect its manifest has been compromised. What if there are safeguards?"

Juke sighs. "Mila, let me worry about the technical part of our plan. I might look young, but I've been hacking systems since before you knew what an engine was, and I've never been caught."

Clera listens to their exchange. They talk in the bantering way of old friends. Even her brother seems a part of this inner circle as he jokes, "Now, now, kiddies. I trust both of you to make this happen. You're *sure* we'll have enough fuel to get out of Earth's atmosphere, Mila?"

"The newer shuttles like *Beatriz* don't burn everything up when they launch, and once they're in space, they don't need much propulsion. She should be good to go."

"This all appears too easy." Everyone turns to look at Clera.

Juke says, "Are you always a thrill kill?" He follows this with a teasing smile, but her hackles rise.

Before she can defend herself, Elio says, "Clera's just careful, that's all. In our experience, when things sound too good to be true, they generally are."

"Well, let's hope this time is the exception," Mila says dryly. "Now, if we're done questioning each other and this plan, maybe we should go watch the show."

Clera's appetite has deserted her, and she leaves half her bagel in the box. They emerge from the hangar into bright sunlight. It's a cloudless autumn day, still cool but promising to heat up by noon. *This is the last daylight I'll see for a long time—maybe ever.* She wonders if the others share this thought. Juke's steps are jaunty, like he's going to a party. Her brother slips his hand into Mila's, and she smiles up at him.

Clera doesn't let herself think about Zavi, or blue skies, or the thousand things that could fall apart with Elio's plan. She follows the others out a side gate, where a mass of onlookers armed with binoculars and "Welcome Home" banners await *Beatriz*. The runway the museum uses to land spacecraft sprawls beyond a tall chain-link fence. It's a shocking waste of space in an overcrowded city, but the government supports the museum, which attracts tourism and big donors. Hawkers drift through the crowds, selling bottled water, candies, even Chicago's famous pizza pie, though it's not quite lunchtime.

Juke looks at his Skinpad and offers to find them lemonades. Elio says he'll help carry them, and they disappear among the milling crowd. Mila watches Elio go, then turns to Clera. "Your brother is the best pilot on the sims though he's only been playing them for a few months. Of course, he was there for hours every day until recently."

"I didn't know." Clera feels stupid, like she *should* have known. "He said he had a job at a construction site."

"Well, he probably thought you wouldn't approve." Mila shrugs. She's dressed in a loose tunic and tight pants that end a little past her knees. The pastel pink of the outfit matches her warm skin tone.

Clera understands why a guy would fall for Mila. The dimples alone might do it. She and the mechanic girl must be about the same age, but so different. "Elio used to go off and do things the family didn't approve of. He would hide things from all of us. I was the responsible older sister, the one who always followed the rules."

"He was a real troublemaker, eh?"

Clera smiles, remembering. "But so cute that no one could stay mad at him for long." She pauses, considering. "He's changing, though. Growing up, I suppose, like we all do. This plan of his was well thought out. He said he had a lot of time to fine-tune it while he sat in jail wondering if anyone would come for him.”

“He knew you’d come. That you’d try, at least. I can see how close you two are. Wish I’d had a sibling to share all the crap with.”

“Yes, we are lucky, especially when so many parents nowadays choose to have only one child or none.”

“I’d like children someday,” Mila volunteers unexpectedly. “I want them to have my eyes, though I doubt they will, and Elio’s curly hair.”

Clera can’t control her shocked expression. “I thought you’d only been dating for a few weeks,” she blurts, then bites her lip and starts to apologize, but Mila waves away the words.

“You can’t tell Elio I have plans for him, or you’ll scare him off. But I don’t give myself lightly to any man, no matter what you or he might believe. And I’m loyal. I’ll stick with him. I’ve decided.”

“Oh, so you two have already . . .”

“Slept together. Yes. Does that make you dislike me? I assure you I don’t sleep around. I just make up my mind about people quickly, and I’m never wrong. So why wait? Life is short.”

“What have you decided about me, then?”

Mila flashes those dimples. “You’re cautious, that’s for sure. Like Elio said. And you obviously care about your brother more than anything. I like that about you. It’s something we can build on.”

“You say what you think.”

“And you don’t. So, I’m asking. What do you think of me?” Mila studies an apparently fascinating pebble on the ground.

This wins Clera over. “If Elio loves you, I will, too. We’re on the same side, right?”

Mila half-smiles, squeezes her hands together, then stuffs them in her pockets. “Oh, he doesn’t love me yet, but he will.”

She's wrong. Clera has been watching her brother, and if love means a willingness to sacrifice for someone and follow them anywhere, Elio is quickly becoming all Mila's. Maybe circumstances have accelerated their strong feelings. They need each other. Juke and Mila are *both* essential to Clera's and Elio's future, but again Clera wonders, *where do I fit in?*

It's like Mila hears her thoughts. "I'm glad you're coming with us, Clera. We can use someone steady like you on this adventure. Juke's brilliant but flighty, as you can see. I tend to get in people's faces or fly into a rage. Elio still has some growing up to do, though he's a wicked good pilot."

Steady. Is that to be her only contribution?

53

CLERA

Mila looks at her Skinpad. "I have a countdown timer going for *Beatriz*. She should be coming in at any minute from that direction." She points into the sun and glances around. "Where are those lemonades? The guys better hurry, or they'll miss the best moment. To see a ship start as a winking dot, then grow bigger and bigger until it's a beautiful bird gliding down to meet you—well, that's something you don't want to miss. I hate taking them apart, but I love the moment they fly home to me."

"You talk about the spaceships like they're your pets."

"More than that. You'll see, when—" She casts a furtive look around. "You know, when the time comes."

Before Clera can answer, a glimmering dot blinks to life in the sky. It grows larger and larger. Are flames shooting from the back? Is that normal as a shuttle descends through Earth's atmosphere?

Mila grips her arm so hard it hurts. She hisses, "Something isn't right. *Beatriz* is past reentry, but she's burning up! Oh, hells!"

People shift around them. Murmurs break out, and some in the crowd edge away from the runway. A small child calls, "Look, Mommy! The shuttle is on fire!"

Clera grabs Mila's hand and pulls her toward the back of the crowd. "Excuse me! Move aside, please!"

Mila lets herself be carried along without a fight. She cries out with a hint of panic in her voice, "What about Elio? What about Juke?"

"Nothing we can do for them," Clera gasps as black bits fly off *Beatriz*. Fire blossoms from them as if Bendurin's birthday fireworks have exploded early.

"Oh, hells," Mila exclaims again. She frees her hand from Clera's and presses forward.

The blazing ship has grown from a speck into an actual spacecraft, but any recognizable form rapidly deteriorates. Some observers flee toward the parking lot at the front of the museum. Others stare up, openmouthed and dumbfounded. There's no cover except behind cars or inside.

Clera and Mila make it past the fence. The solar prototype shuttle sits to their right. Its blue sides resemble a gleaming, beached whale. Chains attach landing gear to rings in a concrete pad, and its broad underbelly sits fifteen feet above the ground. While most people run for their vehicles, Clera tugs Mila toward the display ship. They duck beneath its sheltering wings just before an explosion rocks the ground.

The earth trembles. A cacophony of yells, breaking glass, and crunching metal meld into a terrible symphony. Fires spring up wherever bits of blackened wreckage land. Panic climbs up Clera's throat. Where are Elio and Juke? Her chest tightens. *Breathe deep. Fight it, Clera!* She inhales, holds her breath, exhales slowly.

Several high-rise buildings across the street erupt in fire and smoke. Shrapnel from the shuttle must have hit them. A car alarm in the Arcade parking lot adds its wails to the melee, and a piece of *Beatriz* pierces its roof. The air fills with oily smoke. Mila clutches Clera and calls for Elio. He'll never hear her above the chaos of stampeding feet and screams.

Emergency sirens add their off-key song to the chaos. Clera wonders if she and Mila should head toward the Arcade but watches several women and children fall under the panicked mob's stampede and changes her mind. A few spectators make it to the boulevard. Cars honk and brakes squeal.

Clera peers from beneath the far side of the tethered spacecraft, where dry autumn grass blazes—and a few people along with it. They run in erratic circles and set others on fire. The majority of *Beatriz* rests in that field, a clump of melted metal. The crowd thins, and she spots Elio and Juke running toward them. Her heart leaps. She steps into the open and waves with both arms. Mila joins her, puts two fingers to her lips, and emits an eardrum-rupturing whistle.

Juke's head jerks around. He points their way, and Elio and he set off toward the prototype ship. Elio holds his arm against his side like it hurts. Fire trucks turn down a side street that leads to the burning field. Their long, low honks join the turmoil. Ambulance hovercraft trail in their wake but hang back, away from the flaming airstrip, probably waiting until the fires are doused.

Juke runs under the display craft's wing, followed by Elio.

Mila pushes past Clera to grab onto him. "Are you hurt? What happened? Where were you two? You could have been . . . you could have been . . ." A sob overtakes her words. Elio folds her into his side and rests his chin on her head. "Hey, it's all right."

Clera should have been the one to run to her brother and check him for injuries. Elio's eyes find hers. He scans her from head to foot. She does the same for him and smiles in relief. No blood or burns. Her brother returns the smile, yet there's a grim set to his lips. He's trying hard to contain his emotions, but she knows him. He wants to break down as his dreams go up in smoke.

Beatriz. His plan. Destroyed before it had a chance to work.

It's so unfair. It was such a *great* plan. Clera can't even comfort him properly because Mila's there, leaking tears into Elio's shirt, stealing her place.

Juke tries to explain why they didn't return in time to watch *Beatriz* come down. "There was this huge line at the lemonade kiosk. Elio wanted to give up, but I was really thirsty. And then something looked wrong with *Beatriz*, so we did break out of line, but there was such a crowd, and some of them were already trying to get away. Someone ran into the kiosk. There was this big pile up. Elio got knocked down, but I hauled him back to his feet before he could be trampled."

Elio confirms this with a nod.

It dawns on Clera that his hurt might be adding to his drawn expression. She moves closer. "Did you dislocate something, Elio?"

"I don't think so. Just a sprain. My arm twisted funny when I went down."

"If something's broken . . ."

"Nothing is," he replies hurriedly. "I'm fine."

Plumes of water spray across the field, and smoke billows up in a concealing curtain. Shadowy figures of emergency workers rush here and there. Someone with a bullhorn yells, "Please leave the museum grounds in an orderly fashion. This situation is under control. Staying to help will only put more people in harm's way. Give the emergency teams room to work."

"We *should* be helping," Clera murmurs.

Juke nods agreement but adds, "I don't know how. I couldn't even manage to bring you girls *lemonade*." It's a weak joke, and no one laughs.

Mila says, "If they don't want us near the wreck, we might as well go back to my apartment. I have drinks there and a sling for Elio. There's nothing we can do out here."

"You two go." On impulse, Clera turns to Juke. "We'll see what help we can offer to the people who were trampled as they ran for their cars."

Juke looks from Elio and Mila to Clera. Elio drapes his good arm around Mila's shoulder.

"Umm . . . okay?" Juke says.

Elio and Mila edge toward open air and the entrance to the museum.

Clera darts from under the ship and races for the first humped form on the ground. It's a woman. She kneels and turns her onto her back. The lifeless face looks like a bowl of lumpy beets. Broken bones distort its shape, and blood drips from the woman's ear. She stares blindly upward.

Clera turns aside. Bile rises in her throat, but she doesn't vomit. She reaches for the woman's wrist, feels for a pulse and finds none. Footfalls shuffle behind her.

Juke walks past Clera to kneel by another unmoving form. Maybe ten bodies, mostly children, litter the cement walkway that leads to the museum's glass doors. Limbs bend at impossible angles. Shoe soles stamp patterns onto skin already black with bruises.

The screams fade away. Sirens trickle to a stop. Those that could escape have done so, and an eerie hush falls over the grounds. Piercing that silence, a small voice cries out. Juke beats Clera to its source—a little girl of around five. She peers at them from beneath a body. Whoever fell on her probably saved her.

Juke pushes the corpse aside and swings the girl into his arms.

Tears dribble off her chin, but Clera can't find any scrapes or bruises. "It's okay, little one. We'll find you help."

By the time they flag down a free paramedic, the fires are out. Ambulances scream away. Someone closes the gates leading into the Graveyard. There will be no speeches today, no welcome home ceremony for the flight crew. *Beatriz*'s prepared pad gapes like the space left by a pulled tooth.

Juke hands the little girl to a paramedic who checks her pupils and feels her limbs for broken bones before settling her inside the open back of his vehicle. He turns to Clera, his ashen face reminding her of the dead. She realizes he's been protected from death, from blood and pain. She offers her hand. "Come on. Let's join the others."

54

SOLAST

Boom! An explosion reverberates through the thick walls of the *Blue Goose*. Sol jerks awake, peels the face mask from her eyes, bolts upright. The faint shouts of a large crowd filter through the hull. Screams, thuds, and sounds like metal colliding with concrete continue to shatter the quiet. She's instantly alert, throwing off her blanket, and lifting the shade enough to peer out. All she sees is the front walk that leads to the main museum doors. She watches, listens. It isn't long before people come into view. They run and push, mouths and eyes opened wide in terror. Soon the few become a mob, thick and roiling, like some giant, unstoppable ocean. Sol covers her mouth as people falter and fall beneath churning heels. A little boy goes down. She should close the shade, but she can't make herself move.

There's nothing she can do. If she leaves the shuttle, she'll only be caught up in the panic. Whatever those people are fleeing from, she'll meet it here, inside the *Blue Goose*.

55

ELIO

Mila makes Elio lie back on her bed. He'd rather go out there and—what? Save *Beatriz*? There was never a chance of that, and with his arm injured, he can't help anyone. His elbow joint is on fire, but he broke an arm once in a fight, and this feels different. Not the sharp, I-can't-breathe sort of pain. More of a slow, steady burn.

Mila leaves him but returns moments later with a glass of water and a bottle of pills. She sets them down on the bedside table and helps him lift into a sitting position. She props a pillow behind him and hands the drugs over.

He eyes them. "What am I taking?"

"Pain pills and anti-inflammatory meds."

"Will they make me tired? I don't want to zone out."

"I'm saving the muscle relaxers for later. So, no. You'll be fine."

He downs the drugs and sets the empty glass back on the table. Elio stares at the ceiling, barely noticing when the mattress sinks next to him, and Mila's cool hand strokes his cheek. He glances toward the soot smudge on her temple. "You just can't seem to stay clean, can you?"

She pretends to punch his shoulder. "I'm a mechanic at heart. What can I say?" She looks down at her pink outfit, which is as grimy as her face. "I should give up and walk around in grease monkey suits all the time."

"I liked you in that black get-up you wore to the sims tournament." Elio traces a smear of dirt along her thigh.

Their light banter feels false, like a sheet draped over a body to hide what's obvious to everyone.

"I'm so sorry this happened." Mila's eyes shine bright with tears.

She's never seemed the crying type. Elio hides his surprise and goes back to staring at the ceiling. "I can't say I didn't expect something to go wrong. When do my plans ever go right? I should have known."

"You couldn't have." Mila takes his hand. "Nothing like this has ever happened here before. The shuttles are so safe. NASA's safety checks are crazy detailed. I can't imagine why *Beatriz* crashed."

"Maybe sabotage? This whole *Beatriz* extravaganza was supposed to be part of some elaborate presidential celebration, but not everybody likes President Bendurin." He lets that idea hang for a minute. "We're missing the mandatory parade right now. Think they'll arrest us?" Attempting flippancy seems better than breaking down. He doesn't want Mila to see that side of him.

"Screw the parade. I'm just glad one of those flaming pieces of metal didn't hit you."

Her fierceness pulls a real smile from him. He brushes a strand of hair from her eyes.

"What will we do now?"

"What do you mean?"

"Come on, Elio. This isn't the end. We'll make a new plan."

"Right." He stares at a crack above his head.

"You aren't going to fall into some pity party at the first sign of defeat, are you?"

He huffs a laugh. "Of course not." But isn't that exactly what he's doing? Self-loathing stirs in him. It coats his tongue and burns in his belly and makes his pain somehow worse. The bitterness isn't against Mila or even fate, though. It's directed at himself because she's right. He's better than this, not that kid anymore but an adult, and he'd better act like one. For Mila, Clera, and Juke, but most of all for himself. He needs to step up and be the leader they need.

His head hurts, and he's drowsy despite Mila's assurances that those pills won't put him to sleep. "Need a little nap and time to plan," he murmurs, closing his eyes.

She runs a hand through his hair. "You sleep, Elio."

He's pretty sure she lied to him about those pills, but he doesn't care.

Shall we go, then? Like children who have spilled drinks upon the carpet and left crumbs and wrappers in the couch? Too much work to clean up. Best to leave, find a new home without the mess. And what then? Will history repeat itself?

> *– Mons Vega, Prophet for the earth*

56

■ ● ■

CLERA

Clera and Juke slip into Mila's apartment to the sound of soft feeds playing on her big screen. Mila leans forward on the couch, arms wrapped around a pillow. A 24-hour news channel shows footage of *Beatriz* breaking up.

Juke flops down next to Mila and asks, "Any conjectures about the cause of the crash yet?"

"The investigation's only starting. There are lots of maybes being floated." She clicks off the news footage. "Could have been sabotaged by some anti-space group like the Earthers or someone wanting to ruin the president's birthday bash. Could have been a ship malfunction. We probably won't know the truth for weeks if ever."

Clera looks around for her brother and sees him passed out on Mila's bed. His foot twitches, but he doesn't wake. "Is Elio okay?"

Mila puts the pillow aside. She twists around to follow Clera's gaze. "I gave him some pain meds to put him out. Nothing serious, but he needs to not think for a bit. *Beatriz* crashing was a big blow, plus he's hurting. Just a sprained arm, I'm pretty sure. We'll see how he is when he wakes up."

"Thanks for taking care of him." Clera sits on the other end of the couch. She pushes her boots off and leans her head back. The horrible sights of the last hour are sinking in. She reacted on instinct during the crash, shock shielding her from emotion, but now images of broken bodies flash before her eyes. More people might have been trampled than killed by the pieces of wreckage scattered across the airstrip. What does that say about humanity, anyway?

"Are the fireworks still on for tonight?" Juke asks.

Mila says, "Yep. Nothing will sway our illustrious leader from celebrating his birthday. The parade is still going. The news folk were showing clips of it, too. Quite the contrast!"

"Then it's over." Juke jumps up and paces. "This whole dream of sailing to the stars! Was it ever going to happen, or were we pretending?"

"Of course, it was going to happen." Clera glares at him.

"We could have done it," Mila agrees. "With your computer skills, Juke, and Elio's flying ability." She falls silent. The only sound is Juke's feet shuffling back and forth, back and forth.

"You two sound like you've given up," Clera scolds, her voice cold and measured. "Like one hiccup ruins everything. Plans go wrong all the time. We regroup. Revise. Start over if we have to."

"But *Beatriz* was destroyed," Juke objects. He pauses his pacing to stare at her, and when she stares back stone-faced, he turns to Mila for support, but she only shrugs.

"*Beatriz* isn't the only shuttle in the world," Clera says, then asks Mila, "What about all those ships in the Graveyard? They used to fly."

Mila shakes her head. "No. I've scrapped them. Cleaned out their insides. They're only husks now. Even if I had the parts, it would take a long time to put one in working order." She pauses. "I could do it, but Uncle Bas or one of the other mechanics would notice. And when does *Calliope* leave? In a week? Two weeks? Whatever we do would have to be quick."

"What about that blue ship out front? The display shuttle?" Clera recalls how its tiles sparkled in the sun, how the underbelly curved above

Mila and her, protecting them like a momma bird.

Mila's eyebrows go up. "The solar ship? She's a prototype. Those aren't in production yet, though they're supposed to be up and flying soon."

"Does that mean they're still being tweaked? Is something wrong with them?"

"No! The prototype came to us a year ago on loan from NASA to promote production and draw in visitors. Since then, I think the holdup has been financial. You know, working out the roll-out bugs, distribution, pricing. I don't know anything about the money side of things, but that's what I heard on the news."

Clera gnaws on her lip as she listens to Mila's answers. What started as simple curiosity and the need to distract herself from the crash burgeons into something more. "That prototype shuttle looks so different from the retired boats in your yard. Would it raise red flags if we showed up at *Calliope* on it wanting a berth?"

Juke stares at Clera, mouth half open. He bursts out, "No! The tractor beams and landing sequences are AI-controlled. All the starship cares about is a shuttle having the proper credentials. You need to be on the manifest, and your ship must be registered. We can do that with any ship. Well, I can do it." His mouth tilts upward in a slow-spreading smile. "Clera, you're bril!"

She ignores him, her attention centered on Mila. "Will that shuttle fly? Does it really not need rocket fuel? Is it as hollowed out as the ships you worked on?"

"I've never been in the prototype." Mila jumps up. "But to answer your question, those solar panels have been soaking up sunshine for months and storing it in batteries. She's only on loan to us, so I'm assuming NASA will eventually come get her to sell or send on a mission. She's a science vessel."

"Can we look inside her?" Clera asks.

"Fec, yes!"

"Right now?" Juke chimes in. He looks like a little kid waiting to hear if he gets to open his Christmas gift a day early.

"There's no time like the present." Mila grins with dimples.

"But what about my brother? He'll want to see, too." Clera glances at the bed where Elio twitches again in sleep.

Mila says, "Let's see if this ship is even a possibility before we tell him. He can't take another disappointment."

Clera gets up, liking Mila more and more. Any jealousy she felt has vanished. "Let's go."

They head out the front doors of the empty museum. Mila carries a square, hand-sized device from the cubbyholes in the staff room. There's a label on it: *J-Bird C Class Science Vessel.*

"Will we be seen?" Clera asks.

Mila shakes her head before the question ends.

"The parade," Juke murmurs.

When they reach the shuttle, Mila bends to examine how its landing gear is attached to the manacles securing it to a pad beneath. "Electronic bolt cutters will snap these chains, no problem," she says. She points her device up at the hatch. It opens, and a stairway rolls out, unfolding as it descends.

57

SOLAST

Sol has just settled onto her bunk when faint voices accompanied by grating sounds alert her. She clutches her blanket, then pushes it aside. In an instant, she's on her feet. Outside her cabin, the main hatch releases with a whoosh. A whirring sound follows. The stairway. She gathers her pillow and blanket and is about to scramble from the cabin when she remembers the plant. She snags it and peers into the hallway. Empty. But there's a rectangular hole of sunlight where the exit leading outside used to be.

Sol's heart pounds so hard she's sure the intruders can hear it. She's got seconds, not minutes, to hide. She darts toward the cargo hold, slips inside. Sol trips on the trailing blanket and almost goes sprawling. Recovering her footing, she tosses the blanket and pillow down and sets the tiny plant nearby. She tugs on the floor compartment's latches while the murmuring voices grow in volume. People are on the rollout stairs—at least two, maybe more.

The latches click, and she slides back the panel. Sol throws her bed things down, cradles the clay pot, and jumps into the compartment. She's filled it with too many things, and she barely fits. Pushing her chamber pot into a corner, she maneuvers onto her back, reaches up, and pulls the cover over her. She can't latch it from the inside, so she holds onto the straps that run along the interior. Footsteps sound in the corridor. *Please don't let them find me.*

The cargo compartment is shallow, dark, and tight as a coffin. Sol's breathing comes in ragged gulps, and she wills herself to slow it by counting under her breath. *One, two, three, four, five, breathe out. One, two, three, four, five, breathe in.* Slivers of light pierce the cracks where the panel meets the hold's floor. If light can get in, so can oxygen. Still, she feels stifled, air-starved. She waits and tries to understand what's happening above.

58

——— • ———

CLERA

The streets are deserted and emergency crews on the airstrip hidden from view. Buildings hit with shrapnel still snake wisps of smoke, but the fires have been quenched.

They climb twenty steep stairs and enter the shuttle. Mila pushes a button. The stairs retract, and the door slides down. She taps a panel next to them. Clera holds her breath as lights flicker on. *So far, so good.*

It's hot inside, and the air smells like plastic and just-out-of-the-factory materials. Everything is pale gray except for a shiny, metallic floor that makes their shoes squeak as they shuffle forward. "This is so lux!" Mila whispers, leading the way down a narrow air lock. Like she's their tour guide, she takes them into a hallway and points out rooms that branch off both sides. Her voice is low, a reverent whisper tinged with excitement: "Workroom, the head, crew cabins, storage bay."

Clera counts six tiny cabins, three on each side, equipped with bunks, storage cabinets, desks, and one chair each, bolted to the floor. Mila leads Juke and her into the empty space of the forward bay. "What's a 'head'?" she asks. "It looked like a communal bathroom to me."

"That's exactly what a 'head' is." Mila tries to look in every direction at once.

She leads them back the way they came, past the airlock, where another open space half the size of the bay boasts couches, a long table and chairs, and a large vid screen built into one wall. There's a kitchen area along the side but no equipment in it, no utensils in the drawers, no food—even freeze-dried packets—in the refrigerator. Everything is locked down, spotless, *waiting*.

For us, a voice in Clera's head tells her.

Mila saunters to one side of the lounge and points out three identical cubicles. "Escape pods," she explains. "And engineering is past them."

"Everything is so symmetrical," Clera observes, running her hand along a curved corner.

"Yes, it's an impressive design," Juke agrees. "But I want to see the bridge."

Mila points to a metal stairway that disappears through a hole in the ceiling. "Up there." They climb and emerge onto an upper floor not much bigger than the common area below. Two smart chairs of white leather sit before a console of screens and buttons. Panoramic windows offer a view of the boulevard, Arcade, and skyscrapers beyond. Other chairs and computer stations are scattered throughout this operations level.

"The bridge." Juke sinks down into one of the white chairs. "It's like in the sims. Well, only a lot bigger."

Clera casts a worried look over the flight console. "Elio will know how to operate all that?" She gestures.

"Oh, yes," Juke assures her. "They may have changed this baby's outsides and her mode of propulsion, but they haven't changed the standard controls. At least not radically, I don't think." He casts a sheepish look over his shoulder. "I'm not much of a sims player myself."

"I need to take a better look at engineering," Mila announces, and they hear her descending the stairway.

Clera sits in the other leather chair and tries to imagine she's in outer space. Everything not nailed down will float. She'll bob like a bouncy ball from wall to wall, hair drifting across her eyes. Outside, Earth will seem to float past the viewscreen, a blue and white orb, impossibly small and growing smaller every second.

Juke interrupts the daydream. "It's hard to believe this is going to work."

Clera jolts back to reality and looks at him in alarm. "You don't believe it will?" She doesn't realize she's holding her breath until he grins.

"Of course it will! I believe in Mila, and I believe in Elio. Furthermore, I have the hacking skills to tie this ship's signature to our names, which I already programmed into the manifest." He pauses. "And we have you, Clera. The leader of the operation. The girl who saved the dream."

She flushes and laughs, shaking her head in denial, but she likes the sound of that. *The girl who saved the dream.*

They stare out the windows at New Chicago. Far off, streets buzz with traffic. Maybe the parade is breaking up. "We should go tonight," she tells Juke. "When darkness falls and the fireworks start."

"Good idea," he agrees.

A short time later, Mila's head pops up through the stairwell. "Life support seems functional, and the batteries read 'full.' This ship isn't stocked, so we should spend the time we have left gathering what supplies we can. We'll need blankets, pillows, toiletries, food." When Juke and Clera don't move, she snaps her fingers. "Come on, people. There's work to do! And someone better wake up Sleeping Beauty and tell him he's on call to fly us out of here. I can't believe we're stealing the prototype! Wish I could see Uncle Bas's face tomorrow morning!" Her head disappears.

59

SOLAST

The voices fade. Have the intruders gone? Sol pushes up on the panel, then remembers she hasn't heard the whir of the stairway retracting. The visitors can't have left. She's losing it. *Focus. Think.* They could be up on the bridge. Yes, of course. If this is a tour, they'd go there. Her grip tightens around the strap. She waits.

Soon, footsteps and voices sound again. Sweat trickles down Sol's temple. *Clunk. Clunk.* Footsteps approach. She feels their vibrations through the floor. She listens.

Is the museum opening the prototype for tourists? That would make sense. Or maybe it was only on loan and is about to be returned to NASA for its virgin flight off-world. Sol feels a twinge of envy. She's *definitely* losing her sanity to feel jealous of a boat. *Good for you,* Blue Goose, *if you finally get to fly. But as for me—.*

She'll have to leave, find a new home. Again.

They're talking just outside the hold. Two females and one male. Young-sounding. She can make out words now, but they tell her very little. Only what she already knows about this ship.

Whir. It's the sound she's been waiting for. The rollout stairway. *Clunk, clunk, clunk. Whir.* And she's alone again.

What should she do? Run? No. Too risky. Anyone could see the stairway coming down. They might be right outside, watching. She'll have to wait until her normal "wake" time. Midnight. She shifts and tugs at her blanket, then slides a pillow beneath her head. But she can't sleep.

60

ELIO

All the noise wakes Elio.

He gingerly stretches his arm. It feels a lot better, so possibly the pain pills are still working. The others bustle about. Mila swears. Juke dumps what looks like packages of crackers into a box by the table. Clera ticks things off a list. He kicks away a blanket, slides out of bed, and runs a hand through his hair. "What's going on?"

Mila rushes over to him and grabs his cheeks in both hands. "Your brilliant sister has thought up a new plan!" She grabs his good arm and leads him to the table, where she pushes him into a chair. Juke and Clera barely pause to acknowledge him. They seem intent on filling crates now. "Are you moving out?" Elio asks Mila. "And what did you give me? My head feels thick."

"It'll wear off soon." Mila slides into the chair across from him and fills him in.

Elio doesn't interrupt. Amazement and hope rise by inches as Clera's idea takes form on Mila's lips. When she finally finishes, he glances at his sister. "Clera?"

She pauses in front of him, a crate in her arms. She blows hair out of her face. "Yes?"

"I . . . I love you."

Her eyes go wide. She smiles a tired, excited, nervous smile. "I guess that means you believe we can do this."

"Well, I know *I* can. I *did* win the Sims Tournament." He looks around, opens his mouth to speak, then hesitates.

"What is it?" Clera asks.

"Just that, well, what happens when Uncle Bas notices the shuttle is missing? I mean, won't he call the clinks?"

"I suppose so," Clera admits, dragging out the words.

They look at Juke. Mila knocks a fist against her forehead and swears. "Why didn't I consider that?"

Juke says, "What? We'll be in outer space. No clinks can follow us there."

Mila bites her lip. "No, but these ships have trackers. At least the ones in service do. The clinks will call NASA, and they'll use their tech to track down the prototype. When they discover the shuttle is at the U.S. Space Station, it won't be a stretch to realize what happened, even for them."

Elio frowns at Juke. "Tell us you can disable the tracker."

"Um . . ." Juke offers a shaky smile. "Probably?"

"We'll need you to do it before we go," Clera adds.

Juke clears his throat. "I'd better do some research on my Skinpad in that case." He waves them away. "Go on. Keep packing. I'll just be over on the couch. Don't talk to me while I work."

Elio shares a look with Clera. Will she back out now she knows they could be caught?

But she only shrugs. "You heard him. Let's keep working."

He sighs in relief. His eyes shift to a box on the counter. "I suppose these supplies are for the journey?"

"That's right." Clera picks up a pile of blankets. "It's amazing how much stuff is packed into that break room and in good old Uncle Bas' office! He could live here if he wanted."

"He has on occasion." Mila rolls her eyes. "When his current girlfriend gets tired of his bullshit. Are we almost ready?"

Clera sighs. "I'm sure we're forgetting something. Probably several things. But we're only breaking orbit, right? It's not a long journey to *Calliope,* and *she'll* be well-stocked, though Elio and I don't have any credits to spend."

Juke says, "I'll float you what you need until we all get assigned work and can start earning salaries. Maybe I'll even have a legit job." He shrugs. "Although what's the fun in that?"

"Should we start loading the ship?" Elio asks.

Mila answers, "It seems so exposed out there. I don't want anyone asking questions or calling the clinks to investigate."

"This is all going to take a while to transfer to the shuttle." Clera looks around at the piled boxes. "I mean, if we have to put everything away."

"We can't leave supplies sitting out loose," Elio adds. "In a ship, things that aren't tied down become missiles."

Clera frowns. "Can we secure our supplies somewhere on board until we have a chance to go through them?"

Mila snaps her fingers. "I noticed straps connected to the cargo bay's walls. They'll be perfect for holding our boxes in place."

"So, we wait until dusk anyway, then move out." Clera smiles.

Elio whispers, "We're really doing this." Doubt hides behind his words. He's afraid to believe, can't take another letdown.

Juke looks up from his Skinpad. "I'm starved. How about some famous Chicago pizza pie while I work. A celebration dinner before takeoff."

Elio, Mila, and Clera all exclaim, "No!"

"Wow!" Juke clutches his chest and lurches backward.

Elio tells him, "We can't contact anyone, even the local delivery service.

No one can know we're in here, Juke."

He holds out his hands. "Well, you can't blame me for trying. I haven't worked this hard at anything since—well, forever." He adds almost apologetically, "We had a robo-maid. And electronic movers. Wish I could have taken one of them here."

"I hope this works." Elio drops down on the couch. There's a twinge in his arm, but nothing major. He can ignore it.

Mila rummages in the refrigerator and brings out cartons of day-old takeout. She divides the food on plates, warms up each individually, and passes them around with sets of chopsticks. "This'll have to do," she tells Juke.

He doesn't answer, just digs in with enthusiasm, eyes never leaving his Skinpad. Chopsticks in hand, he taps and scrolls, takes a bite, taps and scrolls.

The minutes crawl by. Everyone falls silent. Mila cuddles up to Elio and takes his hand, which is nice for a while, but soon he gets twitchy. He rises to escape the trapped, restless feeling of waiting. He could go into the shop, but he doesn't. Instead, he retraces his footsteps back and forth across the room.

Clera stares at the wall, and he wonders what she's thinking. Juke's forehead wrinkles while he works. Time feels like a rubber band stretching, stretching, until he's sure it will break.

"Aha!" Juke makes everyone jump.

"What?" Clera scoots to the edge of the couch and clasps her hands. Elio freezes.

"I've been roaming around inside NASA's space program. Finally found the blueprints for our prototype solar ship. Hang on a minute." Jukes fingers fly across his Skinpad.

It's more than a minute before he emits a satisfied grunt.

Mila says impatiently, "Tell me where the tracker is, and I'll go out with my tools and remove it."

"No." Juke finally glances up, blinking. "The tracker is within the onboard computer's software. Keep your tools in your belt." A radiant smile breaks across his face.

"So you can do it?" Elio rasps.

"No problemo, hom. I'll disable the tracker when I set our course and contact *Calliope*."

Clera's plan is really a go. Elio's stomach clenches even while elation makes him dizzy with excitement. He forces himself to relax. *You can do this. So do it.*

His sister jumps up and bends to collect a box. "Mila, you go first with the door lock remote. We'll be right behind you."

Mila picks up the device from the counter along with a pair of bolt cutters.

Elio nods at the cutters and tells Mila, "Good thinking." He gathers one of the smaller boxes filled with towels, soap, and toothpaste, and follows Mila into the shop. She looks around, then continues into the museum. Emergency lights glimmer, paving their way down tomb-like halls, through the vast, empty main room, and out the front door.

The sky beyond glows pink with dusk. He looks over Mila's head past the empty parking lot, the boulevard, the towering buildings. Streetlights gleam, but all the businesses are closed on this Sunday night. Most people fill Presidential Square waiting for the fireworks to start.

Mila draws an audible breath and heads to the shuttle. Its portal slides open. The staircase unravels, and while he, Clera, and Juke climb into the boat, she works on the chains with her electronic cutters. It doesn't take long to store their loads in lockers. Elio missed the tour earlier, and he wishes he could take it now, but there's no time.

Mila lets them back inside the museum with her master key. The prototype has been unshackled, a barely noticeable fact in the gathering dark. They make two more loading trips before something goes wrong. Mila's about to push the button that opens the exit door so they can disembark when Elio hears a low whir. He grabs her wrist with one hand and signals complete silence with the other.

Their eyes widen in the dim passage. "Wait here." He slinks toward the crew quarters and ducks inside the first cubicle. An oval pane of radiation-protectant glass looks out on the parking lot where a hovercraft sidles up to the curb near the shuttle.

A voice speaks at his elbow. He rears back and almost hits his head on the low ceiling.

Mila edges in front of him for a better view. "It's Uncle Bas' vehicle. What's he doing here so late on a Sunday?"

"In trouble with the girlfriend?" Elio tries to joke, but she doesn't laugh. He doesn't feel like laughing, either.

"Let's hope not. If he stays all night, we're going to have to take off anyway and trust he's a sound sleeper. Or scrap our plans for another day. But tomorrow's Monday. Lots of people will be around, plus the fireworks are providing a nice distraction if we can leave tonight."

Elio is so anxious to take off he can barely stand it. "What else could your uncle be doing here?"

Mila doesn't answer.

The others join them in the tiny cabin, so close he feels their heat, their sweat, the barely contained panic rippling off them. Elio says, "Maybe Uncle Bas came in to check on the Graveyard. Make sure all those fires are really out at the airstrip?"

"I sure hope so," Mila says.

"What do we do now?" Juke asks. "The fireworks start in five minutes, and we have one more load to haul out."

"No, we don't," Clera says. "It's nothing essential. Let's watch for that hover car to leave, then launch. To go back outside is too big a risk."

No one argues. Juke ponders a minute and says, "Once we power up, I have to hack into the manifest and add our ship's signature and ETA to *Calliope*'s system. Not to mention deal with the tracker. I could do that now, but I suppose you don't want me to."

"Absolutely not," Clera replies.

Elio asks, "How long will all that take you, Juke?"

"Five minutes. Maybe ten."

He watches out the shaded glass. More long minutes tick by. The last bit of color fades from the evening sky. Something booms in the distance, followed by *pop, pop, pop.* Red and green showers of sparks explode over New Chicago.

The front door of the museum opens, and Mila's Uncle Bas steps out. He's carrying two bottles of champagne, and he looks to be in a hurry. He opens his car door and disappears inside. The car whirs to life, lifts on its cushion of air, and zooms out of the parking lot.

"That jerk," Mila murmurs almost fondly. "If I'd known he was hiding his best liquor at work, I would have packed it on board the shuttle!"

"Let's go," Elio says.

They hurry up the metal stairs and onto the bridge. Elio and Juke slip into the white leather pilot and copilot's chairs. Elio studies the controls in front of him. It's not exactly like the sims, and he looks over the console carefully to make sure he knows what's what before he reaches for the main power switch.

He flips it.

There's a beat of silence. Then the overhead lights blink on, and the control panels light up. Juke whoops and starts tapping on his screen. The prototype's specs appear. Juke taps some more.

"I thought you didn't know how these ships fly," Mila asks over Juke's shoulder.

"This isn't flying, baby girl. It's just working the computer."

His hands flutter like birds. Tap, pause, tap some more. "I'm into *Calliope*'s brain," he murmurs. After that it's only moments before he exits the screen and slumps back. "*Calliope* is waiting for us with open arms. We won't look like any other shuttle, but she won't care that we're the first of our kind. All her AI knows is the data I put into her. We're already cleared."

"And the tracker?" Clera asks.

"What tracker?" Juke blinks, wide-eyed.

"Good work, Juke," Elio murmurs. He might sound calm, but his heart hammers, and his palms feel slick. "Now it's my turn. The space station isn't stationary. It circles Earth every few hours to keep from being dragged down into Earth's gravity, but I should be able to program a path. And if this ship is as smart as she looks, she'll do the rest. You won't hardly need a pilot unless aliens attack as we hit the black."

"Very funny, Elio." Clera hovers behind him. She radiates confidence, and knowing she's there settles his stomach and focuses his mind. As long as they're together, everything will be okay. He knows this.

He's got this.

There's a tense moment when the ship's computer digest the directions Elio tapped in. Then a mellow female voice wafts through the speakers. "Your flight plan to the United States Space Station is confirmed. Once you reach proximity, starship *Calliope*'s automatic pilot system will engage. Is this agreeable?"

"Yes," he tells the ship without bothering to type.

She answers with a jaunty, "Have a pleasant trip, captain."

It's up to him now. *Pretend you're in the sims.* "Juke, Mila, and

Clera—sit down and buckle up."

He checks his systems one last time. They all read green.

Elio grips the throttle, and they move off the pad, through the parking lot, and turn left. The airstrip stretches before them. No emergency vehicles remain, but debris litters the burned field. He steers past the museum and finds the tarmac. The ship bumps onto it, and in seconds he's zooming down the runway.

Fireworks explode. *Pop, pop, pop.*

The moment the landing gear leaves solid ground is like nothing he's ever experienced. The sims can't come close to this feeling of weightlessness. His stomach drops as they rise. The ground falls away. New Chicago falls away. They're flying at such a vertical angle that he's shoved back into his chair, held in place by the force it takes to push past Earth's atmosphere.

Life support sends him a message that it's adjusting oxygen flow and temperature as their air thins, then disappears altogether. The ship's nose rushes upward through an inferno of fire. She rattles like she's coming apart at the seams. Is that right? Before he can form an answer, they burst into a darkness so complete and pure and *right* that it takes his breath away.

61

SOLAST

Later, the strangers return. They walk back and forth overhead, banging and scraping and murmuring. What are they doing? The light where the panel connects with the floor disappears. She realizes someone is about to lift the compartment door just in time and pulls hard on the straps. Whoever it is gives up and moves away. She doesn't let up on the straps until all is quiet again.

Time stalls. Probably only a minute or two has passed since the others left, but Sol's leg cramps from the necessity of absolute silence. She rubs the clenched muscle into submission. She's sick of listening. Waiting. Trying not to breathe loudly. Has she made the right decision to wait until midnight to escape? Her mind feels sluggish.

Explosions like guns shooting drift to her ears. No, not guns. Fireworks. It's dark in her compartment. Then a jolt, a hum, and track lights flicker near her head. The *Blue Goose* has awakened.

Oh, dear gods.

Sol's stomach growls. She has to pee so bad it's a physical pain. More minutes pass. What should she do? The ship jolts again and rumbles beneath her. *We're moving.*

This lasts for seconds that feel like hours. Suddenly, everything tilts. The chamber pot knocks into her head. She braces against the compartment's sides as gravity presses her down. Pressure pounds against her eardrums. The shuttle shakes. Hurricane winds hurl against the outer hull. She hears them like the screams of ghosts coming for her.

Urine trickles down her leg. She doesn't care. *Make it stop.*

The shuttle levels out. The screaming winds die, and her ears pop. Then the oddest thing happens. Sol floats off the bottom of the compartment and bumps her nose on the lid.

Oh, gods. Fec all! Savage rat piss hot hells slashing . . . fec!

I'm in outer space!

———◆———

Minutes pass. She isn't here. Can't be here.

Her life is on Earth.

Slummer. Earther. Orphan. Avenger. Those are who she is. Her purpose lies back in New Chicago's crowded streets where a fanatic plans his next speech, builds his following, arranges terrorist cells and studies which form of destruction will further his cause best. A scream builds inside her head and swirls into a tornado of conflicting thoughts, stinging missiles that pelt and pummel. The rage wants out. What does she care if those feckless strangers above hear her? She can take them. She'll kick and punch until she's the only one standing.

That won't get her anywhere, though. *Maybe* she can take on several combatants at once, but then what? She can't fly this boat, and dying won't fulfill her goal. Probably nothing will, now, but she's not ready to give up. The rage won't let her.

Sol realizes the storm in her brain has quieted. Rational thought creeps back alongside a dull sense of loss. Failure. Bitterness. Those familiar emotions ground her like the weightless air cannot. She won't stay in this fecking cargo compartment until someone finds her. Best to face her new enemies like Father would have, with resolve.

She presses up on the lid. It opens, exposing her to a room now filled with boxes and crates strapped to the wall. No one is there, and she realizes they must be up on the bridge. Crawling out, she grabs onto a nearby crate. Her feet leave the floor. She drifts, bumps into a wall, and finds a railing there to grab. Sol's stomach turns, but she refuses to vomit. Not in this vacuum. Not anywhere. She swallows, lets her eyelids close, breathes in the artificial air that whooshes through ceiling vents. When she opens her eyes again, she feels better. Well, not totally. Her pants rub damply against her thighs, and she stinks, but who cares? She wasn't going to make a good impression on these people, anyway.

Better get it over with.

Hand over hand, she maneuvers out of the hold and toward the stairway leading upward into the unknown.

62

ZAVI

After he leaves Clera and Elio, Zavi parks at his bungalow and walks to the arboretum offices. He's got loose ends to wrap up if he really does leave soon. But will he obey Grandfather's orders? He told Clera he would.

Zavi rubs his neck where the tension of the last twenty-four hours has settled. He pauses outside Albero's door, grits his teeth, and knocks.

"Come on in." The director's muffled voice drifts through the panel.

Zavi expels his breath and enters.

Albero sits at a desk dwarfed by a mound of papers. He looks up with a broad grin. "Hello, there."

Zavi relaxes a little and even smiles back as he sits down. Albero has that effect on people. They exchange pleasantries. The director mentions that the apple tree grafts are taking hold, and he's secured a grant to experiment with frost-hardy tomatoes. The words slip in and out of Zavi's consciousness, pushed aside by the weight of possibly leaving Clera and Grandfather.

Finally, Albero frowns. He folds his big brown hands. "Something's on your mind."

"Is it that obvious?"

Albero only cocks his head, waiting.

"It's Gab." The story of Second City's ties to Fadel Industries spills out.

Albero blinks a few times but otherwise remains silent.

"Did you know?" Zavi finally asks.

Albero shakes his head slowly. "Maybe I should have suspected. The gangs never caused a problem here though that wasn't the case elsewhere."

"Second City murdered your sister. I figured you might not want to work at the arboretum and greenhouses anymore if you knew Grandfather had made a deal with them."

Albero rubs his long, hooked nose. "That sadness happened in the past. Doesn't mean I'm happy about this situation, though." He pauses. "Sometimes you end up making deals with the devil to secure a greater good. I used to be an idealist, but now I'm just a middle-aged man doing his best."

"Grandfather should have told you. Maybe he was worried you'd leave, and I'm sure no one wants that." Zavi spreads his arms. "This place is successful because of you."

"Thank you, Zavi. I appreciate that. Gab will have to be replaced, and I'll talk to your grandfather about the rest of it. I truly wish you were staying."

Zavi thinks of Clera and almost blurts, *so do I.*

"But director of *Calliope*'s biosphere! What an opportunity! Imagine the chances for ground-breaking research you'll have on a new planet. If I were twenty years younger, I would have given you a run for your money to get that job."

"I didn't exactly apply." Can Albero hear the dryness in his voice? The director seems too caught up in the dream of a new planet to notice.

Their conversation moves toward speculation: What sorts of flora exist on Vishnu? Will there be a whole new arsenal of medicinal plants? Carnivorous ones? Something so new and strange scientists will have to create a new phylum to contain it? Albero's enthusiasm stirs something deep inside Zavi. Populating a new planet *should* be exciting. But there's Clera. Their relationship was just budding. Now it will wither and die before it can blossom.

Plus, how can he leave Grandfather? Zavi only returned from a visit, but he needs to see the old man again. They have things to discuss that require the intimacy of in-person contact. He can catch a quick flight to Grandfather's guarded compound outside the city this afternoon and return in time for the president's birthday celebration tomorrow.

⸺◦⸺

The glass elevator delivers Zavi to his grandfather's top floor penthouse. As a boy, Zavi loved looking through the polished panes to watch the ground drop away. He'd wondered if blasting off in a spaceship felt like that. Back then, he would have been ecstatic to board a starship and take charge of such an important project as the biosphere, which will replenish oxygen and supplement food rations on the journey.

But a lot has changed in the last year. An image of Clera's face floats before Zavi. Gentle, cautious Clera with her hidden backbone of steel. From the moment they met, he felt that opposition locked within her: a quiet strength twined with vulnerability and grief.

He breathes deeply and exhales. *Let her go.* That isn't so easy. He remembers dropping Clera off after rescuing Elio. When she and her brother got out of his jeep and waved goodbye, he'd longed to call out, *Wait, Clera!* Why hadn't he? She'd turned away and followed Elio inside. After the door closed, he slumped in the driver's seat, defeated.

He was leaving. Best to make a clean break. Yet it didn't feel clean. Or right.

His eyes blur with tiredness. When did he last sleep? The elevator cruises to a stop. A disembodied voice announces, "Penthouse floor. Visitor not expected. Retinal scan required to exit."

Zavi turns his gaze to the scanner. A laser swipes across his eyeball, and the door chimes and opens. A short hallway bordered by floor-to-ceiling terrariums filled with exotic plants leads to Grandfather's front door. Zavi pushes the doorbell and speaks into the intercom. "Grandfather, it's Zavi. We need to talk." The door swings open on automatic hinges.

"Zavi? What are you doing here?" the old man calls. Zavi follows the sound through a sitting room and an arched passage that leads to the study. Grandfather sits behind his desk, flanked by bookshelves and original Georgia O'Keefe oil paintings. Sunlight streams in from the UV-filtering glass wall behind him, casting the old man in shadow.

Zavi stands before that massive desk like so many times before, but this instance feels different. He hasn't come to receive instructions on how to live his life. He's come to object to them. He loves Grandfather, but the old man moves people around like chess pieces. This tendency has only gotten worse since the air rail accident that killed Zavi's parents. Grandfather's strong will has one focus now—Zavi. Family money funded his education and surgeries to fix his spine, for which he's grateful, yet the weight of gratitude feels like chains.

Grandfather gestures to a leather armchair. "This is an unexpected pleasure. Sit down, Zavi. If you forgot to tell me something on our last visit, you could have simply called." His thick eyebrows draw together. "Unless something has happened. Are you all right?"

Zavi finds himself following instructions. If he can't even resist a command to sit, how will he say what he's come to say? "I'm fine, Grandfather. I know it's weird to see me again so soon, but I've had time to think, and I wanted to speak to you in person."

Grandfather frowns. Vented air ruffles his snow-white hair. His hands remain folded loosely on the mahogany desktop, but something in those brown eyes hardens. "You don't want to become a pioneer. You're refusing the job advancement on *Calliope*. A posting any botanist with so little experience would jump at."

Zavi isn't surprised Grandfather has guessed. He's always been canny, especially when it comes to his grandson. Zavi's mother used to call them *two peas in a pod*. He doubts this description applies anymore. "We'll talk about that, but first, why did you lie to me?"

"Excuse me?"

"You've been doing more than making deals to keep Second City away from the arboretum and greenhouses grounds. You've been *housing* them inside, and yet you never told me." Zavi grips the arms of the chair.

"A lie of omission only." Grandfather shrugs. He rubs at his whiskered chin. "I did what was necessary to secure the park so we could create better housing for the poor, not to mention the community gardens. The pay-off more than made up for the price."

"Might makes right, or something similar?"

Grandfather shrugs again. "Perhaps. When you're as old as I am, you'll shed those black-and-white ideals you wear like a cloak, Zavi. It's commendable, but it doesn't get things done. People are starving right now on the streets. We can give them food. We can shelter them from the snow. All for the small cost of letting a gang run its business alongside ours."

Zavi reaches for anger but can't find it. Grandfather's philanthropies are many. Maybe making deals with the Second City *is* a price worth paying. More leth in New Chicago but less homelessness. And the Steelheads would have kept the drug business going even if Second City hadn't been housed by Fadel Industries. He closes his eyes and says nothing.

"You're growing up." A note of surprise colors Grandfather's speech.

"Thinking things through before lashing out. I wish the world was different, but it isn't. We do what we can and let the rest go, no?"

Zavi's eyes flash open. "I wish you had told me everything."

"You weren't a supervisor at Fadel Arboretum and Greenhouses, only a worker."

"You didn't tell Albero, either."

A pause. "No." Grandfather drops his hand. "Of course not. That would have been cruel."

"Because of his sister's murder."

Grandfather inclines his head in answer.

"But I'm your grandson."

Grandfather refuses to engage, simply regards Zavi with a penetrating gaze that has always seen too much.

Zavi ends their stare-down with a sigh. "There's more."

"I assumed so. Would you like a drink?" Grandfather gestures to the cut-glass array of liquors on a sideboard.

"No, thank you." He takes a breath and speaks in a rush. "This won't take long. I just wanted to say that I've no wish to fly away on *Calliope* next week. I don't understand how you could want to send me to a place where I can never see you again. I'm your heir, your only close living relative. Won't you miss me?" Hurt makes Zavi's voice crack.

Grandfather gets up and edges around the desk. He ignores the cane propped against it and pulls a second armchair close to Zavi. He squeezes Zavi's knee. In a husky voice, he whispers, "I'm an old man. I was middle-aged when your father came into the world, and that was forty years ago. There's not much time left for me on this earth."

"All the more reason you should want to spend what remains with me!"

"I want to." Grandfather's hand falls away. "But more than that, I want you to be safe, to have a better future than this old Earth can give. I'll keep fighting for her until my last breath, but you don't have to. You can do something I would have given up everything for if I were young. Travel to another solar system. Help establish human life on a brand-new planet, and hopefully encourage the colonists not to make the same mistakes we made on this one." He stares at Zavi with solemn, sad eyes. "I trust you to do that. Your parents and I raised you to be just such a leader."

Zavi swallows the lump in his throat. "If you won't abandon Earth, how can you expect me to?"

There's a long pause. "Humanity needs you, Zavi. We don't always learn from our mistakes. I know you'll fight to preserve and protect whatever habitat you find on Vishnu. I can't vouch for many others to put a planet before their own self-interest. We humans have a history that, unfortunately, speaks otherwise."

"That's a big ask, Grandfather." Zavi pictures Clera. Half the reason he wants to stay on Earth is because of her. He wants to find out what they might become to each other. That seems a weak reason to reject Grandfather's grand calling, though. "You really think I will do the right things to protect Vishnu when we colonize?"

"I'm counting on it."

"But surely there are others who . . ."

"None I know so well as you." Grandfather falls quiet. He stares at the carpet. "What do you believe your parents would wish for you?"

Zavi's chest pinches. He can't answer for a moment, but finally he finds his voice. "They'd want me to go."

63

— ◆ —

CLERA

Stillness.

They've come through the fire like Persephone rising from hell to take her mother Demeter's hand and usher spring into the world. But there is no spring out here in the black. There's no color at all. Juke cheers, and Mila joins in. Elio warns them to stay buckled. They aren't wearing grav boots, and the shuttle has no artificial gravity.

Clera unbuckles anyway. Her body tries to float. She holds onto the chair back and shifts her grip to a railing on the wall. She pulls herself along until she's at the pilot's chair. Thick windows curve around the prow, offering an expansive view of space. Freed from New Chicago's polluting haze, stars twinkle brighter than she's ever seen them.

She drifts next to her brother and tries to stay still though her body keeps drifting away. Elio glances sideways at her but says nothing about violating his orders. He might be pilot on this boat, but she led them here. In that sense, she's the captain. Without her quick thinking, this blue-winged bird wouldn't be flying.

Clera kicks off toward the wall, grabs the railing, and follows the curve of the ship. Earth comes into view as the shuttle changes trajectory to catch up with the fleeing space station. The planet looms large and beautiful, the only color in this void except for the prototype herself. Clera recognizes the United States though smog obscures large portions of the surface like a tattered cloth laid over a gypsy's crystal ball.

The sight leaves her speechless. Some emotion too large for words rises in her throat. She pulls her way back to Elio. He finds her hand, and they watch together. She remembers where they started, in Armour Square on the south side of Chicago, and sees how far they've come. The past shrinks like their planet, diminishing every second. They aren't the same people anymore. She imagines Zavi somewhere below, so tiny he isn't even a speck. Yet he still looms large in her heart. He'll be flying out soon, too. *Calliope* is a city where thousands of adventurous people gather, ready to ship out to a new world. Will they meet again?

She drags her thoughts away from him, forces them in a new direction. Is this how Christopher Columbus or Magellan felt when they set out on rickety schooners to weather storms and cross an ocean with no end in sight? Clera can't see her end, either, but maybe that doesn't matter. She imagines a beginning for Elio and herself. She sees the world—literally—in a new way, and it's so small. So, *she* must be miniscule, right? But she feels big inside, stronger than she's ever been, powerful enough to step outside her familiar world and into something new.

She thought this ship was like Persephone rising from darkness, but now she realizes that's not true. *She* is Persephone, once a captive to her own fears, now soaring above clouds into sunlight.

Clera doesn't know what comes next, but she's not afraid. Already, the prototype feels like a home. Elio is here, and Mila, and Juke. Together, they'll rise to join the stars.

64

EPILOGUE

Zavi

Zavi sleeps on the flight home, then more after he stumbles into his house well after midnight. The next day, it's almost noon by the time he rises and sees the newsfeed videos of *Beatriz*'s explosion. He gulps strong coffee, showers, and heads to Clera's cottage. When no one answers his knock, he tries the doorknob. The door swings open.

Foreboding curls in Zavi's stomach. It's Sunday, and the Diaz siblings should be home. If they'd gone out, surely, they would lock their door? The place looks like its occupants just left, with a few dishes in the sink, laundry in the dryer, and a forgotten drink sitting on the kitchen table. Zavi calls out, but only silence pushes back. He looks for a note or some other sign to indicate where they went. When he finds nothing, he walks down the row of printed homes to Gab's cottage. It's deserted, of course. What did Zavi think he would find there?

He scratches his head, replays every conversation he's had with Clera, and realizes how little he knows about her. Still, he has two other places to search. Zavi leaves a note at the cottage in case Clera returns. He goes home, unpacks, waters his plants, and returns to Clera's place after a couple of hours to find it's still empty.

He's worried now, so he follows up on his other leads. He walks through Slavland, past the cellar where he rescued Clera and a burned-out building with shattered glass littered across the sidewalk. Maybe it's the place Clera and Elio briefly stayed? After a few more blocks, he finds himself in front of the Boba Tea Cafe, but the door is locked. A sign in the window reads, "Closed." The wrought-iron tables have disappeared, as has the pink and blue-striped awning. *That's right. Soo Yun mentioned they might leave with her sister.*

He hails a smartcab and heads for South Side. Zavi stares out the window while the close-packed downtown businesses slide by, the river dotted with ferries, and public parks littered with cardboard shacks. Perkine Skinpad Industries flashes past, then a homeless shelter, row houses, and brownstone buildings with sagging stoops.

"Stop!" Zavi directs. The smartcab pulls over. He pays and climbs out. Just ahead, yellow caution tape flutters in the breeze. The tape walls off a dirt field wedged between two apartment buildings. A few faded flower bouquets lie before a concrete path that goes nowhere.

Zavi pauses. He *feels* Clera here. It's where her mother died, he's sure. That explosion sent Clera running west and into his arms, if only for a short time. He tries to imagine what her life was like before the Housing Authority's wrecking machines pummeled her childhood home into dust. So many questions he should have asked! But there wasn't time.

He finds a bench across the street and sits there for hours. The sun blinks out past concrete and brick buildings. Daylight fades to dusk, then nightfall. The stars come out. A firework explodes to the north, followed by another. That's right! Today is Bendurin's birthday celebration. He's supposed to be on the broad, grassy strip before the presidential palace along with the rest of New Chicago's residents. No wonder it's so quiet here.

Zavi gets up and faces the pyrotechnics. Red, green, and yellow flowers glitter and die in the deep blue heavens. Movement catches his eye. High up, something glows bright for a few seconds and disappears. His heart lurches for no reason. He shakes his head.

A trick of the eye. That's all it was. Not a spaceship leaving orbit.

Zavi's thoughts shift to the future. To *his* future. He's got a lot of packing to do. Best get home so he can begin.

⸺◦⸺

If you enjoyed *Persephone Rising*, please leave a review on Amazon!

Coming Soon!

Book II of the Genesis Planet Trilogy

Erebus Unleashed

In *Erebus Unleashed*, book 2 of the Genesis Planet Trilogy, Solast Bahri has become an accidental stowaway aboard a stolen space shuttle. As she embarks on an unwelcome journey to meet the starship *Calliope*, she renews her vow to seek revenge against the man who murdered her father back on Earth. But fate has other plans. *Calliope* is bound for an ancient Martian-made wormhole leading to the green planet of Vishnu, where pioneers hope to start anew. Odds are low they will ever return home.

As Sol navigates living in close quarters with suspicious shipmates, she uncovers unexpected friendships, too, as well as a stoic archeologist whose quiet manner and dedication to his mission challenge her resolve. Caught between a thirst for vengeance and the growing bond with her new companions, Sol must confront the darkness within herself.

Will she embrace the chance to become a savior for passengers seeking a fresh start, or will the shadows of her past consume her? In this riveting space opera, Sol's inner conflict intertwines with the struggle for survival in a galaxy filled with peril and possibility.

65

AUTHOR'S NOTE

While I love a good dystopian novel, I dislike the idea of abandoning Earth as a solution to climate change. Even with future advancements in space travel, the vastness of the galaxy makes reaching a habitable planet within our lifetime, or even centuries from now, unlikely. Only by solving the tough problems of a warming world can we find a real solution.

But speculative fiction is just that. Such novels (like all fiction) wonder, "What if?" Thus, in *Persephone Rising*, advanced alien technology offers the protagonists a way out. It allows them to abandon a world that has turned its back on them and sail through a wormhole to a brighter future. But fear not, Earth lovers! By book 3, our brave pioneers will have determined to travel back through the wormhole and rescue their former home. Yes, they will need alien help, but who doesn't?

Mild-mannered, escapist Clera will have self-actualized into a proper leader by then. She'll be joined by a host of new characters including water dragons and a sentient fungus determined to ruin everything. Spoiler alert! Book 3 will fulfill Zavi's grandfather's hope that survival on the home planet is, in fact, achievable. Hang on, Earth! We're coming back for you!

But what about book 2? Well, Clera and company must *reach* the genesis planet before they can learn from it and find the solution to Earth's woes. And before they can colonize, they must survive a fanatical leader's plot to bring down the starship *Calliope* using a secret—wait a minute! I can't tell you that! You'll have to read *Erebus Unleashed*, book 2 in the Genesis Planet Trilogy, if you want to unmask the dastardly villains waiting to ensnare Clera, Elio, Sol, Mila, Juke, and Zavi in its tangled web.

ACKNOWLEDGEMENTS

I'm grateful to my writing groups for their fresh perspectives and honest advice. Your comments strengthened my beginning, made Clera stronger, and encouraged me to create Zavi's and Sol's points of view. Thanks for bringing my subliminal doubts to light and giving me the chance to acknowledge and deal with them.

To my cherished beta readers, Pete, Jackie, Kathy K., Connie, Nellie, Robin, and Terrell—thank you for diving into my world, catching errors big and small, and extra thanks to Kathy K. for double-checking the geography of a city I've never explored.

Finally, to my former science teacher husband, Howard, whom I consult on all things scientific before putting pen to paper, a very big thanks for all your years of service!

About the Author

Kate Glass (Kathy Bjornestad) is a retired public-school teacher and librarian. She has won a Wyoming Fellowship for Creative Fiction, placed in multiple writing contests, and published widely, including, most recently, in Sally Port Magazine. Kathy is part of South Dakota's Speakers Bureau and has completed four children's books. You can find her at redheadswrite.net.